J. Evan Johnson

When It's TOO DARK to see THE LIGHT

A Novel

2⁰ Theory Books

Chapter One

MARK Cooke watches his wife strut toward the large church building as he fumbles with his keys in hand. He pretends to grab something from inside the car as she looks back and smiles. He looks at her and smiles. Watching her walk away is like watching the formation of a work of art: smooth and fluid in every way. She pulls her Bible from her purse, but stops again and turns around completely. She meets his eyes with hers. Even at the considerable distance, it feels like she is right in front of him. He can't help but grin ear-to-ear. She waves him over as if to say, "Hurry up. We're going to be late." He makes his way over to her and places a strong hand on the small of her back.

"What were you waiting for?" she asks.

"I wasn't really waiting; I was admiring."

She looks at him with a wide smile as he opens the front door for her. "Admiring what?"

"You. Your beauty."

"Yeah, right. You were looking at my booty."

He chuckles. "That, too." They get to the front door of the sanctuary of the church. "But seriously, I love you."

She smiles and looks at him. He opens the door to the sanctuary for her and she walks in. His smile fades just a bit. It is imperceptible to everyone he walks by and greets in the sanctuary. Little by little, he feels a heaviness hook itself into him. He loves his wife. He loves his kids. He loves his church and Pastor.

But he hates himself.

"I know you two are busy, but I had to bring you into my office for a few moments."

"Oh, no, that is perfectly fine, Pastor."

Pastor Brentwood smiles as he takes his glasses off and cleans them with a cloth. He slides them back on, maintaining his genuine smile. "It's been a couple weeks since our final session. I wanted to know how you were doing."

Mark glances at his wife Jade and looks back at Pastor Brentwood. "I'd say we're doing well. What do you think, Jade?" He looks at her with pleading eyes. He is a bit uncomfortable with how much he still needs her validation.

Jade glances at Mark and smiles. "I think we are exceptionally well."

Pastor Brentwood nods.

"It seems like a distant memory . . . those times," Jade continues. "Thank you for helping us."

"No thanks necessary. You two did the work. I just guided."

"I know . . . it's just . . . it's just . . . ." Jade stares at the floor. "The way we were back then. There's no way we should have made it."

Mark looks at his wife as she pauses to reflect. He holds out his hand, palm up. She looks at his hand and places hers in his gently. Mark then moves his fingers in between hers and grabs her hand. He lifts it up and kisses the back of her hand.

"Our God is a restorative God," Pastor says.

"He is. He sure is."

"And when He restores things, they end up better than they were before," Mark says.

"Amen to that."

"Well, I'm glad to hear you two still doing so well. It does my heart good. I told you many moons ago that I pray for you two . . . maybe even more than others. It is good to see some of my prayers answered." Pastor looks down at his watch. "I know you were on your way to Bible study. Jade, do you mind if I talk to Mark alone for a second?"

"Not at all." Jade turns toward Mark. "I'll be at our usual spot." She smiles and gives him a kiss on the cheek. "Love you."

"Love you, too."

Jade leaves Pastor's office with Mark watching her walk away. As she gently closes the door, he turns around. "What's up?"

"How are you doing?"

"I'm okay." Mark smiles.

Pastor eyes him curiously. "You sure?"

"Yeah, I'm fine. Everything is alright."

Pastor gives Mark another discerning look before continuing. "I wanted to know if there's any more word on that . . . other situation."

"Other situation?"

"With her."

"Oh." Mark pauses. "The locals found something else to poke at."

"And what about her directly?"

"I haven't heard anything . . . not since she got out of jail. I'm not too worried, though."

"You shouldn't be worried . . . just aware."

Mark nods.

"And the job search?"

"Nothing . . . but I'm still hopeful."

Pastor nods with a satisfied look on his face. Yet, there's a shadow of concern making its way through. "You sure you're okay?"

"Pastor, I'm fine. Trust me."

Pastor nods and gets up from the edge of the desk, unwilling to press the issue any further. "Let's get out of here. We both have wives to get to."

Mark and Pastor walk out his office. Before Pastor could get too far away, Mark calls him. Pastor Brentwood turns around.

"Yes, Son?"

Mark pauses at what Pastor called him. He never realized this until now, but Pastor Brentwood is the closest thing he ever had to a real father. He wishes he came sooner in his life. Maybe some things wouldn't have gone the way they did. "How long have you been married?"

"Forty-two years."

"You know where Jade and I are. You know what we've been through. This may be a stupid question, but . . . what do you think?"

"What do I think?"

"Yes . . . like, do you think we are going to make it?"

Pastor pats Mark on the shoulder. "You're making it now, Son. Did you see the way Jade looked at you?"

Mark smiles. "I did."

"That should be all the answer you need." He takes a deep breath. "But I'm not going to shortchange you here: it's still going to be some work. Marriage is work." He smiles. "But work well worth it. Understand?"

Mark nods.

"Now you move along. I have a hot date tonight."

"Pastor, you're sixty-four years old. You don't date, and it isn't hot."

"That's what you think." Pastor smiles. "Just ask the missus."

Pastor trots out the church's front doors.

Later in the night, Mark and Jade are on their way home from Bible study. Mark notices every few seconds, Jade stares at him. He finally decides to say something.

"Something up my nose?"

Jade chuckles. "No, silly. Why?"

"You were staring at me this whole ride."

"No, I wasn't."

"Yes, you were. If it's not a snot rocket . . . you are just so captivated by my looks."

Jade slowly turns her head to look out the window. "You are too much."

Long pause.

"It was nice that Pastor wanted to see how we were doing."

"Yeah, it was nice."

Jade adjusts her seatbelt and slides closer to Mark. She places her arm around the headrest of his seat.

"Uh-oh. What are you coming over here to do?"

"Nothing," Jade says in a not-so-innocent voice. She slides her feet into her seat and moves even closer. She places her mouth right to his ear. "You know I love you," she whispers.

"I do know this."

"You are the only one, other than Jesus, who can make my soul jump for joy."

Mark smirks as he feels the warmth of Jade's breath on his ear.

"And I don't know what I would do without you," Jade continues. "You have given me three beautiful children, a roof over our heads, food to eat. God has been so good to me . . . to us."

"Even though I'm out a job?"

Jade pulls back a bit. "I'm not worried about that, Mark."

"I know. I know. It's . . . just . . . I mean, I thank God every day for you having your job and it being enough to support us . . . and I'm not so sexist to think that I should be the main breadwinner because

I'm the man. But I couldn't find a job? No teaching job anywhere? Nothing."

"But you still do so much."

"Yeah, but none of that helps our family. I work in ministry. Three of them, to be exact . . . but none of them supports our finances."

"Maybe it is just part of the plan. Maybe it's a test, even. But you still get to do what you dreamed of and more, unless your dream was under the presupposition of getting money for your work."

"It was never about money. I just wish I played a bigger part in the success of our family."

"You play the biggest part, Mark. You know our success doesn't have anything to do with money."

"I know . . . I just—"

"You have your moments, I know. But you have to remember, the kids and I love you not because of the money you brought in. God loves you not because of the money you brought in. It's your heart, Mark. You are a good man . . . a strong man. That's important. That's what matters."

Mark gets silent. He pulls into the garage of their home.

"We all need the strong Mark, not the wallowing in self-pity Mark."

"You're right."

"I know I am." Jade moves close to his ear again, and in a low and sultry voice says, "And I planned on making love to the strong Mark tonight, but if he isn't anywhere to be found . . . ."

Mark raises an eyebrow. "Tonight?"

"Yes, tonight. Pay the sitter and put the kids to bed early. I'll be waiting." Jade gets out and walks in front of the parked car. She sits on the hood of the car and glances back at him. She hikes one shoulder up, bringing it close to her cheek, and purses her lips. She hops off the hood of the car and walks to the door that leads into the house. Just before she gets there, the door swings wide open and Charles stands there with a big smile on his face. Jade short-steps her way over to him and picks him up, shutting the door behind them.

Mark still grips the steering wheel, as he hasn't let it go since parking in the garage. He takes a deep breath and gets out of the car. He makes a quick promise to himself to shut his brain off for the rest of the night.

Chapter Two

"Okay, hold on, hold on. Be still. Ready?"

"Take it already."

"You look mean. Smile or something."

"I am."

"No, you're not. Show some teeth."

"Fine."

"That's better. Okay here we go, one . . . two . . . three."

SNAP!

Alberta Barlow pulls the camera away from her face and smiles. "That turned out well."

Her husband, Craig, smiles. "Now you have a picture for your desk at work."

They both walk along an empty beach, enjoying the sights and sounds of the area that surrounds them. Craig, in his Hawaiian-print shirt and shorts, lifts Berta up into his arms. Berta laughs as he carries her back to their towels. He lays her down first and then lies next to her.

"Chivalry is dead, huh? Liars," Berta says.

Craig laughs. "So, where to next?"

"Where to next? What do you mean where to next? Home, that's where."

"I know that. I mean after home . . . our next vacation."

"Craig, we've taken at least ten vacations since we got married. My job is starting to give me that sideways look. You know, the one before they fire you. I mean, we went to Paris, Rome, Fiji, that cruise on the Mediterranean . . . the Bahamas. We've traveled the world in a couple years."

"I told you that was what we were going to do."

"Yeah, but I thought that was one of those figurative sayings. You know, like that mushy poetic stuff."

"Well aren't you glad you were wrong?" Craig smiles.

Berta's face is straight. "I am, but we are on an island in the middle of nowhere."

"Bora Bora, to be exact."

"Yes, Bora Bora . . . and it's wonderful here, the hut over the water and everything . . . it's all great, but how about we stay home for a while. I may be all vacationed out."

"Or how about we go somewhere a bit closer to home . . . like Alaska."

"Alaska sounds nice . . . no, wait. First, Alaska isn't a bit closer to home. It's still on the other side of the US. And—"

"Alaska will be the last one for a while. Just let me take you to Alaska."

Craig looks at Berta with a pitiful look, pleading with his eyes.

"Fine. Just stop looking at me like that."

Craig lies on his side, resting his head on his arm, and stares at Berta. Berta, lying on her stomach, propping herself up with her elbows and forearms, dips her head and looks at Craig. She smiles. Her hair falls to the towel as her turquoise-colored earrings sparkle from the rising sun. The wind blows the back of her skirt around her legs. "What are you thinking?" Berta asks in a soft voice.

"I'm thinking that you are the most beautiful person I have ever seen."

Berta smiles and looks away shyly. She plays with her hands and continues smiling. "You're not so bad yourself," she says without ever looking him in the eyes. For a second, her face flashes of seriousness.

"What's wrong?"

"Nothing. Nothing is wrong. I just . . . I just wish Daddy was still alive to see us . . . married."

"I don't know, Berta. I'm not so sure he would want to see what's about to happen to you right now." He places his hand on her lower back.

"Stop it, Craig. I'm serious. Plus, if that were the case, he would only have to look away for a second or two."

"Hey, I get excited," Craig says while laughing. "In all seriousness, I think he knows. I'm not sure how . . . but he knows how happy we are . . . together."

"You think?"

"I do. Here, give me the camera. Move closer."

Craig takes the camera from Berta and flips it around to face himself. He lies on his back and pulls Berta in closer to lie on his chest. "Look at the camera and smile."

"Are you smiling, too?"

"I always am when you are around."

"You have about one more time to use a corny line on me."

"I'm smiling."

SNAP!

Craig turns the camera around to look at the picture he just took. He shakes the camera a bit. "For Mr. V. I'll drop it off when I go to visit his grave."

Berta lies on Craig's chest for some time before saying anything. Craig sets the camera down at his side.

"Craig?" Berta sounds muffled as she talks into Craig's chest.

"Yes, dear."

Berta moves to get up and whispers in his ear. "I think Daddy should be more concerned for you. I highly doubt he would want to see what is about to happen to you right now." She presses on his chest with her hand as she stands up and starts walking up the beach, hoping Craig is staring at her. Just before she could get out of his reach, Craig grabs her leg. She trips and falls into the sand.

"That is not romantic, Craig," she yells.

"I know." He crawls up to her. "But this is." He places his lips on hers and kisses her slowly, with care.

"What are you doing?"

"Kissing you."

"Well, come on. Let's go back to the hut."

"No." Craig continues to kiss Berta.

"What do you mean no? Where are we g—No, Craig. Not out here."

"Why . . . there's . . . no one on this side . . . of the . . . island." Craig starts working on her neck.

"Because . . . we might . . . that feels good." Berta groans. "Wait, Craig, wait." She stops him and stares at him for a few long moments, reading him. "I love you. You know that? No matter what we go through . . . despite what we're going through, I will always love you."

Craig whispers one last thing to her before making love to her on the beach.

"I love you more."

CHAPTER THREE

WHEN she saw the picture, she froze. Memories flooded her mind as her husband held the picture with a shaky hand. He, too, found himself unable to move as he stared at the picture in disgust. She snatched the picture from him. A pounding headache and the metal taste of blood in her mouth . . . the smell of antifreeze leaking from a crashed car . . . an unbearable pain raging up and down her broken arm. She ripped the picture in half and crumpled it up in her fist. Shortly thereafter, she left her husband crouched by the box in the attic. She wasn't necessarily angry with him, but she did fear what other items remained in the dusty, worn cardboard box in the attic.

That was a few days ago, but the memories still fill her gut with angst.

"Jade, you okay?"

Jade Cooke is snapped out of her daydream and stares at a short and skinny girl, seemingly fresh out of college.

"Pardon?"

"Are you okay? You were just staring off into space."

"Oh. Yes, I'm fine. What do you need?"

"Just wanted to let you know that all the materials are set for the presentation later today."

Jade, still sounding as if she is somewhere else says, "Okay. Thanks."

The young woman looks at Jade, attempting to read her again. "You sure you're okay?"

"Of course. Why wouldn't I be? Look, I'm going to head out for an early lunch." Jade gets up from her leather executive chair and grabs her navy blue blazer hanging on the back of it. She slides the blazer on and looks at the young woman again. "Karen, I'm fine."

"I hope so. Big presentation later."

"I'm ready. Don't worry."

Jade goes into her desk, one of the side drawers, and pulls out her purse. She grabs her keys and leaves her office, sliding on a pair of sunglasses and closing the door behind her.

It has been a little over two years since Jade's marriage was on the brink of failure. Half of that time was spent in counseling and recovering from what most marriages would crumble over. Every now and again, she puffs her chest out and smiles, for she knows she and her husband did bend, but they did not break. Although today . . . today is a different day; as different a day from any other. Call it intuition, some good foresight, a prophetic occurrence, or plain and simple fear, but something is off. Today, she doesn't feel as confident.

Jade leaves the marketing wing of a midsized pharmaceutical company, thinking about how just recently, she was promoted to the position of Vice President of Marketing, a drastic difference from the pharmacy-tech job she held years ago. First entering the company with a low-paying internship-type job, she quickly worked her way up the ladder by showing she knows how to bring in and handle the larger clients. In a way she was forced to take the aggressive approach to climbing the job ladder, because Mark, her husband, lost his job. After word about his indiscretions on school grounds broke out, the school board immediately asked for his resignation. He tearfully obliged, but everyone knows—probably even the school board itself knows—that Mark Cooke was the best teacher in town. Jade continues walking through the main office floor and out the building.

The sun is bright and warming while a cool breeze swirls around her, making the fabric of her pants flap around. It's almost the end of summer, and soon that breeze will get even cooler. She gets to her car, a burgundy S-class Mercedes Benz, and gets inside. She feels somewhat silly for spending so much money on a car, even though Mark, Berta, and Craig urged her to do so. They said she deserves it. Still to this day, Jade doesn't see how. Needless to say, her new position pays her well; very well, considering the size of the company and the current economic environment, to the tune of a hundred and ten thousand dollars a year. She finds it to be a miracle that she has a job to begin with. Stories of pharmacy technicians getting into marketing for a firm are few and far between, but to get to VP of marketing . . . Jade is sure that has never happened before, at least, not in a two-year time span. She starts the car and quickly turns down the radio that she had playing before she got out of the car in the morning. The leather seats yawn at her every movement. She presses a button on the steering wheel and sets her cell phone on the passenger seat. A few moments later Mark's voice comes in through the car speakers.

"Hey, Babe," he says.

"Hey, Love. I'm on my way."

"Okay. I'm pulling up now, so I'll grab us a table. Inside or out today?"

"Definitely out. It's good weather."

"You good? You sound a little down."

"I'm fine. Just a little tired . . . and this hot and cold weather has my nose stuffed a bit."

"You want me to pick something up for it?"

"No, no, don't worry about it. I'll probably work it out by the time I get home."

"Okay . . . for two please . . . outside . . . thank you." Mark pauses. "Got the table. We're good to go."

"Okay. I'll see you in fifteen."

Jade presses the button on her steering wheel again and straps on her seatbelt. Just as she is about to pull off, a silver Maserati coupe pulls up and parks next to her. Jade stares at the car and makes a face, though no one could see her expression through the tinted windows of her car. A tall man steps out and grabs his suit coat from the back of his seat. He has fair skin and a perfectly shaped haircut and goatee. As if he knows Jade is looking right at him, he flexes a bit as he puts on his suit coat. Jade blinks at the way his pink dress shirt fits snugly over his muscular chest. To most women, Calvin Gaffney is a heartthrob, the most eligible bachelor in the state, sending all types of women into a visual coma because they set their innocent and unsuspecting eyes on his greatness. To Jade, this guy is a reason to be nauseous, as everything about him makes her sick. Unfortunately, he is the CFO of the company, and she has to interact with him daily. Jade sighs and rolls her window down. She knows it would be rude to just pull off, and she knows she couldn't hide inside a running car, so she says hi.

"I've heard of coming in late, but man, this is a stretch, isn't it?" Jade says.

The man looks at Jade and smiles a big smile, showing off his obviously bleached, bright white teeth. "Not at all. I just got back from a conference. Where are you headed off to?"

"Lunch."

"Oh, yeah? Can I tag along?"

"Actually I was meeting with my husband . . . like we do every day."

"Oh, okay. Well, tell him I said hi."

"Will do." Jade knows she won't. "But let me get out of here before I have no time for lunch."

The man nods and smiles again. "As always, it was a pleasure, Jade."

Jade smiles a fake smile and rolls up her window. She pulls off.

"Yeah, you can tag along . . . with my fist in your mouth and foot in your behind, you arrogant jerk." Jade says to herself what she wanted to say to him.

CReD

Mark sits outside looking over a menu. Few people sit at the tables outside as a cool breeze flows around him. This past summer was a good one, one that he could never forget. A waiter comes up to his table and takes his order. He orders for himself and for Jade the same meals they always eat: a tuna club for her, and a turkey burger for him. Mark hands the menu back to the waiter and smiles, then leans back in his chair. Every day for the past year and a half, Mark and Jade have met at this restaurant for lunch. Rain or shine. Even in a blizzard. This every-workday rendezvous is part of a concentrated effort to repair their marriage. Though it was a small step, its benefits outweighed many other things they've attempted.

His mind shifts to the box in the attic. He looked through the rest of the box after Jade left a torn-up picture of that woman in her wake. The whole box, the entire box, was filled with different keepsakes and things that came from Alicia.

Alicia: the very same woman who, at the time, seemingly popped out of thin air to widen the already monstrous canyon that separated him and Jade.

He didn't know he even kept any of those things, let alone brought them into his house and stuffed them into a box in the attic. There were different pictures and love notes written by both him and her. It seemed as if he was trying to hold on to what he had with Alicia. At least, he imagines that is what it looked like to Jade, who has every right to be upset. He has to clear the air because he knows something like this could cause a rift, and he doesn't want anything to do with that after the journey they had.

Mark hears the clock of dress shoes on the concrete and they abruptly stop behind him. The back of his neck gets warm as he feels someone staring at him. He doesn't turn around. Slowly, Jade's beautiful face comes into his peripheral vision. He smirks as she gives him a kiss on the cheek.

"Hey, Handsome," she says, smiling.

"Afternoon, my love." Mark gets up from his seat and pulls out Jade's seat, allowing her to sit comfortably in front of him. He gets back to his seat.

"Did you order already?"

"I did. Got us the usual." He slides his chair closer to the table. "How's work?"

"You know . . . work. Nothing new or exciting ever happens in that place." Jade slightly turns her lips to the side. "I do have a presentation to give today. Some pretty big clients I have been courting for months now."

"Yeah?"

"Yeah. I thought I would be more excited than this, but I'm not."

Mark shifts in his seat. He watches her fidget for a brief moment before realizing why she isn't all that excited. "The box?"

Jade stares at Mark as if she were shocked he knew, though it doesn't quite come as a surprise to her. They have been in tune with each other for a while now. She nods.

"Sweetheart, I did not keep ahold of those things for any reason. I didn't even know those things were up there."

"I know, hon. But back then . . . you held on to those things for a reason, right?"

"I guess so."

She stares at Mark for a few moments before shaking her head and chuckling. "It's just a box . . . that's what I told myself. Just a box with direct reminders of that psychopath and what she did to us . . . of what we did to ourselves."

"We aren't those people anymore. We are a different couple now."

"I know. But that feeling I had when you opened that box hasn't left. I can't even tell you why."

"What is it? The feeling, I mean."

Jade stares Mark straight in the eyes. "Fear."

"Aww, come on, honey. There's nothing to be afraid of."

"Don't you think I know that? I don't even know what I'm afraid of. Although—"

"What?"

"We have no idea where she is."

"She's in jail." Mark knows that's untrue and he knows Jade knows as well, but he says it anyway as a means of dismissing the subject.

"No, she was in jail. We have no idea where she is, what she's doing."

"She moved on just like we did."

"She still could be living in the area."

"She isn't."

"How do you know?"

Mark stares at Jade for a moment. "I don't. But what I do know is that it doesn't matter and that I love you. So you have nothing to worry about."

"She tried to kill us."

Mark gets silent. The waiter comes to their table with their meals. Mark blesses the food and they begin to eat.

"Look, Jade, you have nothing to worry about. You can count on that. Before, I know, that wouldn't mean much to you. I was a weak man with even weaker excuses, but hear me clearly: I will die before I let anything happen to you or the kids."

Jade looks at Mark and the fierce determination in his eyes. She knows what he said is true, and finds comfort in it.

"Well, that's a shame. Because I planned on having my husband for at least twenty more years." She smiles.

"You will. I'm not worried about Alicia . . . or anyone else that wants to act stupid. Jesus is on our side. So stop acting so skittish." Mark sniffs the French fries he ordered with his burger, and then shoots a look up at Jade. "No worries."

"No worries." Jade grips her sandwich. "What did you do with the box?"

"Burned it . . . all of it."

Jade nods and takes a bite of her sandwich.

CHAPTER FOUR

CRAIG Barlow sits at work at his desk, unable to concentrate. He twirls around in his chair a few times before grabbing the phone and calling his wife Berta.

"I wanna go back to Bora Bora," he says.

Berta chuckles. "Already? Why? What's wrong?" she says in a quiet voice.

"Nothing is wrong per se . . . I just can't concentrate, that's all. How is your day so far?"

"Busy."

"Well, mine isn't."

"That's because you aren't doing any work."

Craig leans back in his chair. "I can't wait to see you tonight, though."

Berta chuckles again. "Is that why you can't concentrate?"

"Maybe. Just thinking about that move you did in Bora Bora. Completely blew my mind."

Berta pauses. "I'm so embarrassed. Your face afterwards was one of pure shock and happiness. Oh, my goodness, I'm so embarrassed." She exhales loudly.

"Don't be . . . because I'm not." Craig hears Berta's contained laughter as if she's far away. *She must have set down the phone*, he thinks. A few moments later, Berta speaks again.

"You really liked it?"

"I have never . . . in my entire life . . . I mean you . . . Yes, Berta, I liked it . . . a lot. I need you to do that again tonight."

"So now you *need* me to do it?"

"Yes. I don't even care. I'm strung out on a move. I'm afraid to ask, but . . . where did you learn that?"

"I didn't. It was a spur-of-the-moment thing and I was"—Berta lowers her voice to a whisper —"feeling extra creative. I can't believe you have me talking about this. I'm at work."

"I am, too."

"Yeah, but you can talk on the phone all day if you wanted. I can't."

"All right, church girl. I'll let you go."

"Church girl?"

"Yeah. I've called you that before."

"But now? You call me that now?"

"I dunno . . . I never knew church women to know how to do . . . stuff like that."

Berta tries to whisper even more. "You've never known church women to please their husbands?"

"Not like that."

Berta sighs, then snorts. "Your naiveté is cute sometimes."

"Cute enough for the move?"

"We'll see. Anyway, I have to run to the church after work."

"You know we have that charity dinner to go to."

"I know. I'm only running in really fast to talk to the women's ministry leader."

"Oh. That's fine. I'll see you later tonight."

"Alright, Baby. I love you."

"Love you, too." He goes to hang up the phone but jerks it back to his ear. "Wait, Babe."

"Yes."

"Do you miss it?"

"Miss what? You better not be talking about what I think you are talking about."

"No." He chuckles. "I'm asking if you miss working here."

"Sometimes. Yeah, sometimes I miss it. Why?"

"Because I do. I miss being able to tell you stuff while working without having to rush off the phone. I miss the small things, ya know. Like how you used to get me ready for a terrible date. Or how we would just sit there and talk about all the airheads I dated."

"I do miss those conversations . . . those times, but Craig, we can still have those times and better. We . . . just . . . don't."

"Yeah." He rubs the back of his head. "Maybe we have to fix that."

"We do."

Awkward silence.

"Craig, I have to go. I'll see you tonight."

"Alright, Babe. Love you."

"Love you, too."

Craig hangs up the phone and leans deeper into his seat. A few moments later Ted, his assistant, sounds through the intercom.

"Mr. Barlow, you have a second?"

"What's going on, Ted?"

"Three things. One, Mrs. Tolliver wants to meet up. She sounded a bit nervous about this retirement thing."

"Call Mrs. Tolliver. Check. What's next?"

"Mr. Collier . . . his wife is pregnant."

"Oh, boy. Gotcha. Next?"

"I'm not sure who this is. Her name is Patrice Stafford. She wanted to meet and discuss business, but she didn't say what exactly."

"A new client?"

"Yes, sir."

Craig taps his pen on the desk. "Did she say anything else other than meet on business?"

"Nope."

"Okay. Thanks. You still studying for these licensing exams?"

"Of course, sir. I'm thinking I'll be ready to take the series seven next week."

"Good. That's good to hear. Now get back to work . . . slacker."

"You're the one talking on the phone all day."

"Touché Ted, touché. Back to work."

"Yes, sir."

Craig clicks off the intercom and leans back into his chair.

⊗

Berta hangs up the phone and gets up from her desk with a stack of papers in her hands. The pages have different tabs sticking out, denoting where a signature is needed. She trots through the office, the top floor of an insurance company—the underwriting floor—and gets to a large double door. She knocks first, then gently opens to see a man sitting at a large desk looking through some more papers. A man of few words, John Bromley glances up at Berta, then looks back down. Berta walks over to his desk and places the stack of papers in the corner. He looks at the papers. The white-haired man then grabs the stack and places it under the stack that he was already working on.

"You have a three o'clock and a four o'clock today, Mr. Bromley."

"Thank you, Berta."

Silence.

Berta stands there for a few moments before heading to the door.

"Berta."

"Yes, Mr. Bromley."

"How's your family?" The man asks without removing his gaze from the papers.

"Good. My family is good."

"Good. The holidays are just around the corner."

"Yes, sir, I know."

23

The man says nothing else.

Berta walks out of the office, finding the interaction strange, but after two and a half years of working with Mr. Bromley, she feels she is used to his much-introverted ways. She gets back to her desk and looks around the floor. A bunch of people run around handing off papers, picking up papers, very few people stopping to talk or interact. She sighs and gets together a few more papers for the other underwriters.

"Hey, Berta."

Berta looks up to see a short woman in black slacks and a blouse standing in front of her desk.

"Do you have my packet ready for me yet?"

Berta tries to smile but knows it comes out looking more like a snarl. "I was headed over to your office in a few minutes, Angelina."

Angelina Crosby, the second of the two underwriter managers Berta assists, is the one Berta doesn't mesh with too well. She stands at around five-foot-three and barks orders at anyone under the sound of her voice. In most cases, Berta is the only one under the sound of her voice. She reminds her of a Chihuahua. *Just yap, yap, yapping away,* Berta thinks.

"I need my packet rather soon, Berta."

Berta doesn't say anything, a trick Berta uses on her often. If she ignores Angelina, she usually goes away. This time, she doesn't move. Berta keeps working and she pulls up a chair to sit in front of her. Berta doesn't look at her at all, knowing that it would give her great satisfaction to see Angelina's angry stare.

A few minutes later, Berta clamps together a stack of papers and places it at the corner of her desk. "There's your packet."

Angelina grabs the papers and skims through them while still in front of her. "You know, Berta," she says while still flipping through the papers, "I could have used this information quite some time ago. But you weren't here. Where were you again?"

Berta internally groans. "On vacation."

"I see. Where was it this time?"

Berta stares at the woman and makes attempt after attempt to restrain herself from jumping over her desk and wringing the woman's neck. Angelina glares with a look as if to say, "Well, out with it."

"Bora Bora."

"Ahh, that's it. Bora Bora. I don't remember ever approving *another* vacation for you. So I was wondering . . . ."

"You aren't my boss. You're not my supervisor. You're simply another coworker that I am trying to be nice to. But to reference your point, my vacation was approved *by my boss*. Mr. Bromley had no issues."

"Let's clear something up, shall we?" Angelina adjusts in her seat. "You are executive assistant to not only Bromley, but myself as well. You were in the room when the decision was made. For some odd reason that is beyond me, you seem to forget that."

Berta takes in a deep breath and exhales slowly. "What is the problem? What is the point of your little rant?"

Angelina grips the papers in her hand and stands up. "You take a lot of vacations. That's valuable time from the office."

"Are we really having a debate over my company-given vacation days?" She chuckles. "Sounds like you need more to do. Plus, they're my vacation days. I can use them whichever way I want." Berta notices Angelina doesn't look her in the eye. Instead, her focus is on a picture of Berta and Craig, which is sitting on the desk.

"We aren't debating. I'm telling you how it is." Angelina places her hands flat onto Berta's desk. "A word of advice: I wouldn't take off for anything anytime soon. You might just find yourself looking for another job."

Before Berta has a chance to respond, Angelina trots away. Berta decides not to tell Angelina that she has to be in the meeting with Mr. Bromley at four.

CHAPTER FIVE

JADE walks through the office with her briefcase on wheels behind her, after her presentation. Karen seems to have trouble keeping up with Jade as she motors her way through to her office. Once inside, she and Karen begin to celebrate. Jade gently closes the door.

"That was big. That was huge," Karen says.

"I know. It sure was. And they all were eating out of the palm of my hand." Jade begins to jump around in her heels. "It's been a while since I had to do this . . . especially for such a huge group."

"But you pulled it off."

"Man, that was fun."

Someone knocks on her door and in comes Calvin with a big smile on his face.

"Vineland Health Pros, huh? You lit it up in there. I watched them as they left the room. They were confident, giddy almost. You must have given one heck of a presentation."

"Thank you, Calvin. It was a good couple hours."

"Hey, Karen, do you mind leaving me alone with Jade for a second?"

Karen looks at Jade, then at Calvin. "Sure, no problem. Good job again, Jade."

Jade nods as Karen leaves the office. Calvin waits to speak until he hears the click of the door.

"Twenty-five healthcare professionals . . . one network . . . one deal . . . and you reel it in for us. You are amazing, you know that?"

"Thank you." Jade walks around her desk to take a seat.

"We should go out to dinner . . . and celebrate."

Jade's face turns to a slight frown. "I will celebrate . . . with my husband. He will be pleased to know how I got the big deal."

Calvin smiles and begins to chuckle. "I'm sure he would." He sits on the edge of her desk. "How was lunch?"

"Very well. Thank you." Jade keeps her tone formal.

He pauses and looks down at the ground. "No prob. Listen, I have a few files on my desk, a couple projects that I need to run by you."

"Well, I'm getting ready to leave, so . . . ."

"Oh, okay. Yeah, sure, I'll get out of your way."

"Thanks. That would be great." Jade smiles a blatantly fake smile.

Calvin leaves the office and a few moments later Karen comes back in. She stares at Jade.

"He did it again, didn't he?"

"As usual."

"I don't get it. What makes him think he can just say what he wants to whomever he wants? What makes this guy think he can get with any woman any time?"

"I would have to say those women that lie down for him and the men afraid to say anything do."

"Well, not me. I don't play that. My boyfriend would tear him to pieces, as I'm sure your husband would." Karen looks around. "You have to tell someone. Tell the CEO."

"Right, Karen. I've been in this position for a little over a few months . . . Calvin in his for ten. Think about it. Officially, I am the only high-up woman in the company. They wouldn't believe anything I say and Calvin has a bunch of people waiting to line up and virtually testify in court and vouch for his so-called good character."

"Someone has to believe you."

"No one will, Karen . . . and even if they do, they'll be too scared to say anything for fear of losing their jobs. Calvin has this place wrapped around his manicured finger."

"So we just let it happen?"

"We?"

"He doesn't try to get at me, but it feels like he watches me, too."

Jade smiles. "But you don't play that."

"That's right."

"Look, Karen, I'm not at all worried about Calvin and his groupies. If it gets to be any more of an annoyance, I'll get Mark on him. But that is only if it gets to be more than I can handle."

"He knows about it?"

"Of course he does. But I asked him to ease up. I don't need my husband going to jail."

"I understand."

"But my advice to you is this: keep working hard and keep your high moral and ethical code. Wherever you end up, keep those with you."

"Wherever I end up?"

"You know more than I do that you are by far the most skillful here. But you wouldn't have gotten noticed because you won't sleep with Calvin. Because of that, you will always be at the bottom rung here . . . until he's gone." Jade shuffles some papers on her desk. "I wanted you on my team for your skill and ethics and I felt you deserved it. I'm not sure how much longer I'm going to last here, but while I'm here . . . you're secure . . . once I'm gone . . . I can't make any promises."

Karen continues to look at the ground. She doesn't say anything for a while.

"Karen?"

"We are supposed to be celebrating. All that other stuff we can worry about later." She smiles. "I guess though that means you and your husband aren't going to the office party this year?"

"I haven't talked to him about it yet."

"Well, what are you waiting for? The party is soon . . . like next Friday soon."

"I know. I'm still debating."

"On what?"

"On if I want him anywhere near Calvin after I tell him what happened just ten minutes ago."

"I see . . . Well, you guys should really come. You two are the perfect non-drunk company my boyfriend and I need."

Jade smiles. "I'll talk to him about it tonight."

◌₈◌

Mark sits in the copy room of the church waiting for his print run to finish. He sits alone. Lately, that's the way he would have it. For the past two years, all he's heard is people wishing him well, giving him job leads, saying how great a teacher he was—how great a teacher he *was*. Mark impatiently gets up from his seat to see if his copies are complete. He grabs one and skims it, checking the quality. *Setting up for back to school drive*, he thinks. He places the paper back in with the rest and goes back to his seat.

He misses teaching. He misses his students. Every now and again he goes on his search to find out how they are doing, without anyone ever knowing. They're all moving on to seventh grade now. Frankie Simms, his outspoken C-average student is now an A student who loves to write. Betty-Ann Lawrence is still doing great in class and is now part of the debate team. Donald Francis is still unbelievably cocky and plays basketball. Mark then remembers Tim, the only one he couldn't and wouldn't track down. Tim, Alicia's son, a student who quickly became his favorite in the short time he was here. Mark shakes his head at the memories.

"Hey man, you good?"

Mark looks up to see Reverend Hudgins, Pastor Brentwood's righthand man.

"Oh, yeah, I'm good. How are you doing?"

"I'm good. You sure you okay? You look down."

"Naw, just tired."

Reverend Hudgins steps into the copy room. "Everything is going to be okay, Mark. An opportunity will pop up."

Mark, being angered by the comment he has heard a thousand times, simply nods. Reverend Hudgins notices his shift in demeanor and changes the subject. "You going to the men's retreat?"

Mark smiles a faint smile, feeling badly for letting even a slight annoyance show. "I decided against it."

"Really? You know it's a multi-church retreat. Should be some great seminars and classes . . . and Brentwood is preaching."

"I know."

"It isn't too late to register." Reverend Hudgins eyes the copier that has finished running copies for Mark. "And it's in your hometown. You're from Philadelphia, right?"

Mark gets up and grabs the papers from the copier and sets them on a table next to it. "Yes, I am."

"Maybe it would be a good time to see some family, maybe?"

"No, it wouldn't." Mark puts the papers in a box and grips the box in his arms. "Look, thanks for the concern, but I'm fine. Really, I am." He makes his way out of the room without saying goodbye.

CHAPTER SIX

"MR. Barlow, we thank you again for your generous donation. Every time we hold one of these dinners, you have shown up and helped us in a major way."

"It isn't a problem. This donation is from both me and my wife."

"Your wife? When did you get married?"

"About two years ago."

"No way."

Craig, wearing a tux, stands in the corner of a large ballroom at the charity dinner. He talks to a short blonde-haired woman. Everything about her says librarian: the tight bun in her hair, the glasses, the sweater and blouse, the skirt just below her kneecaps; though she isn't a librarian at all. Craig doesn't remember exactly what she does, but he knows she works for the state and every three years or so, she puts together this charity dinner to help rebuild different parks and public areas. Craig was always a big contributor because his mentor, the late and great Raul Valencia saw it fit to help as well.

The blonde-haired woman smiles at Craig. Craig shuffles his feet a bit.

"You don't believe me? You thought it would never happen, huh?"

"I didn't say that, I just . . . wow, who is the lucky woman?"

"You ready for this?"

"I think so."

"I married Berta."

"Berta who?"

"Berta, Berta. Mr. Valencia's Berta."

"Oh, my goodness." The woman gushes. "That is so wonderful. I bet she's making a real man out of you now, huh?"

"What's that supposed to mean?"

"I mean," the woman laughs, "that before . . . you weren't exactly the . . . settle-down type of guy . . . or so it seemed. Obviously I was wrong."

"So real men settle down?"

"Gosh, Craig, you know what I mean. Don't take everything so literal. Why wasn't I invited to the wedding?"

"It was a private affair. We only had a few people there."

"And I couldn't have been one of the few?"

"I uhhh . . . ."

"I'm going to talk to Berta about this." She smiles a bigger smile. "Just kidding." She pats Craig on the arm. "I'm happy for you two. You take care of her, you hear? That's my baby. Has been ever since Raul brought her along when she was a child."

"I know. Trust me. I've made it part of my purpose to take care of her."

"Good." She turns to look behind her. "I have to go, but I'll see you two before the night is out."

"Sounds good." Craig starts to walk off.

"Thanks again for the donation."

Craig smiles. "Indeed it is my pleasure." He slides his way through the crowd to get to the other side of the ballroom and finds Berta sitting by herself at one of the tables. Not for one second does she look lonely or out of place. Rather, she looks like she owns the place. That's one of the things that Craig loves about her. Wherever she goes, she is sure of herself, but not in an arrogant way, not in a way some may call "prissy." Craig calls it a shy confidence. He looks at her, observing even the slightest detail, like how one corner of her mouth goes up a bit higher than the other when she smiles to greet people, or how she folds her hands and rests them in her lap as if she is posing for a picture, or how she crosses her legs under her long and sleek evening gown, which Craig notices is a different color than what she normally wears. The gown is bright red and she has on matching bright red pumps and wears bright red lipstick. It's a classic look that works well with her complexion. The part that he observes on her the most is the five-carat diamond ring and wedding band that glisten in the dim lighting from the chandeliers.

She notices him approaching and smiles. Craig gives her a kiss on the cheek and slides into the seat next to her. Neither says anything for a while.

"You're quiet tonight," Craig says.

Berta looks over and smiles. "Sorry. Just thinking too much. As usual."

Craig takes a sip of his drink. "What's on your mind?"

"I dunno . . . stuff."

"And this 'stuff' has you thinking so hard on it because?"

Berta shrugs her shoulders, still maintaining her regal look. Craig slides closer to her and puts his hand out on the table for her to grab. She touches his hand with her index finger, tracing along his palm, before setting her hand in his.

"What happened?" Craig asks.

"Work." Berta sighs. "It was a rough day."

"That Angelina chick again?"

Berta nods. "I'm getting tired of playing this game with her."

"Then don't."

"What choice do I have?"

"You can always quit. You know that money isn't an issue for us."

Berta looks at Craig for a few moments and smirks. "But you know I can't just quit."

Craig smirks. "I know."

"Plus, what am I going to do all day?"

"I don't know. Stuff for you. Do more at the church. House stuff maybe. Maybe take care of kids."

"I don't know." Berta glances at Craig. "I like how you threw kids in there, though."

"Yeah? I'd thought I'd sneak that one in."

Berta smiles. Shortly thereafter, her face turns serious. "You know we're not ready for them yet."

"I don't see why we aren't."

"You know we have our issues . . . issues that we need to deal with before bringing someone else in on them."

Craig sighs. "So we have our quirks. What married couple doesn't? That doesn't stop half of America from having kids."

Berta stares at Craig incredulously. "We're not half of America."

Craig nods. "Okay. Let's talk them out."

"Now you want to talk them out? I have been urging you to talk to me about these things for months now, even during the trip to Bora Bora."

Craig says nothing.

"I really don't get you sometimes."

"It's the job, isn't it?"

"What?"

"What happened to the Berta who made jokes, who smiled more than anyone I've ever seen, whose laugh almost always causes someone else to laugh? This job is taking away those things that make you Berta. It's sapping you of all life."

Berta stares off into the crowd. "It's not the job, Craig."

"I think it is."

"So what do you want me to do?"

"Quit."

Berta shakes her head. "That's not happening."

"Then I don't know." Craig takes a sip of his drink, his face showing clear frustration. "Find a balance somehow. So you can be yourself again."

CS8O

Berta looks away from Craig, a bit disappointed in him, for he never asked what he could do to fix the problem.

"Look," Craig says. "Why don't we forget about this stuff for tonight and enjoy the evening?"

Berta moves a strand of hair from her face. "Sounds good." But in her mind, she's telling herself that they are always forgetting about it and fake-enjoying things, just to come right back to it some other time.

CHAPTER SEVEN

MARK gets back home, carrying Amber in his left arm and holding a diaper bag in his right hand. Charles comes running around Mark and heads straight to the TV, flipping his book bag off and sending it flying into the couch.

"Did you do your homework?"

Charles stops in his tracks. "We didn't have any."

"What did I tell you about lying?"

"But D—"

"Homework. Now."

Charles makes a face and sets down the remote. He begrudgingly grabs his book bag and goes upstairs. Mark walks around the corner into the living room and sets the baby in her playpen.

"Daddy, I need help," Charles screams from upstairs.

"I'll be there in a second. See what you can get done by yourself first."

"'kay."

A few moments later, Mark hears the garage door opening again, knowing it is Jade just getting home as well. Amber stands up in her playpen, holding on to the edges, and looks toward the door.

"You're excited, huh?"

Amber looks at Mark for a second, then back at the door. As soon as Jade comes in, a big smile comes over Amber's face, showing but three teeth. She starts making noises and shaking the rails of the playpen.

Jade comes in with a smile and gives Mark a kiss. "The rest of your day go good?"

"Yeah. Not bad."

"Good." Jade smiles. She looks over to Amber and makes a surprised face at her. Jade hops her way over to the playpen and picks Amber up as Amber gurgles random words.

"I'm going to help Charles with his homework."

"Okay. Getting started on dinner now. Kalina isn't home yet?"

"Nope. Bus didn't come yet. Must be running late."

Jade disappears into the kitchen, still holding Amber. Mark goes upstairs to help Charles with his homework when he sees Charles sitting at his desk, falling asleep.

"Charles."

Charles jerks his head up and looks around, trying to see if anyone saw him sleeping.

"You don't do that at school, do you?"

"No." Charles looks at him earnestly.

"Yeah, I bet. And how the heck are you falling asleep already? It's only been five minutes. Anyway, what happened to you trying it by yourself?"

"I did try. I don't get this stuff."

"All right, well, let me help you. First, wake up."

"Dad, when can I play football again?"

"When you bring your grades up."

Charles grunts, then growls. "Kalina can do whatever she wants to do. Why can't I?"

"Kalina has straight As. And she can't do whatever she wants to do. She earns certain privileges by working hard."

"I'm not as smart as she is."

"Yes, you are. You're just lazy."

"This stinks."

"Mmm-hmm, I know." Mark smirks. "What number are you on?"

"One."

Mark sighs, then he hears the school bus driving by the house. He goes to the window to see Kalina up the street walking toward the house . . . with a boy . . . and his hand is in her back pocket.

"What the h—"

Mark jerks away from the window and rushes out of Charles' room. "Keep working. I'll be right back."

Mark bounds down the steps loudly enough to get Jade's attention.

"What's wrong?" she asks while standing at the kitchen entrance.

Mark doesn't answer and opens the front door. Just as he gets to the top of the driveway, Kalina and the boy see him. The boy snaps his hand out of Kalina's back pocket and freezes. Both stand a few houses away, frozen as Mark marches toward them. Mark, grumbling to himself, makes it to Kalina and grabs her arm.

"Bye," he says to the boy in an indignant tone and turns his back on him. He pulls Kalina along until they are both in the house.

"Explain," Mark says.

"I . . . he . . . ." Kalina doesn't know what to say.

"What happened?" Jade yells from the kitchen.

"Your daughter is home," Mark says. "And she was trying to bring us a present . . . in her back pocket." Mark walks to the kitchen.

"I don't get it."

"Somebody was feeling on her booty."

"What?"

"She was walking home, with a boy's hand in her back pocket. The little gremlin was cupping my Kalina's booty, Jade. I wonder if he is still out there." Mark starts to go outside again.

"Hold it."

Mark stops at Jade's command.

"Go upstairs and help Charles with his homework. Kalina, come help me with dinner."

"Yes ma'am," Kalina says and heads into the kitchen with Mark staring her down.

Mark goes upstairs.

❦

"Was it Gerald?" Jade whispers to Kalina.

Kalina nods.

"Why don't you invite him over for dinner? That would be nice, wouldn't it?"

"No. Daddy is gonna kill him."

"So it was better to have your father see his hands on your butt?"

Kalina stares at the ground.

"He won't kill him. I won't let him. But if you call this guy your boyfriend, I think it would be a good idea to invite him over."

Kalina looks at the counter. "Spanish rice and beans?"

"Yup."

Kalina nods. For a moment, she stays silent.

"Mommy, I really like him."

"I know."

"But he isn't a bad guy. He's smart and athletic. He's quiet and loud at the same time."

"Are you getting poetic on me?"

Kalina smiles. "No. I just really like him. And he's the only one I know who can consistently beat me in chess. Daddy can't even do that anymore. And Gerald tries, Mommy, he tries."

"He tries what?"

"He tries to impress me. To be around me. Guys at school act so macho, like I'm supposed to worship the ground they walk on." Kalina puts a finger up. "Uhhh, no. Sorry, I'm not that type."

"I know that's right." Jade says with her back to Kalina. She tries to hide the smile that creeps onto her face as she fiddles around with the stove.

"Gerald asked me if he could put his hand in my pocket. I said yes. But neither one of us meant any harm. I mean, it's not like I'm going to jump into the bed with him or anything."

"I know, Kalina. But I think your father has some reason to be alarmed. For starters, he doesn't know Gerald. As far as he is concerned, he sees Gerald as just another hormone-driven punk who is trying to make you not-so-innocent anymore."

"But that's not who Gerald is."

"Your father doesn't know that."

Kalina stares out the kitchen window. "Was his hand in my back pocket that bad?"

"You don't see your father's hand in my back pocket while we walk down the street."

"But Mommy, you don't have any pockets. Either you wear those business skirts, which look really good on you by the way—"

"Thank you."

"Yup. Or you wear business pants like today. No butt pockets."

Jade chuckles. "The point is, you need a bit more modesty. You are still just fourteen."

"Yeah . . . just fourteen." Kalina grabs a stepping stool and goes into the cabinet to grabs cups for everyone. "When can I have what you and Daddy have?"

"What do you mean?"

"Daddy worships the ground you walk on. He, like, carries you, and you carry him. I don't know how to explain it."

"I think I get you just fine. We put in years for it to be this way, Sweetheart. Years of highs and lows. It doesn't come overnight . . . or over a week . . . or over a month . . . you get what I'm saying."

"Kinda."

"It takes time."

"But I want it now."

"Just be patient. You are such a wonderful person. We see it. God sees it. That someone is out there for you. You just have to wait for things to grow."

Kalina stays quiet. "You trying to make me cry?"

Jade laughs. "No. I'm not. I'm just telling you like it is."

"Hmm. Well, can you tell Daddy about Gerald for me?"

"I'll think about it."

"Thanks, Mommy."

"Yeah, yeah. Set the table. Oh, and no more back pocket booty feels."

Kalina chuckles. "Okay."

∞

Later in the night, after the kids have been put to bed, Mark and Jade sit up in their bedroom talking.

"I don't know, Mark. I think you should ease up on her."

"Why? She still hasn't said anything about him to me."

"I know. She's scared."

"Scared of what?"

Jade smiles. "Look, here's your opening. You've finally seen him. Now you can ask questions."

"But why should I? Why is it that she told you months ago about this supposed boyfriend, but she hasn't said a word about any boy to me?"

"Because you're her father."

"And?"

"And she thinks you would kill whoever steps to our porch."

Mark sighs. Jade crawls up behind him and wraps her arms around his waist, placing her chin on his shoulder. "Just talk to her."

41

Mark stares at the tan carpet for a few seconds. "Fine."

Jade kisses Mark on the cheek and slides back to her side of the bed, her satin pajamas making hissing sounds as she skims under the covers. "How are things at the church?"

"Fine. They're still trying to get me to go to that men's retreat."

"Why don't you go?"

"It's in Philly. I promised myself some time ago that I would never go back. Bad stuff happens every time I do."

"I think you should go. It could be beneficial."

"Beneficial?"

"Yes. Maybe there's a message there for you, a word to keep you going. You never know."

"I guess."

"When is it?"

"Next Friday."

Jade props up her pillow and lies gently on it. The retreat starts on the same day as the office party. She wants Mark to go with her, but she knows it is more important for Mark to go to this retreat. *Maybe this will break him out of his funk. Since he lost his job, he hasn't been a hundred percent, no matter how many times he smiled to cover it up.* "I want you to go. If not for yourself, go for me."

Mark turns to face her and looks at her with an expression that makes her insides melt. She pushes Mark's face to turn away from her.

"Don't look at me like that."

"Like what?"

"Like that."

Mark smiles, then slides under the covers. "I'll register tomorrow . . . for you."

"Thank you."

Mark lies down and nudges closer to Jade. Jade flattens her pillow and lies down, inching closer to Mark so that he can wrap his arms around her.

"So did you get those clients?" he asks.

"I did."

"Did you?"

"I did."

"Why didn't you tell me earlier? We could have celebrated."

"There's nothing to celebrate. I know it's a big thing, but it felt so hollow."

Mark keeps silent.

"There's that office party next week."

"When?"

"Friday."

"You want me to go to that and the retreat?"

"No. I'm just stopping by to show my face at the party. I don't really want to be there, anyway."

Silence.

"Mark."

Still not a word.

Jade turns around to see Mark sound asleep.

CHAPTER EIGHT

THE sun sprinkles rays of light through the window of the bedroom, waking Jade before her alarm goes off. She moves around a bit, removing the sheets from herself. She turns around to see Mark staring right at her.

"Good morning," she says.

"Morning." Mark's voice comes out deep and gravely. "Ready for prayer?"

"Yeah." Jade moves close to Mark, as if he's the sheet and she wants to cover herself with him.

"Whose turn is it to start?" Mark asks.

"I don't remember. I'll start anyway."

"Sounds good."

Jade closes her eyes. "Lord Jesus . . . thank you for giving us another day, and another chance to do Your will . . . ." Jade continues her prayer, giving thanks and asking for protection for their marriage. Mark eventually finishes off the prayer. Prayer: another often-used and highly beneficial recovery tool for their marriage. Every Saturday morning (even after those late night Fridays) Mark and Jade pray together. They always believed they should do it, but rarely did they. That is, until the bottom fell out of their marriage. Now, it is like second nature for both of them, something that Jade says brings them closer every week.

Jade looks Mark in the eyes. She kisses him on his lips softly. Mark smiles and places his hand on her thigh. Jade looks at his hand, then back at him.

"We can't right now," Jade says.

"Sure we can. It's morning. You know what happens in the morning."

Jade gets up from the bed. "I know, but we can't. Not this morning."

"Why not?"

"Berta and Craig are coming over, remember? And I have to take Kalina to school."

Mark sits up. "School? On Saturday?"

"Yeah. She joined this community service group. I think they're going to a retirement home."

Mark gets up from the bed and walks toward Jade. "It will only take ten minutes."

Jade moves away from Mark. "You always say that. But ten minutes turns to thirty. Next thing you know it's two hours later and we're late for ev"—Jade's alarm goes off and she slaps the top of it to shut it off—"late for everything we planned."

Mark chuckles. "As I recall, we were late the last few times because of you."

"I don't remember that."

"We were late to the high school orientation for Kalina because you were feeling 'bad,' remember? And we were late to church last Sunday because you had some 'things I needed to handle.'"

Jade laughs. "Shut up. I'm going to check on the baby." She walks up to Mark and kisses him again. She traces her finger along his chest. "But later tonight, if you want, we could have some fun." She smiles. "And if you're really good, I might put something nice on and give you a little show."

Mark smiles. As Jade pulls away from him and turns around, he slaps her on the butt, making a loud 'smack' against the satin of her pants. Jade hops a bit and smiles.

"If I'm really good, huh?"

"If you're really good."

Mark sighs. "You know, I can imagine this is how Eve got Adam to eat a piece of that apple."

Jade stops and looks at Mark strangely. She smirks. "What?"

"Eve came up to Adam and was like, 'You should take a bite of this apple.' And Adam, seeing Eve standing there naked and enticing and all, was thinking, 'If I take a bite of this apple, maybe she will do that upside-down thing hanging from a tree branch.'"

Jade laughs. "Mark, what are you talking about?"

"I'm just saying. Eve used sex to get Adam to eat that apple. There's no other way it could have happened. Eve shakes her booty in front of him and Adam takes a bite so she can shake it some more. Boom. The fall of man. You want me to be 'really good' and I'll get some. I say we should just do it now so we can balance out the universe."

"The universe?"

"Yes, the universe. Eve messed things up because she used what she had to get Adam to take a bite. Adam was scared he wasn't gonna get it anymore. Truth be told, he probably wasn't gonna get anymore because Eve already took a bite of the apple. She was already"—he makes air quotes with his fingers—"enlightened. She wouldn't want anything to do with him because she was smarter than he. Don't do me like Eve did Adam." Mark smiles. "For the sake of everything that is right and just in this world . . . Jade . . . I need you to get naked. It's the right thing to do."

Jade stares at Mark with a blank expression. "You're an idiot. I'm going to check on the baby." She leaves the bedroom laughing.

ೞ

Berta has been lying awake for the past few hours, most of that time spent watching the beams of sunlight crawl their way across the bed. She stares at Craig, who still sleeps, and places her hand on his face. Craig stirs for a quick moment before waking.

"Morning, Sunshine," Berta says.

Craig groans and stretches. "Good morning." He sits up in the bed. "How did you sleep?"

"Not the best."

"Really? After last night," Craig smirks, "I thought . . . you know . . . you would have slept pretty well."

Berta smiles. "Someone is proud of themselves, aren't they?"

"Shouldn't I be?"

"You know, you weren't always this cocky."

"I was. You were just love-struck then."

Berta lightly elbows Craig in his side. "What was I thinking?"

"I'll tell you what you were thinking. You saw me every day at work and had all these freaky fantasies about me. You were like"— Craig pitches up his voice, but it still sounds gravely— "'Oh, Craig, you are so big and strong, and you dress so nice. I just want to be around you and bask in your glow.'"

Berta grins. "Is that right?"

"That's my story and I'm sticking to it."

Neither for a few moments says anything as Craig holds Berta in his arms.

"At least I can still make you laugh," Craig says.

"Yeah. That isn't going to change. No chance."

Another moment of stillness surrounds them.

"So why the little sleep?"

"Worry, I guess."

Berta feels Craig take in a deep breath and exhale slowly.

"Worry about what?"

Berta moves from Craig's arms. "I don't know."

Craig looks at her with a confused expression.

"Just tell me something, Craig." Berta says. "Do you love me?" Her voice shrinks down to a whisper, as if she's about to cry.

Craig looks even more confused. "Of course I do, and I always will."

Yet Berta still senses a layer of uncertainty in his voice.

"Why you ask?"

"I just . . . I just needed to hear it, that's all."

"Well, I'll do you one better."

He pulls her close to him, covering her with his bare body, and makes love to her, but even that isn't enough to quell the pesky something troubling her soul.

∞

"Baby, hurry up. They're almost here." Jade runs around the house picking up some things and rearranging others. "And I still didn't get ready yet."

Mark clops downstairs in his workout gear. "I don't understand why you are cleaning now. Everything is clean . . . and it's just Craig and Berta. They've been here before."

"You know how I like this place to be clean when we have company."

"But it isn't company." Mark gives Jade a blank stare. "It's Craig and Berta."

Jade stops what she's doing to stare at Mark. She holds a cloth in one hand and spray in the other. "Here," she says while handing him both. "You clean. I get ready."

Mark stares at Jade for a bit longer before taking the cloth and spray. "Fine." He watches her as she walks away. "You need any help?"

Jade stops and stands with one foot turned out to her right. "With what?" She tries to conceal her smile.

"You know." Mark smiles back at her. "Don't act like you aren't tempted."

"By what?"

"By all this muscle you see. I'm all ready for a workout." Mark winks.

"Oh, goodness." Jade flips around and hurries upstairs.

"Come here, girl," Mark yells. "Where you going?" He doesn't wait for an answer but starts on spraying and wiping down the dining room table, though it already looks cleaned. He puts the cleaning items back under the kitchen sink and heads toward the living room when he feels it again. The same feeling that has been dragging him down since the incident with Alicia. Even after two years, he still doesn't know what to call it. After the first year, he likened it to a panic attack, but he knows that isn't what it is. Everything could be going normally. He could be happy as can be, but like a flash of lightning, this feeling of dread overtakes him. This feeling, this terrible feeling of profound sadness has consumed him many a time before and here it is again to take him down a road he'd rather not travel today.

The doorbell rings.

"Mark, can you get the door?"

Mark snaps back to reality, thankful for the reprieve from his descent into self pity, and goes to the front door. As he opens it he sees Berta smiling widely.

"Hey, lady." Mark smiles and gives her a hug. He sees Craig walking up the driveway toward the door.

"Hey, hey. How are you doing?" Berta moves past Mark.

"I'm good. Jade's upstairs getting ready." Mark looks back outside to see Craig stopped in the driveway. He looks back at Berta. "You can go ahead upstairs."

"Okay. Hey. You okay?" Berta looks at him, slightly squinting.

"Yeah, I'm good. Why? Do I look that out of shape?" Mark smiles.

"I'm not saying that. I'm just making sure, that's all."

"Oh. Well, yeah, I'm fine." Mark looks outside. "Nothing to worry about."

"You ready yet, man?" Craig yells.

Berta starts up the steps while shaking her head. "Sounds like someone is impatient."

Mark puts up his pointer finger then walks to the coat closet to grab his gym bag. While throwing the bag around his shoulders, he pulls out the running stroller for Jade.

"Jade, I'm outta here. Call me if you need me."

"Okay, Baby. Love you."

"Love you, too." Mark closes the door behind him.

Once near Craig, he gives him a fist bump and they get into his Porsche.

"What's good, man?" Mark asks.

"Ah, you know how it is. Work. Wife. Church. The norm. You?"

"Same."

For a while, both stay silent.

CHAPTER NINE

"HEY, Berta." Jade peeks her head out from the closet. "I'm almost ready." She ducks back into the closet. "Just need to find a pair of sneakers . . . to . . . go with . . . what . . . I have on." A shoe comes flying out of the closet. Jade eventually walks out with a pair of sky-blue sneakers to go with her sky-blue yoga pants and T-shirt. "So how are you?"

"I'm great. How are you?"

"You know. Busy as ever. So . . . ." Jade purses her lips and smiles. "How are the two lovebirds?" She slips her sneakers on.

"We're okay."

"Just okay?"

"You know. Still learning. Still getting used to each other's quirks."

"I see."

Berta looks at Jade as she goes to the baby's room to wake her up from her nap.

"Craig thinks it's a good idea to quit my job," Berta blurts out.

"Why?"

"He thinks it's changing who I am."

Jade gently rubs the cheek of the sleeping child. Amber opens her eyes and immediately smiles when first seeing Jade.

"Hey, baby," Jade says in a high-pitched voice. "You awake now? Wanna go on a run?" She lifts the child out of the crib and turns to Berta. "Well, is it?"

"Yes. Kinda. Well, yes and no."

Jade stares at her.

"It makes me tired, yes. And maybe I'm not as chipper when I come home because I'm frustrated. But it's a bit less stressful than it is at home. At least at work, I can keep my mind off things and just focus on work."

"But why would you want to focus so much on work? And why is home so stressful?"

Berta says nothing.

"Hold on for a sec." Jade knocks on Charles' door and creaks it open to see him doing schoolwork. "How many do you have left?"

"Three."

"Okay. Take a break and come walking with us."

Charles hops up from his seat, excited. "Okay." He runs to Berta and gives her a hug. He races downstairs ahead of them.

Jade and Berta head downstairs. Jade stops at the foyer to see the running stroller by the door.

"Awww," she says.

Berta looks at Jade, the softness in her face, and the smile that forms. She then looks back at the stroller.

"Here's a tip, Berta. Learn to appreciate even the small things Craig does. It goes a far way not only for him, but for you." She grabs the baby's jacket and hat and sets her in the stroller. "But anyway, what else is bothering you and Craig?"

"I guess nothing, really." Berta says, for fear of sounding off with too many complaints.

Jade looks at Berta, trying to read something off her. "You sure?"

"Yup."

"You seem . . . like there's more that you're not saying."

Berta shrugs off her jacket, revealing her black tights and T-shirt. Jade looks at how muscular Berta looks.

"Berta, what size are you?"

"A six. Why?"

"No reason. Skinny heifer."

Berta smiles. "You don't look bad, Jade."

"Yeah, whatever. Come on so I can get my size six back."

০৪৪

Craig looks at himself in the mirror while curling dumbbells. He lifts a few more times before placing the weight back onto the rack. He taps Mark on the arm and points to the heavy bag.

"Spot?"

Mark nods and they walk over to the heavy bag.

"So how's married life?"

Craig gives Mark a look. "Confusing."

"Yup. Welcome to marital bliss."

"No seriously. I am so confused, I don't know when I'm right . . . or wrong. Or what to do . . . what not to do."

"What happened?"

"Berta, that's what happened."

Mark laughs. "Okay. You're gonna have to give me more than that."

"Okay, so Berta and I . . . we've been off lately."

"Yeah."

"And for a while I didn't want to talk about it. Primarily because it wasn't such a big deal then. Now it's getting bigger, and becoming a major annoyance."

"Wow."

"I'll admit, I didn't think it was going to get this big. But I think it has to do with the job."

"You sure?"

"Yeah. But man, this is the tip of the iceberg here. I just. I don't know how you do it."

"Do what? Marriage?"

"Yes. It's not as exciting anymore. I mean . . . ."

"You've finally left the honeymoon phase."

"I guess. But Berta is great and I love her to death . . . this married life thing is . . . a monster . . . and I know that sounds bad. And with Berta being the way she is right now . . . it's wearing on me."

"And how is that reflecting upon your relationship with Christ? Or vice versa?"

"I still love Christ. And I still pray and go to church. It's just marriage. It isn't what I thought it was going to be."

"You know what you sound like?"

"What?"

"A man that has a bit of growing up to do. It sounds like you're stuck in your old days."

"I don't think I am. Though, I get how it seems that"—Craig hurls his fists into the heavy bag—"way."

"You remember when you told me that your purpose is to take care of her?"

"Yeah. But—"

"And remember how happy you were when you finally found 'the one?'"

"Yeah. But I never expected her to change so much in this way."

"It sounds to me that you are failing your purpose."

Craig stops. "What?"

"In a good marriage, you get out of it what you put in it. Berta strikes me as a woman who gives back what you give her . . . like a mirror, almost."

"So her acting strange towards me is my fault?"

"In part maybe. I mean, you don't really know what's wrong, do you?"

Craig looks down for a few seconds. "Nah. It can't be. I really think it's because of her job." He goes back to punching the heavy bag.

"Well let me give you this advice."

"I'm listening."

"Both of you are going to change. Change is inevitable, especially in a marriage. Just understand that you married Berta, the spiritual being, not Berta the body. If your purpose is to take care of her, make sure you're doing it spiritually as well as physically. And emotionally, too. This helps in her feeling secure. Because when you're both old and gray, God willing, you won't have that body to look at anymore, and the foundation you built in the beginning comes into play even more. Trust me on this."

Craig stops and looks at Mark. He nods. "So you think she feels insecure?"

"Maybe. But there's no real way of knowing if you don't genuinely talk to her about it. Don't run away from your problems, Craig."

"I'm not running."

"You've always ran. We both did . . . since we were little."

"I guess. Don't take this the wrong way, but that seems to be more your M.O."

"Maybe. Either way, don't run away from this one. It's only going to get worse if you do. If your marriage is on the line, you have to do whatever it takes to keep it."

"Gotcha. I hear you." Craig punches the bag more. "But you do know that at the first hint of gray I'm dying everything . . . even chest hairs."

Mark chuckles. "Man, shut up and switch. I might have to send a few haymakers to you instead of the bag."

⟋⟍

"Okay Berta, so what is it?"

"Huh? What is what?"

"It. You said home is more stressful than work. Why?"

Jade and Berta sit on a bench at the park after their jog. Up ahead is Charles, playing with the neighborhood kids.

"No reason. It's no big deal."

"You sure about that? The whole jog was silent. When we got back to the house, silence. On the way here, more silence. It's like you're in some deep trance."

"Am I that bad? I'm sorry. But I'm good."

Jade gives Berta a skeptical expression, but she presses no further. For a while, they both watch as Charles learns to play baseball.

"So you ready for one of these yet?" Jade asks as she picks up Amber from her stroller.

Berta looks over and smiles. "I should be, right?" She chuckles. "But no, no, I'm not ready for kids."

"Do you want any?"

"I know my clock should be ticking." Berta slides more onto the bench. "But I have no desire to have any."

"What does Craig think about that?"

"He wants a son, of course. Someone to teach things to and so on."

Jade nods, but gets silent.

"You still trying to figure out if there's anything wrong?"

Jade snaps out of her train of thought. "Nope. I figured you would tell me if there was something really wrong."

Berta smirks. "Okay, well maybe there's something else."

"Well, talk it out, chica, talk it out."

Berta looks up at the sky. "Craig . . . Craig has been different lately. He isn't the same as when I married him. Before he was romantic, he was caring, he was attentive. But now . . . we barely talk. He's been getting distant. It's like he isn't interested anymore."

"Craig will bounce back. It takes time."

"It seems Mark was always like that. I told you this once before. I'll say it again. You got the very last good one."

"No, I didn't. Mark is a good one, but I almost messed that up."

"You know. Sometimes I wish Craig were more like Mark. So intuitive, so caring."

"But minus the unfaithfulness, right? Minus messing with the crazy ex, right?"

"Of course."

"You missed my point, Berta. No man is perfect. No being is. He'll fail you time and time again, and you'll fail him time and time again. But that's okay, as long as you two work together in striving for perfection."

"But what if one of us is the only on striving for that goal?"

"Then you have to get on the same page somehow."

Berta stands up and wraps her arms around herself. "You see? That's part of my issue." Berta looks at Jade. "I need your honest opinion on something. I need just a straight-up answer, but I need to know your true feelings on something. Okay?"

"Sure."

"Do you think Craig would ever cheat?"

"No."

Berta takes in a deep breath and exhales slowly. "Elaborate."

"Craig? Cheat on you? No, I don't think Craig would cheat. He's a good man and he loves you. Plus, he doesn't seem like the type."

"Then why else . . . Why else would he let me feel like this?"

"Maybe because he doesn't know."

"But he acts like he doesn't want to know. And you and Mark are good people . . . but . . . ."

"Mark and I made mistakes . . . mistakes I don't think Craig would willingly walk into. Not since his best friend showed him the major pitfalls."

"So you don't think Craig would cheat on me?"

"No. And let's stop calling it cheating. You cheat in a game. Marriage is not a game. You cheat with the idea of getting ahead or for some gain . . . to prosper. But when you are unfaithful or when you have committed adultery there is no gain, no matter which way you look at it. Cheating it is not. Sinning it is."

Berta gawks at Jade. "Okay. So you don't think Craig would commit adultery?"

Jade winces. "Sorry. Some of the counseling stuff Mark and I attended kinda seeped through."

"No, that's fine." Berta takes a deep breath. "Maybe I need to hear the hardcore Christian stance." She pauses. "This is all silly anyway. I am worrying about nothing, right?"

Jade scrutinizes Berta's face. "Berta, I know you too well, now. I know you're worried about this, as you should be."

"I am." Berta puts her head down. "It's this and . . . I'm worried about . . . everything. I thought marriage was supposed to be different. I thought it was supposed to be more. Never would I have thought that marrying the man I love would leave me so—"

"Empty."

Berta turns toward Jade as if she just had an epiphany. "Yes. Empty. I mean at first, we burned so bright. It was so passionate, so romantic. And now it's just fizzling out. The bad part is we have to take vacations, like, all the time just to try to rekindle some of that stuff. We are barely passed our second year, Jade." Berta shakes her head. "He's setting something up for us to go to Alaska. I don't want to go, because if we can't get our normal everyday lives straight, the vacations seem so . . . fake."

Jade nods. "Charles, time to go," she yells. She puts Amber back in the stroller. For a few moments she stares at Berta as Charles makes his way over. Berta looks off into the distance, seemingly in deep thought.

"Just talk to him. Keep the lines of communication open. Whatever you do, don't shut him out. I can tell you firsthand the horrors of not telling him what you just told me. Keep on his behind about it. He'll talk."

"And then what?"

"Make a decision, make moves . . . together."

"That's it?"

"That's never it. But first things first, make sure both of you understand the situation for what it is."

Berta nods. "That counseling thing helped?"

"It sure did."

"You think someday you and Mark . . . ."

"We're in your corner, Berta. We want you and Craig to have a successful marriage. Just let us know when and where and we'll be there."

"Thanks," she says, but she was thinking of something else.

CHAPTER TEN

THE ride is silent. When they get home, they remain silent. Berta steps into the shower while Craig gets something to eat. He tries to figure a way to talk to Berta, but he doesn't know what to say. She gets out of the shower, puts on a silk poncho and long skirt, grabs the newspaper, and heads out onto the balcony. She opens the French doors and a gust of wind snakes through the living room, the sheer white curtains flowing around her. She lies on the cushioned chaise and opens the paper to the headline news. Hurricanes, floods, and more natural disasters. War. Berta flips to the small business section next. What she sees stuns her.

⚜

Craig stands in the shower thinking about what to do next. He figures just to ask her what he can do to be better, what they can do to be better. He knows it probably won't answer every question their marriage has, but it's a start. He shuts the water off and grabs his towel. Time seems to slow as he begins to get nervous about bringing anything up to her. He dries off and leaves the bathroom. After putting on a pair of sweatpants and a tank top, he goes to the kitchen to get something to drink. He looks out at the balcony through the flapping sheer curtains to see Berta leaning on the rail of the balcony, her hair and her skirt blowing in the wind. Sometimes, he tells himself, he forgets how beautiful Berta really is, even in the simplest things.

The more he looks at her, the more he gets the feeling that he is in the wrong. He replays what Mark told him at the gym. He needs to be there for her because she may be insecure. This could all be his fault. He is failing at what he called his purpose. He feels embarrassed for the way he talked about his marriage earlier. *How could marriage to such a wonderful person be a monster?* Maybe he had the wrong idea about marriage. Maybe he went into it thinking it was going to be all about how much fun they would have, in a superficial way, not in a lasting, meaningful way. Maybe he is running.

Craig pours a cup of water, but leaves it on the counter and walks out to the balcony.

"Did you want anything to . . . ." He looks down to see the newspaper scattered on the floor and he sees Berta, staring out at the skyline. She doesn't say anything, and that makes Craig feel that the talk will be worse than he thought. He looks out at the skyline as well. He glances to the side to see a tear flow from her eye and is confused.

"He's dead," Berta whispers. "He's dead."

"Who?"

"Courtland DeVries."

Craig looks concerned. "Your biological father?"

"They called him a beloved businessman. Those two words don't even go well together. He was as dirty and as crooked as they come . . . and they call him beloved." Berta says "beloved" with hate. "That man raped a little girl and took her innocence from her. Didn't go to jail. Didn't get punished for it."

"How did he die?"

"The article says natural causes. He didn't even suffer. He died peacefully. How does a man like that deserve to die peacefully and respected?"

Craig doesn't know what to say.

"His funeral is next week. On Saturday." She stops leaning on the rail. "I don't know why, but I think I want to go."

"I don't see what good that will do."

Berta stares at Craig with tear-filled eyes. "I don't know. Maybe I need to see him dead. Maybe I need understanding."

"But I thought he was dead to you some time ago."

"He was."

"So what do you want to go for? I don't get it."

"Like I said, I don't know. I mean, shouldn't I be there?"

"No. Why?"

"Because I'm his daughter? Right? I should be there because of that, right?" Tears stream down her face. "Whether I like it or not, he was my real father. And . . . and I don't know why I feel the way I do. I don't know why I had this wave of emotion come over me when I found out the devil himself died. I don't know. I don't get it. I . . . ." In midsentence, Berta stops talking, leaving her mouth wide open. She slowly shuts her mouth as her chin quivers. She turns away from Craig and leaves the balcony.

Faintly, he hears Berta sobbing in the bedroom. He just doesn't understand what for.

Chapter Eleven

"**Y**OU should have been out on the road, Mark."

"I know. I wanted to spend some more time with you before I leave."

"You mean cash in on that promise I made you."

Mark grabs a duffel bag and hangs it on his shoulder. In his other hand he grabs a suitcase and carries everything downstairs. Jade follows closely behind him.

"Yup. And it was great." Mark disappears outside to put his bags in the car. He comes back moments later. "The little dance was cute, too."

"Little dance? Cute? You were drooling halfway through the routine. You mean that smoking hot dance of visual ecstasy."

Mark smiles. "Or that. Where are the kids?"

"They're all downstairs waiting for me. It's movie night tonight."

"Oh. Well let me run downstairs and say goodbye." Mark walks past Jade and into the basement.

"Okay kids. I'm out."

Kalina and Charles get up off the couch and give Mark a hug. Amber sits on the floor and plays. Mark kneels down in front of her and gives her a kiss on the forehead. "See ya later, Munchkin."

"You gonna bring me something back?" Kalina asks.

"Nope."

"Why not?" Kalina asks, smiling.

"'Cause I don't like you."

"Daddy, you love me. You know you do. You can't deny it. I'm the best thing that has happened to you."

Mark smiles. "Yeah, you're a thing, alright."

"That's why your head is big."

"Yeah, yo momma."

"You married her."

"I'm telling," Charles says.

"You see. Now you're gonna get in trouble," Kalina says.

"Trouble? Little girl, don't you know that I run this? All of this."

Out of nowhere, Amber laughs. Everyone pauses and looks at Amber, then starts laughing themselves.

"Alright kids. Gotta go."

"Bye, Dad." Kalina gets up and gives Mark another hug. "I love you."

"Love you too, Babygirl."

Mark goes upstairs to see Jade standing by the front door waiting for him. He strolls up to her and grabs her by her waist. He pulls her in close and gives her a long kiss. While kissing her, he takes one hand and runs it through her hair, also massaging her scalp. When he pulls away, he looks her in the eyes, but says nothing.

"I think I may have something you need to handle," Jade says.

Mark smiles. "Well, if you're good, maybe."

Jade laughs while still in Mark's arms. She crosses her eyes and in a goofy voice, says, "But it will balance out the universe."

Mark chuckles. "I'll call you when I get there." He gives her another kiss.

"Sounds like a plan." Jade moves from Mark's grasp. "Hold on a sec." She skips to the basement door and yells down. "Kalina, start the movie. I'll be down in a few minutes."

"'kay."

Jade then runs to Mark and grabs his hand. She leads him into the garage and to the car. But instead of opening the driver's side door, she opens the back door.

"Get in."

"What?"

"Get in. You're not going to leave me here all week after kissing me like that."

"What?"

"Don't play dumb. Get in."

"Jade, what was earlier, then?"

"Pregame." Jade starts pushing Mark into the backseat of the car.

"I'm going to be all tired on the road."

"No you won't. Let mama do all the work. Next time, you give me a peck on the cheek. No one told you to kiss me all passionately like that. But that's okay, you'll learn."

Jade scoots into the backseat with Mark and slams the door.

☙

After a long five-hour drive, Mark makes it to Chestnut Hill, PA, to a hotel where he and other church members are staying. He's pretty sure people thought he was a no-show as it is already ten o'clock in the evening. *It doesn't matter*, he thinks. Yet, while driving over the cobblestone street, trying to stay straight while the trolley tracks force his car to the side, Mark begins to feel nostalgic. There aren't many cars out on the road, and no one behind him, so he slows the car down to take in the scene of the historic area. He eventually comes up to the hotel and pulls over to the side.

Just before he stops the car, his stomach complains of being empty. Mark recalls passing a WaWa that seemed to be open on his way up, so he turns the car around and heads back. Even seeing the WaWa brings up memories, as he hasn't seen one in ages. Back when he was younger, for him, it was always Roy Rodgers for breakfast (the hash browns were his favorite), and a WaWa hoagie for lunch. But with those good memories, uniquely bonded to them, are the bad ones.

The reason he had WaWa and Roy Rodgers virtually every day was because his mother was rarely home to fix any real meal. When she was home, he was the least of her worries. For dinner, he was always over at Craig's house, his foster parents being better parents to Mark than his own. He pulls up into the parking lot and shuts the car off. For a moment he sits, still thinking about the past. Thoughts of his brother creep into his memory, and instantaneously, that heavy feeling returns. Mark's hands begin to shake and it feels like the car is closing in on him. The more he thinks of his brother, the smaller the car seems. Mark rests his head back onto the headrest.

"Lord," he whispers as a tear traces down the side of his face.

Mark holds in a cry with all of his might, swallowing it down, pushing the pain deeper inside of him, but the more he pushes things down, the more new things come up. Regrets of mistakes made and pain over wrongdoings leave Mark sitting in his car looking stunned. A car pulls up next to him and a man gets out and enters the store, never looking Mark's way. Mark tries to steel himself to get out of the car, to no avail. He takes a shaky hand and starts the car. For now, his growling stomach is going to have to wait.

Maybe the hotel has a vending machine.

Mark wakes up in his small hotel room to someone knocking on his door. He wipes at his eyes to look at the clock and sees that he is already a half hour late for the first session. He pops out of bed and swings open the door to see no one there. He swears he heard knocking on his door. He shakes his head and swings the door shut, making haste to get in the shower.

Once showered and dressed, Mark grabs his notebook and Bible and rushes to his car to get to the church. He follows the directions he wrote out for himself two nights before and gets to a monstrous-sized church with a fenced-in parking lot that is more than halfway filled. Mark looks at his watch. He knows he already missed Pastor Brentwood making the opening remarks. He gets into the parking lot and is directed by a man wearing a neon-green vest to a spot relatively close to the church. Mark turns the car off and stares at his agenda for a few seconds before exiting the car and rushing into the church.

Once inside, Mark walks through the crowd of men to see everyone filing out of the sanctuary. He knows he missed the opening remarks and prayer, but knows he could be early for the first thing he signed up for. He separated the retreat out into three sections for himself. He figured if he is here, he may as well make the most of it. He rushes to the first class to see it already filled. He looks around the room to see a few empty chairs way in the back and moves his way to a seat. He sits and gets comfortable, nodding to the man sitting next to him.

"I'm Roland." The man sticks his hand out.

"Mark." He shakes the man's hand.

"Someone told me this was going to be a good class. I know the teacher. He's a good guy. Really knows his stuff. Real holy-spirit filled, you know?"

"Yeah." Mark just lets the man talk.

"And the Lord knows I could use a pick-me-up. My kids are acting a fool. My wife is threatening divorce and I'm living with my parents."

"I'm sorry to hear that."

The man shrugs his shoulders. "But I'm not worried. The Lord has made ways for me before. I know . . . I know He will do it again. I just need some direction. That is what I need." The man pulls out a picture from his pocket and shows Mark. "This is my family."

Mark looks at the picture. *Nice looking family*, he thinks.

"Yeah, my oldest, my son, he's selling drugs. My daughter, she's a prostitute, but she thinks I don't know what's going on. And here"—he points at the woman standing next to him—"here is my old lady. Yup. She doesn't want to be with me anymore, I know. We were wrong for each other from the start, but we still stayed together. Well, we were forced together in a way. I got her pregnant and there was no way I was leaving then." The man chuckles. "I tried to make the best of a bad situation and look at me now. Living with my parents again."

"Oh."

"So, what about you?"

"I'm sorry?"

Roland smiles. "You don't come early to a class called 'Moving past your past' for kicks and giggles."

"I'd rather not talk about it."

"Fair enough." Roland looks around the room and ends up looking at Mark again. "So which of the big three is your pastor?"

"Brentwood. Pastor Brentwood."

"I heard him preach before. He definitely knows his word. Very technical, he is."

"That's why I like him."

"So you prefer the ones who talk about the Hebrew and Greek meaning of certain words and things like that, huh?"

"I prefer the more complex preachers . . . the ones that force me to think and simply don't just shout, then spoon feed everything to me."

"I see. That's cool." The man waits for Mark to ask him who his pastor is, but when Mark says nothing, he changes subject.

"So what do you do for a living?"

Mark frowns. "You ask a lot of questions."

"Always did. Ever since I was little. It's how I came to a better understanding of myself and the world. You don't have to answer if you don't want."

Mark glances to the side, being hesitant to say anything more to the man. "I'm . . . I'm a teacher."

"Really? What grade?"

"Elementary." He tries to keep things simple.

A short man in a suit enters the room and everyone gets quiet. Everyone focuses their attention on the man as he scans the classroom full of supposedly broken men. His face is stern, but he quickly flashes a smile and greets the class.

Chapter Twelve

Jade is already late for the office party, not that she cares. She parks in the parking lot of the hotel and walks in. In the lobby that is adorned with various works of art, Jade looks toward the front desk. The only sound is the echoing of her shoes on the marble floor. The front desk attendant is a cheery man in a blazer.

"I'm looking for the ballroom for Raynard Pharmaceuticals."

The man smiles. "Just down the first hall, at the end of the hall through the double doors."

"Thank you."

Jade walks past the desk and looks at her watch. Eight o'clock.

"They seem to already be having a good time."

Jade stops. "Sorry?" She looks back at the desk attendant.

The man puts his thumb to his mouth and sticks out his pinkie as if he's drinking from a bottle.

Jade nods. "Ah. I see. Thanks for the heads-up."

"No problem, ma'am. If you need anything, please don't hesitate to let me know."

"Okay. Thanks." Jade turns around with a smirk on her face.

As she gets closer to the ballroom, she hears the thumping of loud music. When she finally opens the doors, she is greeted with a rush of sounds. Music, laughing, loud talking. Jade walks in and looks for a place to sit. Walking through the crowd, she is greeted by people who are sober enough to recognize her. She finds Karen, who looks bored, and her boyfriend, who looks even more bored.

"It's just another office party. It's not the end of the world," Jade yells over the music.

Karen looks up, annoyed at first, but then elated to know it was Jade. She pops up and gives her a hug. "I thought you were standing me up."

"No. I wouldn't leave you here." She looks at Karen's boyfriend. "You holding up there, guy?"

The burly man looks up and smiles. "Barely. I want to shoot myself."

Jade and Karen sit down, their backs toward the wall.

"So here's what you missed." Karen points across the room to a stick-thin woman with long blonde hair. She wears a business suit without the blazer, but a short-sleeved blouse instead. "Brooks and"—she points to the opposite side of the room at a plain-looking man in a dress shirt and tie, everything still neat and in place—"Almodovar have been secretly seeing each other."

Jade's face tunes up.

"Yes, I know." Karen continues. "Both are married. Both have their spouses here as we speak."

"How do you know this?"

"Almodovar's wife came over to our table, drunk out of her mind and started telling all their business. And speaking of spouses, where's yours?"

"He had something to do with the church."

"Gotcha. Anyway, that's just the beginning. Wait until later on. Everyone's business will be out."

"And then everyone goes back to work as if nothing happened," Karen's boyfriend says.

"Of course. All I can say is that there is a lot of dirt under the fancy imported carpet of our company lobby."

Jade grunts.

"All the bigwigs were looking for you earlier."

"Yeah? What for?"

"Don't know. I'm sure to congratulate you on the account."

Jade shakes her head.

"What's up?"

Jade nods her head in the direction of a group of women. All professional women, acting like school girls in the presence of one man.

"Calvin," Karen says in disgust. "This is what he's been doing the whole time since the party started. At one point he was grinding on the backs of some young girls on the ballroom floor."

Jade stares at him. He talks it up with the group of women, adding in jokes here and there to make them laugh. His movements are that of an arrogant man, Jade believes. A man whose type she was ashamedly interested in at one point. She shakes her head again and looks down.

"Excuse me, Jade."

Jade looks up to see the CEO of the company, Martin Lawson. He's a short old man, but moves and speaks with every bit of vigor as a twenty-year-old.

"Mr. Lawson." Jade starts to stand, but Martin waves her off.

"Please. Be comfortable. I just wanted to thank you for your hard work. I heard the news about the big account and I am excited to see where this deal takes us."

"Well, thank you, sir."

"You are very welcomed. You are an incredible asset to this company. Incredible."

"Again, thank you for your kind words."

"But, I must bid you adieu. I have to catch a plane to San Francisco." The old man gives Jade an informal salute and walks away from the table. The crowd splits to move out of his way and closes in behind him. Appearing from the crowd, as if he phased right through them, is

Calvin. Jade notices that Karen and her boyfriend tense up the closer he gets to their table.

Calvin smiles that fake and cheesy grin and eyes Jade. "How did you sneak in here past me?"

Jade stares at Calvin, not amused. "I just walked in. I think you were a bit preoccupied with the throes of women."

"Throes of women? Ouch, Jade. These are all our wonderful employees here." He glances next to Jade. "Hey, Karen. How are you?"

Karen glares at the man in a perfectly pressed suit. "I'm good."

Before Karen could get out another word, Calvin turns his attention back to Jade, also purposefully ignoring Karen's boyfriend. "So, Jade. I just wanted to congratulate you again for your big catch. The boss seems to be very pleased."

Jade nods slowly, sensing he has some more to say.

"He asked me to run the numbers for this partnership one more time and everything looks solid. You should be proud of yourself."

Jade nods.

"So where's your husband?"

Suddenly, Jade feels Karen's hand rapping her on the thigh.

"He couldn't make it."

"Hmm." Calvin nods. "I would think he would be here to celebrate with you."

Karen raps on her leg harder.

"Is there anything else you need?"

Calvin smiles. "There are a couple more projects on the horizon, from what I hear."

"I know. VP of marketing, remember?"

"Yeah. I'm just offering a helping hand. If you need some numbers run . . . you know who to call."

"Yup."

Calvin nods and walks away from the table toward the bar. Jade looks over at Karen, who looks at her brooding boyfriend.

"Just give me the word," the burly man says. "Just give me the word and I'll wipe this ballroom floor with his face. Just give me the word."

"It's okay, Baby," Karen says, "Calm down." She looks at Jade. "Well, that was completely disrespectful."

"Yeah, it was. He feels he can get away with anything now. In part, he can." Jade stares at Calvin as he takes back three consecutive shots in a row of some clear liquid. "I didn't know Calvin was a big drinker."

"He's not," Karen says. "I think maybe your rejection is finally getting to him."

"You think enough to stop?"

"Probably not."

"Well, how much longer do you guys want to stay?"

"I don't," Karen's boyfriend says. Karen hits him on the arm. He just shrugs his shoulders.

"I think we stayed long enough," Karen says. "We're ready to go when you are."

"Okay, well let me go to the ladies' room first. I'll meet you two out in the lobby?"

"Sounds good to me."

At once, Jade, Karen, and her boyfriend get up from the table and leave the ballroom. Jade splits to the left, down a dimly lit hallway to the restrooms. Her heels thud on the carpeted flooring as she makes her way down the hall that seems to go on forever. The closer she gets to the restrooms, the more uncomfortable she feels. She enters the ladies' room. No one is there. *I should have asked Karen to come with me*, Jade thinks. For a brief moment, she thinks she hears something, but ignores it and goes to the bathroom.

Upon exiting, Jade is startled by someone sitting on a cushioned bench right outside the restrooms.

"Calvin . . . why are you ju—"

"I don't get it, Jade." Calvin doesn't smile. Rather, he looks down at his hands, sitting slumped on the bench, his suit coat off, but otherwise looking well put-together.

Jade gives him a look and turns to walk away, but before she could even take a step, Calvin leaps up toward her and grabs her arm. He pushes her into the wall.

"You should be thanking me—"

Jade squirms and Calvin's grip becomes vice-like. Jade screams, but not loudly enough for anyone to hear over the ruckus of the ballroom. Calvin lets go and moves in her way, stopping her from going down the hall.

"Calvin, I'm only going to tell you once. Let me pass." She steps away from the wall.

Calvin looks at her and smiles. He doesn't look of a man who has had too much to drink, though his breath says otherwise. He looks like a man who is fully aware, fully aware of what he's doing and what he wants to do.

"You know how you got to be VP of Marketing? You think it was because you are so skilled and talented?" Calvin chuckles. "You had no skill for this position. You got here because of me." He slaps his chest. "On my word. And you act so prissy. All I want is a bit of respect."

"That's not what you want. I don't know who you think you're fooling, but I'm not stupid. I know what it is . . . that you want."

Calvin smiles again, this time a more sadistic smile. "Then why haven't you given it to me?"

"A number of reasons, the most important being I'm married."

"What does that mean now? Better yet, what does that mean to me?"

"It means the world to me. What it means to you is irrelevant."

Calvin nods and takes a step closer. Jade moves back, again being pressed to the wall. "You're still not convinced? You still think you got here on your own merit? Ask the entire executive board what they think of Jade Cooke. Ask Vineland Health Pros. You know what they'll say? That's one fine piece of ass."

Jade stays silent, frantically thinking of how to get out of this situation.

"Just ask Mr. Lawson." Calvin changes the tone of his voice. "You're an incredible asset to this company, Jade." He chuckles. "Asset indeed."

Jade's face becomes flush.

"Does it make sense now? Did it click yet? You are the pretty face in this company. Football has cheerleaders. Boxing has those ring girls that walk out in bathing suits. We . . . have you."

Jade looks at Calvin and eyes his movements, being cautious, and looking for a way to get away from him. He reeks of desperation in what he says, in his frantic movement. The slight twitch of his hand. It all lets Jade know she isn't in a good spot right now.

"How much longer do you think you will be with the company?"

Jade still remains silent.

"Just a wild guess. Five years? Two? A month? A day?" Calvin sighs. "Look, Jade, I don't want to play hardball. I didn't want it to come to this, but you're forcing my hand. You want to stay VP. How badly do you want to stay VP? You need the money, right? Your good-for-nothing husband doesn't help, I heard."

Calvin takes a few more steps, backing Jade into the corner of the hallway, the darkest part of the hallway.

"It's just me and you here, Jade. No one would know."

Jade slaps Calvin hard enough to leave a red imprint of her hand on his face. Calvin stops in his tracks. He feels his face and nods. "Okay. I get it. I'm no animal. I'll leave you alone." Calvin steps back.

For a quick moment, Jade feels relieved and lets her guard down. That moment gives Calvin enough time to bound over to her and grab her again, this time with more force. He pulls her hair and yanks her into the men's bathroom. She trips and bangs her knee into the hard floor of the bathroom. Calvin locks the bathroom door. Jade's screams echo throughout the bathroom, yet still no one seems to notice. Calvin grips Jade and slams her into the wall, and she lands on the floor with a thud. She can no longer scream; her throat hurts. The edges of her vision go dark because she hit her head on the wall hard. Calvin lifts her up from the floor and pushes her forward into the sinks. She flies into the counter, the edge of the counter digging into her stomach, her forehead hitting the mirror so hard it cracks it. Jade slumps, powerless. Her vision fades in and out even more and when it is clear, she sees the blur of tears. To stop her from falling to the floor again, Calvin presses his body behind hers and mashes the palm of his hand to the side of her head.

"Please, Jesus," Jade whispers, and begins to weep.

Calvin traces his finger along the back of her thigh as he repositions his body against hers. He slowly pulls up the back of her skirt. Still pressing against her skull with one hand, he fumbles around with the other. Jade hears the clinging of his belt buckle. In order to undo his pants, he releases his positioning on her just a bit and Jade seizes the opportunity. With a quick switch, she gets one leg free and with all of the energy she has left, she lifts her leg as high and hard as she can in between his legs. Calvin lets out an awkward scream and crashes to the floor. Jade falls to the floor in front of him and watches him squirm in agony. He is already beginning to recover, so Jade rushes to the only weapon she sees, the metal top to a trashcan. She yanks the dome top off and hits Calvin in the face with it. She hits him again.

And again.

And again.

She hits him more times than she can count. The next and final time she lifts the top into the air, blood flies from it. Jade now begins to take in what just happened . . . and what she has done . . . what he tried to do. A barely moving Calvin lies on the bathroom floor with blood flowing from his face. She drops the top and in a knee-jerk reaction, runs to the trashcan to vomit.

Slowly, Jade unlocks the men's bathroom door and limps out.

The hallway is exactly as it was before: dark, and completely empty. She grabs her purse from the floor by the cushioned bench and limps her way down the hall, leaning on the wall for support. When she gets around the corner, the only people in the lobby are Karen, her boyfriend, and the front desk attendant. Karen spots her first.

"Oh, my God, Jade, wh—"

"Men's bathroom." Jade is barely able to talk. Her voice comes out hoarse.

Karen looks to her boyfriend and he looks to the desk attendant. The attendant points down the hall and Karen's boyfriend rushes off.

"What happened?" Karen asks.

"Calvin," is all Jade can muster.

"Call the police," Karen says to the attendant. "Hurry, call the police."

"And tell them we need an ambulance," Karen's boyfriend yells out.

Jade plops on the ground and Karen goes down to hold her. She steals a look at her boyfriend, who has a look of grave concern.

"Did I kill him?" Jade asks.

"No. But he doesn't seem to be in good shape."

Jade nods and leans into Karen's arm more as tears slide down her face.

CHAPTER THIRTEEN

AFTER a full day and night of experiencing what the conference has to offer, Mark leaves the church feeling a bit renewed. But when his stomach murmurs in protest, he decides to try for the WaWa just down the street from the hotel again.

He pulls into the lot and parks. This time, he feels no dragging feeling, no feeling of deep despair, so he gets out and goes in. The bell above the door chimes, announcing his entrance. He goes to the deli and orders a sandwich, his all-time favorite: a meatball sub. He then goes to the back of the store to grab a few snack cakes and some chips. Not the healthiest meal, but it will have to do. The bell above the door chimes again. Mark walks to the register to pay for his stuff and walks back over to the deli to grab his dinner.

"Hey, man."

Mark turns around to see Roland grabbing a bag of chips.

"Got the late night munchies too, huh?" Roland says.

"Something like that."

"It's funny running into you again."

Mark does find it strange that he ran into this guy again. "Yeah?"

"Yeah." Roland looks at Mark strangely. "Can I ask your opinion?"

"Sure, I guess."

"You think that first class we had was helpful?"

"My honest opinion? No. The class wasn't much help to me."

"It didn't much help me, either. I was shocked because it had all of these glowing reviews from others I know. I know the guy teaching, but I don't know, it just didn't do it for me."

"No, I fully understand. It was too much 'pray and wait' for me. Not that there is anything wrong with that idea."

"It's just that you've been doing that the whole time and you were looking for something a bit more substantial."

"Exactly."

Roland nods. "I was talking to my wife a few hours ago." He walks to the register to pay for his things. Mark reluctantly follows him.

"I was talking to my wife and I was telling her how good I was doing. I was promising her that I would become a better man. I was almost pleading with her to give me a bit more time. She never answered me. Instead she just changed the subject and asked me if anything interesting happened." Roland thanks the cashier and both men walk to their cars. Roland is parked next to Mark.

"She changes subject and asks me if anything interesting happened. Anytime I want to talk about us, she changes the subject. It's been like that for years." Roland grabs his bag of chips and pops them open. He sits on the back bumper of his SUV and looks out into the street. "And now that I'm not in the house . . . I don't know. Sometimes I feel like this isn't going to work. That no matter how much work I do, it's not enough to outweigh the harm I've done." Roland looks at Mark. "And I've done a lot of harm. Sometimes, I feel like I can't make things up. I've lost too much ground. The class gave me nothing for that."

"We all have a lot of ground to make up. But, maybe you can't make up ground . . . maybe all we can do is make things better."

"Maybe. I really love that woman, you know. I can't just take all this stuff going on with my family lying down. Even if it is my fault."

"I understand."

Both men get silent for a few moments. A car with all its windows tinted pulls into the lot and parks next to Roland. A woman gets out from the passenger side and goes into the WaWa.

"Why did you tell me all that?" Mark asks.

"I'm not sure. Because you're here. And it's weird. And through my experience, things don't happen just because. And you seem like a cool dude. I don't think you would just go around the whole retreat putting my business out there. Would you?"

"No."

Roland nods. He turns around to look behind him. The woman leaves the WaWa and slides back into the tinted-window car. "I guess I ought to thank you for listening."

"No prob. Listen, I'm going to go. Have this sub here and it's gonna get cold."

"Oh, yeah. Sorry for holding you up."

"I'll uhhh, see you tomorrow, I guess."

"Yup yup."

Mark gets into his car and turns the engine on. For a moment, he looks at Roland. Roland stares blankly out into the street. Mark then faces forward and stares into the store. It's obvious the guy just needs someone to talk to. Mark looks back at Roland again. He then turns off the car and gets back out. He sits on the back of his car and starts chomping into his sandwich.

"So how is everything your fault?" Mark asks.

Roland looks at Mark for a second, trying to see if he is serious. After a few more moments, Roland answers.

"My son is a drug dealer, like I said. But he only learned that stuff from me. I was the one running the streets when he was younger. The sad part is the fact that I taught him this stuff. He saw too many things. My daughter saw some of those things, but most importantly, she learned how to be treated by a man from me. And I failed at setting the proper example. I treated my wife badly. She was never up for the thug baby-daddy thing. She wanted something real. I couldn't, and at many times wouldn't give her that. I put that woman through things no woman should go through. And both of my children saw most of it. The abuse, the arguments . . . the cheating. Everything. Everything I put my wife through, my children went through with her. I didn't get it until it was too late. I got saved too late." He turns to look at Mark. "I guess that pretty much explains it?"

"I see."

"What about you?"

"Huh?"

"What were you in the class for?"

"I was curious."

"Yeah, you looked more than curious. You looked desperate."

"For?"

"Answers."

Mark takes another bite of his sandwich and thinks for a few moments. "Yeah, maybe I am looking for answers. But I kinda figured I wouldn't find any here. I was more or less forced to come here."

Roland nods.

"Oh, and let me come clean about something. I'm not an elementary school teacher. I was one . . . but things didn't work out in the end."

"What happened?"

"A whirlwind of crap. My ex comes back. We start starting fires if you know what I mean, even though we were both married. I taught her son. Things go bad, or good, depending on which way you look at it. But she was abusing her son and there was a case, and guess who has to go to court as a witness?"

"You."

Mark nods. "The problem was, you can't expose one thing without the other. So it got out that things went on between her and me and the local news got ahold of it. The board got nervous and didn't want the added attention, so they gave me the boot, or put me in a position where I had to leave. That's the abridged version."

"Wow."

"Yup. They tried to get me to serve some time. I honestly didn't think the kid was being abused. I guess good thing they believed me . . . And don't get me started on why I hate coming back to Philly."

"Back to?"

"Yeah. I grew up here. East Oak Lane. But no fond memories to go off of. My parents sucked, and my brother was killed. And I spent most of my time by myself or with my homeboy Craig . . . who is also from Philly. He didn't have the best time here, either, but he fared a bit better than I did." Mark takes the last bite of his sandwich and stuffs the trash into the plastic bag. "So I have no job, and can't get one. I can't seem to shake my past, and there's this woman out there . . . who could be angry with me."

"You still with your wife?"

"Of course. We worked hard to get to a place where we are both comfortable with ourselves, each other, and our marriage. It took us two years, but we did it."

"So if you are still with your wife, and everything is good, why is it that one of things that you are concerned about is this other chick?"

Mark thinks for a second. "I think because she's a big question mark now. She's completely shrouded in mystery. And, I don't know, call it a gut feeling."

"Did you love her, this other chick?"

"That's not the first time I've been asked that one, but at one time, when we were younger, I suppose I did. At least, I did by my definition of love back then. It sounds kinda confusing, I know—"

"Naw, I get it. The way you saw things then . . . you saw them veiled by your immaturity. What you thought was love then, the younger you, before you were saved, turned out to be something different, older you, after you were saved."

"For the most part." Mark looks at Roland. "You seem to know what you're talking about."

"I know enough about messing up. I just don't know so much about fixing it. But look, I took up too much of your time. Let me get back to my parents' place . . . before they start to worry." Roland chuckles and shakes his head. "Again, thanks for the talk."

"No problem. I'll see you tomorrow?"

"Yup. Closing day." Roland gives Mark an informal salute. "I'll be praying for you, man."

"Thanks. I'll send up a few for you, too."

Roland disappears around his truck. Moments later, Mark hears the rumbling of the engine and Roland pulls out of the lot. Mark gets into his car and leaves.

CHAPTER FOURTEEN

"ARE you sure about this?" Craig asks Berta. They both sit in Craig's car, which is parked in front of the doors of a small church. Berta looks around to see a number of people walking the streets and filing through the doors.

"This many people," Berta says. "This many people for this . . . rapist."

"Berta, I don't know if this is the best idea."

Berta stares at Craig for a few moments before opening her door. "Then go home," she says before exiting and slamming the door shut.

Berta walks into the church and immediately finds a seat in the next-to-last row in the back. She looks around at the sea of unfamiliar faces, obvious supporters of her tyrannical biological father. Craig slides into the pew and sits next to her. They are the only two in the row.

"What was that about?" Craig asks.

"What do you mean?"

"Just storming off like that. Look, I'm here to support you, not to ruffle any feathers."

"Look, Craig, I'm just as confused as you are about this, but what I don't need right now is someone nagging me, commenting on everything I do."

Craig doesn't say anything, but his face shows a struggle to keep quiet a few choice words he has for her.

Berta sits back and thinks for a moment. *There's never going to be a good time for this*, she thinks. *And while I have his attention . . . . No. Not now. Ask later.* But as Berta tries to coach herself, she finds herself caring less and less about the fact that they're at a funeral and focuses more on the simple fact that she wants answers.

"Are you cheating on me?" she blurts out. She knows that was likely the worst thing to ask Craig, especially now, but she couldn't stop herself. Now, she feels like she is unable to close this can of worms. She is unable to stop her anger.

Craig looks stunned and pained as if someone punched him in the gut. "What?"

"I need to know now. If you are, we can make this process simple. Cut our losses and move on."

"Berta, I'm not cheating on you. Why would you ask that?"

"Because, Craig. I know you said that I wasn't the same . . . and blamed it on the job, but truth is, you aren't the same. You haven't been the same Craig that I looked forward to seeing every day. You act . . . you act bored . . . like I'm not exciting enough for you. That makes me wonder . . . maybe you're getting your excitement somewhere else."

Craig looks down, feeling a bit guilty. "This is crazy. I'm still the same me I was years ago."

"No, you're not."

"I am."

"Craig, I am telling you that you are not the same man that I married. I'm not going back and forth with you on this."

Craig is visibly frustrated. "I'm not cheating on you. Maybe I have a ways to go before I'm a super husband, but I am not a cheater."

"Yeah, but in the past—"

"In the past, what?" Craig raises his tone, but lowers it back down to a whisper. "Are you being serious right now? I have never cheated."

"You just dated everyone in the state."

Craig stops and doesn't say another word. He stares at Berta in complete shock. Berta catches his look, but then faces forward as the funeral is set to begin. Craig shakes his head.

"Look," Berta says, "I'm sorry f—"

But before Berta could finish her sentence Craig gets up from the pew and leaves the church. Berta knows she made a mistake in her comment, and feels badly for it. She feels even worse knowing that she is now at this funeral by herself. She knew it was going to happen. She knew she was going to explode if they never talked about it. She just wishes that it didn't happen here and now. She turns around and looks through the double doors that open up to the lobby, hoping to see Craig.

The lobby is empty.

Nervously, Berta flips through the program, reading the 'About Courtland' page and finding that he started a completely new family, and that there is no mention of herself or her mother anywhere in the program (though this was to be expected). She looks at various family pictures that were printed in shabby form onto the page. The woman next to him (who surely isn't her mother) smiles, and the two kids, one boy and one girl, look exactly like him. Berta crumples the program in her hand and surveys the crowd again. She first spots the wife, a tall but plain-looking woman. Her looks pale in comparison to the beauty her mother possessed. She wears all black with a veil to cover her face. Berta then spots the children; the girl, now a young woman, seems to be distraught. The son, a lot younger, sits in between the mother and his sister. Berta shakes her head. She doesn't get it.

For the entire service, Berta listens carefully to each portion, trying to understand how so many people could be deceived. Especially this new wife of his. Berta finds herself wondering if Courtland has done to his new daughter what he did to her. If so, how could she just sit there and act like she is really hurt over this "loss." Again, Berta doesn't get it, but at this time, she has had enough. Only a few moments are left before this part is over and everyone is to proceed to the cemetery for the final goodbye. Berta grabs her purse and pulls a tissue from it. She fakes like she is crying, dabbing at her eyes, and exits the church. She hopes Craig is just sitting in the car and didn't drive off anywhere. At the bottom of the steps Berta hears her name being called. She stops in her tracks and turns around to see Izabel Rego, her mother.

"Alberta?"

Berta doesn't know what to say so she stands there, frozen. It's like she is looking into a mirror; Berta is a spitting image of her mother.

"Hello . . . Izabel."

Izabel moves a step closer to Berta but she backs away. "Why are you here?"

Izabel looks hurt by Berta's movements. "You look wonderful, Alberta. So beautiful."

"Why are you here?"

Izabel remains still. "I should be asking you that very same question. No?"

Berta looks at her in disgust. She turns her back on Izabel and steps away. Berta keeps walking in the opposite direction from where she knows Craig parked the car, but she doesn't care. She just needs to get away from that woman.

Eventually, a few blocks down the street, Berta comes to a bench and takes a seat. Her mind is racing, and she can't form a complete thought. She looks back where she came from to see Izabel walking up to the bench. Berta looks away but doesn't move.

Izabel takes a seat next to her and for a while says nothing. People walk by and stare at them, likely because they look just alike. Berta sneaks a glance at Izabel to see her deep in thought, as if she is looking for words to say. At the very next instant, Izabel looks at Berta. Both women stare at each other for a long, uncomfortable moment.

"Were you compelled by God to come?" Izabel asks.

Berta frowns. "No."

"Well, I was." The older woman moves her purse to her lap. "I read the little obituary in the paper the other day. I read it three times. After the last, I sat there, thinking. I asked myself again and again, 'Why do I have this urge to go? Why do I feel so strongly about seeing this man . . . into the afterlife? It makes no sense.'"

Berta doesn't break her stare.

"I didn't know until now. Now I know for sure. I didn't come for him . . . I came for you. Call it an answered prayer."

"Well maybe God should have left this one unanswered."

Izabel nods. "Maybe. But He didn't. Here you are. Here I am."

"I still don't understand why."

"For truth, Alberta. For truth."

Berta chuckles. "Truth, huh? That's what I came here for? That's what you came here for? Okay, here's some truth for you. You cheated on your husband who is dead now and you left your only child with him to get molested and raped." A tear traces down her cheek.

"Alberta."

Berta gets up from the bench and heads back toward the church.

"Alberta, I didn't know."

Berta snaps around. "You did," she yells. "You left me there with him. You want truth? You were a selfish and inept mother who let your one-and-only daughter suffer through the most horrific experiences a child could go through. And now you want to bring up God? The nerve . . . ."

"I was forced t—"

"You were forced? No, you didn't care. All you cared about was whatever that golf instructor guy was giving you. I know when I have a child, nothing on this planet could force me to let them go. I don't care what anyone says or does."

"It's not that simple. I—" A tear traces down Izabel's face. "There is so much for you to know. So much for me to tell."

"Well, that sucks . . . because I'm not convinced that anything you have to say will be of use to me."

Berta leaves her mother sitting on the bench alone.

She gets back to the car to find no one there and wonders where Craig could have gone. She rummages through her purse to see if she has her set of keys to the car, but comes up empty-handed. Berta then goes back to the church and sits in the lobby.

Sun shines through the numerous stained-glass windows as Berta waits. She feels exhausted and it is still early. While in deep thought, Berta unknowingly plays with her hair, twirling it in between her fingers. *What am I going to do? Can't stay here. Jerk Craig takes the keys to the car.* She tries to analyze everything that has happened and finds that she still can't keep a single train of thought. When she thinks about Craig, her mother quickly pops up, and when she thinks about her mother, Craig pops back up, and back to her mother again. Berta rests her head in her hand.

Moments later, she hears someone entering the lobby. She turns to the side to see Craig strolling through, not noticing her. He strolls right back into the sanctuary of the church.

A few moments later Craig comes out of the sanctuary and spots Berta. He strolls over and sits next to her. Berta looks at him as he stares forward.

"Do you still want to be married?" Craig asks.

"What? Craig, we need to talk about this later. There's too much going on right now." Berta is being completely honest; she can't think of answering anything right now.

Craig looks at Berta. "Later? Just say yes or no. No need to elaborate. Just one word will suffice."

With every thought that runs through her mind, Berta gets weaker and weaker. "Craig, please."

"So you find it necessary to ask me if I were cheating on you, starting this whole debate, randomly, just blasting off on me, at a funeral no less, but I can't ask you a question that's on my mind?"

"I'm not saying that. I just needed to know at that time. It was a terrible attempt to get us talking. Wrong time, I know."

"But you still didn't answer my question." Craig's voice is grave.

"Because I'm unsure."

Craig doesn't move, but even Berta is shocked by her response. *Could it be that bad?* "No. I didn't mean that."

Craig puts a hand up and shakes his head. "I asked, right?" He digs in his pocket and pulls out the keys to the car. He places them in Berta's hand, gets up, and leaves.

"Craig, wait. How are you going to get home?"

"Cab."

A few long strides later, Craig is gone, and Berta stares at the car keys in her hand. She shivers a bit, not knowing what just happened. She then saunters to the outside of the church, just in time to see Craig in the back of a cab driving away. She squints as the sun beams directly on her. Having had enough of her biological father's funeral, she walks to the car.

Once at the car, Berta finds a slip of paper stuck to the windshield, held there by the wiper blade. She thinks it's a ticket and braces for the worst. Instead, the paper is a note written in handwriting that looks more like art. Immediately, she knows who it is from.

Please, just ten minutes of your time.
I can explain everything.
In front of the church.
Tomorrow at 7pm.
I love you.
-Izabel

Berta plops into the car and slams the door shut. *How did this lady know what car I was in?* She starts the car and lets the hum of the engine soothe her as she gently lays her head back on the headrest.

 G3&0

Craig decides not to go home. Instead, he pays the cab driver to take him to the building where he works. He thinks to himself that work will take his mind off things for a few moments. He gets out of the cab and enters the building, waves at the guard in the lobby, and takes the elevator to his office. Once inside, Craig looks at Ted's desk. Completely spotless. Craig then walks into his office and leaves the doors wide open. He takes off his suit coat and throws it on the chair. Then, the pacing begins.

"Okay, gut check, Craig. What is going on here?" Craig asks himself. He continues to pace back and forth across the floor. For a couple of minutes, his mind frantically searches for an answer, a cure-all maybe, anything to ease the intensity of the current situation. Craig stops in his tracks at the sound of the elevator bell ringing. Someone getting off at this floor? And the guard let them through? Craig continues to stare at the doorway, waiting for someone to come around the corner. Part of him expects it to be Berta. The rest of him is hoping that it is.

"Hello?"

Not Berta's voice.

"Is anyone here?"

Craig simply stands in the doorway, waiting to see who it is that comes around the corner. He doesn't recognize the voice, a woman's voice.

The person who appears from around the corner is someone he has never met before. She is an average-looking woman, dressed in jeans and a spaghetti-strap shirt, with a lace shawl. She has a purse hanging from one arm and a few other bags from the other. It seems as if she's just gone shopping. She stops at Ted's desk and stares for a few seconds.

"Can I help you?" Craig asks, startling the woman.

The woman jumps slightly and turns to face Craig. "I'm sorry. I'm looking for Craig."

"Craig? Okay, hold on for a sec. I'll go get him." Craig walks out of the doorway and to the side, and then walks back into view. He walks to the woman a holds out his hand. "Hi. Craig Barlow."

The woman smiles, chuckles a bit, and shakes his hand. "Patrice Stafford."

Knockout smile, Craig thinks.

"Patrice . . . Stafford. You called not too long ago, correct?"

"I did," Patrice nods. "I thought my phone call was a bit unprofessional. I was going through a few things . . . but that doesn't matter." Patrice shakes her head vigorously. "What I'm here for today is to correct that . . . on a weekend." Patrice sighs. "Look, I was recommended to you by Marlon Jones."

"Oh, Marlon. One of my favorite people. Good guy."

"Yes, Marlon is a good guy. Beautiful family, too."

"Yes, indeed. So what can I do for you, Patrice?" Craig walks over to his desk, offering a seat to Patrice. She sets her bags down next to her seat and sits.

"I need financial advice . . . a lot of financial advice."

"Okay." Craig grabs a pen and paper. "I'm all ears."

"Well, I came into a lot of money as of late."

"From what? Job? Inherited?"

"Divorce settlement."

"Craig scribbles on the notepad. "I'm sorry to hear that . . . I think."

"No, don't worry about it. It was the best thing for me to do. Anyway, I have a bunch of money from that and things have been picking up with my job."

"What do you do?"

"I'm a writer."

"Really? What do you write?"

"Erotica."

Craig smirks. "Seriously?"

"Yes, seriously."

"Okay. So a divorce settlement and book sales. All right." Craig opens a drawer and pulls out a few papers. "This packet of paper contains my contract and some other helpful bits of info. Also included is a list of the things I'm going to need from you. This basically helps me form a financial profile for you."

Patrice looks at the stack of papers. "When do I need to get this back to you?"

"Whenever you're ready."

Patrice stares at Craig. "You don't strike me as a financial advisor type."

"If you're wondering if I can do my job, please have no fear. I'm licensed and I have years of experience in this."

"I'm not saying that. I mean that . . . you're not stiff . . . or boring."

"Not all finance or accounting guys are stiff. Just most of them are." Craig smiles. "Look, I take this approach: My clients aren't just clients, they're family. I know information about them that few do: their financial situation. Millions of people hide that from others. This group of people finds me worthy enough to reveal this info to, and for me to give them advice on it."

"I like your approach."

"Well, it's not mine exactly. It was my mentor's philosophy to this business. When I took over the company, the philosophy remained unchanged."

"Tell me more." Patrice gets more comfortable in her seat.

"Huh?"

"I want to know more. You find it necessary to know my financial situation; I find it necessary to know who I'm giving this info to."

"Fair enough. What do you want to know?"

"For starters, why do you do this?"

Craig gets up from his desk and walks to the window. "That's actually a good question. I do it because it's good money. Of course that isn't the only reason, but coming from where I came from, money was big on influencing my decision."

"Let me guess. An inner-city kid looking to make it big?"

Craig stares at her. The silence that takes over the room just starts to become awkward when Craig answers. "Kinda like that. Raul Valencia owned the company before I did. And he plucked me from the depths of darkness to teach me the ins and outs of this business. He paid for my way through school."

"He sounds like a good person."

"He was. But even more than that, I suppose he wanted a son . . . and I needed a father . . . so there he was . . . and now, here I am." Craig turns back around to face Patrice. "Will that do?"

Patrice smiles. "For now." She gets up from her seat. "I'll get the papers back to you on Monday. Is it okay if I stop by?"

"Sure. I'll be here."

"Perfect. I'll see you later, Craig."

"Be safe, Patrice."

Patrice leaves the office and takes the elevator to the lobby.

Craig stares out the window again, going over a few things in his mind. *A normal client meeting. That's what that was. Plenty of clients have asked me why I do this, and I've given that very same answer a number of times. Why does this time feel so . . . different?* He sees her walking in the street below, heading back across the street to her car. He waits for her to drive away before leaving his spot by the window and coming up with some work to do. At this point, he sits at his desk again, doing everything he can to avoid going home.

CHAPTER FIFTEEN

AT seven o'clock in the evening, she thinks of it as stupid. At one after, she thinks it is a good idea, right until she sees her mother stepping out of a cab. Berta now figures that traveling across town again to meet her mother outside the church was a bad idea.

She spent the rest of yesterday after the funeral thinking about everything, and the most predominant thought that came of it is that she should meet up with her mother. She came up with that first, primarily because it was the simplest conclusion. But now, as the sun is almost completely down, Berta stands, wrapped in a long coat, staring at her mother, a woman whom she hasn't recognized as such since childhood, walking toward her.

Izabel gets to Berta and looks as if she wants to hug her but refrains. Instead she nods. "Thank you for coming."

"Don't thank me. I still may just leave you here."

Izabel nods and begins walking down the street. Berta follows. As they walk, a cold wind blows through the streets, sending a chill up and down Berta's spine.

"Where are we going?"

"Just right here." Izabel points to a giant building a little further down the street.

"The public library?"

Izabel nods.

"That place should be closing soon, shouldn't it?"

"Not if you work there . . . and have a key."

"You're a librarian?"

Izabel nods again. "Come."

Berta follows Izabel to the front doors of the library and unlocks the doors. Both she and Berta rush in as Izabel puts in the security code so the alarm doesn't sound. She locks the doors again. Berta hears the humming of a floor buffer and the strange sounds of a man singing. As they step to the main lobby, Berta sees a man with large headphones, dancing while moving a buffer across the floor. He looks up to see the two and gives a confused expression. He cuts the buffer off.

"Bell? People told me you weren't working today." Then man speaks in a strong Hispanic accent.

"I'm not. I just need a few moments to spea—"

"Oh, my goodness. Is this your daughter? She looks . . . she looks just like you. I know this is your daughter. Just like you. She looks just like you. I'm Renaldo." The man places his hand out. Berta slowly shakes it.

"Renaldo, slow down. Yes, this is my daughter. We need a few moments, though. This is the only place I could think of that would be empty . . . and free."

"Oh, yes, yes. Please, take the upstairs. Grab a room. I just finished cleaning those."

"Thank you, Renaldo."

"Uh-huh. Hey, Bell, you know Tera is going to be mighty upset that I got to meet your daughter and she didn't."

Izabel pats Renaldo on the shoulder. "That's why she's not going to know about it. Right?" Izabel nods. Renaldo nods with her.

"Sure. Yeah, okay. My lips are sealed. But don't be a stranger, miss . . . Alberta, right?"

Berta nods.

"Yes. This is going to be a good night. I met Bell's daughter. Alberta from the stories."

Izabel and Berta walk past him to the stairs that lead to the rooms. A few moments later, Berta hears the buffer running again, accompanied by Renaldo's terrible singing.

"He knows my name? Alberta from the stories?"

Izabel nods but says nothing. Instead, she ushers Berta on to the first room they get to at the top of the stairs. She opens the door and cuts on the lights. Berta is first hit by a smell of old books and cleaning chemicals. It's a weird and dizzying mix of smells. She then sees a large conference table, eight chairs around it, and a bunch of books on shelves behind it. Berta sits in the first seat she can get to, an old wooden chair that creaks. Izabel shuts the door and sits across from her. Both just gaze at each other. Berta realizes she looks more like her mother now than ever before.

"I thought this was some kind of prank," Berta says. "Part of me still feels that way. Like this is some big joke."

Izabel's face remains warm, calm. Berta feels her gaze piercing through her, making her feel uncomfortable in her own skin.

"So I'm here. Now what?"

Izabel snaps to. "I talk about you all the time. I tell stories of when y—"

"You said something about you not knowing about the situation with the monster. You implied that I didn't know the truth. Let's talk about that stuff."

Izabel pauses, taps her chin, and sighs. She grabs a tissue from her purse. "Have you ever wondered how Raul got to you? Have you ever wondered how he knew?"

"No."

Izabel smiles. "You're lying, Alberta. You know how I know? Your lip still quivers, just like when you were a child."

"Can we move on with it?" Berta is embarrassed for being found out so easily.

Izabel stares at Berta. "What kind of person do you think I am? Do you think I'm a good person . . . a bad person . . . a confused person, maybe?"

"What? Mom, stop with the games. You—" Berta stops herself; both she and Izabel realized what she just said. "Izabel, please, stop with the games. If you have something to tell me, tell me straight."

Izabel starts to say something, but stops. "Am I 'Mom' to you?"

Berta doesn't answer.

"I always thought of you as my daughter. It's interesting . . . some part of you still connects to me . . . on that level."

"I never said that."

"But you called me 'Mom.'"

"If this is what this little meeting is about, I can just leave. I didn't come here to debate who you are."

"But who I am is important, at least in this instance."

"Why?"

"Because I am not who *you* think I am. I am not who you were led to believe."

"Then who are you?"

"A broken woman, yes, but not this terrible person you think I am. There is very little truth to this whole golf instructor thing."

Berta smiles and leans back in her seat. "Then what is the truth, Izabel?"

Izabel stops, noticing the disbelieving smile Berta has plastered on her face. She continues anyway. "The golf instructor thing was a lie."

"Of course it was."

"Courtland saw an opportunity to get rid of me, and he took it. He told you that I slept with the golf instructor and just up and left with him, right?"

"Maybe."

"At least, that's what he led you to believe."

Berta stares at Izabel blankly, waiting for her to continue.

"Courtland and I weren't on good terms at all. He abused me. He raped me. He did many, many bad things to me." Izabel looks up at the ceiling as if she were reading something on it. Then she blurts out, "I was talked about like a dog, then forced to stay away, then talked about again. It all started with Courtland. We had a rocky marriage . . . an abusive marriage. It ended when he kicked me out, leaving me in the streets to fend for myself. He came up with the rumors, and they spread like wildfire, all an elaborate scheme to get me out of the house, to get him out of the marriage, to shut me up.

"He had connections to every high place and many low places. All he had to do was make a phone call and whatever he wanted was done. But by the time you were three, the police started picking up on his activities, and he had to be more careful. If it weren't for that, I'd likely be dead."

"Wait, you're all over the place here. Slow down. So the golf instructor thing, the selfishness, every negative thing that was said about you was a lie." Berta smiles that same incredulous smile. "And it all started with the monster and his treatment of you. A bit convenient, don't you think?"

"But it's the truth. I threatened to let the world know of his penchant for abusing his wife and he got scared. He figured he would, for lack of better words, beat me to the punch and make me seem crazy and selfish, so his reputation remains intact." Izabel pauses and looks at Berta for effect. Berta seems unfazed.

Berta squints her eyes. "Even if all that were true . . . You weren't there . . . you weren't there when I needed you the most . . . when I needed a mom the most. And let's be transparent here: I remember the crappy way you treated me when I was little. Remember, I was there firsthand to experience that."

Izabel hangs her head in shame, unable to say anything to what Berta just said.

"So where does Daddy come in on all of this?" Berta decides to keep the conversation moving.

Izabel sends a crooked smile toward the table and for a moment, everything stills. "You still call Raul 'Daddy.'" She looks away. "Raul was a good, good man. Sometimes I wish I had married him."

Berta looks at Izabel in confusion.

"Raul is your hero, yes?"

Berta says nothing.

"Raul is my hero as well. When I was living in the streets without a dime to my name, it was Raul who gave me shelter . . . and love."

Berta still says nothing.

"For a little over a year, I hid in Raul's mansion. Rarely did I ever leave the beautiful place. Luckily, Raul had some connections as well, and that allowed me to stay hidden from everyone. Not that it mattered. As far as people knew, I was with the mysterious golf instructor in some other country. Anyway, Raul helped me to my feet in so many ways." Izabel looks to see if Berta is paying attention. "He was the complete opposite of Courtland. Where Courtland was a crooked businessman, Raul was always on the up-and-up. Where Courtland was uncaring, harsh, and abusive, Raul was ever-present, kind, and, loving. And somehow, they were business acquaintances." Izabel furrows her brow. "But Courtland was good at covering up his second life. He was good at covering up his alter ego, the one you call the monster. Raul, you could take him at face value. He was the only one who believed me. Why he did, I don't know. He was really good at reading people, I suppose. But I eventually told him everything about me and Courtland . . . and you. Though I thought nothing was going on, he feared the worst. And it turned out that the worst was happening. That's when I found out about what Courtland did to you." She sighs a slow and long sigh. "I know there's a lot to the story that I don't know about, like exactly how he did it. There are parts that Raul never told me because he feared it might change the way I perceived him. What I know is he left one morning and came back in the evening carrying you in his arms. And he said nothing more of it."

"I don't remember seeing you at the mansion."

Izabel puts her head down and is unable to look Berta in the eyes. "I left."

"Why?"

"Because I couldn't stand to look at you without feeling guilty." She looks up at Berta. "If I had known, I would have fought harder, for you."

Berta stares at Izabel for a few moments. Then she gets up from her seat, her chair making a loud creaking noise.

"Alberta, please stay. You have to know this is the truth."

Berta stops and stares at the ceiling. "What if I don't really care anymore?"

Izabel leans back in her chair. "Then you can leave. But something brought you to that funeral. Something brought you here tonight. And I can tell, Alberta, you are scared. But it's okay to be scared. I'm scared, too."

"Scared? You think that's what it is? Fear?" Berta glares at Izabel. "Goodbye, Izabel." She turns on her heels and walks away.

How often do people hold truth in their hands, or stare it down face-to-face, but cower away or let it go? Why do people do this? How often do people choose ignorance over truth simply for the sake of a false freedom and selfishness?

SLAM!

Berta is snapped out of her daydream on a sermon preached this past Sunday by Angelina slamming a stack of papers on her desk.

"I need these copied, stapled, and set out for the managers' meeting today."

Berta looks up at Angelina abruptly. As each day goes on, Berta dislikes Angelina more and more. Berta grabs the stack of papers and heads into the copy room. Everything is a fog to her. She can only focus on the events of the past couple of days, and the issues rotate, each vying for its share of her attention. She slams the papers on the copier, thinking about how she ridiculously accused Craig of cheating. She sets one part of the stack in the worn-out machine and presses the glowing green button to copy. She grabs the stack of paper from the tray and sets them on a table next to the copier. She sets the final part in the machine and jabs at the glowing green button again. Then she thinks about her mother and her story, and how those things she once came to terms with are starting to feel uncomfortable again.

Berta massages her temples. She feels a pulsating so strong inside her head and wonders if she's thinking too much, if she's worrying too much. *I'm going to worry myself to a stroke,* she thinks. She takes a deep breath and makes a few snap decisions, for her own sanity. *First, I'm going to talk to Craig as soon as I see him. I'll pull him off to the side and we will talk this out, whether he wants to or not. Second, I'm going to talk to Izabel so I can rid myself of the what ifs and move on with my life. Done. And. . . .*

Berta turns to the side to see Angelina standing near her, watching her every move.

"Almost done."

Angelina doesn't move, and waits for Berta to finish before snatching the papers from her and storming off. Berta ignores her, focusing more on what she has to do after work. She looks at her watch. A few hours left before the end of the day. With very little more to do for the day, Berta stares at the clock on her computer monitor for a few minutes. She thinks back to her conversation with Izabel, slowly drifting away into her thoughts. A few thoughts press themselves forward to the front of her mind. She knows there was a seemingly strong relationship between Raul and Izabel. How far it went, she doesn't know. She also knows that she is the only one who knows what happened the night Raul came to get her, that is, if what Izabel says is true. The more

Berta thinks, the more she feels she is missing something. She tries to piece things together, but her thoughts are quickly becoming sporadic. And then there's the feeling. It hits her hard in her stomach and every time she gets it, it forces her to move. Berta grabs her things and heads out of the office for the day, three hours early.

Berta gets to the library and calmly walks in. She goes to the checkout desk, though no one is there. She looks around the vast main floor to see mostly students studying, some whispering to each other. She passes by the front desk and begins her search. She begins by looking through every aisle, but realizes that she is getting nowhere fast. She needs to find someone else who works there. She looks back at the main desk to see a man stepping behind it. Berta makes her way over, her footsteps being drowned out by the echoing of pages turning.

"Excuse me."

The man looks up and smiles. He takes his glasses off for a second and cleans them with a microfiber cloth. "What can I help you with?"

"I'm looking for Izabel Rego. Is she in today?"

The man furrows his brows. "Bell? I'm not sure if she is. Hold on." The man disappears again through some other door. He comes back out a few minutes later. "She's on the top floor, in what we call the dome room. You know, you look a lot like her."

Berta takes a few steps back. "I know. Thanks for checking for me." She turns and walks away.

Once at the top level, Berta immediately spots Izabel stacking books onto the shelves. Berta just stands there watching her, observing every movement she makes. She is graceful in almost everything she does. She's dressed like a librarian, but there's a sort of flair with what she has on that Berta spots as well. Though she went on this search for her, Berta is finding it hard to move to say anything. What Izabel has told her thus far is in direct conflict with what she believed about her all these years. She needs answers, though. Berta takes a step into the room, noticing that no one else is present but her and her mother. Izabel sees Berta and stares. They stare at each other as if trying to see who would first blink.

"Why didn't you fight for me?"

Izabel, without taking her eyes off Berta says, "Because I couldn't."

Berta walks to the table in the middle of the room and pulls out a chair on one side, then the other. She sits down and folds her arms.

Izabel stacks another book on the shelf and pushes a cart closer to the door. She looks at her watch, then glides over to the table. She sits down. "Well, let me thank you again for listening." She clasps her hands together. "I understand if you are angry with me. You have every right to be angry." She looks down. "I was angry at myself as well." Izabel looks at Berta's hand to see her wedding ring. "I wish I could have been there for you. Who gave you away?"

Berta looks at her ring, twirling it around her finger with her thumb. "No one."

Izabel nods. "I'm sorry."

"Yeah, me, too."

For a few more moments, both look at the wood grain on the table. They say nothing.

Berta's cell phone sounds off inside her purse. She snaps to it and turns the ringer off, but not before noticing that Jade called her. She stuffs the phone back into her purse. The cell phone allowed a break from the intensity of the situation, and allowed a window for Izabel to speak.

"I love you so much, Alberta. My fear, which has also become my truth, is that you will never know how much."

Berta nods and cuts to the chase, yet again. "You didn't fight for me. Why?"

Izabel pauses. "A number of reasons. I guess a mother who simply leaves her child doesn't have much of an excuse, but here's what I thought. I was scared to show my face because I thought I'd be killed.

Even if I wasn't afraid of that, I simply didn't have the resources to give you any semblance of a good life. And . . . I was jealous of you. A large amount of guilt came with that."

Everything inside of her freezes, but she manages to speak. "Jealous?"

"Yes." Izabel clears her throat to stop the tears from flowing. "Yes. I am ashamed to say, but I was jealous of my own child. Courtland and I were doing terribly. Everything he said in our vows turned to dust. But according to him, we put on a good show." She pulls her seat from the table a bit and crosses her legs. "We would go out to these upper-class dinners and laugh at things that weren't funny, act like a close husband and wife team. We would put on a good show, I will admit. But then, when we got home, if that's what you want to call it, the abuse resumed as normal. Sometimes he would beat me so badly I couldn't move. And when he saw me there, battered and broken, he would take me. Right then and there. He craved power, especially over me."

"Why didn't you leave?"

"And go where? I knew no one. I had no friends but his friends. And he owned a couple cops then. I could run, but they would easily find me. Then the abuse would have been worse. He would have killed me. And my focus was simply staying alive. And if I ran away with a child . . . the results would have been worse."

"But still, you didn't try anything?"

"No." She sighs. "At one point later in the marriage I believe he finally succeeded at brainwashing me. You see he treated me like a slave, like a common whore. After a while, I believed that was what I was. As sick as it was, I eventually looked forward to the abuse. It was the only connection I had with him, and for some odd reason, I needed a connection to him."

Berta shakes her head.

"So, one day, I wind up pregnant. And the abuse stops. I thought that was the end of it, that he finally saw the error of his ways. But I could never leave the house. He put security on the house just in case I tried to leave. The sad thing is, I never wanted to leave. I just was happy for my baby's upcoming arrival. And it seemed that he was, too.

"So you finally came, perfectly healthy, and it seemed that things were going to be good forever. We would have dinners together, us three, and it didn't feel fake. People would see us and envy what we had. I soaked it all up. And there you were, little Alberta, with a smile that made everyone smile. The true love of my life. For that moment in time, I was in heaven.

"But one night, late in the night, I found myself in the bed alone and wondered where Courtland was. I walked all over the house just to find Courtland in his office, sitting there, brooding, with a weird and distant look I remember well. I should have just left him alone, but I was deceived yet again, this time by my own machinations.

"The abuse picked up where it left off, but I was different this time. I began to fight back. We fought all the time, but never around you. Actually, he never treated you wrong at all. And that's where my attitude toward you changed. I loved you so much, yet I didn't understand how he could have such a good relationship with you and not with me. You adored him, and he loved you for it. I adored him, and got pummeled. Eventually, a rift formed between us, me and you. You felt it. You knew I was jealous of you."

Berta shakes her head, but still listens carefully. Izabel looks at her watch again.

"My shift is almost over. Meet me in the lobby?"

"Fine."

Izabel gets up and goes to the cart full of books. She sets a few more on the shelves before rolling the cart to the elevator. She turns around, smiles, and walks into the elevator. The doors shut, but Berta remains still.

Berta can't help but feel angry about this story that Izabel is telling her. She tries to sort through her feelings, attempting to be as unbiased as possible, but she can't shake the feeling.

This woman left you there, stranded, knowing what the monster was capable of. She didn't care and she left you because she was jealous. Maybe there really wasn't a golf instructor, but she is still the same selfish person.

Berta gets up from the chair and slides it in under the table and pauses. She takes a deep breath and releases the chair, deciding to take the stairs instead of the elevator. She needs a few more moments to think. Berta gets to the lobby of the library and finds Izabel talking to a few of her coworkers, bidding them a good night. She spots Berta and paces her way over.

"Did you want to get something to eat?"

They begin walking.

Berta slowly shakes her head. "Not really."

Izabel nods, then looks down.

"This is . . . all of this is just too much. I called myself giving you a chance, giving you the benefit of the doubt . . . I haven't seen or heard from you for years. Years. Now, you come out of nowhere and tell me of your guilt, your jealousy. Then you go on and make yourself out to be someone who is the complete opposite of who I know. This is just too much. Now all of a sudden, you're caring. Now all of a sudden, you're loving. And why on God's green Earth would you leave me with a psycho who abused you? What did you think he was going to do to me?"

Berta and Izabel walk out of the library. Izabel seems to be collecting her thoughts. Out on the streets, people stroll by, some on cell phones, many carrying briefcases and bags of some sort. A man by himself on the bench draws her attention. He just sits there in tattered clothing, watching everyone go by. For a brief second, he looks at Berta from across the street. He smiles. Berta quickly turns away and blinks a few times. She looks at Izabel, noticing that her mouth is moving, but Berta doesn't hear any words.

"Wait, what?"

"I'm sorry."

Berta stops walking and stands as people move around her and Izabel.

"I did not mean to overwhelm you, though I knew this was going to be a lot for you to handle. I'm sorry for the decisions I made. If I could do it again, I would. I wouldn't have let you go. But I can't take anything back. It took me years to realize that I can't take anything back, and I can't necessarily make up for it. What I have done is what I have done. All I can hope is that you and God forgive me." She looks down the street. "All I can do is change from being that person I was years ago."

Berta wraps her arms around herself, not knowing what to do next.

"Alberta, just take your time. When you're ready to talk, I'll be here." Izabel calls for a cab. One pulls up almost immediately. "You know where to find me." She gets into the cab and a few moments later, the cab drives away.

Berta stares off into the distance. She doesn't find it awkward that Izabel left so abruptly. Rather, she finally believes what she is saying because the look on her face when she was leaving confirmed everything for Berta. The look plastered on Izabel's face was one of shame, and Berta knows that she couldn't fake it even if she tried.

Berta still stands on the sidewalk, looking around. She begins walking to her car, thinking to herself that she really needs Craig right now. But with the way things are between them, it wouldn't be a good idea to drop more issues in his lap. She needs someone to talk to, someone who could make this feeling of being in a dream go away. She trots her way to her car, trying to hold in the tears that force themselves out, and she pulls out her cell phone. The first person she calls is Jade.

No answer.

Berta gets in her car and sits there for a few moments before finding it necessary to pray. She begins to pray for everything and everyone that is on her heart, but most of all for guidance concerning her mother. A few minutes into her prayer, her phone rings. She snaps it up and answers it, expecting to hear Jade on the other end. Instead, she hears the voice of someone she hasn't talked to in some time.

"I . . . I didn't expect you to pick up so quickly. Actually, I didn't expect you to pick up at all." The woman on the other end sounds shaky, unsure of herself. "So how have you been, Berta?"

"Candace?"

"Yeah. Weird time to call, I know. I just . . . Something was telling me to call you . . . and you've been on my mind real hard lately."

Berta chuckles as she wipes the tears from her eyes. "Lately. I've been on your mind lately. Not for the past year, but lately." Berta shakes her head. "What do you want?"

"I'm just calling to see how you are doing, that's all."

"And what stopped you from doing the same, let's say, a year ago? A month ago?"

"Look, I didn't call to argue, and I didn't call to anger you. I—"

"Well, what did you expect? You thought it was going to be jokes and giggles? You completely cut me off . . . a year later, you expect us to pick right up where we left off? Are you serious? I called and called, tried to set up lunches, dinners, girls' night out, whatever, and you didn't do as much as give me a call back to say you were alive. So, yes, I'm angry, but even beyond that I'm hurt at your feeble attempt to see what's going on with me, as if nothing happened."

Berta hears Candace sigh over the phone. "Maybe this wasn't the best idea."

"Maybe? No, this clearly wasn't the best idea, point-blank, period. So again, I ask, what do you want?"

Silence.

Just before Berta hangs up Candace talks again.

"I'm sorry, Berta. I truly am. I just called to see how you were."

"Well, I'm just dandy. Anything else?"

"No . . . I guess not."

"Okay, well, I'm getting off the phone now. I have some important things to handle."

"Okay . . . I'll, I'll uhhh, talk to you sometime."

"Yup."

Berta slides her thumb to the end button, but before she presses it she hears Candace still on the other end. She puts the phone back to her ear.

"What did you say?"

"I got a divorce."

"Okay."

"That's what was going on. I was getting a divorce from Jack."

Berta stays silent.

"I caught him cheating on me with his high-school crush . . . or whatever he said she was. I didn't tell you because, well, you and Craig were just married, and I didn't want to rain on your parade."

"Rain on my parade? Candace, I considered you a friend. I was there for you like you were there for me. You could have told me and I would have been there a hundred percent. Instead, you choose to cut me off without a word. No heads-up, no goodbye, nothing. Why?"

Candace sighs again. "I just couldn't handle it all. Easily, you and Craig are the most envied couple I've ever seen. You have everything I never had. Craig treats you like a queen."

Correction, he did treat me like a queen. Now he treats me like a peasant.

"And after all the years of getting looked over by guys who were running toward you, I just felt worthless. You walk into a restaurant or store or something and the whole world falls at your feet. With me, I would be lucky to get a glance. That stuff wore on me after a while, and after the divorce, seeing you and Craig made things worse. I mean, in a few short months, your husband treated you like you two were together for years. He was so on point. I couldn't . . . I couldn't take it. It was a struggle for me just to get my husband to touch me."

"So . . . you were jealous?"

"Unfortunately."

Berta still says nothing.

"Nothing much to say, huh?"

"What do you want me to say?"

"I don't know. Something."

"To be honest, there isn't much more to say."

"Could you ever forgive me?"

"I already have. I've forgiven you a long time ago."

Candace pauses. "Well, why don't we meet up for lunch or something. You know . . . like it used to be."

"Nope. No. No. No. Not happening. You see, I've forgiven you, but that doesn't mean I want you in my life. My life is fine without you."

Candace pauses. "I see. Okay, well—"

"And furthermore, I think that was an incredibly selfish question to ask. You cut me off without saying another word. You made your choice. You just can't jerk me around. One day you're my good friend. The next you're jealous and not talking to me. Which Candace would I get?"

"Berta, I promise, I—"

"No. No promises. Like I said, my life is fine without you. You can move on with yours. I hold no ill will. And again, I have forgiven you. So your conscience can be free."

"Oh." Candace sounds like she's holding back tears. "Well, if you ever need someone to talk to . . . you can give me a call." She hangs up the phone.

Berta throws her phone to the passenger seat and starts the car. She bristles a bit, collecting her thoughts. Her determination sets in and she puts the car in drive to get to Craig's office.

CHAPTER SIXTEEN

"OKAY, so we have all the paperwork signed; we have your goals clearly outlined, here,"—Craig points on a sheet of paper, explaining what's on it to Patrice—"here, and here."

Patrice smiles. "What's this number here?" She points on a different sheet.

"That's my fee. But if it's too much, I can work with you on it."

"If it's too much? Craig, I'm worth millions."

"I know, but . . . through my experience, the more people have, the tighter they are with it."

"And you were willing to accommodate that. You would reduce your fee because I'm potentially a cheap, uptight person?"

"I didn't say all that. I'm just looking at the situation for what it is: a woman who is going through some rough times, who was essentially thrown into this situation, who needs help getting used to the new situation. That's it."

"But do you look at everything as if it needs saving?"

"What do you mean?"

"I'm the woman; the situation is this crazy divorce mess, which leads to another situation of having all this money and not knowing what to do with it. You kinda act like you're my knight in shining armor. I mean, in a weird, roundabout way."

"Trust me, I'm no knight. I like helping people. You came for my help based on recommendation. I'm going to make sure I help you. After all, it's my job."

"But do you treat all your clients this well?"

"I do." Craig senses a slight turn in the conversation. The air is filled with another long moment of silence, this one being more awkward than the last. "It's what keeps the business going."

"Oh." Patrice smiles. "Okay, so where do we go from here?"

Craig grabs a folder from his desk and scans a few papers. "From here, you live your life as normal, and the only time you hear from me is when you make too many purchases, when investments change, or other special circumstances—like maybe you saved money on something and have a bit extra to play with, whatever."

Patrice looks down. Her shoulder–length hair slides to the front of her face. She pushes a few strands behind her ear. "I'm not sure what living life as normal is." She looks up at Craig, who sits by the window. "You know what I mean?"

"I follow you. But that's up to you to figure out now. No one else can tell you how to live now. It's all on you. You have options. Weigh them out carefully and . . . be free."

Patrice scoffs. "I halfway expected you to tell me that I should pursue God now. Now would be the best time to see what plans He has for my life. That's what most Christians would say, right?"

"Maybe. But it sounds to me that you already know that."

"Maybe. But seriously, what does a woman in my situation do?"

"Pursue God. See what plans He has for your life." Craig smiles. "But I don't think writing erotica fits in that mix."

Patrice smiles. "Then I doubt I'm going to God."

He looks plainly at her, but in his mind, he prays for her. He doesn't know what for exactly, so he just prays for her wellbeing, for her healing.

"Did I hurt your feelings?" Patrice interrupts his thoughts.

"No." Craig smiles. "Not at all. It's just interesting to hear someone say that."

"Well, I have my reasons."

Craig opts to change the subject a bit. "So you were a football wife, huh?"

Patrice's eyes twitch. "I guess you can call it that."

"What else would you call it? You were the wife of a football player who makes millions."

"The shoe fits, but I never liked being called that. It's like I had no identity of my own."

Craig nods. Patrice stares out the window.

"I guess this conversation has taken a turn. Quite a few turns. Money to God to football ex–wife. Interesting topics . . . but enough about that. I'm supposed to live life as normal, right?"

Craig nods.

"Fine." Patrice gets up from her seat. "I can do that."

"You don't look so sure."

"I'm not . . . but I'll manage. I have books to write." She heads to the door, but stops. "It was nice talking to you."

"Why don't I walk you downstairs?"

Craig opens the office door for Patrice only to see Berta standing at Ted's desk. He makes eye contact with her as Patrice moves around him and out of the office. Patrice stops and stares at Craig.

"Patrice, please allow me to introduce you to my wife."

Berta cautiously walks to Craig with a slightly annoyed expression.

"Berta, this is Patrice. Patrice, my wife Berta."

Patrice shakes Berta's hand. "Nice to meet you. Craig, I know my way out of here. I'll talk to you soon."

"Okay. Talk to you soon."

Berta walks into Craig's office without saying another word. Patrice disappears around the corner. Craig looks at Ted.

"Something's really bothering her," Ted says.

"I know. Isn't it time for you to go home yet?"

"As you can see, I'm packing now."

"Well, I'll see you tomorrow." Craig goes into his office and shuts the door.

He sees Berta sitting in his chair, her legs crossed, staring at him, but not saying a word. Craig stands there, waiting for her to say something.

"One of us is going to have to start this off," Berta says.

"So start it off."

Berta sighs. "Why does it always have to be like this with you?"

"Always like this with me? What do you mean?"

"I mean why do you make things so difficult?"

"Correct me if I'm wrong, but wasn't it you who accused me of cheating, at a funeral for a man you despised? I think it was. Also, it was you who storms into my office when I'm with a client."

"You were done."

Craig stares at Berta, saying nothing.

Berta shakes her head. "We need to talk this out. There are a lot of things we need to talk out."

Craig sits down. "Fine."

"I know the conversation I brought up at the funeral wasn't appropriate, and for that I apologize. But I don't apologize for asking in the first place."

"But Berta, why would I cheat on you? You know me. You know I wouldn't do that. You know I couldn't do that."

"You see, that's the thing. I did know that. But now, cheating is the only thing I could think of to explain why you changed."

"How have I changed?"

"You're not as romantic. You're not as caring as you once were. Something happened and I don't know what."

"We just came from Bora Bora. I planned another trip to Alaska. I'm not romantic?"

"Yeah. You know, just like I know, that the vacations don't mean much anymore. We both act like things are good, just so we can have a somewhat okay time." Berta squints her eyes. "But once we come home, you act like a complete stranger. We don't talk, we rarely make love. What would you think if the shoe were on the other foot?"

"I don't know. But I know I wouldn't think you were cheating."

Berta looks out the window. "I think we need counseling."

Craig sighs. "I don't. I think we can solve our issues by talking them out just like we are doing right now. We have more than enough tools to do so."

"But look at how long it took to get you to sit down and talk."

"That doesn't matter. The point is we are talking right now. We can fix it right now."

"But nothing like this is ever fixed right away."

"Jeez, Berta," Craig shakes his head. "Can't you just for a second stop over-thinking things?"

"I can do that when you stop taking things so lightly."

Both pause and stare at each other.

"So is this a stalemate?" Craig asks.

"No. I'm setting up an appointment with Pastor for us. If you decide not to show up, I know where you stand, and I will act accordingly."

"What does that mean?"

"That's up to you." Berta gets up from her seat. "But let me say this: I love you. I love you with all my heart. But I love myself, too, and I know what to stand for and what not to. I'm trying my best to be a good wife. But I can't have a great marriage alone. I'd much rather be by myself than carry an entire marriage on my shoulders." She walks toward the doors. "Especially with all of this other stress. I'll see you at home."

Before Berta opens the door, Craig stops her. He turns her around and pulls her in close. He kisses her deeply, as if he's thirsty and she is his water. Moments later, he pulls away. "You think I don't love you, too? You think I'd rather be with someone else? You're wrong. I do love you, and I want to be with you and you only for the rest of my life. What I said in my vows remains true."

Berta starts to go limp in his arms. A tear traces down her face.

"I get it, Berta. I get it. You think I'm not interested in you anymore, and that leads you to believe I am cheating. But I'm not cheating. It's taking me a bit to catch up to this marriage learning curve, but I'm trying."

"Are you? Are you really trying?"

"I . . . I . . . ." He slowly releases his grip on Berta. "No. I haven't been." He takes a few steps back. "I haven't been . . . and I'm sorry."

Berta stares into space with tears in her eyes. "Why?"

"Why am I sorry?"

"No, why haven't you been trying?"

"I guess . . . ." Craig turns around. "I guess . . . I don't know . . . I figured marriage to be different. I always thought that in a marriage, you just are happy and things will be good. Treat your spouse well and things will be fine. All that other stuff to me always muddled things up. Marriage is real simple to me."

"But it isn't that simple. It never was."

"No, marriage to you isn't that simple." Craig faces Berta again. "I thought it would be. We were friends for years. We knew each other. We knew the other's quirks. We knew what made the other mad . . . and what made them happy. It was supposed to be simple."

Craig rubs the top of his head and paces back and forth in front of Berta. He thinks of the conversation he had with Mark last week. "It's all on me. Okay. That's fine. I'll be different."

"How?"

"I'll think of ways. I can fix this."

"Craig, I want to go to counseling."

"No."

"Why not?" Berta yells.

"Because all they do is give you a platform to talk. We have that. We're talking now."

"But that's not all they do. They give tools to help. They make it easier to figure out how. Don't be so pigheaded just because you don't want anyone looking at your marriage as a failure."

"That doesn't bother me."

"It does. I know you."

Craig plops into his seat. "You're wrong."

"Then why don't you want to go?"

Craig looks at Berta. "Because we aren't that bad yet." He looks at her with a softness that makes her insides melt. "I didn't fail you yet."

Berta can't stand to look at him because every time she looks into his eyes, she wants to cry. "I'm not saying you failed me," she says to the floor. "I'm saying I don't want us to fail. I'm saying that getting a few pointers doesn't hurt. Please, Craig, I want to do counseling."

Craig thinks for a second. *Whatever it takes.* "Fine."

Berta grabs a tissue from her purse and dabs at her eyes. "I'll set the appointment for sometime next week."

Craig give a curt nod.

Berta looks at Craig, who now seems to be in a daze. "Craig."

He looks up.

"I love you."

"I . . . love you, too."

CHAPTER SEVENTEEN

JADE sits in her parked car in the Raynard Pharmecuticals lot, trying to steel herself to go in. The front of the building looks strange to her, like she's never been there before. She looks around the lot, but doesn't see Calvin's car anywhere. *First step, get out of the car.* She slowly places her hand on the car door handle, but freezes as she tries to open it. As if she were being tortured by being forced to watch a continuous stream of images while being tied to a chair, she relives the night of the incident. In vivid detail, the whole night comes to mind. Certain occurrences come to mind stronger than others, such as the clinging of his belt buckle . . . the revulsion she experienced as he touched the back of her thigh . . . the relief and fear she felt when she broke from his grasps.

The police came and surprisingly arrested Calvin, and then asked her a billion and one questions. With Karen sitting with her, stroking her back, Jade answered every one of the officers' questions, though she found it to be more of a formality. The idea of pressing charges continuously came up, but she didn't want to think of that. She just wanted to get home to her kids . . . and Mark. She almost curled up in a ball and cried knowing he wasn't home from the retreat. Karen drove her home while her boyfriend followed behind. Jade appreciated the burly man, as he went into protection mode for her, backing up all the onlookers and others trying to find out what happened. That was another thing that made the situation uncomfortable. By the time the police came, many people were leaving the party to go home and do Lord-knows-what. A good-sized group started to form right around the time the cops were putting Calvin in handcuffs, and Calvin—being Calvin—even while being cuffed, soaked up the attention. He flopped around, yelled, screamed, threatened, and demanded, while the cops used as much self-restraint as possible. With the forming crowd, the last thing they needed was a video of them beating Calvin to a pulp.

Before Jade got home, she checked herself in the small mirror on the visor. She had a bruise on the right part of her forehead. She couldn't let the kids see it, so she packed on makeup over it. She got home and thanked Karen and her boyfriend, then entered the house. The kids were watching TV and she quickly gave them a hug and a kiss. She rushed upstairs to the bathroom and turned on the shower. She stayed in the shower for a least a half hour, letting the warm water wash away the night and her tears. She tried to keep her sobs quiet, but at a few moments, she knew one of the kids must have heard her.

Saturday and Sunday were nothing eventful, and that's how she wanted it. She needed time to think. Monday, she was too depressed to go to work, so she shut off her work cell phone, kept her laptop closed, and called out sick.

Jade snaps from her trance and takes in a deep breath. She slowly opens her car door. A gust of wind gives her resistance, but she stands tall. She walks through the front doors and straight back to her department. As soon as she walks into the marketing wing, it takes all of a few seconds for everyone's eyes to be on her. She walks to her office and closes her door. A few moments later, a knock.

"It's open."

Karen walks in and gently closes the door. She stands there staring at Jade. "Are you okay?"

"I'm better." Jade makes a face. "But not perfect."

"Listen, whenever you want to talk, you just call me, okay. If there's anything you need, just let me know. My boyfriend and I are here for you. I can't believe that bastard sh—"

"Karen. Slow down. I appreciate the support." She sits on the edge of her desk. "Has Calvin showed up?"

"Nope. Chatter around the office is that he took a few days off."

"A few days off?"

Karen nods.

"What other stuff have you heard?"

"A bunch of nonsense."

"Like what?"

"The gossipy stuff . . . like you led him on . . . mostly women saying that. Many say it was a setup to get him out . . . like you had this whole plan devised."

"What would I do that for?"

"Money, I guess."

"What does my schedule look like today?"

"Pretty clear. You have a meeting at ten. I can cancel it if you want."

"Who is it with?"

"Hold on, let me check." Karen leaves her office and comes back a few minutes later. "Mr. Lawson."

Jade nods and gets up from the edge of her desk. She looks at Karen, who stares at her in confusion. "I think my time is up here, friend."

"What? Don't say that. You've done nothing wrong. He just wants to talk, probably about the accounts, and if he does bring the party up, he just wants to understand your perspective."

"Karen, let me ask you something. How do you think I got this position?"

"Hard work. Rather smart and aggressive work."

"That's what you think?"

"It's the truth."

"I thought it was, too, at one point. But like I said, I had some time to think. Calvin said a few things that . . . I'm starting to believe."

"Like what?"

"Like me being hired for my looks. Calvin wanted me from day one. He thought if he helped me to this position, I would help him in return . . . sexually."

"But Mr. Lawson wouldn't have fallen for that."

"Maybe. But we know Calvin is like a son to him. A son he would do anything for. And what if he liked what he saw as well?"

Karen says nothing.

"Think about it. With my skill set when I first got the position, would you say that I was a perfect fit, or was it too far of a reach? If you were in Mr. Lawson's position."

Karen still says nothing.

"My blessing . . . my miracle . . . was a trap."

"Jade, maybe things will end differently."

"They likely won't. So I'm going to push this meeting up a bit so I can get this over with. At least I can leave with a speck of dignity."

Jade straightens her suit coat and walks out of the office and to the second floor, which is Mr. Lawson's office. She knocks on his door and his secretary opens. As soon as she sees Jade, her smile turns to a slight frown. She offers Jade a seat and calls Mr. Lawson on the phone in the lobby. Every three seconds or so, the curly haired woman glances at Jade. When she hangs up, she tells Jade that he will be right with her. The door to his office suddenly opens, and the other VPs walk out. A usually jovial bunch, neither had anything to say to Jade. Then, behind them was Calvin in street clothes. None of them looks her way. The secretary walks Jade into the office and leaves, closing the door behind her. Mr. Lawson sits in his giant leather executive chair with his hands folded in front of him. As Jade nears a chair in front of his giant wooden desk, he stands. He places out his hand, offering her the seat. Jade looks at his face and is unable to read anything from it. She sits.

"Jade, I'm sorry for what transpired at the party on Friday. I feel in a way personally responsible for this, as I have always tried to foster a safe work environment full of classy, hard-working people."

Barf. Barf.

"But some things wound up out of my control, and as CEO, that shouldn't happen. So to rectify the situation I had to make some . . . tough decisions." He slides a piece of paper in front of her. "Please let me know if this is agreeable."

Jade lifts up the paper and begins to read. It's turning out to be exactly as she thought. "You're letting me go."

"It's the best choice ongoing for us. But as you see, we aren't leaving you high and dry. I could never do such a thing for such a great employee. I hope you find the seven months' severance well enough for you and your family."

"What about him?"

"He has been demoted."

"That's it? You're firing me, but he just gets a demotion, even though he is the one who is wrong."

"Again, I said this was a tough decision."

"You do know that this is completely wrong and I will be pressing charges?"

"I'd advise against that."

Jade pauses.

"I'd advise against that on a number of levels. Please, read the specs of the severance."

Jade reads the paper. "I can't sue the company." She looks up with a fire in her eyes. "Or anyone associated with the company."

"If you do, the severance is null and void. We would owe you nothing."

"This is so wrong."

"Jade, you must understand that a sexual assault case would surely put a blemish on this company's record. And for him . . . ."

"Why should I care about him? He tried to rape me. Do you get that?"

"I understand fully the magnitude of what I am asking of you. But please don't look at it in that light. Call it another blessing in disguise."

"What?"

"Jade, look at the situation for what it is. I'm saving you the trouble, the money, and maybe even the jail time."

"Jail time?"

"You assaulted him, did you not?"

"I defended myself from him."

"Word against word, Jade." He adjusts in his seat. "Look, I'm deeply sorry for all of this. But I have to operate in the best interest of the company."

"So you fire me?"

"Both of you are getting just punishment. Calvin is like a son to me. But I do not, nor will I ever condone his actions. But I just can't have that blotch on this company's sterling record."

He sounds like a freaking broken record. "And how am I a blotch?"

"You are not a blotch per se. It's just that people will always remember. It detracts from the morale of this place. And the rest of the board agrees."

"They never wanted me in this position in the first place, so I figured that much."

"That isn't true. They thought you to be a wonderful candidate, and they were right. We were all right."

"You're lying. Why did you hire me?"

"Because we saw potential."

"Tell me the truth." Jade looks Mr. Lawson in the eyes. "All of it."

"Jade, I assure you, I have been nothing but transparent with since you started with us. Please, don't make this more difficult than it has to be. I am operating here in your best interests."

"And if I decide to sue anyway? If I say screw this severance and take Calvin and this crooked company for everything it has? If I reveal all of this to the local media?"

Mr. Lawson's face remains the same, straightforward. His voice presents a different side of him. Something more menacing. "Then we will crush you." He shifts his voice back to pleasant. "But Jade, please understand that this is not the path that we recommend. We would like this business relationship to end amicably. I mean, think about it." He leans back in his seat. "We could easily get a team of high-powered attorneys. Attorneys that could flip a case like this and make him seem like a saint and you a strung-out sinner. Attorneys that would know why you really left your position at the pharmacy." He smiles at her. "What attorney would you get? We have a bunch of people willing to vouch for his character, where he was the entire night, and anything else. What people would you get?"

"Wait. Why did I leave my position at the pharmacy?"

Lawson smiles yet again. "Jade. Come on now. We knew about your indiscretions with, what was his name? Boley? Is that what you called him?"

Jade's mind immediately shifts to Karen, the only person she told about her past issues at the pharmacy. "Karen, huh? What did you offer her?"

Mr. Lawson chuckles. "Who do you think agreed to take your position when you are gone? She won't have anything to say about that night, trust me. Just tell her you are thinking about suing the company . . . see how she reacts."

Though Jade's inside are flipping inside out, her face shows calmness. "So this is hush money."

"Look at it however you want, but I think the package is fair."

"None of this is fair." Jade, finding that she has hit a brick wall, stands up and makes her way out of the office. Before she exits, she turns around.

Jade nods. "Amicable." She leaves the office.

"It has been a pleasure working with you," he says.

Jade glances back as she walks away, catching Mr. Lawson staring at her legs.

"Good luck to you in all your future endeavors, Jade."

Jade gets back to her office to see Karen sitting in front of her desk.

"You waited here the whole time?"

"I can't go back out there." Her eyes are puffy, as if she were crying.

"Karen?"

"Please say it wasn't what you thought it was. He didn't fire you."

Jade looks at Karen sadly. "He did."

"I don't understand why. I don't get it."

Jade understands everything well, but she cannot bring herself to say it. Calvin was right . . . and she couldn't feel any lower than what she feels now. And to have Karen play this innocent role for her now. Jade could rip the skin off her, but she remains professional. "I have to pack my things."

"Jade, I'm sorry."

"It's okay. Don't worry. I hope—"

A booming knock on Jade's office door fills the room. Karen jumps. Jade opens the door to see two large men . . . in security uniforms. Jade just nods.

"I just need a few seconds to get my things."

One guard looks Jade in the eyes while the other looks away. The guard looking right at her asks, "Would you like any help?"

"Please."

The guard grabs the box handed to him by Jade and waits by the doorway. Jade looks at Karen, who looks at her in shock. "That's a wrap, kiddo."

Karen gets up and gives Jade a tight hug. "I'm so sorry," she says, on the verge of tears again.

"It's fine. I'm still pressing charges against Calvin."

"Good."

"And this company. I'm taking them both for everything that they have." Jade scrutinizes Karen's face.

Her face is soft at first, but as the seconds pass, the edges become hard, and her face contorts into a pained snarl of sorts. "You sure that's a good idea?"

Jade looks at Karen blankly. "You thought selling me out was a good idea. At a time like this, why?"

"What are you talking about?"

"They put a wad of cash in front of your face and you tell all? Well here's some news, they're going to use you, then throw you to the side."

Karen's face turns to one of shock. A few moments later, she hangs her head, and slumps her shoulders. "What was I supposed to do?"

"Not sell me out for some money. Dirty money at that. At the very least you would still have your dignity . . . and my respect."

Karen looks at Jade in anger. "That's easy to say for you. But for me, I have to worry about the crap apartment me and my boyfriend live in. I have to worry about my boyfriend coming home with no money because most of his check goes to child support. I need the money. You said so yourself: I was safe while you were here, but when you're gone. I needed to set up for the future. *My future.* I—"

Jade puts her hand up, stopping Karen. She looks at the guards and follows them out of the building, without giving even a single glance toward anyone there, though Jade knows they were all staring at her anyway. The guard carrying her things places her box in the back seat of the car and nods.

"I'm sorry, Mrs. Cooke."

Jade doesn't say anything. She gets in the car and drives off, never to step foot in the Raynard Pharmaceuticals firm again.

Chapter Eighteen

After a long drive, Mark gets home to his family, excited to see them. When he finally gets into the house, he sees it decked out in party decorations. Suddenly, Jade and the kids pop out from behind the couch and yell "Surprise."

Mark smiles. "You do know I haven't been gone for even a week."

The kids rush over to Mark to hug him while Jade shrugs her shoulder and gives him a kiss on the cheek. "The kids wanted to do it," she says.

After a short night of celebration (the kids have school tomorrow), Mark and Jade retire to their bedroom. Mark starts to unpack while Jade watches.

"How was the retreat?"

Mark pulls a bunch of dirty clothes from a bag. "It was okay. I learned a few things. Met a couple of nice people. You know." Mark stops unpacking to sit next to Jade. "But I'd much rather have spent that time with you." He kisses her on the forehead. As he pulls away, he stares at her for a bit longer. His expression turns to a frown. "What happened here?"

Jade says nothing at first. She knew he would see right through the makeup cover up. She stares into Mark's eyes, trying to find the right words to say.

"Jade, what happened?"

"The office party didn't go so well. It didn't go well at all."

"Okay . . . ."

"I got into an altercation with Calvin."

Mark says nothing.

"He assaulted me."

Mark pops to his feet. "What?"

Tears come to her eyes. "Mark, please, the kids will hear." Jade gets up and closes the door. "He . . . he assaulted me and tried to . . . tried to . . . ."

"He tried to what?"

Jade looks into Marks eyes, seeing a growing fire behind them. She can't bring herself to say anything more.

Mark's face shows he knows what she is talking about. "He tried to, but he didn't." He looks to her for confirmation.

"No. I fought him off."

He starts pacing back and forth. "You're not going back there. And I'm going to have a talk with Calvin. Did you call the police? We have to go to them tomorrow and file a report."

"Wait, Mark. Listen. There's more to this."

Jade goes to her nightstand and pulls out a piece of paper and hands it to Mark. Mark reads the paper, his eyes still ablaze.

"They're letting you go? I don't get it."

Jade looks at Mark. She tells him about what happened between her and Calvin. She tells him about her conversation with Mr. Lawson. She tells him about how she feels about everything—about the assault, the firing, about Karen selling her out. By the end of it, Mark plops on the bed and looks blankly out into space.

"What do you want me to do?" he asks.

"Right now, I just want you to hold me."

She curls up into a ball and presses back into his body. A few seconds later, she feels his arm wrap around her and pull her in close.

"I'm thinking of taking the money," Jade says.

"Jade, no. We're going to pin these bastards to the wall."

Jade dismisses him with a wave of her hand. "We can't afford it. And my income was the only consistent income."

"I'll find a job. It doesn't matter what field. I'll get a job."

"But that won't be enough to pay the attorneys we would need for a case."

"Come on, Jade. You stopped me from handling the situation before and it got worse. Now you're asking me to keep my hands tied again?"

"What other option do you have? What can we do, really?"

Mark pauses. "I'm going to pay this Calvin guy a visit."

"Mark, please don't."

Mark sits up. "And you're not taking that money."

"Mark, I understand you are mad, but don't mess this up."

"Mess what up? Do you hear yourself?"

"I do, and I had plenty of time to think about it. Just listen for a second."

"No." Mark gets out of the bed. "I told you to let me handle it. It would have never gone this far. I don't know what you were trying to prove. I don't know what you were thinking."

"So this is all my fault. That's what you're saying?" Jade sits up.

"I'm not saying that at all. I'm saying we should fight, because up to this point, we haven't."

"But don't you get it? If we do that, what do we lose in the process? Here we go with another case, another way for the media to dig into our lives. Another few months of lost privacy. Think about the kids. They couldn't do it. I can't do it. I just want to move on."

Mark sits up on the edge of the bed, still visibly fuming. Jade notices he got himself so worked up, he's shaking. She goes to put her hand on his, but he snatches it away.

"Can you really move on?" he asks.

She lies back down and curls back up. "I have to. We have to."

CHAPTER NINETEEN

2MORROW. Midday. Meet with pastor.

Craig looks at the text message from Berta. Then . . . .

Sorry bout the short notice. Only slot open.

Craig leans his head back and starts to massage his temples. He slams his phone on the desk and calls for Ted. Ted appears a few moments later.

"What's my schedule look like tomorrow?"

"Packed. You have about five meetings. A few investment changes."

"Okay. I need you to clear half the day for me."

"Are you okay, sir?"

"Irritated, Ted. Just . . . irritated."

"Care to talk about it?"

"Not really. I'm sure I will be doing plenty of talking tomorrow." Ted frowns.

"Anyway, you take the series seven?"

"I did."

"And?"

Ted puts two thumbs up.

"Good. Soon, I'll shift a few clients to you so you can build your resume. Then, you can write your own ticket."

"Before you do that, we need to talk."

"What about?"

"Well—"

Craig's phone rings. "We'll pick up on this later. Okay?"

"No problem." Ted leaves the office.

Craig answers the phone.

"Hey, Craig."

"Hey . . . Patrice. What's up?"

"Big change to the plan. I don't want to sell the house in Florida."

Craig leans back in his seat. "Okay. You do know that a good chunk of your money is tied up into the place?"

"I do. But I thought I'd rather move down there than stay up here."

"You sure?"

"I've been thinking about it for the past few days and I thought it would be a better idea. Plus, I grew up in Florida. Most of my people are there."

"How did you end up here in the first place?"

"My ex got traded."

"I see." He flips through a folder. "I'll run those numbers for you. Any other change?"

"Nope."

"And you are really sure about moving to Florida? In the same home you and your ex built?"

"Well, my ex was never home, so there aren't many places he built. It was always just me in the house."

"And what of the life you built here?"

"What about it? If anything, I had the worst experiences up here. Plus, the condo here doesn't suit my tastes. We can just sell this one instead. But if I'm not mistaken, it sounds like you are trying to keep me here."

Craig hears it in her voice. She's smiling. "No, no, I'm just making sure you are making the best financial decision. My job, remember?"

"Of course."

Long pause.

"Listen, would you like to go out and get a bite to eat?" Patrice asks.

"A bite to eat?"

"Yeah, you know, like, lunch or something."

"L—like a date?"

"No. Nothing like a date. I know you're married. I wouldn't dare try to step on that. I mean like two friends going out and catching up or something like that. Nothing intimate. Nothing that would cause your wife to hunt me down with a bowie knife."

Craig feels embarrassed. "Uhhh, I don't know."

"Tell you what, forget I asked. I just saw you as someone who I could talk to about stuff. Maybe I pushed the limits of professionalism too far. I'm sorry if I made you uncomfortable."

"Naw, that's cool. Ummm. I'll work out those numbers for you and give you a call later?"

"Sounds good."

"Okay, cool. I'll give you a call. Take care." Craig rushes off the phone.

He pauses to take a few breaths. *What was that?* He gets up from his desk and paces back and forth. *Like a date? Really, man? Idiot.* In between bouts of putting himself down, he tries to figure Patrice out. He doesn't understand it, but there's something about this Patrice woman that intrigues him. Right off the bat, he knows that is a problem, especially given the current state his marriage is in.

Chapter Twenty

BERTA sits at her desk working on a spreadsheet on her computer when Angelina stands in front of her. Berta looks up, but looks back down, ignoring the woman.

"Berta, I need you to set up an appointment for me."

Berta looks up. "Okay."

"Send the invite out to myself, Bromley, and yourself."

"Anyone else?"

"Nope. That's all."

"What's the point?"

"Excuse me?"

"What is the point? Why the big production over a meeting between us? I've never had to do this before."

"Well, this meeting is important . . . and I don't want you forgetting."

Berta grits her teeth. "What is this, really?"

Angelina smiles. "A performance review. Set it up for two in the afternoon."

"I won't be here then."

"You ought to be."

"I have already talked to Mr. Bromley about it. I have somewhere I need to be. I have the time. Mr. Bromley had no issue with it."

"And if I did have an issue with it?"

"Does it matter? I already have permission from my boss." Berta smiles.

"You don't just work for him. You work for me as well."

"Really? I must have forgotten."

"Well, I think it is in your best interest to remember that tidbit of information."

Berta smiles. "Noted."

For a moment, both stare each other off.

"Look, I don't have time for this, and neither do you. If you still want this meeting, I'll set it up, but it will have to be before eleven." Berta starts clicking on her computer. "Mr. Bromley has ten-fifteen open, and"—a few more clicks—"so do you. So do you want to set it up then?"

Angelina glares at Berta. "Fine."

"Good. I'll see you in a half hour or so." Berta looks back at her work. When she hears Angelina storm off, she can't help but smile.

Berta never really understood the performance reviews. She understood hers even less. Her performance review consisted of Angelina making things up about her, twisting up others, and Mr. Bromley describing what exemplary work she does. Mr. Bromley wants to promote her, Angelina wants her gone. So, according to the company as a whole, Berta is a lukewarm employee. She hates that.

And it's all Angelina's fault.

Berta packs up her things before she leaves and makes a quick trip to the bathroom. She gets in to see Angelina at a sink washing her hands. She glances at Berta, then lets out a loud "hurmph." Berta enters a stall.

"You know, Berta, eventually you have to face the facts."

Berta says nothing.

"You aren't a good fit here."

Berta comes out of the stall and walks to the sink, still ignoring Angelina's babbling. She is almost out the door when Angelina asks something that gets Berta's complete attention.

"How's Craig?"

Berta stops at the restroom door. She slowly turns around to see Angelina leaning on the wall near the sinks. She has a smug look.

"What?"

"How's your husband?"

Berta thinks for a second. *She said his name with an air of familiarity . . . like she knew him . . . or knows him.* "I don't see how you care."

"You're right. I don't. But he's another one who has to face the facts." She gets off the wall. "He could have been so much happier in life. He could have been with a woman of power, a woman to complement his strengths, a woman to build an empire with . . . not someone's assistant." She chuckles. "I wonder how long your marriage to him will last when he realizes you clearly are not the best one for him."

Berta is stunned into silence. She stands in front of Angelina, filled with so many emotions it paralyzes her. Sadly, what she says resonates with her more than she would like. Her marriage is in a weird place right now, but how would Angelina know that? *She couldn't know that. Could she?*

"How exactly do you know him?"

"I slept with your husband," is what Berta heard, but what Angelina actually said was more confronting, more vulgar, to drive in her point.

Berta shakes her head as if she pities Angelina. "How far are you going to go to shake me? How low will you sink?"

"You don't have to believe me. Ask him." She chuckles again, while shaking her head. "But he chose you. Life is funny." She walks past Berta, leaving her in the women's restroom alone.

CZ&O

"Ted, can you get Patrice on the phone for me?"

"Of course, sir." Ted comes through on the intercom again. "She's on line three."

Craig grabs his phone and switches to line three. He presses the speaker button.

"Hey, Patrice?"

"Yes?"

Craig hears a bunch of noise in the background. "I'll make this quick."

"It's not good news, is it?"

"Well, here's the situation. You can keep the house in Florida, but half of your net worth is in the place. I doubt you could sell something that much anyway, so from that perspective you're okay. Selling the condo is going to be hard, and it's likely you will have to take a loss on it."

"Will I go broke?"

"No."

"Okay, then go for it. I really just need to get out of here."

"Is everything okay?"

"I'm fine."

"Patrice, I'm serious. Are you okay?"

"Of course I'm not okay. How could I be okay?"

Craig pauses. "I'm sorry for being insensitive."

"It's not you. You aren't my problem, and you aren't being insensitive. If anything, you are the only one I know who is showing some kind of compassion."

Patrice gets quiet. Craig doesn't say anything.

"The fool just up and left. Gave me money and went about his business . . . like I was an extended hoe."

"Do you have any family to help?"

"None that could really help me. And now movers are here to get the rest of his things. They're cleaning the whole place out. You want to know what they're taking right now as we speak? The bed. They're taking the bed in which I sleep at night. The only thing they were told to leave was a couch."

Craig doesn't know what to say.

"And he hired this cop to come and make sure I don't do anything crazy, like stop the movers from taking his things." She stops talking.

Craig looks at his watch. "You still want to go out for that lunch?"

"What? No." Patrice's voice is strained. "I don't want it to seem like something it isn't. And I don't want you to be uncomfortable."

"I won't be. I just stuck my foot in my mouth yesterday. That's all."

"But I understand how it would look. And I understand that could potentially put you in a bad position. The fool used to do that all the time without a second thought. I hated it. I don't want that for you or your wife. And all we would need is your wife to see us or something. Drama. Too much drama."

"Well, you shouldn't be in there. Not while that's happening."

"I'll take a walk."

"How about a drive up this way. You know Stan's, the steakhouse a few blocks from here?"

"You still trying?"

"I want to help."

Patrice pauses for a moment. "Fine. I'll see you there in fifteen minutes."

"Good."

Craig hangs up his office phone and grabs his cell. He quickly texts Berta and leaves the office for the day.

Cʒℰᴅ

Before Berta gets to Pastor's office, she is already on the verge of tears. There are simply too many things going on for her to sort through. Her thoughts have become erratic lines, one leading to another. None of them end anywhere there's closure. Her phone beeps as she walks through the hallways of the church. She digs in her purse, fumbling around for her phone, and grabs it. It takes only a few seconds for her to read the message, and the anger to nearly overtake her. *Going to be late. Out with client.* That is all the message reads, but it's enough to ignite a rage in her that she is sure she has never felt before.

"Berta?"

Berta snaps back to reality. "Yes? Oh, Pastor Raines, hi."

The pastor of the church, the church Craig first found himself in when trying to realign his life, is a plump man, though he has lost a few pounds over the years. He smiles brightly at Berta, but immediately picks up on the scowl Berta had on her face.

"We have an appointment, yes?"

"We do."

He nods and takes big steps to the back offices. Berta has to almost speed-walk to keep up. He stops.

"I thought it was going to be both you and Craig."

"He's going to be late."

Pastor Raines nods, and off he is again.

When they get to his office, the pastor ushers Berta in and he gently closes the door. He doesn't sit behind his desk, but in a chair next to her.

"So what's going on?"

Berta takes in a deep breath. "Well, Craig and I . . . we need . . . we need counseling."

"Okay. Did you want to wait until Craig gets here to start?"

"I did, but I know we only have an hour slot."

"Let's give it ten minutes." He gets up from the chair. "I have to grab a few things. Would you like anything to eat, anything to drink?"

"No. Thank you." Berta gives a half smile.

"Be right back." Pastor says, and walks out of the room.

Berta goes for her phone again and texts back to Craig, asking him how late he's going to be. She sits and waits. No answer. The longer she waits, the more her blood turns to acid.

"Alright." Pastor comes back with a book, presumably a Bible, and a stack of papers. He looks at the still-empty seat next to Berta with a disappointed expression. He sits behind the desk now, but leans in, his tone soft. "What's troubling you, Berta?"

Berta stares at him, her face emotionless, as tears slide from her eyes and down her face. She shakes her head, then looks to the side. "Craig and I aren't in a good place right now. Nothing is in a good place right now."

"Talk to me."

From there Berta proceeds to tell Pastor Raines about everything: about her struggles at the workplace, about Craig, about her mother, about her dead father's second family, about Candace, everything. Pastor Raines allows Berta to get speak freely as he listens intently. He makes a few key comments here and there, offering Berta places to start with each situation, while trying to understand what she is saying. At some points, his face is one of shock, because of what Berta is going through. When she is done talking and crying, she looks at him.

"Craig still isn't here," she says.

"Maybe that was a good thing. I think you needed to get this off your chest first, to release some of this vitriol beforehand. Maybe this will mean a more productive meeting when he is here."

"That's pretty optimistic. I doubt he's ever going to come to one of these."

"If I know Craig, he will. But in the meantime, I will set you up for a few more meetings. I feel there are some things you still need to work out, outside of your issues with Craig."

"I know."

"And I can't do much to help the marriage without helping the people in it first."

"I understand." Berta looks down. "Do you think Craig and I got married too soon?"

"There's no real way of telling. And even if there were a way, I wouldn't be the one to tell you. Every person is different, making every marriage different. We have guidelines, sure, but it all comes down to the two of you and if you were ready, or not."

Someone knocks on the door. Pastor gets up from his seat while looking at his watch.

"Excuse me for one moment." He leaves the room.

Berta sits still, thinking she told pastor a lot, but feels no better about any of it. In fact, she feels even more upset because Craig never showed up.

Pastor comes back into the room. "Sorry about that. Listen, what days are good for you to continue this?"

"It doesn't matter."

"Hmmm. All I have for a weekday is nine in the morning on Tuesday. It's a two-hour slot. Is that okay?"

"Yes, that's fine." Berta gets up and grabs her purse. "I'll let Craig know."

"Good." Raines lays a hand on Berta's shoulder. "Berta, don't make any decisions based on today alone."

Berta knows what Pastor is talking about as she told him earlier on that she gave Craig an ultimatum. If he didn't show, she was filing for divorce. She nods. "I'll see you in service Sunday."

Pastor Raines bows his head and Berta leaves to go home.

C13 80

"Thanks for getting me out of the house. Or, what's left of it."

"Hey, no problem. I heard over the phone that it was getting pretty intense for you."

"It was. It sure was."

Craig and Patrice sit and enjoy lunch. Craig incessantly looks at his watch.

"It seems you have somewhere to be." Patrice smiles.

"I'm sorry. Actually, there is somewhere I should be. I'm already fifteen minutes late. But . . . ."

"Oh, don't worry about it. I'm fine. I'm just thankful that you had lunch with me. I know you're a busy man."

"Are you sure?"

"Yes. Yes. Go do what you have to do."

Craig gets up and grabs his wallet. He pulls out a fifty-dollar bill and slides it under the table centerpiece.

"You're a good tipper," Patrice says.

"It's for both the meals and tip."

"But I can pay for my own meal."

"I know." Craig says as he walks away from the table. "If you feel that bad about it, I'll add it to my fee later on."

Patrice smiles. Craig looks back to catch a glimpse of her smile. It nearly stops him in his tracks.

Once in his car, Craig sits there. His heart races, but he doesn't know why. A few minutes later, he sees Patrice coming out of the steakhouse. Quickly, Craig grabs his cell phone and pretends to talk on it. Patrice walks toward him. Craig realizes that she parked right next to him. He starts randomly talking about numbers so it seems like he is actually having a conversation. He stares at Patrice the entire time. She wears a navy medium-length trench coat, slacks, and heels. As time goes on, Craig realizes she isn't as average-looking as he originally thought. She isn't muscular, but soft. Thick thighs. Full chest. Full lips. She's a powerhouse and she walks like it. Each step forward seems to move her body in wonderful ways. Craig catches himself. He looks down. He hears Patrice's BMW start up and looks to the side. Her passenger side window is open and she is staring at him. He smiles. She blows him a kiss and mouths out "thank you." He bows his head and mouths "you're welcome." She drives off.

His phone beeps loudly in his ear from an incoming text message. He didn't realize he was still holding the phone up to his ear, even though Patrice was gone. He snaps the phone away and reads the message. It's from Berta. He throws the phone on the passenger seat and starts the car. He knows he's late, but the only thing he can think about is how much fun he had with Patrice. Craig isn't completely blind, though. He knows having lunch with her was a huge mistake. He knows having any more contact with Patrice could lead to something . . . bad. His best friend went through the same exact thing. He tells himself the same thing he told Mark back then. The problem is, he doesn't want to hear any of that right now. A large part of him simply doesn't care.

Eventually, Craig gets to the church and parks behind Berta's car. He hops out and rushes inside only to see Berta headed his way. He comes to a stop. Berta keeps walking, completely ignoring his existence. Craig calls for her, but she says nothing and walks right by him. She gets into her car and drives off, with Craig watching her car turn into a dot on the horizon.

"Give her some time."

Craig turns around to see Pastor Raines.

"Yeah."

"What's going on with you, man?"

"Nothing. Besides this stuff, I guess."

"You sure?"

"I'm sure."

"Did you do it?"

"Do what?"

"Sleep with her coworker."

Craig eyes Pastor Raines curiously. "With her coworker? No. She told you that?"

"She didn't say it directly, but it's a question she has. Did you know about her mother?"

"Her mother? What about her?"

Pastor Raines looks down. "Do you know about anything that's going on with her?"

Craig senses a bit of an accusatory tone. He doesn't say anything.

"Craig, I need you to do two things. First, talk to her tonight, but listen to her even more. Second, I want you to be here next Tuesday at nine in the morning. That's the next session."

Craig nods. "Thanks."

Pastor Raines gives Craig a hard pat on the shoulder and heads back into the church. Craig simply stands there, still trying to figure out what's going on.

CHAPTER TWENTY ONE

MARK hasn't gotten much sleep over the past couple days. With both Mark and Jade home, each day has been filled with a sort of tension stemming from what each wants to do with the severance situation. Mark feels the right choice is to sue for harassment because the money in the severance is essentially dirty money. Jade comes from the perspective of one who is tired of the media. She can't intentionally put her family through what they went through with the fallout of the Alicia situation, even if it was on a small scale compared to other "scandals." The media scrutiny and the lack of privacy turned out to be too much for them to handle. One would think that Mark and Jade were celebrities the way newspapers and local shows hounded them for interviews. Mark isn't completely oblivious to Jade's argument, but he is angry. He's asked himself many times over: which is greater, his anger, or his love for Jade. He thinks his answer is a simple one.

He walks up to Jade, who is at the kitchen counter with her back turned toward him. He places his hand on her shoulder, and that's when he feels it.

A flinch.

Jade snaps around and stares at Mark. Mark frowns a bit. He realizes that Jade is still living the situation over and over again. He notices her hand trembles slightly and grabs it. He pulls her in close and embraces her. At first, holding Jade is like holding a rock; every muscle is hard. She is stiff. He strokes her back while holding her. As time passes, Jade softens and once again fits with Mark. Mark holds her protectively as if he is her armor. He feels more of Jade's weight as she slumps to the floor. Mark slumps with her, not letting her go. They both sit on the kitchen floor, Jade curled up in between Mark's legs.

"What are we going to do?" Jade asks. She speaks in hushed tones, though no one is in the house with them. Her voice comes out soft, as if she's scared and vulnerable.

"First, you're going to sign those papers and get them to the company. Then we are going to find a way to keep moving forward."

Jade looks up at Mark with glassy eyes. "You don't want to sue them?"

"Of course I still do. I want to see them burn, but our family can't take that type of storm . . . not again."

She lays her head on his chest. "Thank you."

Mark says nothing at first. He sits in silence and continues to stroke her back. He looks to the side.

"But you know I'm going after Calvin . . . eventually."

Jade tenses and for a moment, she moves with the motion of Mark's chest as he breathes. "I know."

"And I don't know what I will do."

"I think you should leave this one to God, Mark."

"I want to . . . I really do. But I can't."

"Don't be brash. Nothing good can come from you approaching him."

Mark thinks for a second. He doesn't want to press the issue any further because he already knows what he is going to do. "I suppose."

"You said we are going to find a way to keep moving forward. If you engage Calvin in any way, we'll be taking a step backward."

"You're right."

"I am right. But I know you. I know you're going to think of a way around it and approach him anyway."

"How you figure that?"

"Any man would." Jade looks up at Mark again. "But please, I'm begging you, please, don't do it. For my sake . . . for our kids' sake."

Mark looks away from Jade. "Fine." Mark shifts away from Jade. "I got to go get Amber."

And just like that he gets up and leaves.

ଓଞ୍ଚ

Later in the night Jade cleans up the kitchen after dinner with Kalina eying her curiously.

"Mom, what's wrong?"

"Huh?"

"Ever since that thing for your job, I don't know, you've been off."

Jade turns and smiles at Kalina. She secretly hopes that Kalina doesn't see right through the fake smile. "Nothing's wrong. I'm fine."

"Did you cheat on Dad again?"

Jade frowns. Part of her was always unsettled at the notion of Mark telling Kalina so much. Jade believes Kalina knows too much for a child, yet Jade still answers.

"I nev—" she sighs. "No. I couldn't go through that again."

"Did he cheat on you again?"

Jade sits down on a stool at the kitchen island. "There is nothing wrong between your father and me."

"Then why haven't you been yourself? And why haven't you gone to work?"

Jade looks at Kalina, and opens her mouth to say something.

"We will talk to you about that some other time. For now, get to bed."

Both Kalina and Jade look to the side at Mark standing in the doorway. Kalina looks at Mark, then at Jade, then at Mark again, and

151

finally decides to listen to her father. She leaves the kitchen and goes upstairs.

Jade gets up and goes back to cleaning. Mark is just about to go upstairs when Jade stops him.

"Are you mad at me?" she asks.

Mark slightly tilts his head to the side and looks at Jade strangely. "No. Why?"

"I don't know. I just get the feeling that you are." She focuses on washing dishes, trying not to look at Mark.

Mark walks up behind her and wraps his arms around her waist. He places his chin in the crook between her neck and shoulder. Jade feels his warmth, and his breath smells like mint. Jade can't help but smile.

"You remember when we did all those Bible studies back in the day?"

"Around when we first met?"

"Yeah. You remember your little addiction."

Mark pauses for a second, then chuckles. "Mint candies."

"Mint candies. Every time I saw you, you were popping a mint something in your mouth. Tic-Tacs, Lifesavers, peppermint patties . . . ."

"Don't forget those weird mints that old people put in their candy dishes."

"The fifty-year-old mints from the dollar store."

"Yeah, those."

Jade smiles more and takes a few seconds to revel in the memories . . . the good ones, anyway. She then feels the vibration of Mark's cell phone in his pocket.

Mark takes out the phone, grunts, and places the phone on the kitchen counter.

"Who was it?"

"Restricted number. Been getting a few of those lately."

"Oh."

Silence.

"Look, Jade, I'm not mad at you at all. I'm frustrated that I can't do more. I want to do so much more. You think we would be in this position if I had a job?"

"There's no way of telling."

"Yes, there is. If I had a job, you wouldn't have even worked at Raynard. There would have been no need. And now that all of this has happened, I mean, I'm so far out of the loop it's embarrassing. I just want to wipe this situation away, not for my sake, but for yours."

"I understand. But you know what I was thinking about earlier? We have to realize that this situation isn't just going to disappear tonight, but by taking this money, we are ensuring at least enough time for me to get another job."

"Or for me to get a job."

"Yes, for both of us to get another job, less all the distractions that would be present if we took this whole thing to court. It's not the choice I want to make. Quite honestly, I don't like either choice. It's the proverbial rock and a hard place. The choice to take the money is the one I have to make. Would I like to be an advocate of sorts for women in the workplace, make an example out of Raynard? Of course I would. Do I feel like trash for taking the money and not fighting to stop the abuses of Raynard? Sure do. Do I want to see Calvin vaporized for what he did? For what he tried to do? I sure as hell do, but I have a family to worry about." Jade turns around to face Mark. "We have three kids to worry about."

Mark nods and looks down. "I know."

Jade pats Mark's chest, turns around, and starts washing dishes again.

"You're one strong lady, you know that?"

"I try to be. But it's pretty easy to be strong when you have someone stronger backing you up." She glances over her shoulder.

"I know what you mean." Mark smiles. He wraps his arms around her again and whispers into her ear. "We're going to be okay." He then kisses the nape of her neck. He holds her as they gently sway side-to-side.

"Do that again," she says.

"Do what?"

"My neck. Again."

Mark kisses her neck again, this time softer. Jade holds on to Mark's forearms for support as she leans into him more.

"I can't tell you how safe with you I feel," Jade whispers.

Mark doesn't say anything, but he holds on to Jade as tightly as he can without hurting her. Jade slinks from his grip and hops up onto the island.

"I didn't get a chance to welcome you home." She swings around and lies on the countertop, her feet on the edge of the counter, her back arched.

"You just cleaned the kitchen."

Jade opens her shirt, slowly turns her head, and grabs Mark by the waist of his pants. "I'll clean it again, afterwards."

Mark and Jade make love in the kitchen, then they sneak upstairs to not wake the kids and they make love on the bedroom floor. They continue their night in the shower, where Jade couldn't help but be loud on a couple of occasions. By the time they actually get to the bed, they both are right for sleep.

Jade lies in the bed next to Mark, still feeling the electricity between them. Her whole body doesn't just pulse, it surges, leaving her feeling tingly all over. She looks at the clock.

"You know we have to get up soon."

Marks voice comes out deep, gravelly. "I know."

She slides closer to Mark and rests on his chest. "You're a beast."

"And you just saved the universe."

She feels his chest contract while he chuckles, but after a few seconds, his chest moves with more even movements—deep, even movements. She knows Mark is sound asleep. She closes her eyes, but is still buzzing with energy. *We haven't made love like that since . . . since . . . we've never made love like that.* Jade ponders on the night, but she can't help but think more into it. There is an air of finality about the night. It was loving. It was passionate. It was fun. It was exciting.

And it feels like their last.

CHAPTER TWENTY TWO

CRAIG saunters to the front door of his home. After the failed counseling session, Craig went back to work. He had some things to do and he wanted to let Berta cool off, but he knows that there is nothing that he could do to avoid her anger toward him. He slides the key into the door lock, listening to the teeth of the lock and key press against each other. For Craig, everything moves in slow motion. Every sound is amplified. He opens the door, and for a moment he thinks he sees Berta in the kitchen, cooking. The smell of basil rises to his nose. Craig stands at the doorway as a silent Berta smiles and glides over to him. She kisses him on the cheek and says something, but Craig can't hear her. Her mouth moves and she smiles as if carrying on an entire conversation with him, yet he hears nothing.

Craig realizes he is daydreaming about how things used to be, and snaps back into reality. His home is dark and quiet. He cuts on a light and sees Berta lying on the couch, curled up in the fetal position. Her eyes are wide open and puffy. She must have been crying for a while.

"Berta."

She doesn't answer.

"Listen, I'm sorry. I got caught up at work and . . . ." He stops talking because he knows it all sounds like an excuse. He grabs a chair and sits in front of her. When he moves to pat her on the shoulder, she jerks away.

"Why weren't you at the church?"

"I was with a client."

"Since when can't you maneuver your client meetings around?"

"It was a type of emergency."

"And our marriage?" Berta looks directly at Craig. "We aren't in a *type* of emergency to you?"

"I didn't say that. I just . . . ."

"I'm disappointed in you. You said you were going to be there. Instead, you hid at work. While I sit there looking stupid, embarrassed." She curls up into a tighter ball. "Then you come at the end as if you made an effort to get there. You made no real effort."

Craig feels numb. "I'm sorry."

"Sorry means nothing to me." Berta sits up. "Nothing at all."

"Pastor told me about the appointment on Tuesday. I will be there. I will do whatever I can to make this right."

"There are a lot of things you need to do to make this right." She rolls her eyes. "Did Pastor tell you anything else?"

"He said a few more things, but glazed over the details."

"Did he tell you about my run-in with Angelina?"

"Sort of."

"Well, she was being her usual self, trying to run me down, and she popped up with this news that she had slept with you."

"I don't even know who Angelina is, other than your terrible supervisor."

"But, you had sex with her." Berta says matter-of-factly.

"Berta, where did you get this from?"

"Angelina herself."

"She's lying."

"I don't think she is. My gut is telling me that she is telling the truth."

"I did not cheat on you."

"I never said you did."

"Then what is this about?" Craig finds himself getting annoyed.

Berta sighs. "Angelina Crosby. That name doesn't ring a bell?"

"No. Not in the slightest."

"Well, here's what I think. I believe that Angelina was one of those 'airheads' you used to date. You tried her out for a week or two, then dropped her. Now she's gunning for me because I married the man who didn't want her. She's jealous."

"So without a second guess, you believe her? So any woman who comes up to you and tells you I screwed them, you will believe."

"I'm not saying that, and you know it."

"No, I don't know it, because I don't know what you are saying. You're running around accusing me of stuff I didn't do." Craig takes a deep breath. "You know me. You know my past and every single woman that I slept with. I revealed everything to you. I hid nothing. Nothing. And I find it odd that you are so quick to believe someone who doesn't even like you, over your husband. And even before that, asking me if I'm cheating, at a funeral." Craig frowns. "Seriously, Berta, where is your head?"

Berta says nothing.

"I mean, even if I did sleep with Angelina in my past, what does it matter now? There's nothing either one of us could do about it." Craig bows his head and pinches the bridge of his nose. "But I think I'm starting to get it now. You put more weight on my past than you let on. Now when things get tough, you can always go to my past and pick some issue to blame. Maybe you always did that and I never noticed."

"That's not true."

"Then where is this mess coming from?"

"Stop. Don't turn this on me. Everything would have been fine if you didn't change how you acted toward me."

"But I already told you my reasoning for the change. Why are you adding your own spin on it?"

"Because the crap reason you gave doesn't fit."

"Crap reason?"

"Yes, crap reason. You said you are trying to catch up to the marriage learning curve, but when it comes time to actually do something, you fail to show up . . . because you were with a client. What client emergency was so important that you left your marriage aside?"

Craig says nothing.

"I meant that as a serious question. What client emergency kept you away from our counseling session?"

"They were taking her stuff away. She doesn't even have a bed to sleep on."

"She? She who?"

"Patrice."

"I see." Berta says in hushed tones. "The same woman who was staring at you all googly-eyed when I came to the office?"

"I know where you are going with this, and it isn't like that at all."

"So what did you do? Run to her place?"

"No."

Craig offers no more.

"You know, I don't think this is going to work."

"What do you mean?"

"I mean this . . . this marriage. I don't think we are going to make it."

"We can make it if we fight for it."

Berta stands up and sluggishly walks to the kitchen. She leans on the counter. "You are right. We can make it if we fight for it." She turns back to him. "But you haven't begun to fight . . . and I don't think you will."

"You can't say that, Berta. I've messed up, I know, but I can, and I will make this better."

Berta smiles a weak smile. "Craig, I know you. I've known you for years. It's not in your makeup to fight. You run. You talk a good game . . . you always have, but when it gets time to do something . . . ."

Craig takes her comments like a slap in the face. "What have I run from? Every situation I was presented, I stared down and I conquered. What have I run from? And you, the nerve of you to pin that on me. You're the one who ran and made everyone believe you were in some other state. Remember that?"

Berta stares Craig down but says nothing. She laughs off what he said and grabs a glass and fills it with some wine. "I still have things I have to take care of. You can do what you want, but I'm still going to meet with Pastor."

Craig takes her comments as her resignation of their marriage. She's done everything short of filing the papers. Though her comments hurt him deeply, more deeply than he would ever admit, he knows he still loves her. He just doesn't like her too much right now.

CHAPTER TWENTY THREE

BERTA sits at her desk, unable to finish any task. For the entire day, she has done a good job of avoiding Angelina, but somehow she still feels her watching. Berta sighs. She asks herself why she is fighting this battle, this asinine battle with Angelina. She asks why no one has done anything to help.

Berta has allowed herself some time to think about the accusations Angelina made, and remains stuck on the fence. On one hand, she believes Craig when he says he didn't sleep with her. At least, that is what her heart is telling her. But her mind says something different. Her mind says that it makes perfect sense that Angelina is targeting Berta and no one else because Angelina is jealous. She is jealous, like everyone else seemed to be at one point in time. Candace, her own mother . . . Angelina targets Berta because Berta has what she wanted . . . what she thought she deserved in Craig. That's why Angelina would scoff at the vacations, and stare at her wedding picture in disdain. Berta sighs again, and this time, shuts her computer down. She gets up from her seat. She walks to Mr. Bromley's office and gently knocks on the door and pokes her head in.

"Mr. Bromley, I need to talk to you for a second."

The old man waves Berta in. "Have a seat. What's on your mind?"

"That won't be necessary, sir. I just . . . I needed to let you know that . . . that I decided to resign from this position. It's out of the blue, I know, but . . . ."

Mr. Bromley's face shifts into a perplexed one. He leans back in his seat. "Close the door for a second," he says plainly. "Please, take a seat."

Berta does as he asks.

Bromley sits in his seat, seemingly trying to find the words to say. "Why are you resigning?"

"It has become too much to deal with. I have a lot on my plate right now . . . and this job doesn't really help."

"I see. So you're just going to let her win?"

"Uhhh. I don't follow."

"You get me. You're leaving because of Angelina, and that is a terrible mistake."

"I'm not leaving because of her."

"So the performance review where we tell you that you have done everything right, but still are doing everything wrong, had nothing to do with your decision?"

"It played a part. But it isn't the whole."

Bromley gets up from his seat and walks to his bookcase. "Can I be frank?"

Berta nods, but is a bit thrown off by his forwardness. Mr. Bromley may have said no more than ten words to her per year. Now, it seems he's getting set to give a speech.

"There are some people on this planet who do something and you can tell they've worked hard at it. Then there are those who you know it's pure talent shining through. But there are those who have this natural ability to do something, and they work hard at perfecting it. Berta, you are one the hardest-working people I've met, and on top of that you have this knack for helping people, for assisting, for making things organized when there is nothing but chaos."

"Thank you, sir."

"Hold on, I'm not trying to schmooze you or anything."

Berta nods.

"But then you have people like Angelina; people who seem to lack any real skill, who lack any talent." He looks at Berta. "You know I have more talent in my pinky than she has in her entire body?"

"I believe you."

"But here's the problem. She is a deceiver. She has manipulated her way to a high position, a position she doesn't deserve. She has manipulated her way, and insulated herself from being canned. All that and she hasn't done a day's worth of work." He sits back down. Berta notices his breaths are heavy.

"This floor was so different before she came. This company was different, too. Before, it was about hard work . . . about being good to people . . . about loyalty . . . now, it's all about what the other can do for you, and this floor is like a machine . . . completely lifeless."

"And you blame Angelina?"

"She has played her part. Maybe I have as well. I could have said more, maybe I could have done more; but no one could have predicted it would be like this." He gets a far-off look in his eye. "But I'm getting off track here. Look, take some time off. Heck, take the rest of your time if you must. But give this decision some thought. Maybe take that time to lessen what's on your plate outside of here."

Berta looks down at the ground. "Okay. Thank you, sir." She looks back up, confused. "Why does it matter what I do? I'm just an assistant. You can get another."

"No. You're more than that. There's something about you that goes beyond your position. When you are here, things are . . . different. I'm not the only one who notices it, either. People smile more. They laugh more. Angelina notices it, as well. You know, I talked to her for a moment before your review. She reeks of jealousy."

"No kidding."

"She stoops to very low lows to get what she wants, Berta. She lies. She uses her body in . . . unprofessional ways. She plots, she schemes.

There's nothing it seems she wouldn't do. But with you, she seems completely flustered."

"It doesn't seem that way to me. She seems to know exactly what she is doing. She knows what she wants . . . who she wants."

"I'm sorry?"

Berta shakes her head. "Nothing. I'll take some time off and handle what I need to handle. I will let you know what I decide to do. Thank you."

"You are very welcome. I should be thanking you, really, for considering staying."

"Your words are very kind." She gets up from her seat.

"Berta."

"Yes, sir?"

"How is your family?"

Berta's heart drops. "I'm not so sure how much a family I really have." She looks down, and without letting Mr. Bromley say another word, she says. "I'll see you in a couple weeks."

CげʘౖⅭ

Craig leaves work early to get to Berta's work building. He parks in the back of the lot, but has full visibility of the front doors. He sits in the car, blending in with the various other high-end vehicles, and waits. He sees Berta coming from the double doors at a hurried pace. Even from afar he sees how worn out she is. He looks away, but he doesn't know why. Guilt? Shame? Disgust? Either way, he isn't here to see Berta. As he sees Berta drive off, he steps out of his car and heads to the doors of the building. A few people leave the building and eye Craig curiously. No one says a thing, though. He walks through the lobby area to the receptionist desk. A young blonde sits at the desk, seemingly annoyed by Craig's existence.

"Hi. I'm looking for Angelina Crosby."

"Do you have an appointment?" The blonde asks in a monotone voice.

"I'm a friend. Just dropping by to see her."

"Name?"

Craig hesitates. "Brandon. Brandon . . . Jones."

The woman rapidly punches in numbers on her phone and slaps the phone to her ear.

"Angelina." The woman pauses. "I mean Ms. Crosby. Sorry . . . yes, I know . . . you have someone here to see you. Your friend, Brandon Jones . . . uh-huh . . . yup . . . ."

Craig sees the woman flash a glance toward the security guard standing at his post in the far corner of the lobby. Craig looks the guard's way and notices his hand on his side. He can't tell if the guard is carrying a gun or a walkie-talkie. The woman gets off the phone.

"She will be right with you. Please, take a seat over there." She points to a row of seats against the far wall. Craig lets his gaze linger on her for a bit more before taking a seat. He grabs a *Fortune* magazine and flips through the pages. He gets aggravated after flipping through the fifth magazine. He sets it on the table next to him and looks up. He catches the security guard eying him. After twenty minutes of waiting, Craig starts to feel this was a bad idea. He walks to the front desk, startling the receptionist.

"Can you let her know I will catch up with her later? I really have to be on my way."

"Oh . . . I'll give her a call."

She picks up the phone and punches in numbers again.

"She's not answering. She must be on her way down."

Craig nods. "Well . . . ." As he looks to the side, he sees a short woman approach the security guard. The guard glances his way yet again, this time, not so discreetly. After a few more moments, the short woman makes her way to Craig. He turns to the receptionist.

"Listen, I can't wait any longer. I really should get going." Craig turns and heads for the door.

"Wait. She's coming up to the desk."

That was the last bit of confirmation he needed. As the woman shows a hint of recognition on her face, Craig tries to conceal his disgust in this scandalous woman.

He's disgusted because he has never seen her before in his life.

"So we've got you on camera, and a few witnesses . . . just in case you want to act funny. What do you want?"

Craig looks unfazed. "Why have you been telling my wife lies?"

"Lies? Awww, you don't remember me? You don't remember that passionate night?"

"I've never met you before." Craig eyes the receptionist. "Can we go somewhere else?"

"Nope. We can stay right here and talk. This conversation is almost over, anyway." She pauses. "Look, Sweetheart, this is nothing personal. It is all business. I need her out. Period."

"You want her out so badly you would stoop so low as to lie?"

Angelina smiles. "That's what business is. You should know that."

"I don't handle business that way. I don't need to lie to get my way."

"Well, to that I say you are your own worst enemy." She pulls up her sleeve and looks at her watch. "Your time is up. Now, you can either leave here on your own, or be escorted out by security. But one last word of advice . . . Stay the hell out of this building." She turns on her heel and storms away.

CʒꙄ

Berta doesn't go straight home. Instead she goes to the church. She knows few people are in the building on a Friday evening besides a few janitors and maybe a few others. She heads straight into the sanctuary and looks around. No one is present. She walks down the main aisle, her footsteps echoing across the wooden floors, and stops. The setting sun shines through the skylights. She takes a seat in the pew closest to her to pray, but nothing comes. Every time she starts, she finds it a great labor to continue, so she says nothing. She thinks nothing. For a brief moment, she allows herself to rest.

Moments later, she hears a group of voices in the back of the sanctuary. She doesn't bother to turn around to see who it is as the group of deacons walks by her toward the back rooms. Each one greets Berta by name before leaving the sanctuary. Directly next to her, the sound of the wooden pew being depressed resonates in the air. She knows it's Pastor Raines.

"Are you okay?" he asks.

Berta doesn't look his way. She clinches her jaw repeatedly to hold back tears. "Nope. I'm falling apart . . . making stupid decisions . . . saying stupid things . . . believing anything."

"Have you talked to Craig?"

"Not in a way that helped. I yelled at him. I insulted him on a number of different levels. I never even told him what I really feel."

"Why?"

"Because he's part of the problem."

Silence.

"Truth is, I've been afraid of this day since I first started dating him."

"This day?"

"The day our pasts come up to bite us in the rears."

"Is that really the case, or is that the way it is perceived?"

"I don't see the difference."

"Well, let me say this: The enemy has a really good way of distorting what is perceived and making us believe it's reality. Fear plays a major part in that. Fear essentially changes the way we look at things."

"I see." Berta shifts in her seat. "Maybe that's true for what's going on with Craig. Maybe even my job, but when it comes to my Mom, I see the reality."

"But the fear is all the same, no?"

"Maybe."

"From what I can tell, your mother comes back into your life and changes what you thought was a rock of your past. It was solid. It happened. End of story. But I'm guessing her appearance isn't so much what bothers you as what she said. What she told you about herself revealed to you a different person than the one you once hated. You now see a person who was battered and broken . . . one who aided in saving your life. That shakes the foundation of who you think you are in a way. Maybe even makes you feel guilty. But this is all conjecture. I'm just poking in the wind."

She glances in his direction. "So if you were me?"

"What I would do?"

Berta nods.

"It depends on what I want for myself. A marriage, a job, and a mother/daughter relationship are at stake initially. Ask yourself, what do you want? Do you want to be married to Craig?"

Berta shrugs her shoulders. "I love him. I really do, but our marriage is nothing like what I thought it was going to be."

"Is there a chance that, over the ten years you waited for him, you built up the idea of marriage to such an illustrious standard that no one could ever reach it?"

Berta shrugs her shoulders again.

"What about your job? What do you want on your job?"

"I want to perform my duties in peace . . . and I want to be rewarded for a good job, not put down for made-up stuff. And things would be easier if Angelina weren't there."

"You think Craig slept with her?"

"I'm leaning toward no. But I don't know for sure. Craig said he didn't . . . and I'm trying to believe him. I'm trying harder not to believe Angelina."

"Well, let's say Craig didn't. Why is Angelina the way she is toward you?"

"Because I smile at her the same as I do for everyone else. Because people like me more. Because I threaten her. Because she's jealous of me."

"Why would she be any of those things? And why does any of that matter? Why can't you work somewhere else?"

"Because getting a job isn't that easy nowadays. You know that."

"I don't want to pry too much, but I never knew you two needed the money."

"We don't."

"So what keeps you there?"

Berta doesn't answer.

"And for you and your mother, what do you want?"

"Don't know. She has opened up doors I shut long ago. It feels strange, but I guess a part of me wants the truth. The whole truth, not the abridged version. And she wants to tell me the truth. So I guess it should be easy."

"Are you content with your life?"

"Obviously not."

"Are you content with yourself?"

"No."

"Well, change it. We have the ability to change ourselves, and our environment. It's a God-given ability. Ask for guidance. Then make change." He gets up from the pew, the wood creaking. "I'm still praying for you and Craig. Make sure you keep me updated on what's going on."

"I will."

Pastor gets up and starts on his way, but stops to look back at Berta.

"It will all be okay."

Berta nods, then looks down, because she isn't so sure of that anymore.

♋

Craig moves around the house with urgency, setting the dinner table with a meal he prepared as soon as he got in. He flips on the radio and digs in a drawer in the kitchen to grab a candle and matches. Just as he sets the tip of a match to the candle wick, he hears Berta's keys in the door. When she comes in, she scans the house and settles her focus on Craig. For a few long and silent moments, Craig and Berta stare at each other.

"I made dinner. Are you at all hungry?"

Berta nods and goes to the kitchen to wash her hands. Craig waits for her to sit before he sets their plates with food. He then grabs two wine glasses and fills them halfway with red wine. Once finished, he sets the bottle on the table and sits. They bless their food and eat, remaining silent the entire time. Berta cleans her plate, but doesn't touch the wine. Once finished, she gets up from the table and grabs her plate to set it into the dishwasher.

Craig watches her as she operates as if he isn't even in the room. He switches his focus to the still-full glass of wine.

"Thank you for dinner. It was delicious."

Craig notices her voice comes out strained, forced.

"Berta, I didn't sleep with her."

Berta walks back over to the table and sits. "I believe you."

"But do you know it?"

"What do you mean?"

"You say you believe me, as if you're still unsure for yourself. It's like saying I know two plus two is four because it's a fact, as opposed to I believe my teacher that says two plus two is four. There's still room for doubt."

"Sounds like you're being a bit nitpicky."

"I am. Because it's important to me. Do you just believe me, or do you know it as fact?"

Berta looks at Craig. Her voice comes out as soft. "I believe you. That should be enough."

Craig nods, disappointed.

Berta gets up again to go to the back rooms when Craig gets up and grabs her arm. He swings her around and kisses her. For a few moments, they kiss, but something different happens. Their kiss ends awkwardly with them simply pressing their lips against one another's. Craig pulls away slowly, dreadfully. A tear wells in his eye. Berta looks at him straight-faced, but her eyes tell him that she knows the same thing he just found out.

There is nothing there.

Craig lets Berta go and continues to look her in the eyes. Many thoughts run through Craig's mind, trying to explain what just happened. How did their kiss go so flat? How did their marriage go so flat? He feels angry . . . and he feels guilty. On the inside, he starts to panic.

Berta blinks a few times, but maintains her expression. She grabs his face, cupping it as if she were holding the most valuable item in the universe, and kisses him. She kisses him deeply, causing Craig's tears to fall even more. When she lets go and looks him in the eyes, she tells him that she loves him, and that she always will. Craig says the same and watches her leave into the back rooms.

Stunned, Craig saunters over to the dinner table and takes a big gulp of wine. After two gulps, he finishes his glass, then he drinks the other glass that was set for Berta. He wipes away the tears and pours himself another glass. He knows not to drink anymore, because he knows there isn't enough alcohol in the world to soothe the pain he feels at this moment. The gut-wrenching agony of a truth he has come face-to-face with forces him into a type of catatonic state.

His marriage is over, and Berta sealed it with what felt like a goodbye kiss.

CHAPTER TWENTY FOUR

MARK stands at the front window, peering through the blinds to see when Kalina comes home. He has made it a routine to watch her as she comes home ever since her boyfriend's hand made its way into her back pocket for an extended stay. Though he told Jade he was going to talk to her about this boyfriend he isn't supposed to know about, he remains silent. He still can't wrap his mind around the fact that his little girl, the one he dropped an entire life to protect and nurture, is interested in dating and having boyfriends. It's all happening too fast for his taste.

Mark sighs.

"You looking out that window again?"

Mark glances back and sees Jade holding Amber in her arms.

"Yup." Mark retrains his focus on the school bus stopping at the corner of their block. He sees Kalina come off the bus. A few seconds later, her boyfriend does as well. Mark waits a few seconds for them to split, but when they don't, he gets anxious.

"Mark?"

"Hold on a sec." Mark continues to watch them as they near the house, both of them . . . together. When they both get to the door, he hears Kalina's key in the lock. Mark steps away from the window and eyes the door. As soon as she gets in, she calls for him. Mark looks at Jade.

"She invited him for dinner."

"Why didn't you tell me?"

"You would have found some way to make it not happen."

Mark grunts and walks to the front door. As soon as Kalina sees him, she lights up. Mark looks at the boy standing next to her. Unknowingly, a snarl comes across his face.

"Daddy, this is Gerald. Gerald, this is my Dad."

"Nice to meet you, sir." The boy puts out a hand.

Mark reluctantly shakes Gerald's hand. He eyes the boy again. Gerald stands a bit taller than Kalina, and he wears glasses, a sweater vest, and a bow tie. Mark also notices that the boy wears skinny jeans and basketball sneakers.

"What are you, a nerd?" Mark blurts out.

"Mark." Jade grabs Mark's arm, but before Jade could get him away, Gerald answers.

"No, sir. Well, yes, sir. In some respects I am, sir."

Mark shakes Jade's grip off. "In what respects?"

"I guess I would qualify. I get good grades. I'm exceptional at chess. I speak like this."

"You get bullied, boy?"

"No, sir. Many people like me."

"Why, because you help them cheat on tests?"

"No, sir."

"You do their homework?"

"No, sir."

"Then why?"

Gerald shrugs his shoulders. "Maybe because I play basketball?"

"You play ball?"

Gerald nods.

"Are you any good?"

"My friends seem to think so."

"So you're a nerd who plays ball and has friends?"

"Yes, sir."

"Okay, I think that's enough of the questions," Jade interrupts. "Mark, help me in the kitchen; Kalina and Gerald, you two have any homework?"

"Yes," Kalina says.

"Well you can go into the living room and start it while we get the food ready."

Mark looks back at Jade and grunts. "Did Charles finish his homework?"

"He's in the kitchen. Both of you are helping me with dinner."

Mark grunts again and heads for the kitchen. He sees Charles stirring sugar into a pitcher of tea.

"I don't like him, Daddy," Charles says.

"I'm still trying to read him. Have you ever heard of a popular nerd? A popular nerd who plays ball? That's not a nerd, that's a jock . . . or a kid with some really good game."

"I beat nerds up."

Mark smirks. "Charles, are you a bully?"

"No. But I would be one on him. I don't like him."

"Okay you two, cut it out." Jade enters the kitchen after getting Kalina and Gerald situated. "Gerald is a nice boy."

"But tell me something. Since when is it cool to be a nerd?"

"Different times, Mark. Different times."

"I don't like him, Mommy."

"And why don't you like him?"

"He touched Kalina on the butt."

Jade sighs. "Look, you two. Get to know the boy first before you pass judgment."

"I know I want to punch him in the face," Charles says under his breath.

"How about you punch your grades in the face? How about that? How about you punch in some As."

"Awww, Mommy."

"Awww, Mommy nothing. Leave the boy alone. You finish stirring the tea?"

Charles nods.

"Good. Now go wash your hands."

Charles hops down from the stool he was on and runs to the bathroom.

"What about his parents?" Mark asks.

"They're nice people."

"So you've already met them? Without me?"

"It was for the best."

Mark grunts.

"And what's with all this grunting?"

"Mom." Kalina calls for Jade. "Can you get Charles?"

Kalina comes to the kitchen, holding Charles' arm. "He asked Gerald what his intentions were with me."

Mark directs a nod of approval toward Charles.

"Did you wash your hands?" Jade asks.

Charles nods.

"Did you finish your homework?"

He nods again.

"Then sit down, right in front of me where I can see you."

On Charles' way to a stool, Mark gives him a high five.

The house phone rings.

"You two are being ridiculous right now. Mark, you gonna get the phone?"

"They'll leave a message."

"Speaking of which, did that restricted number ever leave you a message?"

Mark grabs his cell phone. "I don't think so." He scrolls through his phone call log to see that he has two missed calls. "And it called again today." Mark squints. "Craig called, too. I'll call him back later."

"Yeah, I have to call and see how Berta is doing. We've been playing a bit of phone tag lately."

"We should set up a dinner or something. Seems like we haven't been able to catch up with each other. But hold on a sec, let me see who called the house."

Mark gets up and grabs the house phone to access the voicemail system. He listens to the message that was left and as he does, a smile creeps onto his face. Immediately he calls the number back and talks on the phone for a few minutes. He hangs up and strolls back to the kitchen.

"Who was it?" Jade asks.

Mark says nothing.

"Mark? Mark?" Jade turns around.

"I got an interview."

"What?" Jade drops a spoon on the counter and walks over to hug Mark. "That's great news."

"Well, let's not get too excited. It's just an interview."

"What job?"

"The community college a few counties over is looking to fill an academic advisor role as soon as possible."

"Yeah?"

Mark nods. "Interview is next week."

"I didn't know you sent them your resume."

"I didn't."

Jade looks at Mark conspicuously. "So they just stumbled upon you? How?"

"A guy I met at the retreat. He knew a few people that knew a few people. He must have put in a good word . . . I know it sounds weird. I don't really believe it myself."

"We should celebrate."

"Let's celebrate after I get the job . . . if I get the job."

"You'll get it. No worries." Jade smiles. "Things are already starting to look up."

"Yeah. The only downside is this little hooligan sitting in my living room with my daughter."

"Mark."

"What?"

"Give him a chance."

"Yeah, yeah. C'mon, Charles, we're gonna stand guard."

"Sounds good to me." Charles hops off the stool. "I'm locked and loaded. No more booty grabs. Not in this house."

Mark smiles and looks back at Jade.

CHAPTER TWENTY FIVE

BERTA wakes up early Saturday morning and leaves the house while Craig is still asleep. She glances at him as he lies on the couch. His chest rises and falls with each breath. For a moment, she forgets about the strain of their marriage. She forgets about the pain. For a moment, she allows herself to be at peace, just her and Craig. Everything around them is still as she focuses more and more on his breathing. Abruptly, she snaps out of it.

Berta tiptoes out the door and closes it gently.

Within the hour, Berta gets to the library and sits on the bench just outside the front doors. The morning air is cool and fresh in her lungs. At an instant, she wants to break down and cry, but she composes herself. She's hoping to see Izabel to talk to her for a few minutes, and came before the library is due to open. Berta ends up waiting for a half hour after the library opens before going in to see when Izabel is set to work. She walks to the front desk, approaching the same man she did before, and asks if 'Bell' is in.

"Bell's daughter, right?"

Berta nods.

"She wanted me to give you something." He digs around behind the counter and pulls out an envelope. "She wanted me to give this to you whenever you showed up."

Berta grabs the envelope and thanks the man. Once she gets to her car, she opens the envelope to see a small piece of paper and an address, along with a phone number written on it. Berta calls the number, nervous.

"Hello?"

Berta hears Izabel's voice, but says nothing.

"Hello?"

Berta stays silent. Even shocking herself, she finds it hard to say anything. She bites her bottom lip. A tear forms in her eye.

Izabel hangs up.

Berta takes a deep breath and exhales slowly. She dials the number again. This time, it takes Izabel a bit longer to pick up, but when she does, she sounds just as polite and calm as she did the first time.

"Hello?"

"Hi."

Long pause.

"I'm so glad you called, Alberta."

"Is there somewhere we could meet?"

Berta decides to meet Izabel at her apartment on the north side of town. By the time she gets there, the midday sun beams brightly above. She gets to an average-looking complex. It's clean, but it isn't pristine. There are flowers and shrubs all around, but you can tell a professional landscaper hasn't done anything to it. It reminds Berta of the apartment she lived in before she purchased the condo. As soon as she pulls up into the lot, she sees Izabel sitting on a bench by the main office.

Berta gets out of her car and heads over to Izabel. Izabel gets off the bench and greets her with a hug, shocking her.

"Thank you," Izabel says. "Come." She starts walking to one of the buildings.

Berta follows her into one of the larger buildings and up a set of carpeted stairs. They walk past a few doors before stopping at Izabel's apartment. She opens the door and allows Berta in.

"Please, have a seat. Would you like anything to eat, drink? I have loads, I mean loads, of snacks. I do some babysitting for the neighbor's kids every now and again so . . . ."

"No, I'm good. Thanks."

"Okay, then." She sits down in an armchair. "What's on your mind?"

Berta looks at Izabel, noticing her tense expression. "You're nervous."

She smiles. "A little."

"Why?"

"Because I want this to go right. Because I thought that you would never want to talk to me again."

Berta starts to say something, then pauses.

"But how good is God? Since the day I left Courtland to this very day, I have prayed for the same thing: Just another chance to tell my daughter how much I really love her."

"God is good . . . but you had plenty of those chances when I was younger . . . but you left . . . even from Daddy's house after he came and got me."

"I couldn't face you. It was . . . it was . . . too much." She presses a strand of hair behind her ear.

For a while, both stay silent.

"Are you sure you didn't want anything to drink, or munch on?"

Berta stares blankly at her. "I'm sure." She doesn't move her gaze.

"I see."

"I'm here because—"

"You want the truth."

Berta nods. "The entire truth."

"Very well."

"Now let me make sure I have this straight. You were abused. You had me. You were jealous of me. You left me. The monster raped me. Daddy saved me. You never contacted me again . . . until the funeral."

"If you wish to put it simplistically. But allow me to clear something up. I didn't leave because I was jealous of you. I left because I was forced to. The jealousy only was for a quick moment. Once I was gone, things became clearer."

"And that's when the guilt and shame kicked in?"

"Yes."

"And that's why you left Daddy's place?"

"Yes."

"Because you couldn't look me in the eye."

Izabel nods.

"So what happened? How did you survive?"

"Raul helped me to my feet. He found me a nice place away from everything and everyone. I would talk to him every now and again to check up on you. To see how you were doing. Each time he would tell me to stop by and see you. I couldn't."

Berta's eye twitches. "So you and Daddy . . . you two were close?"

"We were . . . intimate . . . if that's what you were asking."

"You and Daddy made love?"

"On a few awkward occasions. I loved Raul for who he was . . . and he loved me for who I was. But all he saw was Emily, and all I saw was Courtland, so much so that we would both break down into tears right in the middle of it. We would stop and wonder what was wrong with us. Me, wondering what is wrong with me to think of Courtland while making love to another man, and him feeling bad because whenever we were intimate, he could only think of Emily. He called her name a few times . . . but I didn't care. He was so loving. So gentle. So passionate." Izabel shakes her head. "It was a sad state of affairs."

"So you're out there on your own. Daddy is taking care of me, trying to convince you to show up, and the monster is out marrying some other fool?"

"So it seemed."

"How did you get caught up with the monster in the first place?"

"That is an interesting question. I was young . . . stupid, naive, gullible, you name it, I was it. I grew up in a village in Brazil. Nothing was out of the ordinary about my upbringing, at least in terms of Brazilian culture. My father, your grandfather, wanted to move to America. He always believed there was more opportunity for us there. So we go. My father gets a job and we live well. We lived in Texas for years before moving to Florida. I loved it in Florida, but my father found very little opportunity there. Eventually he wanted to go back home, back to Brazil. At the time, I was in my teens, and I was in school. I didn't want to leave my friends. Texas was great, but Florida felt like home."

Izabel grabs a tissue and balls it up in her hand. "After a huge argument, my father told me to stay, but that he, my mom, and my sister were leaving, going back home. Now you have to understand, I was pulling a big no-no by disobeying my father. But either way, he and the rest of my family left, and there I was, alone, in school, with no job." Izabel smiles awkwardly. "But I had lots of friends. And I stayed with friends for years until I finished school. I just rotated amongst them." Izabel stops.

Berta stares at Izabel, trying to figure out why she stopped talking. She just stares at the table. A tear drops from her eye and onto the table. Berta knows now that Izabel is reliving every detail, even the bad ones. Berta stays silent.

"I never went to college . . . couldn't afford it. So I ended up getting a job in a restaurant. I thought it was the easiest job to do, serving people and smile afterwards. I never understood what my coworkers complained about after each day. Of course some of them didn't like me. I was the Brazilian beauty that got all the tips. I got offers for so many things, but me being so shy, turned everything down. Modeling. Movies. Relationships. One night stands. Everything, every offer, I turned down. All but one." Izabel wrinkles her nose.

"He came in one day, not at all like most businessmen. He was quiet, shy almost, and for a millionaire, I thought that was . . . endearing. Everything between us at the start of that first night was as it should have been. I was the waitress, he was the customer. I'd ask him if the food was to his liking, he'd say yes and ask for another napkin. Nothing about our interactions lended anything towards me falling in love with a Dutch businessman, until the end of my shift.

"I was set to leave and almost out the door when I see him still sitting in the booth in the back of the restaurant. He was nursing the same cup of tea I brought out to him earlier in the night. His face was distant. I stare at him for a few moments as another employee asks him if he needed anything else. He smiles and says that he's good with the same cup of tea, but then he catches me staring at him. He looked away but not even half a second later he stares back. I don't know what that was, but at that moment, I knew I was hooked.

"I walk over to his booth and ask him if he was all right. He, of course, said he was, but his face . . . his face said more than his mouth could. So I sat with him for a while. In a few moments we learned about each other, and for me, it was amazing. I never had this type of interaction with anyone, much less a man. He came around the next weekend, and the one after that." Izabel stops to see if Berta is still listening. Once she knows she has Berta's full and undivided attention, she continues. "Long story short, we ended up getting married. Here's where things changed. Here's where he changed."

Izabel starts grinding her teeth. The look on her face changes so quickly it surprises Berta.

"I should have known, back then, that distant look of his meant trouble." Izabel shakes her head. "He beat me. And it took him raping me to finally catch on to what it really was. It wasn't a marriage. I wasn't his companion to stand by his side. I wasn't the love of his life like he said. I was his slave. I was beneath him as he put his wing-tipped shoe across my neck and stepped down. I was his slave."

Berta stares at Izabel as it takes a few moments for her to come to. "I didn't even know he started another family until I saw them at the funeral. I wonder . . . ."

"You wonder if they went through the same things we did?"

Izabel looks at Berta with glassy, bloodshot eyes, and nods.

"I've wondered that since the funeral as well. Common sense tells me they did, but to what extent?"

Both women sit in silence, pondering on Courtland's second family. Berta ends up breaking the silence.

"I want to know." She stares at Izabel, waiting for her response.

Izabel blinks. "How would you go about finding out?"

"Isn't the family a part of that church . . . where the funeral was?"

"I don't know for sure."

"Well, the way I see it . . . that's our only link to them."

"So . . . ."

"So we're visiting a church tomorrow."

The next morning, Berta gets up early again and dresses for church. She follows the same routine as she did the day before: getting dressed, watching Craig breathe as he sleeps on the couch. She wonders why he chooses to sleep on the couch as it was never brought up by her. He simply did it on his own. She also wonders why he isn't getting ready for church.

Berta gets to Izabel's apartment to pick her up and they both head to the church where Courtland's funeral was held. The idea Berta had was to visit the church in hopes of running into Courtland's widow. As soon as Berta fully told Izabel the idea, Izabel wasn't on board. At first she felt they needed to leave things alone, but the same way Berta was convinced to listen to Izabel: for truth, was the same way Berta convinced Izabel. Maybe curiosity has gotten the best of both of them, but they figure, who knows what type of information she could give on their past? Who knows what Courtland told her? They needed to find out.

Berta parks her car a block away from the church and says a quick prayer. Right now, she believes that her meeting up with Izabel at the church wasn't just by chance, and she also believes the same for her and Courtland's second family.

Both women get out of the car and blend in with the crowd of people flowing into the church.

"Do you really think she is going to be here?" Izabel asks.

"I don't know. But in all honesty, this is the only shot we have."

"And what do you plan on doing when . . . if you find her?"

"Talk to her." Berta glances at Izabel. "It's that simple."

"Even if we do find her, she isn't going to talk to us. Why would she?"

"Let's cross that bridge when we get there."

As people file into the pews, Berta and Izabel concentrate on looking for the woman. Midway through the service, they both realize that she isn't in the church. Berta nudges Izabel as a cue to leave. They get up and walk out the back doors.

"I figured she wasn't going to be there," Izabel says.

"Yeah, well, it was worth a shot."

"I suppose it was. So, what now?"

"I really have no idea. I was putting a lot into this succeeding."

"Well"—Izabel squints her eyes and looks past Berta—"Wait a minute. Isn't that the daughter?"

Berta snaps around to see.

"Yeah, it is." Berta starts that way. "Excuse me."

The woman looks up at Berta and Izabel, and her face drops immediately.

"Looks like she recognizes us," Berta says.

When Berta and Izabel get to the young woman, the woman starts to speak immediately.

"What are you doing here?" she asks.

"I'm sorry?"

"You two don't belong here."

"We just wanted a word with you."

"There's nothing I have to say to you. There's nothing any of us have to say to you."

"Please, it's very imp—"

"Important, I know. It always is." She starts to fidget.

"It's okay, Jennifer." Another woman says. "No need to be so nasty."

Berta looks to the side to see the one they were looking for, Courtland's widow. Berta searches her memory for her name, but doesn't remember.

"We would like a word with you. I'm sorry, I never caught your name."

"Marcella. May I ask why you need to speak with me so urgently?"

"Well, my name is—"

"Alberta . . . and your mother Izabel. Common knowledge at this point."

Berta is taken aback. "Well, we wanted to know if we could sit down with you . . . it's about him."

"About my dead husband, you mean?"

Berta nods.

"So are you looking for some kind of payout?"

"No." Berta shakes her head rapidly. "Not at all. We really just wanted to sit down and talk. That's all."

The woman stares at Berta a bit more, seemingly trying to read her. The lines on her face are pronounced, but her eyes glow with a youthful bright blue fire.

"Fine. But we cannot talk here."

"I agree, but I'm not sure of where to go."

"I know of a place that's private. Did you two drive here?"

Berta nods in uncertainty.

"Then follow us. Jennifer?" Marcella hands Jennifer a set of car keys.

After a few nerve-racking minutes of driving behind Jennifer and Marcella in their Lincoln Navigator, Berta comes upon a long driveway surrounded by woods. They drive along the path for what seems to be forever until they come upon what seems to be a log cabin.

"Very private," Izabel says.

"Yeah, considering it's the size of a freaking Wal-Mart."

"What did we get ourselves into?"

"What do you mean?"

"We are following Courtland DeVries' widow down a long and winding path deep into the woods to her home . . . the same home she shared with Courtland, to talk to her about her life with him and to see if he was abusive toward her or the kids."

"I know it seems crazy. I know. But you want to know like I want to know. Was he the same person toward them as he was toward us?" Berta asked.

"You're right, I want to know, but not badly enough to go to these people's home."

"I don't think there's that much to worry about."

"I don't know. Something's off about that woman. And the daughter. She seemed quite upset at our presence."

Berta glances over as she puts the car in park. "Alright. It's go time."

Izabel grabs Berta's hand and closes her eyes. Berta then closes hers as well. Moments later, both women take a deep breath and step out the car. They watch Marcella as she carefully steps out the passenger side of the truck and smoothes the sides of her dress out.

"You have a beautiful home," Berta says.

"Thank you. But it isn't mine. Not anymore."

"I see." Berta doesn't dig much further.

Entering into the home is like entering a warehouse. Boxes stand neatly stacked up in the multiple rooms. Marcella leads everyone to the back of the house, to the only room that doesn't have boxes. It's a cozy room with a number of soft cushioned armchairs by a fireplace.

"Would either one of you like anything to drink?" Marcella asks.

Both Berta and Izabel decline.

"Very well. Please have a seat."

Marcella sits in a highly decorated chair and Jennifer pulls over a chair and sits next to her. Berta and Izabel find space on a loveseat across from them.

"Are you moving?" Berta asks.

"We have already. Just needed to finalize the sale of this house."

"Someone must have put up a lot of money for this."

"Not as much as you think. Especially in this terrible market. But no bother. We weren't selling the house for the money." She adjusts in her seat. "So what is it you would like to discuss?"

"Well, let us first thank you for meeting with us, though I must say, I am a bit confused as to why you agreed."

Marcella cocks her head back and lets out a laugh that comes straight from her belly. "When I figured you weren't here for money, it made the decision easier." She continues to smile. "But all joking aside, I have my reasons."

Jennifer looks at her mother, then away with a roll of her eyes. Berta notices Jennifer's 'mad at the world' attitude and begins to wonder.

"There's no real easy way of breaking into this conversation so I'm just going to dive in."

"By all means." Marcella waves Berta on.

"We were wondering what kind of man the m—Courtland was to you. I ask because . . . ." Berta looks at Izabel. "Because we were treated like trash. Less than trash."

Marcella's face turns serious, the lines more pronounced. A darkness seems to settle over her face. Jennifer stares at the ground.

"How so?" Marcella asks.

Berta takes a deep breath after glancing at Izabel another time. "My mother was abused . . . by him. I was abused as well. We just wanted to know, did he treat this family"—Berta points in Marcella's direction—"better than this family"—Berta motions toward herself and Izabel—"if that's what you want to call it."

"And what purpose would that serve you?" Marcella asks.

"My thoughts were that it would provide some closure to what happened to us, by possibly shedding some light on it."

"Closure?" Marcella laughs. "There's no such thing."

"Maybe there isn't."

"So let me get this straight," Jennifer finally cuts in. "My father hasn't been dead for two weeks yet, and you are asking us if he was abusive towards us? It's like you willingly took a gamble on him being abusive, but either way, this comes off as highly offensive."

"I must agree with Jennifer. It seems as if you hope that he was abusing us the same way you supposedly got abused, which I find a bit morbid."

Berta looks down. "No. That's not it at all. I never looked at it that way. I just . . . I just needed to know. I apologize. Maybe this was a bad idea." Berta gets up. Izabel follows suit.

"No please, stay. Both of you. Look . . . ."

Berta and Izabel pause.

"We are going through a difficult time right now. So, please excuse us if we seem a bit harsh."

Berta looks to Izabel for what to do. Izabel nods and sits back down. "It is understandable, but we don't mean any harm," she says.

Marcella nods.

"Look," Berta's voice comes out soft. "Courtland raped me. He beat and raped my mother. He put her through hell day in and day out. And if it weren't for an angel, I would have gone through the same."

"Angel? You mean Raul Valencia?" Marcella says.

Berta nods and wonders how this woman seems to know so many of the key players in her life. She glances at Izabel.

Marcella speaks softly as well. "I'm sorry dear, but Raul was no angel."

"What?"

"We all knew about Raul. I haven't seen a woman who could resist him, but that's beside the point. Raul and Courtland ran in the same circles. They had the same connections. For all intents and purposes, they were business partners."

Berta frowns and Izabel shakes her head.

"But Raul was different. He was a straight-up and honest man." Izabel says.

"Maybe that's what he showed you. But I assure you, he wasn't the most honest. He had his dirt."

"I don't believe you." Izabel says.

"It's the truth. They both had their set of paid-off cops, judges, officials. They both had their set of 'not so legal' businesses. Raul and Courtland were nothing short of conmen. From the looks of it, Raul just was better at it."

"Wait, how do you know so much?" Berta asks.

"When it happened, it was big news." Marcella bores a hole into Berta with her eyes. "That's all I'm going to say on that."

Berta notices a different look in her eyes. The youthful fire is replaced by something she can't place her finger on. For a while thereafter, no one says anything. Too many thoughts run through Berta's mind for her to contend with.

"So Courtland abused you, you say? Is that before or after you ran away with that golf instructor?"

"There never was a golf instructor. It was all a lie."

"I see. I never really believed that anyway. When Courtland told me the story, things just didn't add up. And I knew better than to trust a crooked businessman when it comes to matters of the heart."

"But you married him."

"I fell for the same thing you did I presume. The charm, the bravado, the charisma."

Izabel looks away.

"And you, Alberta. Courtland told me once Izabel left him for the instructor, he knew he couldn't take care of a child, and he had no family to speak of to help. He said he knew Raul would be able to do it because he had more of the fatherly touch. Courtland made it seem like Raul had more time to focus on raising a child, which I believe he did. Of course, Courtland didn't mention anything about rape. But maybe . . . maybe Courtland felt some sort of remorse for what he did to you. Maybe he knew the only way he was going to stop was to send you away."

"You believe that?"

"Not at all. I'm just putting that out there as a possibility. What I think is that Courtland was a sick man."

Berta glances at Izabel, noticing she stares at Marcella, seemingly annoyed. Everyone gets silent knowing there's only one thing left to talk about.

"So, to answer your initial question, yes, Courtland treated us the same in some ways . . . but different in others. I was not abused, at least not on a consistent basis." That dark look settles on Marcella's face again. "I was never abused sexually, either. Actually, it took work to get him to be intimate. But later I realized it was because he had no interest in me."

"He was interested in me," Jennifer says with as much vitriol as she could muster. She looks down at the ground and rapidly shakes her leg. "Starting when I was freaking eleven years old."

Everyone stops and lets the weight of what Jennifer said settle on them.

"I'm sorry for what he's done to you," Izabel says.

"Me, too. But no one can take it back now."

"I found out about it only after it was going on for years. Jennifer's grades dropped. Her attitude towards her brother worsened."

"What did you do about him?" Berta asks.

"At first, there wasn't much I could do. I knew of his connections. I couldn't call the police. So I took the kids and ran."

Izabel hangs her head.

"We went to my sister's home out of state. Never told her what happened, though. Just said that me and Courtland weren't working out."

"And that was that?" Berta asked.

"Not quite. We stayed with my sister, but Courtland wanted us back. He would call me, crying about how he messed up and how he would never do it again." Marcella shakes her head. "It wasn't lost upon me that the longer we stayed with my sister, the more danger she was in. And that wasn't fair to her. So eventually we went back. But things were different the second time around."
"All this time, you still didn't call the police?"

"It seemed silly at the time. But we went back and things were good for a little bit. During that time I did some digging into his connections, into his 'businesses. ' I learned about the things he was doing, built up a solid pile of information . . . ."

"And?"

"I buried him under it." Marcella's voice comes out hard, strained.

Jennifer glances at Marcella.

"I'm not sure I follow."

"Well, unfortunately, I can tell you no more." Marcella smiles. "But I think I answered your questions anyway. This conversation has provided some light on a very dark situation."

"Wait. What did you mean?" Berta asks.

Izabel places a hand on Berta's arm. "Let's go, Dear." She faces Marcella and Jennifer. "Thank you for your time." She looks at Jennifer. "Stay strong, young lady."

Berta gets up with Izabel and heads to the front door. Marcella and Jennifer walk her and Izabel out. Shockingly, Marcella gives both Berta and Izabel a hug before seeing them out. Walking back to her car, Berta thinks about the way Marcella hugged her. It was more like an embrace.

The drive back to Izabel's apartment was a long and quiet one as both women were lost in their own thoughts. When Berta finally pulls up into Izabel's complex, she leans back in her seat and sighs.

"He did it again," Berta says.

"What do you mean?"

"The monster. He did it again, because we didn't say anything to anyone about it."

Izabel says nothing, as both of them stare off into space, trying to digest what Berta said.

"She killed him, didn't she?" Berta asks.

Izabel nods. "She fought for her daughter."

Berta doesn't say anything, as she finds it difficult to grapple with the idea of Marcella, while being a church-going mother of two, also being a murderer. An unease settles on her. She hears sniffs coming from Izabel.

"And that stuff she said about Raul . . . ." Izabel's voice comes out deep.

"The stuff she said makes perfect sense. Even you said that he didn't tell you everything for fear of what you might think of him. Daddy wasn't such a great guy like we thought."

"But he was great to us."

"True. But in reality, he was very similar to the monster. We just never saw it. Maybe we never wanted to."
Silence.
"Alberta, I must ask, what were you looking for?"
"The same thing I'm looking for when I talk to you . . . peace."
"Did you find it?"
"No. And I'm afraid I never will."

Chapter Twenty Six

EARLY Monday morning, Berta is wide awake. She sits in the living room across from the sofa that Craig sleeps on for the third night in a row. She looks at him curiously. She doesn't understand what he is doing. *Maybe he is punishing himself for some reason.* But she shakes that thought away, though Craig has been known to be extremely hard on himself when things get tough.

His eyes flicker a bit before opening. It takes a few moments for him to adjust, but when he does, all he does is stare at her. She stares back. She isn't sure what he is doing, but she looks for some visible sign that there is still something there. He smiles, but it's a sad one. Berta knows she has seen that sad smile before, but she doesn't remember when.

"Good morning," he says.

"Morning."

Craig's phone rings. Berta snaps her head toward it and Craig presses the side to silence it.

"Alarm," he says.

Berta isn't so sure. She gets up from her seat.

"Why have you been sleeping on the couch?"

Craig sits up and stretches. "I don't know. For the most part I've been out here thinking while I leave you alone. I just fall asleep while thinking."

"For three nights straight?" She fumbles around in the kitchen.

Craig shrugs his shoulders.

"Well, I'd rather you sleep in the bed. The couch can't be that comfortable."

Craig nods. "I gotta get ready for work."

Berta stays in the kitchen, leaning over the counter all the while Craig gets ready for work. She watches him as he goes into the kitchen and grabs a bagel to eat. She studies him more as he heads to the door.

"I'll see you later," he says, and leaves.

No kiss.

Berta shrugs at the thought, but realizes she didn't stop him, either. She doesn't really get upset because right now, she feels that Craig is a good roommate. And roommates don't kiss. They don't sleep in the same bed. They simply co-exist.

She nods and looks at her watch. Seven o'clock.

Berta knows Jade gets in to work early; around six o'clock in the morning early, so she decides to give her a call, but knowing she could be at a meeting or something even that early, she calls her office phone. After a few rings, someone picks up, and they sound annoyed.

"Hi . . . is this Karen?"

"This is she."

"Oh, hi, Karen, this is Berta. I thought this was a direct line to Jade. I guess she isn't in yet?"

It takes a moment for Karen to start talking. "Jade . . . doesn't work here anymore."

"Oh." Berta furrows her brow. "I didn't know. Sorry . . . sorry to bother y—"

Karen hangs up. Berta decides to wait a bit before calling Jade's cell. When she does, Jade picks up right away.

"So, to end the phone tag, you gotta call me early in the morning, waking me and the kids up?" Jade sounds groggy.

"I'm sorry I—"

"Kidding." Jade's voice goes up a few octaves. "You know I get up super early, Berta. How are you?"

"I'm good. Listen, I just tried to call your office . . . ."

"Yeah, about that . . . I no longer work there. We have a lot of catching up to do. But before that, shouldn't you be on your way to work?"

"How do you know I'm not?"

"You're not cussing people out on the road."

"Good point. I took a vacation."

"Hmmm. What are you doing for breakfast?"

"I was planning on making a great bowl of dust . . . and maybe wash it down with some air. Or maybe have some air. . . and wash it down with some dust. There is no food in this place."

"Well, why don't we grab a bite to eat? We have some catching up to do."

"We do have a lot of catching up to do. I'm down with getting something to eat. Where do you want to go?"

Berta and Jade decide on going to an IHOP for breakfast and meet there within the hour. Berta gets there first and waits. She looks around at the restaurant, attempting to find something to keep her focus off the meeting she and her mother had with Courtland's second family. Each thought that comes up, she suppresses by trying to figure out what someone orders. *Daddy was just as dirty as the monster. Hmmm. Big Steak Omelette. Izabel and Daddy . . . Belgian waffle. Izabel . . . Short-stack with sausage links . . . and bacon strips.* She almost doesn't notice Jade walk in and slide into the booth, sitting across from her.

"Hey, lady."

"Hey, Jade. Long time no see, friend." Berta snaps back to reality.

"Tell me about it. Look, let's order so we can get this food. I'm starving."

Berta smiles.

"I know what you are thinking. So let me tell you the truth in that I haven't worked out since we went on that jog. I called myself trying to be like the boys and have"—Jade makes air quotes—"gym time." She makes a face. "But I couldn't really stay consistent. But the dieting I think I have down."

"That wasn't why I was smiling. It's just really good to see you, that's all."

"Well, it's good to see you, too." She smiles.

"So about your job . . . ."

"Yeah," Jade clears her throat, "I don't work there anymore. Some bad things went down and I was let go."

"What? They let you go? After all you did for them?"

"I can't say too much about it here, but trust me, I was aware of the strong possibility of getting the heave-ho. I knew the volatility of the position, and how difficult it would be to stay in that position. So in some ways I was prepared. I just wasn't prepared for how it all went down."

"Well, it seems like you are taking it well."

"I've had some time to adjust. I'll start looking for a new job soon."

"Do you guys, you know, need any help?"

"Oh, no, no. We will be fine. You know as Mark says, we have backups to backups. But thanks."

"Just let us know. Whatever we can do to help. How are the kids?"

"They're good. Kalina has a boyfriend now."

"Uh-oh."

"He's a nice boy . . . but Mark and Charles don't like him."

Berta chuckles. "Someone is trying to take Mark's baby girl away . . . and Chuck's sister."

"You should have seen it. Charles went up to the boy and grilled him the way you'd think Mark would. I had to keep him occupied in the kitchen." Jade chuckles. "I thought he was gonna tackle the boy."

"Awww, that's sweet. He's protective of his older sister."

"That he is. They've built this strong bond, Kalina and Charles."

"I've noticed. And where does Amber fit in?"

"They're both overprotective of her. And all she wants to do is be around them. It's cute."

"That's good that the kids are so close."

"I'm not complaining. I'm actually taking them to see my parents. I'm planning this special weekend for me and Mark."

"Oooh." Berta smiles. "I guess that means that you and Mark are doing well?"

"It's a funny thing, not having a job. There's so much time to invest in other things . . . into other people."

"Is that a yes?"

"It more than a yes. Mark and I . . . we are somewhere we have never been before. It's such a good place."

"That's good to hear."

"But enough on my up-and-down life. How are you?"

"I'm okay."

"Just okay?"

"Yup."

Berta and Jade stare at each other for a few seconds.

"I guess that means there hasn't been an improvement on the Craig situation?"

"None. It got worse."

"Did you talk to him like I suggested?"

"I did, but it was the wrong time and wrong place. Everything went downhill from there."

"I'm sorry to hear that."

"Don't be. It is what it is, and it's gonna be what it's gonna be."

"Berta, you sound like you're checking out."

"No, I haven't checked out. I just look at things under a new light. A lot has been thrown at me lately and I'm forced to adjust and reevaluate things . . . and people in my life."

"And Craig is one of them."

"He is. Along with my mother and father—the monster—people at my job . . . ."

"What's going on?"

"Long story."

"Tell you what: tomorrow, you and Craig come by for dinner. We can talk about things while the boys do what they do. And maybe Mark and I can talk to you two. Give a few more pointers."

"Thanks Jade, but I really—"

"Wasn't asking." Jade says as she grabs her phone. "Dinner tomorrow. I'm texting Mark about it now."

Berta sighs and starts playing with her food. When she looks back up from her plate, Jade is staring at her.

"You look so depressed," Jade says.

"I think the weight of everything that has been going on is pressing on me. And I still feel . . . so . . . empty."

Jade places her hand on Berta's. "It will be okay. We'll find a way to make this right."

Chapter Twenty Seven

"Mr. Rustinsky, how long have we known each other? . . . And you trust me, right? . . . Exactly . . . It's a good move . . . I am absolutely positive. I ran the numbers three times for four different scenarios. They all turn out favorable." Craig sits at his desk on a call with one of his longstanding clients, nearing the end of his day.

When he gets off the phone, he shuts his computer down, then looks at his watch.

"Ted, you still there?"

No answer. Craig nods, realizing how late it really is. *Ted probably went home an hour ago.* He grabs his things and closes his office door. As he locks it, he hears footsteps approaching him. He casually turns around to see Patrice.

"Hey, you."

"Hey. I just shut everything down. Is it an emergency?"

"No. Not at all. Everything is good. I was just shopping across the street for another pair of shoes." She holds up a bag. "I thought to stop by and say hi . . . and thank you."

"I see three shoe boxes in there."

Patrice smiles. "So you got me. You've found out my new hobby."

Craig chuckles. "Yeah. Hobby. Women and shoes. I will never understand it. Anyway, what are you thanking me for?"

"For being there the way that you have. For helping me get my life back on track."

"Oh. Sure, it's no problem. Just part of my job."

"Well, job well done. You didn't have to put everything on hold just because some guys were taking my bed."

"What did you end up doing?"

"I've been at a hotel. It isn't too bad. Can't wait to hit my own bed." She continues to smile. "I'm leaving to go back home in a couple of days."

"Yeah?"

She nods. "I'm excited, and nervous."

"Well, I can tell you that financially, you have nothing to worry about."

"Thanks. Listen, can I ask you something?"

"Shoot."

"What do you think of me?"

Craig hesitates. "What do you mean?"

Patrice takes a deep breath. "I mean, I know you look after all of your clients. But am I mistaken in thinking that there was something more there?" She steps back a step. "Because I find you very . . . intriguing."

Dammit.

"Uhhhh." Craig smiles. "Look, you are a wonderful woman. But I am a married man and—"

"I know you're married . . . and I repeat I don't want to step on that. I'm not that type. I just need to know, for my own sanity. Do you feel something for me?"

Craig looks into her eyes, but all he thinks about is Berta and how mad he is at her. How he wants to scream at her and tell her to snap back to reality, to break out of this weird funk she's in. He thinks about how much he loves her, and how much he needs her to get back to normal . . . for his sanity.

"I'm sorry. I don't know if I did anything to lead you on, but no, there isn't anything there . . . to me."

They stare at each other for a few moments. Craig fears that Patrice can see right through him. He fears that she can tell that he is lying; that if he weren't married to Berta, he would be ready to whisk her away to some remote island. But she just smiles, and at that moment, Craig realizes her beautiful smile is more of a defense mechanism than a sign of happiness. Her smile is what she uses to conceal pain. He saw it when he first met her, again when they went out to lunch, and finally now as he dutifully crushes any idea of being with her.

"It's okay. I went over this in my head so many times, trying not to ask, but needing to know. I . . . I should go." She turns around in a hurry, but abruptly stops. She reaches for a pen off of Ted's desk and grabs one of his business cards. She writes something on it and hands it to Craig.

"I don't know if you were giving the "good husband" answer, if you really feel that way because you have to, but just in case . . . just in case things don't go the way you planned. Just call me. It's my private line. I will always be there to pick it up."

Craig looks at the card and thinks. By the time he looks up again, she's gone.

Craig gets to his car and throws his briefcase in. He looks up and down the block before getting in his car. *I will always be there to pick it up,* he thinks, going over in his mind every conversation he's had with Patrice. Snapping him out of his thoughts is his cell phone buzzing in his pocket. He looks to see that it's Mark and answers. Mark starts to talk immediately.

"What are you doing tomorrow night for dinner?"

"Probably eating at the office. Why?"

"Scratch that. You and Berta are coming over our place."

"Uhhh, okay. I'll see what Berta—"

"She already agreed."

"Okay." Craig pauses. "What am I missing?"

"I get a text from Jade this morning telling me to talk to you. She was out with Berta for breakfast."

"Breakfast? Both of them should have been at work . . . right?"

"Jade, no. Berta is on vacation . . . But I'm gathering you knew nothing about that."

"Not a thing."

Mark stays silent; an invitation for Craig to talk.

"I don't know what is going on, how it got to be so weird. I tried to be more involved, to show her how much I love her, but things just kept happening. One thing after another. Then she became distant."

"I don't know exact details, but Jade told me it's some heavy stuff going on."

"I know. She doesn't involve me on any of that stuff."

"Then you involve yourself, Craig. You don't get the invite, you start knocking some doors down. Your marriage depends on it."

"My marriage? I don't even know if there's a friendship anymore."

"Sounds like it's an excuse. Listen, ask yourself, do you want to still be with her?"

"I do, but not like this. I think . . . I think I may have made a mis-take."

"What do you mean?"

"In marrying Berta. I think she and I both would have been better off . . . without each other."

"You're joking, right?"

"I'm serious. I think she would have been better off with someone else. I probably would have been better off with . . . someone else. I should have just let her stay at the condo and never come by. I should have just let her go. But that damn Candace, who she doesn't even talk to anymore, by the way, convinced me to go find her. Now look at where I am."

"You done blabbing?"

"Yeah, I'm done. Wait, hold on. She's crazy. Okay, now I'm done."

"Listen, I haven't seen two people more compatible, who are different but complement each other well."

"That's part of my point. That's the way we were. Too many things have gone on, and even I don't know the half of it. I should be the first person to know. Not you. Not Jade. Not anyone at work. Her husband. The one who signed on to be with her forever. But I'm in the dark . . . and I'm expected to do something about it. Not fair."

"So what are you going to do about it?"

"We have counseling tomorrow morning."

"And?"

"That's it, I guess. We have the talk, and we go from there."

"So you didn't take the advice I gave you?"

"I couldn't. I'm being accused of cheating, and my past is being thrown in my face. It's all just ridiculous. She's not the woman I married, and at the same time, she says I'm not the man she married. Ridiculous. I mean, what would you do? If Jade accused you of changing, and cheating, then she shut you out of her life, so much so that you have to hear secondhand about things that go on with her? When you are around her, there's nothing there. Nothing at all. You don't look at her the same, and it's clear that she doesn't look at you the same, either."

"Have you talked about it? Did you tell her what you just told me?"

"I guess I will at this session."

"Well, maybe Jade and I can help ease some of this tension between you two. Maybe we can get you having fun again."

"Yeah. Maybe." Craig rubs the top of his head. "But here's the catch."

"Catch?"

"There's this woman . . . ."

"You didn't."

"No, I didn't. I would call it all off with Berta before I did. But that's the thing. It's hard to put my all into this when I know there's someone else waiting."

"Who is she?"

"One of my clients."

"Whoa. Risky game you play, friend."

"I'm not playing. I just . . . I just find her . . . interesting. And she is interested in me."

Mark sighs. "You think you find this other woman interesting because things aren't good between you and Berta?"

"I don't know. Probably. I initially thought she was just an average woman, but as time went on . . . she looked . . . different. But anyway, what's going on with you? Jade quit that place, huh?"

Mark pauses at the quick change in conversation. "Well, sort of. She was let go, but under some weird circumstances."

"Everything okay?"

"Oh, yeah, everything is fine, now."

"I'm not going to have to knock somebody out, am I?"

"Haha. Not quite. If anyone is going to do some knocking it's going to be me. And I already have a plan for that."

"Fair enough."

"But anyway, I have an interview tomorrow."

"Yeah? Doing what you like to do?"

"A different version of it, but yes. It's as an academic advisor position at one of the community colleges around here."

"That's what's up. So the dinner tomorrow doesn't have to be so depressing now. It can be a celebration."

"Sheesh, man."

"I'm just saying. But listen, I'm going to get out of here. Get back home to the loving wife."

"Yeah, man. And I'll see you tomorrow."

"Good luck on the interview. I'll send one up for you."

"Much appreciated. And good luck on the session."

"Thanks, and Mark? Please don't tell Jade about what we just talked about."

"You mean about the client?"

"Yeah. I just . . . I just . . . ."

"I understand. I'll keep it quiet."

Craig eventually gets home to see Berta sitting curled up on the couch, reading a book. He drops his briefcase at the door and walks by her to the back rooms. Once he changes out of his work clothes, he heads back out to the living room with a magazine in hand. He sits on the same couch Berta sits.

"Hi," he says.

Berta looks up for a second. "Hey." She retrains her focus back on her book.

Craig feels a slight undercurrent of tension between them, which causes him to feel uncomfortable being near her. He wonders if she feels the same.

"I talked to Mark . . . about the dinner."

"That's good. Are you going?"

Craig looks at Berta. She doesn't lift her head from her book. He closes the magazine he was reading and sets it on the table.

"Yeah, I am. How come you didn't tell me you were on vacation?"

Berta glances up again. "Didn't think it mattered."

"Since when does it not matter?"

Berta shrugs her shoulders.

"Look, I'm not trying to start any arguments, but a shoulder shrug isn't much of an answer."

"I don't know what to tell you."

Craig sighs. He gets up and starts toward the back rooms, but stops. "Berta, where are we?"

Berta closes her book and sets it on the coffee table. "I don't know, but we can both agree that it isn't the best of places."

Craig nods and disappears down the hallway.

CHAPTER TWENTY EIGHT

THE next morning, Berta moves around slowly, dragging her feet wherever she goes. Part of her dreads this counseling session now that it's here. She sat up all night getting her thoughts together, approaching the sit-down as if it were a trial. Craig moves as if he's full of life, as if he looks forward to it. For some reason, this angers Berta.

෬෯

After a long and quiet ride to the church together, Craig and Berta sit down in Pastor Raines' office, waiting for him to arrive. Neither says anything to the other. Once Pastor shows up, they greet him and he thanks them for coming. He gets right to business.

"Berta, I've had the opportunity to speak with you, so I'm going to start with Craig, if that's okay with you?"

"I'm fine with that."

"Okay. So Craig, from your perspective, what is wrong?"

"There's a lot wrong. From the way I experience it, Berta and I are not on the same page for anything. She explained to me how she felt at one time, and that was that she felt I was distancing myself from her; that I wasn't as romantic, that I wasn't as into her. This led her to the conclusion that I was cheating."

"Were you? Or are you?"

"No. It's not my style. Never was, never will be."

"So this coworker thing . . . ."

"Lies."

Pastor looks at Berta. "Your take?"

"I believe him," Berta says. "But for the record, I never really thought he cheated on me with her. I mean, I had trouble with it, but it was more so I thought he slept with her at one point before me."

"But here's my problem with that," Craig says, "Why did any of that come up in the first place? Berta knows me. She knows all about me. She knows stuff no one else on the face of this planet knows. Why would she automatically assume that at one point I slept with her coworker and at another that I was cheating? It's a slap in the face—no, it's a kick in the nuts."

Pastor writes something down. "Continue."

"The change happened way before this mess, though. The change happened when she started working for that particular coworker we spoke of."

"Angelina?" Pastor asks.

Berta nods.

"Yeah, Angelina. The first day she was under her, Berta came home, not like herself. She was sad, depressed almost. Every week she had a story of how this woman was tearing her down, how she was trying to put her out. At first, you saw some fight in her, but as time went on . . . ."

Berta puts her hand up. "May I?"

Pastor nods.

"What Craig doesn't understand is that the job isn't my problem, but it's his need to blame the job for all of what's going on. In my eyes the job is bad, yes, but what's worse is not having a husband I can come home and vent all my frustrations to. What's worse is having a husband that seemingly doesn't care about the struggles and frustrations of mine, who doesn't seem to care much about me."

"But I do care," Craig says. "I've always cared."

"It's one thing to say it, but it's another to put action to it. I went to you numerous times trying to tell you how I felt. You always avoided the talk. I tried telling you I wanted to spend better time, not more time, just better-quality time with you. You weren't hearing it. I just stopped trying."

"Let's stay right there for a second. Craig, did she ever try to verbalize what's going on with her, to you?"

"I believe so, yes."

"And how would you respond?"

"For those times I thought something was off, I'd ask her, she'd tell me—"

"You didn't ask me until just recently. At the charity dinner. Before that you acted like everything was normal."

Craig takes a deep breath. "Okay, maybe I did. And for that I am sorry. That's all on me, but I said that before. Like, what do you want from me?"

"I want a husband. I want you to be there for me."

"How? How can I do that when you checked out?"

"Okay, okay. Hold a moment to let things cool down." Pastor puts his hands up. "I know this is going to sound elementary, but Berta, I need you to try again. I need you to dial back in. Craig, I need you to prove to your wife that you can be there. The way it seems, the lines of communication have broken down, and we need those up for anything to work. Now there may be other problems around this one, but at the very least, both of you will be attacking the problem and not each other." Pastor looks at Berta. "Can I count on you to dial back in?"

Berta nods.

Pastor looks at Craig. "Will you be there?"

Craig stares. "How?"

"I have some things planned for that. I just need to know you are on board."

Craig nods. "I am."

"Okay. Now let's set that aside for a second. I want to go a bit deeper. Craig, you said that you never cheated, ever."

"Correct."

"On Berta, or anyone else."

"Correct."

"So Berta, why did you automatically go to that? Why did you think he was cheating?" Pastor turns to Berta.

"Because things like that happen. It happens to the best of us. It happened to his best friend. One of his numerous exes or flings could pop up, and have this completely new and fresh outlook on life and want him back in it. One thing leads to another, and there you go."

"But other than not being as attentive, has he shown any signs of him stepping out on you?"

"No."

Pastor nods. "So the overall feel is that Craig is interested in someone other than you, and if he isn't now, he will be later?"

"Kind of like that."

"You do understand that thoughts like that foster resentment and bitterness toward your spouse?"

Berta says nothing.

"From the sounds of it, Berta, you are afraid of Craig's past, and until you come to terms with it in a *responsible* manner—not saying that you're not responsible, but until you come to grips with what went on in *his* past, you two can't really move forward."

Berta nods.

"But then there's also the part of coming to terms with your own past, isn't there?"

Berta nods again.

"You see, I wondered, after our first talk, if you can't come to grips with what is in Craig's past because you can't come to terms with what happened in yours."

Berta says nothing.

"Well, get back to that later. Craig, help me understand something."

"Yes, sir."

"How is it that when your wife is in need of someone to talk to, to vent, to reveal her feelings to, you aren't there?"

"I don't know."

Berta looks at Craig and opens her mouth to say something, but thinks against it.

"My gut is telling me there's something behind that," Pastor says.

"I'm not sure what. I mean, it does get to be a bit annoying."

"What do you mean?"

"There's always something going on. There's always something taking her down. I think any man would get burned out trying to deal with everything she brings up. I feel that she's . . . very needy."

Berta grunts.

"I miss the days when we were friends. Nothing was forced. We were able to act like ourselves around each other. We just were. Now she needs me to be this ideal husband, so she can be this ideal wife, when all I'm looking for is my friend again."

"Do you think that getting married took that away from you?"

"Well, I thought it was going to amplify what we already had. But yes, getting married I think detracted from our friendship."

"And how does that make you feel?"

"Stupid. Hurt. Angry. Confused. Are there any other negative words I'm missing?"

"You painted the picture clearly. But you must understand that there is always going to be something, no matter who it is. I'm sure Berta isn't asking for you to solve all her life's problems. In most cases, I would say that she just wants you to listen. Berta, am I correct?"

"Yes."

"But there may be something with the friendship thing. When two people get married, you shouldn't lose the friendship. Like you hinted at, Craig, a marriage should in a way enhance a friendship. It shouldn't replace it, so to speak, because years down the line, you're stuck with this person you don't even like. Not a good road to go down. But at the same time, once you add marriage onto the preexisting friendship, that doesn't mean you still act as just friends. It means you have to work harder to be spouse and friend. Make sense?"

Both nod.

"Here's what I want you to do. I want you to go have fun. I know it sounds like some know-nothing psychologist, but it's the simplest answer. You need to get comfortable with each other again. Just you two, go out and do something fun." Pastor gets up and walks while still talking. "And I want you to do something from this list." He grabs two pamphlets from a table. "They're small things, but they work. A successful marriage is all in the finer details." He hands them the pamphlets. "Right off the bat, I see just from what you say, there seems to be a difference in the expectations of your marriage. Craig, you want a perfect friend. Berta, it seems you want a perfect husband. Neither of you is perfect friend or spouse. No one is, so we need to find the middle ground."

Craig looks at Berta, but she doesn't return the glance.

"Now, let's dig a little deeper." Pastor sets two Bibles in front of Craig and Berta and smiles.

Chapter Twenty Nine

MARK sits in his car, stopped at a traffic light, after an interview in which he was offered a position on the spot. In two weeks is his first day. As it turns out, the man he met from the retreat, Roland, has family in the surrounding area, one of which is a director of academic services for the community college closest to him. Some people may say it was chance, that Mark is lucky. Others may call it fate or something like that. He has the music in his car turned up loud and for the whole ride, and he has a huge grin plastered on his face. He knows it was God. When he pulls up into the garage, he sees that Jade's car isn't there. He glances at the empty space with a frown and looks at his watch. *Kalina should be coming home soon.* He assumes Jade ran to the store to grab some things for the dinner tonight. Mark smiles again. He thinks of Jade and the kids; then Craig and Berta. Great family, good friends, and now a good job. Mark is where he wants to be again.

He goes inside to an empty home and runs upstairs to change so he can take his post by the window for when Kalina comes home. He hears slight movement coming from Charles' room. He knocks and opens the door to see Charles sitting at his desk, asleep.

"Charles."

He jerks his head off the desk, a piece of paper stuck to his face, and looks around. He pulls the paper off his face and tries to flatten it on the desk. "Hi, Daddy."

"Were you doing homework?"

"Yes. I'm almost done."

"Where's your mother?"

"Downstairs with Amber."

Mark looks around strangely. He leaves the room and heads back downstairs.

"Jade?"

No answer.

He scans the entire floor before noticing the basement door is open. He goes downstairs to see Amber in front of the TV watching cartoons. She has a handful of her toys and stuffed animals around her.

But no Jade.

Mark goes to grab Amber, who immediately starts to cry because he's taking her away from the TV, and takes her upstairs to her playpen. He sets her down and goes back up to Charles' room.

"How long have you been up here doing homework?"

"A long time. I'm stuck on this one problem."

"Did your mother help you at all?"

He nods. "Then she went downstairs to make dinner."

Mark nods and leaves Charles to finish his homework. Something sinks inside of him, deep within the pit of his stomach, but he pushes it away. He knows Jade has never, and would never leave the kids alone for any amount of time; not without letting anyone know. He checks each bedroom and bathroom, but Jade isn't at any of those places. Mark starts to get nervous and calls her cell phone. After a few rings, he hears her ringtone for him, Stevie Wonder's "Ribbon in the Sky," and starts to get more nervous. He follows the sound to just outside the door to the garage. He opens the door and on the side of the steps, lying in a half-empty crate of Gatorade, is her phone, the screen cracked. He picks the phone up and examines it for a moment before setting it down and calling Craig.

"Craig."

"Yeah man. What's up? You want us to pick something up on—"

"No, no. Did Jade call you or Berta anytime today?"

"She didn't call me. Hold on for a sec. Berta, did Jade call you at all today?"

Long pause.

"No. She didn't. Why, what's going on? Everything all right?"

"I don't know yet. Listen, the dinner might be a no-go for tonight."

"Okay. You need us to do anything?"

"Again, I don't know yet. Give me a moment to catch up with my thoughts. I'll give you a call back."

Mark gets off the phone and goes back in the house. As soon as he shuts the door, Kalina comes through the front door.

"Hi, Daddy."

"Hey, baby girl. Listen, did your mother tell you anything about today? Did she call you at all?"

"Yeah, Uncle Craig and Auntie Berta are coming over. But she told me that earlier."

"That's it?"

"Yup. Where is Mom?"

"She . . . she went out to the store."

"Oh, okay. Well, I'm going to get my homework done."

"Can you check on Charles to make sure he's still doing his homework, too?"

"Yup."

Kalina disappears upstairs.

Mark starts to pace back and forth. He thinks about where she could be, but no logical thoughts come to mind. He grabs her phone and looks through the call log.

Nothing suspicious.

He makes phone calls to people she would normally contact for one reason or another, but still came up with nothing. He even calls

Jade's mother, though the relationship between them has been a bit rocky since the whole Alicia ordeal. Jade's mother hasn't seen or heard from her in weeks.

He then calls Craig back and steps into the garage.

"Craig. I don't know where she is."

"What do you mean?"

"I mean she's gone. Charles was upstairs in his room. Amber was downstairs in the basement, of all places, in front of the TV. But no her. I found her phone and it looks like it was thrown. The screen cracked and everything. Her car isn't here. Now, you know—"

"She wouldn't go anywhere without letting someone know . . . she wouldn't leave the kids alone."

"Exactly."

"Alright, we are on the way."

As each minute passes, Mark becomes more and more nervous to the point of panic, but remains calm for the kids' sake. He prepares dinner and just as everyone is about to eat, the doorbell rings.

"Is that Mommy?" Charles asks.

"I don't think so, buddy. Looks like your Uncle Craig and Aunt Berta."

"Yay." Charles gets up and rushes to the door ahead of Mark.

As Mark heads to the door, Charles bounces up and down in excitement.

Mark opens the door to two grave faces. "Hey."

Berta gives Mark a hug and Craig shakes his hand.

"Listen," Mark says to Craig, "I was thinking we go on a quick search before it's completely dark. If you don't mind staying with the kids for a few minutes, Berta."

"I don't mind at all," Berta says.

"What are you looking for, Daddy?" Charles asks.

Mark looks down at Charles. He forgot he was there for a quick second. He kneels down to look him in the eye. "Your Uncle Craig and I have to go out real quick, but we'll be back soon."

Charles looks at Mark for a second, then smiles. "Okay."

As Mark stands, he sees Kalina from the kitchen staring at him. He gives her a wink, thanks Berta, and heads out the door with Craig. He knows the kids know something is wrong. He could tell by their faces, but he pushes the mélange of emotions deeper into his gut. He has to find Jade.

"Did you call the police?" Craig asks.

"Not yet. I couldn't do anything around the kids."

"I'll drive. Call them."

Mark gets in the passenger seat and pulls out his cell phone. He calls the police and stays on the phone with them for all of five minutes. He hangs up, disappointed.

"They can't do anything quite yet. They said to come to the station first thing tomorrow morning to get a missing persons report filed."

"Why can't they do anything?"

"Too much gray area. If it were one of the kids, they'd all be out on the streets now looking for them. Because Jade is an adult, and because she has a right to go wherever she wants whenever she wants, they have to wait a bit. She could be just taking a breather, according to them."

"What?" Craig looks distraught. "What do you think? You think Jade is taking a breather. That she just . . . stepped out?"

"No. But I guess it's a possibility."

"I thought they had to take these types of cases right away."

"It's different here. Different police force, different jurisdiction. We probably don't even have the police staff to do an all-out search."

Both get silent.

"But at least it's on their radar." Mark says. "So if Jade doesn't pop up tonight, I can get to the station to get things straightened out."

Craig shakes his head. "Man, where could she be?"

"I don't know. Or why would she be there?"

"Nothing tipped you off to something like this happening?"

"Nothing. Turn right."

"Well, someone must know something somewhere, right? How far can you really get with a burgundy S-class without getting noticed?"

"Someone, somewhere . . . yeah. But for now it looks like I have no choice but to turn in for the night, and hope and pray she shows up." Mark pinches the bridge of his nose. "I made some chicken and rice. It's not the big dinner Jade was planning, but you and Berta can have at it."

"Thanks. Listen, Berta and I were talking on the way, and we were going to stay the night to help out."

Mark says nothing.

"Mark? Is that cool?"

"Calvin."

"What?"

"Calvin. This guy she used to work with. I don't know. My gut . . . ."

"Hold on for a second. Who is Calvin and why would he have anything to do with this?"

"Remember when I told you Jade lost her job?"

"Yeah."

"Well, it's because this guy, Calvin, assaulted her."

"You're joking, right?"

"He hit her and dragged her to the men's bathroom . . . forced himself on her. Her company defended and protected him, made her leave."

Craig hangs his mouth open.

"Yup."

"Did he actually . . . ."

"No. Jade defended herself pretty well."

"Okay. But is this dude crazy enough to go into your home and kidnap Jade? I mean, think about what you're saying here."

"I know. Sounds weird. And I don't think he's crazy enough, but I do think he has enough money to pay someone who's crazy enough."

"Wow, I . . . I really don't know what to say."

"He struck me as desperate. And desperate men do crazy things. Desperate men jump states with no money and a child." Mark looks at Craig. "Desperate men try to kill themselves in jail."

The sky is a deep purple, and it is too dark to be able to see well enough to find Jade. Mark directs Craig to turn around and head back to the house. For the short ride back, both stay quiet. Mark stares out the window, hoping to see Jade's car somewhere, while Craig seems to be in deep thought. Craig pulls up in front of the house.

"What are you going to tell the kids?"

"I don't know. The truth? I've always been honest with them. I don't think now is the time to start lying to them."

"You don't think this is a bit much for them to handle?"

"I don't know what else to tell them."

Mark and Craig get out of the car.

"You think she will come back?" Craig asks.

"I don't know. But I'm not getting any sleep either way."

"I'll post up downstairs."

Mark and Craig enter the house and see Berta washing dishes. Mark also hears water running upstairs.

"Thanks for looking after them," Mark says to Berta, "They're getting ready for bed?"

"Yup. Did Craig tell you about us staying to help?"

"He did. Thank you."

"So what happened?"

"I'll explain everything," Craig cuts in. "Mark, you need some rest, man."

"I look that bad already?" Mark quips. "I'll set the guest bedroom up for you, Berta."

Mark bids Craig and Berta a good night and heads upstairs. He walks by Charles' room to see him sprawled out in the bed, fast asleep. Mark says a short prayer that he has a good sleep, one without nightmares. He walks by Amber's room and hears her short baby breaths, and prays the same for her. He knows Kalina is in the shower so he gets the guest room set up for Berta, and grabs a pillow from the linen closet for Craig.

Later in the night, Mark still is unable to go to sleep. In the dark, he stands by the bedroom window, looking out into the streets. He replays everything he saw when he first came home, but comes up with nothing out of the ordinary other than her car being missing and her phone lying in the Gatorade bin, cracked. He already spent the previous hour looking through Jade's phone, trying to glean some information from there but coming up with nothing. She has a few calls in her log, but those were with Berta.

He feels helpless.

He hears light footsteps entering the room and turns toward the doorway.

"You should be in bed," Mark says.

"I can't sleep."

Mark feels his daughter's arms around his waist.

"Is Mom back yet?"

"No."

"Did something bad happen to her?"

"I don't know." He feels like that's his answer for everything right now.

"You said she went to the store."

"I know."

"But she didn't go to the store, did she?"

"As far as I know, no."

"What are we going to do?"

"You are going to go to school. I'm going to find her."

Kalina gets quiet. Her grip around his waist tightens.

"Daddy, I'm scared."

"It's all going to be okay. I won't let anything happen to you. We'll get this all figured out. Here," Mark moves Kalina to the bed and grabs his pillow. "Lie down and go to sleep." He nudges Kalina into the bed and sets the pillow under her head. He sits on the bed next to her.

"I'm not scared for me. I'm scared for Mom . . . and you."

"Nothing is going to happen to us."

"But how do you know?"

"Because I won't let it."

"But you're human. Things happen to people every day whether they let it or not."

Mark pauses. He misses the days when Kalina saw him as a superhero, those days when anything was possible simply because he said it was. "I guess that's where our faith comes in."

A few moments later Kalina says, "I want to cry."

"It's okay to."

Mark rubs her back as she cries herself to sleep.

CHAPTER THIRTY

MARK wakes up to the sun shining brightly into his face. He rustles a bit first before jumping from the uncomfortable position he was in while sleeping in the armchair by the window. He looks at the bed, noticing it's made neatly, and looks at the clock. He overslept. He was supposed to get the kids set for their day, Charles to school, Kalina to the bus stop, Amber to daycare. He rushes out of the bedroom and down the steps. He hears a rustling in the kitchen and heads that way; still half asleep, he's hoping to see Jade. Instead he sees Berta sitting at the island, sipping on a cup of something steaming.

"Morning," Berta says.

"The kids. I was supposed—"

"I walked Kalina to the bus stop. Craig should be on his way back from taking Charles to school and Amber to daycare. Sit. I made breakfast."

Mark looks at Berta strangely. "No Jade?"

Berta shakes her head. Mark sits at the island.

"I have to get to the police station soon, then. File a missing persons report."

She puts a plate of food in front of him. "Do you have all the information you need handy?"

"You mean like photos and addresses of her usual places?"

"Yeah . . . and the info of her dentist." She looks down.

Mark tries not to entertain the thought too much, for he knows the dental records would only come into play if she is dead and isn't recognizable. Those situations are usually pretty bad. Mark then realizes that he shouldn't have tampered with her phone, as it is likely to be evidence. Little by little his mind shifts into thinking about the formalities and the procedures, like one of those crime shows.

He hates crime shows.

"Thank you for breakfast, but I'm not really hungry. I should get moving." He eats two bites and gets up from his seat to look for the most recent photos he has of Jade.

Mark eventually gets to the police station with an envelope full of information and files the missing persons report. Through the blur of questions, Mark remembers one thing distinctly. When asked if anyone would have a reason to take Jade, he mentioned Calvin's name, and referred back to what Jade told him about the night of the office party. He couldn't think of anything else at the time. Before Mark could get out of the parking lot, he gets a phone call to come back to the station.

☙

Craig and Berta sit in the kitchen, absorbing the peace and quiet of the house as the events as of late settle further into their minds. Craig eyes Berta, who stares out the window.

"Can we talk?" Craig asks.

Berta turns and looks at him, seemingly trying to come out of her thoughts. Craig puts out his hand. Berta stares at his hand for a moment before placing hers in his.

"I love you," Craig says.

Berta furrows her brow. "I love you, too."

"And I'm sorry for what making you feel like I'm not there for you."

Berta nods slowly.

"But I need to know: what is going on with you? There are some things that we skimmed over during counseling that I had no clue of . . . like this situation with your Mom."

"It's not much of a situation, Craig. She's just not the person I thought she was. She's a whole lot different, actually. And maybe Daddy was, too."

"Sounds to be a big situation to me."

Berta thinks for a second. "Maybe it is."

"Talk to me."

"I—" She pauses, reading Craig. When she figures he's serious, and not just saying things to smooth things over between them, she continues. "I ran into my mother at the funeral. Don't know why she was there, but we really had no business being there, either. She wanted to meet up for what she called 'the truth' and for some odd reason, I agreed."

"This is the same woman who left you . . . in the monster's hands?"

Berta appreciates Craig's using the same term she uses for her biological father. "The same one."

"The one you blamed for all these years?"

"Yup. So I didn't really have much to say to her, obviously. But she had a world full of information to tell me. She told me how they met, how he abused her, how she was jealous of me, how she was made out to be this nasty person . . . she told me something completely contrary to what I grew up believing."

"You believe her?"

"I do." She takes a sip of her drink. "I really do."

"So where does that leave you?"

"Confused at one point. Curious at another. Angry throughout. But at the moment, my curiosity is taking over. I ask myself every day, if my mother isn't who I thought she was . . . who else falls into that category?"

"And this is how you get to Mr. V?"

"Yes. My mother made it seem that there was this love affair going on between her and Daddy. And we talked to the monster's widow, and she—"

"Wait," Craig frowns. "You tracked down your biological father's widow?"

"My mother and I, yes. And we found out that what he did to me, he did to his second daughter. And we found out that Daddy might have operated under the same shady business practices as the monster."

Craig gives an awkward look. "So when do you stop?"

"What do you mean?"

"When do you stop digging and let the past be the past?"

"When do I stop? I need to know the truth. It's for my own sanity." Berta gets up from her seat. "My mother asked me something similar. What am I looking for? I told her I'm looking for peace. And I know how to get it now. I need to know more about Daddy. I need to know how he got to me. That's the last piece of the puzzle."

"That's what will give you peace?" Craig asks incredulously.

"Absolutely. Absolutely. Let me ask you something. Do you know what it feels like to believe yourself to be this one person, just to find out that you aren't that person? Just to find out that you don't know who you are?"

"Berta, your past isn't who you are."

"I know. But in a way, for me, it is. Everything about who I thought I was is different."

"But it's only different because you are making it different, not because of anything in your past."

"Craig, it's not."

"Look, all I'm saying is that you don't want to go digging in your past looking for things that may not be there. You'll end up disappointed . . . or hurt . . . or worse."

"What? Craig, what are you talking about?"

"The monster was a shady businessman. Now there's a chance that so was Mr. V. Meaning, it's likely they worked with other shady people. You mean to tell me that there aren't people out there who want to keep covered up those very things you are trying to find?"

"Why would they want it to stay covered up? What does it matter to them?" Berta looks at Craig curiously. "What am I missing? What do you know?"

"I know less than you do at this point. I just don't want you to get hurt."

Both get quiet and stay that way for a few minutes.

"You seem obsessed with your past," Craig says.

"Obsessed? That's what you think?"

"That's the way it seems. Could that be a reason why you are so afraid of mine?"

"No. They're not even related. I'm afraid of your past because of the females in it. And like Pastor said, I have to work through that."

Craig winces slightly, but enough for Berta to notice.

"But it seems I have a lot to work through," she says.

"You know what I noticed?" Craig asks.

"What?"

"I remember the Berta who had this faith that was astronomical. It was out of this world. Something would happen to that Berta and she would bounce back so fast because her faith wouldn't allow her to stay down. She had that faith that would stare fear in the eye . . . and smile. I haven't seen that Berta in quite a while. I miss that Berta."

To that, Berta doesn't know what to say.

"That very same Berta used to believe in me a lot more, too. Somewhere along the line, somehow you stopped believing in me. I don't know what I did to make that happen, but it can't just be I'm not as attentive as I once was. The old Berta would have at least slapped me to get my attention." Craig smirks, but it fades away in a few seconds. "It makes me think that you don't want this . . . our marriage, anymore. But those are just my thoughts. You don't have to say anything to it. I just needed to get that off my chest."

Craig still sits at the island. Berta leans on the counter.

"You're right," Berta says. "About how I've been acting. I have lost faith in some things . . . in people . . . in you. I have lost faith in God working things out . . . but I don't know why."

"We can start to go the faith way again. It's not too late … is it?"

"No. No, it isn't. I don't want to leave you."

Berta's cell phone rings.

"Well, let's do this," Craig says. "What can I do to help?"

"Help?"

"Help put the pieces together."

Berta grabs her phone to see a strange number. "Ummm. Hold on for a second." Berta picks up the phone quickly, but moves it from her face quickly and asks Craig to give her a few moments. She appreciates his want to help her, but she feels it's more of a solo gig. She has to figure things out for herself.

Craig leaves the kitchen with a strange expression. Berta turns her attention to who is on the phone.

"Alberta."

"Izabel?"

"We need to meet up."

"What? I can't."

"It's important. Can you meet me at the library?"

"No, I can't. I'm not even in the area. Where are you calling from?"

"A pay phone."

"Why are you calling from a pay phone?"

"It doesn't matter. Can you meet me at my place tonight?"

"I can't. What is this about? And why do you sound so frantic?"

"It's about you . . . and Raul. Alberta, I know how he got you."

Berta pauses, stunned. "What are you talking about?"

"We can't do this over the phone. Is there somewhere closer to you we can meet in private?"

"I'm . . . I'm sorry. No, there isn't any time. I have some major things going on right now and . . . I just can't. Why can't you tell me now?"

"There are some things you need to see for yourself. Listen, tomorrow. How's tomorrow? Can you meet me then? I have a package. I'll just give it to you and be about my way. Alberta, you need to see this."

Berta sighs. "Okay, fine. Where are you going to be?"

"Where do you need me to be that's convenient?"

❧

"Mark Cooke." A man in a trench coat approaches Mark.

For the past twenty minutes, Mark has been sitting at the police station, but for what, he has no idea. For the most part, everyone acted like he wasn't there, just moving along with their daily activities. That all stopped when the tall man in a trench coat stood in front of him. Now, he sees that everyone stares at them.

"Yes, I'm Mark Cooke."

"It wasn't a question." He smiles. "I know who you are. Please, come with me." The man starts toward one of the side offices in the station.

Mark looks around as he follows the man to an office, noticing the glances from other officers. Once inside the office, the man closes the door behind them and takes a seat. He offers Mark the same.

"Seems like you draw a lot of attention," Mark says. "Who are you?"

"I'm Detective Simms." He puts out his hand. "And it isn't me who is drawing their stares."

Mark gives a strange look.

Detective Simms slowly retracts his hand. "Many people in here know who you are. The teacher of the century, fallen from grace for lewd acts on school property. The court case in which one of your students was abused by his mother, the very same woman you were getting with."

"Hey, hold on for a second." Mark still stands, his disposition turning angry.

"Look, you asked. I answered. That's what draws the looks. Now you are in the police station claiming your wife to be missing. It looks mighty strange, Mr. Cooke."

"Strange? As if I did this, strange?"

Detective Simms nods. "And on top of that, you come here mentioning the name that sets this whole place on fire."

"Gaffney."

"The one and only."

Mark sits down. The weight of everything is starting to settle on his shoulders. He slumps.

"But don't worry. I don't hold anything against you. We're men. We make mistakes. We always will. I believe the story you gave one of the officers when filing the missing persons."

"So what is this meeting for?"

"I need to know what you know about Gaffney." He leans in toward Mark. "I've been working on taking Gaffney and his play dad down for years."

"What about my wife?"

"If your story holds true, taking Gaffney down brings your wife back."

"But you seem more concerned about the former."

"They called me in here to solve both." Simms leans back and studies Mark. "I'm sorry. You are right. It does seem like I'm more focused on Gaffney. But this fits his M.O. This is what he does."

"Kidnaps women?"

Detective Simms nods. "I'm sparing you the details. But trust me, it is more important to find your wife. I just tend to get a bit excited the closer I get to taking a bad guy down."

Mark looks at the man. He has a strong jaw and a dimple in the middle of his chin. His hair is close-cut, though with a receding hair-line.

"Do I know you from somewhere?"

"You would know me from a lot of places, Mr. Cooke. I was one of the responding officers when you were in that accident a couple years back. I wasn't detective then."

"But I don't remember any of the officers then. I remember lights, pain, and then a hospital bed. Where else?"

"You taught my son."

Mark thinks for a second, and examines his face even more. "Frankie's father?"

"That's me." Simms smiles.

"I didn't know Frankie's father was . . . ."

"Alive?"

"No, not that, it's just . . . Frankie never mentioned his father . . . ever."

"Yup. I know. His mother and I weren't on the best of terms. We never really saw eye-to-eye . . . still don't. I've done some dumb things. Like focus on work more than my own kid. But again, we're men. We make mistakes. We always will."

"How is Frankie?"

"Don't know. Haven't talked to him in quite some time."

"Oh."

"But anyway, I'm on the case of your missing wife. The first door I bang down is Gaffney's." Simms gets up. "I'm grabbing a coffee. Do you want one?"

"No thanks."

"Suit yourself. Be right back."

"Quick question."

Simms stops.

"How does this normally go? There's more questions to answer, I know . . . but then what?"

"Then I'm on the case."

"And?"

"And I bring your wife back."

"And what do I do?"

"You wait."

Mark looks with a frown as Simms leaves the office.

After a couple more hours of questioning, Mark leaves the police station exhausted. When he gets back home, he sees Craig, Berta, and the kids sitting in the living room watching a movie. He stares at them for a moment before motioning Craig to follow him. They both walk to the laundry room.

"So what's the deal?" Craig asks.

"The police . . . detectives . . . people are on the case. I filed the report."

"And?"

"The detective told me to wait. He's following up on some things tonight and is supposed to give me a call."

"That's it?"

"That's it." He leans on the wall. "I don't know what to do. I can't just sit here, though."

Craig leans on the washer. "We can go on more searches. We can search around for more clues."

Mark smirks. "We're not the Hardy boys. And I'm pretty sure that's what the detective is doing." He sighs. "The detective told me the longer she is missing the greater the chance we won't find her . . . or that we will find her . . . dead." Mark props himself up. "Listen, this is a stretch, I know. . . ." He rubs the back of his neck. "You still have a way to contact . . . those guys you did business with back then?"

"What guys?" Craig squints.

"C'mon Craig, I knew you were into some stuff that wasn't on the up-and-up."

Craig's eyes get wide and he motions with his hand for Mark to lower his voice. "How do you know?" Craig whispers.

"I overheard one of your conversations . . . it always stuck with me."

"When was this?"

"When you first moved into the condo. But none of that matters now. I need your help."

"Mark, I haven't contacted any of them in years."

"I don't mean to cause harm . . . I don't want to stir trouble. But I just can't sit here. I simply can't wait while my wife is out there . . . while he may have her. I'm running out of time."

"So what is it you need? What are you asking me to do, exactly?"

"Information. Maybe some guys to track him. Maybe some more who are willing to get their hands dirty."

"Mark, do you know what you're saying?"

"I do. Do you understand the position I am in? Here's a better question: what would you do?"

"It's not a question of what I would do. I would do the same thing." Craig bites his bottom lip. "Dammit. You sure it's this Calvin guy?"

"I'm not. But, apparently, this is what he does. He kidnaps women and does things to them. Keeps them as slaves."

"But if they know this, how come they haven't stopped him?"

"Because they can never pin it on him. It's always someone else. Plus, he has some people protecting him."

Craig massages his temples. "I left that life alone years ago."

"I know." Mark looks outside. "I'm sorry. It's a desperate move, I know, but I need to find her. I need her back."

"I know you've been asked this before. But are you sure she just didn't take a breather? I mean, maybe things started to weigh down on her and she needed a break."

"I am absolutely positive she isn't just taking a breather. You know even for yourself that's not something she would do."

"I do know . . . I do." Craig takes a deep breath and exhales. "I'll make a few phone calls." Craig looks at his feet. "How far are you willing to go?"

"I don't know yet. I'm just going."

"It will do you some good to consider that from the beginning. Things can get . . . messy pretty fast."

"I will."

"Alright. When I get something solid, I'll call you." He starts his way out of the laundry room.

"Craig."

He stops at the doorway.

"Thanks . . . and I'm sorry."

Craig turns his head to the side, looking back through his peripheral vision. "Me, too."

The kids are asleep and Mark sits at the kitchen island, staring at his cell phone. When it does ring, the vibration along the tile top startles him. He grabs it almost immediately.

"Tomorrow night. Ten o'clock."

"Craig?"

"Tomorrow night. I'll pick you up. We have a party to go to. Wear a suit. Do you have a black briefcase?"

"What? No, mine is brown."

"I'll bring my extra."

"What did you find out?"

"Not much, to be honest. Calvin has professionals on his side. And there are very few people that are willing to dive straight into his do-ings."

"In other words, we are on our own."

"For the most part. But I did get an address, and I know where he is going to be. Every Thursday, he has this party, invite only. We can take some time to search that place, and if Jade isn't there, we move on."

Mark notices that Craig's voice is different, strained.

"We don't have any invites."

"Handled it."

"Do I owe your people now?"

Craig chuckles. "Not at all. They owed me from years back, if you want to look at it that way. Look, I don't want to get too much into the details. Just be ready tomorrow. I'll have a packet of info for you then, too."

Long pause.

"Listen, Craig, again, I am sorry. I just don't know what else to do."

"No. I understand fully. You gotta do what you gotta do. If any-thing, I'm mad at myself for still having these guys' numbers."

"Does Berta know?"

Craig sighs. "No. I never said anything about it."

"Does she know anything?"

"No. Nothing."

"I thought . . . I thought you . . . You didn't say anything to her?"

"I couldn't. I can't. There's more to this story than you think, though. But part of me was hoping that if I simply forgot about that stuff, it would disappear. And it did for a while."

"But it never stays away for long."

"Yeah. Never long enough."

CHAPTER THIRTY ONE

THE next morning, Berta heads to the library to meet up with Izabel. The whole way to the library, she thinks about what she needs to see for herself, this grand information on how Raul got to her. For a moment, she doesn't care, and considers turning around and telling Izabel to drop it. She doesn't change her course, though, because she knows she is almost there. The dots are connecting. But she is still deathly afraid of it.

Berta strolls into the library and asks for Izabel.

"Dome room," the front desk attendant says.

Berta makes her way to the dome room and finds Izabel stacking books in the graceful manner in which she does it. She spots Berta and motions her over. Berta rushes over as Izabel looks to see if anyone else is around. She pulls out a manila envelope and hands it to Berta.

"From Marcella and Jennifer."

Berta starts to open the envelope, but Izabel stops her.

"Not here. Trust me, at your home. Call me later." She gives her a hug and whispers in her ear, "I love you, Alberta. I hope this gives you peace."

And then she pushes her cart to the elevator and disappears. Berta stands there stunned for a few minutes, but eventually leaves the dome room and heads out of the library. *Was she crying?* She sets the envelope in the passenger seat of her car and wonders what's inside. What can this small package tell her? She feels around and notices the imprint of a CD.

Once home again, Berta hurries to lock the doors and she sets the envelope on the kitchen table. She stares at it as if unsure of what to do next. Her hand shakes slightly and she presses it to her chest to stop the tremble. She reaches for the envelope and unties the string. She pulls out a CD and a few pieces of paper, one of which is a small note.

Alberta/Izabel,

Our conversation the other day left us both thinking. When going through Courtland's things, we found this bit of information. He kept individual ledgers for each of the main people he dealt with. His dealings with Raul were extensive, so we gave you the last sheets of his ledger for him. It has some poignant information on it. Courtland also recorded phone messages. We're assuming just in case he needed to use it for something. We went through all of them between him and Raul. On the CD are the last three conversations they had.

By the time you are reading this we will be out of the country. Every other trace of Courtland's dealings will be destroyed. Destroy this information once done with it. We will know if you haven't. Do not try to contact us. You will never find us.

-   M & J

P.S. Alberta, I wasn't ready at the time, but if I could do things over, I would.

Berta gets up and grabs her laptop, scared of what she'll hear on the CD, scared of what's on the ledger. She sets her laptop on the table and grabs the sheets of paper. She looks through the ledger, but the writing is so cryptic she doesn't know what it really means. She does notice that there are many transactions on the sheets. She sets them down and pops the CD into her laptop.

The moment the phone conversations begin to play, a wave of emotion crashes over her. To hear her father's voice, his wonderfully sweet voice, is like a sharp blast from the past. She doesn't even listen to what he says exactly, but reminisces on the great time she had with him. She remembers his smile . . . his laugh . . . all the things he taught her. She is reminded of what he meant to her . . . what he means to her to this day. Berta stops the CD for a moment to cry.

When she starts the CD up again, she is greeted by a voice that makes her skin crawl. She has to pause the CD again because she thinks she is going to be sick. She doesn't even remember Courtland's voice, yet she still has this knee-jerk reaction when she hears it. She listens to the first conversation all the way through. It was mostly about Courtland setting up a big deal and going into a new line of business. Raul inquired, but largely seemed uninterested as there was something already on the table. The second conversation was more of the same.

When Berta gets to the last conversation, the last one Raul had with Courtland, she takes a deep breath. She glances at the papers again, noticing all the amounts are in the hundreds of thousands and millions.

She plays the conversation.

"It's me," Raul says.

"Good friend. What can I say I owe this pleasure to?" Courtland says.

"Your new business venture."

"Ah. You heard of the sales extravaganza?"

"That's a way to put it."

"You don't sound as excited."

"Sorry, but I'm not. I think it's all crazy, to be honest. And that's why I called. I want you to drop it."

"Drop what? Surely, you aren't talking about this new venture."

"I am. It's sick . . . even for you."

Long pause.

"I can't drop it. You hear of the bids I'm pulling in for this?"

"I heard."

"Imagine if I could get word around to other circles."

"They're kids, man. What is wrong with you?"

"Don't judge."

Raul sighs. "Fine . . . Fine. I'm looking for one . . . One in particular."

"You're making a good choice. Which one would you like to place a bid on?"

"No. I'm not placing a bid. I'm buying outright." Raul's voice becomes strained.

"Wait a minute. That's not the way it works. But I'll bite anyway. Who are you that eager to get?"

"Alberta."

Long pause.

"She isn't involved in this," Courtland says.

"I heard from someone else that she is. That there is some private deal going on . . . that you have to because she is no longer . . . pure."

The CD goes silent. Berta sits at the table, her face sideways and flat on the table, with tears in her eyes. She lifts a lazy hand up toward the laptop to stop the CD, but before she could, the CD continues.

"It's a private deal. Why would he say anything?" Courtland says.

"Money makes people do strange things. You should know that already." Raul grunts. "But your own daughter? Really, man?"

Courtland chuckles. "We all have our vices. I must go, old friend. There are some loose ends I must take care of at the moment."

"He's gone. He took the money and disappeared."

"But his money isn't gone. And we both know I can track that back to anyone."

"It will be a waste of your time . . . and money. And we both know how you don't like to waste money."

"Touché."

"I want Alberta. Five hundred thousand."

"What? I pay my accountant that much to hide less than that. Add a million to that. That will get me to consider."

"Two mil. Call it even."

"You really want her, huh? Two mil is what they bid on one who is older than her, and pure. But no bother. I accept your offer. But there are a few conditions."

"There seem to be a lot of stipulations for a child you were trying to shove off onto Marcy."

"My, you are on one today? How did that tidbit of information get out?"

"That's not important. What else is there? Your conditions, I mean."

A long pause.

"First, I need it in cash."

"What? You know it's virtually impossible to get that in cash. Why would I need to? You know I'm good for the money."

"That's how I need it. All transactions of this sort are done in cash. I have my reasons for this."

"Fine. Give me a couple days."

"Before I move onto my next condition, I must ask. How's my wife?"

Silence.

"Now you have nothing to say," Courtland chides. "Answer me. How is my wife?"

"She isn't your wife."

"You're right, but she isn't yours, either. Heck, I kinda miss that woman. She's a fun romp in the bed, I will say that. Don't you agree?"

"What is your next condition?"

"I realized she was with you some time ago, actually. If Emily were here—"

"Don't you dare."

"Okay, okay. Well, here's the thing, *old friend.* I'm starting to notice a trend. Back in the day, when I first started these businesses . . . maybe a week later, you did as well. My wife cheats on me and leaves me—"

"I know what really happened. She didn't cheat on you."

"That's not the point. The point is she ends up in your arms. So you have businesses . . . just like me . . . you have my wife . . . and now you want my daughter. I know imitation is a form of flattery, but this is a bit extreme for you, don't you think?"

"I'm helping them."

"No. No, I don't see it that way. You're *my* friend. But no bother. You know I record these phone calls, right?"

"Yeah."

"Well, here's my last condition. I want you to say out loud, loud enough for it to be recorded, that you want to be Courtland DeVries."

"What?"

"I want you to proclaim for the world to know that you want to be just like Courtland DeVries. That way I can replay this conversation as a reminder of a man who was once a friend, who stole from the only one who was in his corner."

"You self-serving son of a bitch."

"That's not quite what I want to hear. Say it, Raul. Say it." Courtland's voice turns menacing. "You want to be me."

"No."

Courtland laughs. "I know for a prideful man such as yourself, this must be hard. But I have you by the balls, here. You want Alberta? *Say it.*"

Raul grunts. "I want to be Courtland DeVries."

"There we go. Not so hard. Be at my place in a couple of days. I'll have her ready for you. Have my money ready. Come alone."

The phone clicks.

Berta stays motionless, being paralyzed by the emotions running through her body. She slowly reaches for the papers and scans the last sheet, finding the two million dollar transaction. It's the last on the list. She lets the paper fall from her hand and to the floor. Unable to hold in the tears any longer, she weeps, bitterly.

She doesn't remove herself from the table as she contends with multiple bouts of sobbing and cursing. She hates how she feels. She feels . . . not human. She was paid for . . . with money; a ton of money as a matter of fact, yet she feels so worthless. She finally has unlocked the secrets of her past and she couldn't feel any worse than she does now. She wonders to herself, *What was the point?* She constantly asks herself if the information she searched high and low for was worth the trouble. How could she think it would give her peace? *Ignorance truly is bliss,* she thinks. Her thoughts go to Marcella. *Did the monster ask Marcella to take care of me and she denied?* She thinks back to the expression she gave her when she asked how she knew so much. She remembers her eyes at the time. *Full of regret.* She remembers the embrace that was borderline awkward. Then, her thoughts go to Izabel. She's the one who started all of this. Why had she really approached her? What purpose did it serve for her? Berta sits up, grabs her cell phone, and dials Izabel's number.

When Izabel picks up, Berta doesn't say hello. She wants answers.

"Why was it so important for me to know the truth, as you said it? A truth you had no real idea of."

"Alberta, I'm so sorry."

"Sorry? Sorry doesn't even begin to cover it. You did this. You wanted me to know the truth. I was fine without it. You hear me? I was fine without it. I was fine without you."

"I didn't know all of this was a part of it."

Berta's words become more strained. "Well, what the hell did you think came with all of this? You thought it was going to be some fairy tale? That you tell me just enough information to clear yourself from looking like an idiot, but then I would want to know no more?"

Izabel says nothing.

"I hate you. I hated you then . . . I hate you now. Stay out of my life."

Berta mashes the screen on her phone to end the call. Things are moving quickly for her now. Too quickly. The room starts to spin and she falls to the floor, weeping even more.

As her sobs and anger subside, she hears her laptop playing the CD again. She, not having enough energy to stand on her feet, crawls to the table to shut the recording down. As she grips the table for support, she realizes what plays isn't a conversation she previously heard. She flops into the chair and listens. She notices the sound of Raul's voice. It's weak. It's tired. Berta then knows this conversation he had with Courtland was right around his death.

"I must say, I was not expecting this call at all," Courtland says.

"Well . . . ." Raul sounds as if he has trouble breathing. "I wasn't going to call. But it's the right thing to do."

"How's your health?"

"Fading . . . fast."

"Maybe you should get your rest. Save your energy."

"I will. After this call."

"So what can I do for you?"

"Just one thing. Give it up."

"Give what up?"

"This way of life."

Courtland laughs. "Why would I do that?"

"Because your soul depends on it."

"Are you a deathbed preacher now, Raul?"

"No. Nothing like that. I just realized how stupid we were. How stupid the way of life is. We're nothing but two-bit thugs in suits. I have to die realizing I had the opportunity to change, and do good, but I did it too late. You still have time. You can change . . . and do good."

"I admire your attempt. But the only good for me is money. And I make a lot of it. With it comes power. People bend to my will because of it. Why would I want to give that up?"

"I'll still pray for you . . . even until my death."

"Save them."

Silence.

"Well, I guess it's only fair that I tell you that I've been in contact with your protégé," Courtland says.

"I know. And that will not continue. He's a good kid. He had a bit of a rough patch, but he's a good kid. And this life isn't for him. He's not like us."

"I get the impression that he is. I've seen his work."

"As have I. But I have talked to him. He understands my vision for him. He will do the right thing. But just in case you want to test that, I have set my entire network on a final task in protecting him . . . and my daughter."

Courtland chuckles. "Your daughter?"

"You heard me correctly."

"So even on your death bed, you make threats to me? Even after you try to save my soul?"

"These aren't threats, Courtland."

Things get silent.

"I see. Very well, old friend. I don't want anything to do with that slut anyway. And as for your protégé, he's still pretty fresh out of jail. He has the hunger. He'll come to me."

"I doubt he will. He knows what you are about."

"Does he now? Does he know I'm Alberta's father?"

"He does. And he knows why she's with me. He knows the type of man you are . . . the monster you've become."

"What else does he know?"

"He knows enough to know not to deal with you."

There's a rustling over the audio. "Is there anything else I can do for you, Raul?"

"No. I think that's about it."

"Well, good luck in the afterlife."

"That's somewhat cold for someone with so much history with you."

"I'm not much for sentiment."

Raul chuckles and breaks out into a coughing spell. "Do you still record your calls?"

"Every single one."

"Maybe you'll play this one back and realize how foolish you are being. Goodbye, Courtland."

Berta sits for hours at the table, staring off into space, then Craig comes home. He sets his briefcase at the door and starts toward the back.

"Hey," he says.

Berta says nothing. Craig stops and stares at her. He moves slowly to a chair at the table and sits.

"What's wrong? What happened?"

Berta doesn't look him in the eyes at first. She continues to stare off into space. When she does finally roll her eyes to look in his direction, she says, "Why didn't you tell me?"

"Tell you what?"

"That you were a slimeball that claimed to be a businessman."

"What are you talking about?"

Berta rolls her eyes again. "You had contact with the monster near Daddy's death?"

Craig takes a deep breath, but says nothing.

"Your silence says it all. So what was it? What was your thing?"

Craig starts to play with his hands, as a child would do when reprimanded.

"Answer me." Berta slams the table.

Craig stares, but still says nothing.

"I thought you were . . . I thought . . . ."

"The contact was minimal, and I didn't have any form of contact with him after I knew what he did to you."

"Daddy told you."

Craig nods.

"Did he tell you everything?"

Craig looks Berta in the eyes, but only for a few moments before wincing and looking down. "He did."

"So you knew. You knew how he got me . . . you knew for years . . . and never said a word. Even when I opened up to you about it . . . you . . . you tried to convince me that it's a bad idea to try and find out?"

"I'm sorry. I just . . . there was never a way to tell you. There was never a good time. And I simply forgot about it when I thought it didn't matter anymore."

"You don't just forget about things like that." She leans in toward him. "You are so bold as to lie to me straight to my face again?"

"I'm not lying to you."

"But you didn't forget. Mr. Detail-oriented. Mr. Finance. No, you didn't forget."

"Again, I'm not lying to you. I pushed it from my mind."

"But you tried to stop me."

"I panicked."

"But you repeatedly told me you hid nothing from me. You said you told me everything about your past. Correct?"

Craig says nothing.

She brushes her hair away from her face. "So you're just like them?"

"No, I'm not. I haven't been in that game for years. Mr. V told me to drop it . . . so I dropped it."

"And you never went back?"

"I . . . ." Craig winces. "I made a few calls . . . recently . . . for Mark . . . to find Jade."

"Get out."

Craig looks up at Berta. "What?"

"Get out of this house. Don't come back."

"Berta, you have to understand—"

"No, Craig. No. There's no smooth talk. No explanation. You . . . just go. Leave."

Craig slowly gets up from the table. He goes to the back rooms and comes back out with a packed duffel bag and his backup briefcase. He glances back at Berta a final time before grabbing the briefcase by the door and leaving the home.

Chapter Thirty Two

MARK spent most of his day packing up the kids' things to leave for the weekend and tending to Amber. He called Charles and Kalina's schools to let them know they won't be in school tomorrow and made up some vacation excuse. He called Jade's mother to drop the kids off. At the time, she sounded confused and Mark told her that he would explain when he got there. He's getting things in order.

His phone rings.

"Hello," Mark says while trying to finish packing Amber's diaper bag.

"Mr. Cooke, Detective Simms."

"I thought you were supposed to call yesterday."

"I was, and I apologize for not doing so. Look, here's the deal."

"Am I going to like this news?"

"Likely not. We followed up on a few leads on Gaffney, but at the end, he has a strong alibi . . . and a ton of witnesses."

"What are you saying? What does that mean?"

"Knowing what I know about him, it means nothing. He could have easily hired someone to take her . . . or he could have paid all of those people off to lie for him. He has the money. Look, before I pursue this any further, I need to know if there is anyone else on the face of this planet that would do this."

"No. No one else."

"And you are sure she just didn't need a break."

"A break from what?"

"Hey, hey now. I'm not here to ruffle any feathers. I just am asking the questions I need to ask in order to get the most accurate information possible . . . and your wife back in your arms."

"She didn't just up and leave under her own volition."

"Okay. So what I'm going to do is dig a bit more . . . ."

While Detective Simms talks a thought presses its way into Mark's mind.

"Detective. Detective, hold on a second. There is someone else who would possibly do something like this. Maybe."

"Who?"

"Her name is Alicia." Mark thinks. He doesn't remember her maiden name. "Last time I heard, it was Alicia Langley."

"Who is she?"

"You know me so well. You know my story so well. Look through your files."

"Aha. No need. Your sunny disposition says it all. The infamous mistress."

"She wasn't my mistress."

"So, what would you call her?"

"That doesn't matter."

"You're right. When's the last time you've seen her?"

"Years ago . . . in court. But she was just released from prison not too long ago. It just seems too . . . convenient."

"Well, I'll look into that angle before I do anything more with Gaffney. While I'm doing this, I may go dark for a couple days."

"Figures."

"Mark, I'm on your side. Call me if anything changes on your end. I'll be in touch."

Mark gets off the phone and loads up the car to get the kids from school.

Kalina and Charles were excited not to have to go to school to-morrow. Amber was and is completely oblivious to what goes on around her, but she wears a large smile. But as time goes on, Mark notices the cheers fade into silence and the smiles turn to frowns. Kalina is the first to speak.

"Where's Mom?"

Mark glances to his right. "I don't know."

Kalina slumps in her seat. "You're speeding."

"Huh?"

"You're doing fifty. The speed limit is thirty-five." She stares at Mark until he slows down.

"Sorry."

"I don't want to go to Grandma and Grandpa's," Charles says.

"I'm sorry to hear that. But you're going. I need to know you three are going to be safe."

"Why? What are you going to do?" Kalina asks.

"Hopefully, find your mother. But I couldn't leave you at the house by yourselves."

"Why couldn't we have gone to the neighbor's house?"

"Because we aren't on good terms with them anymore."

"What's that mean?"

"It means after our incident of a couple years ago, a lot of people ended up not liking me."

Both get silent.

"Because of the camera guys?" Charles asks.

"Yup. That and other things."

"Like what?"

"It's too complicated to talk about right now, Charles."

"How long are we staying at Grandma and Grandpa's?" Kalina asks.

"I'm picking you up Sunday."

"Why are we staying so long?"

"Look, both of you, enough with the questions." He feels his temper rising and works at calming it.

Kalina and Charles glance at each other for a moment, but get quiet immediately. For the rest of the way, the car stays in complete silence.

When Mark finally gets to Jade's parents' home, no one moves. It takes Mark to step out the car first before the kids even move. Jade's mother waits at the front steps. Mark grabs Amber and hoists her up in his arm. He grabs her bag and starts toward the house, Kalina and Charles following closely behind.

Jade's mother smiles. Mark returns the sentiment, though he is sure she won't be smiling much after he talks to her.

"Is everything okay?" she asks, switching her glance between Mark and the kids. She puts out her arms for Amber. Amber does nothing short of jumping out of Mark's arms and into hers.

Mark looks and nudges Kalina and Charles inside. "Yeah. Everything is fine."

They all walk inside.

Once the kids are settled, Mark sits in the kitchen with Jade's mother.

"So what is going on?" she asks.

"Jade's missing."

"What do you mean she's missing? I just talked to her a couple days ago."

Mark frowns. "I thought you said you haven't spoken to her in weeks."

"I did because she has this whole weekend thing planned for you two. I thought your call was trying to figure out what she was planning."

"What weekend thing?"

"She was planning a weekend for the both of you. She had this whole thing set up for you to spend some time with each other, just to enjoy each other. I'm sorry I didn't tell you then, but what is this mess about her being missing?"

"I go out, she's home; I come back, she's gone, and she hasn't been back since. I went to the police and filed a report, but they came up with nothing so far. It's been a couple days."

Jade's mother gets silent.

"Is there anything else she said that may help? Did she say where she planned for us to go? Anything?"

"No. Nothing. She just asked for us to take the kids. That's all."

Mark sighs and gets up from his seat. "Well, I have to go." He feels a sense of urgency like a burst of adrenaline from deep within him. "I have to make a few phone calls. I'll keep you posted."

He runs to the kids and gives them each a kiss on the forehead. "I'll get you Sunday, okay? I'll have your momma, too."

"You promise?" Charles asks.

"I promise."

Mark leaves thinking about that promise. There are only a couple more days before people will assume Jade to be dead. He won't let her be gone for that long. He can't. He leaves the home, feeling a twinge of sadness for the kids.

ϐࠉ

"So here's the deal," Craig says, "We get in the suits, bring the briefcases; not sure what they are for, but from what I'm told, it's a must. We have to have the briefcase. It's just as important as the invite."

Mark and Craig sit at Mark's dining room table, staring at the various pictures and papers Craig procured from his contacts. Mark looks at Craig and his mannerisms, feeling that something is off. He looks at the beer Craig has been nursing for the past hour.

"You alright, man?" Mark asks.

Craig looks up at Mark's face, but Mark knows he isn't looking him in the eyes. Another sign something is off. Most people wouldn't notice it, but Mark knows Craig. He's known him virtually all his life.

"I'm fine. Why?"

"I can't remember the last time you drank beer."

"Oh. Yeah, I had a taste for a cold one."

Mark stares at him as he looks down and sorts through more of the papers. After a few silent moments, Mark looks back down at the table as well. For a second he sits back and takes the scene in. He finds it incredibly unsettling how easy it was for Craig to get this kind of information on such short notice. Mark flips through the picture of the most recent women he's been with, of his supposed home: a top-floor condo in the middle of the city, and some paperwork. He looks back up at Craig again, starting to realize what he has done for him.

"Craig, I'm really sorry. I know I said it before. But I can't help but feel that I'm . . . throwing the stumbling block in front of you . . . taking you back to a part in your past you would rather forget."

Craig looks up at Mark with a grim expression. "Stop it."

"What?"

"Stop it with this pity mess. You want Jade back?"

"Of course I do. That's not even a question."

"You wanted to search for yourself. You wanted to step into a world you have no idea about."

"You sound like you're blaming me for something."

"I'm not. I blame myself. But there's no time for that. No time for pity. No time for the blame game. You have to become someone else. You need to be cold. You need to be calculated. No emotion. Emotion is messy. It will get us killed." He takes a long gulp of his beer.

Mark lets what Craig said settle in a bit, as his discomfort goes up another notch.

Craig doesn't wait for his point to be made before he continues. "We have good reason to think that Jade is with this man, right? If he has her, she isn't going to be out in the open. She's going to be hidden somewhere in his place. Maybe. If she isn't there, then we search for clues, more info that would lead us to her."

"And if we find nothing?"

Craig sits back in his seat and thinks. "How sure are you . . . of him?"

"As time goes on, I don't know. Why?"

"Alicia. She's just recently out of jail, right?"

"Yeah. I know. I told the detective about her. He's looking into it."

"My question is, why aren't we looking into it? I mean, I'm following your lead here, but don't you think she would be the first person to look into?"

Mark looks down. "You're right." He takes a deep breath and exhales through pursed lips. "I'm just not sure. Like, if we are wrong . . . we could cause her more pain. I'm not up for that. I think I caused enough."

"Are you sure you are looking at this clearly?"

"Clear enough. Look, can you get someone to look into her? Just do it discreetly. She can know nothing."

"Will do."

"What are our chances? Right now, how likely is it that we find Jade?"

"Don't worry about that. Just—"

"Be straight with me."

Craig sighs. "The chances aren't great. We don't have enough information at the moment."

Mark shakes his head. "I don't get it. Why go through all of this? Why agree to hit up your contacts?"

Craig stares at the floor. "Because you need it. Because neither one of us can sit by and let this happen to someone we love. Even if it is just a small chance, I'll take it, if you take it. Ride or die, I said to you years ago. I got your back no matter what. So, if you tell me you need my help finding the most important person in your life, I am there." He takes another swig of beer. "This is Jade we're talking about. It's you were talking about. You . . . my only real friend . . . my only real family . . . ."

Mark takes another moment to get a broad view of the situation, and another to focus on Craig. It takes him back to when Craig was staying with him when he was released from prison. Craig was broken; he was hungry; he was desperate to make something of himself. Mark realizes he sees no hunger or desperation anymore, but the brokenness . . . the brokenness remains.

"What aren't you telling me?"

"I've told you everything I know."

"No. Not about this. About you. What's going on with you?"

Craig finishes his beer and stares at Mark, this time, in his eyes. "Stay focused. You lose focus, you lose her." He gets up from the table and grabs his suit. "Time to suit up. Be ready in fifteen." He disappears upstairs.

Chapter Thirty Three

IT doesn't take long for Mark and Craig to get to Calvin's condo, where a valet takes the car and leaves them standing at the set of doors leading to the lobby.

"You ready?" Craig asks.

"I guess so. You never told me what kind of party this is."

"From what I'm told, this is where a lot of dirty dealings go on. It's like a get-together for the shady and underhanded."

"Of which I am neither."

"Just exude confidence. Stay away from Calvin, just in case he remembers who you are."

Mark and Craig step to the front desk of the lobby, briefcases in hand. A young man stands at the desk, sizing up both Mark and Craig, but stopping at the briefcases. He doesn't say anything to them but calls out the bellboy. Another young man approaches them and stands next to Mark. The man at the front desk nods and motions them to the elevators. The bellboy leads the way.

Mark glances at Craig but says nothing. The three of them go into the elevator, and still, no one says a word. The elevator stops at the top level and Mark and Craig are escorted off and down a well-lit, marble-floored hallway. The walls are adorned with various works of modern art—mostly of nudes, Mark notices. They get to a set of double doors where two large men stand guard. They don't make eye contact, but face forward, as if occupied by something else.

"Invitations," one says.

Mark looks at Craig and pulls out his invitation from his suit coat pocket. Craig already has his in hand. The one man takes the invitations while the other runs a wand around them, presumably for detecting guns. Mark thinks back to his college days for a quick moment. This whole scene feels like he's trying to get into a club again. The man with the scanner nods at the one with the invitations, then stands back in his original position.

For an awkward moment, all five men stand there, as Mark and Craig try to determine if everything is okay. The bellboy turns and leaves.

"Have fun," he says.

Craig is the first to move forward, and after one step, the men open the doors for him. Mark follows closely behind.

Once inside, the two inspect the area. They stand at the front of an immaculate lobby area where people mingle. Mark realizes that the condo doesn't take up just the top floor, but the top two floors. The roof is all glass, and as he traces down the walls, he notices more of the artwork. Again, all nudes. He sees a group of people all in nice suits and understated evening gowns, some mingling, some in cushioned chairs that are scattered along the edges of the room. To his left, a large entryway is covered by a curtain, blocking off more of the large condo.

Mark immediately shoots for that corner of the room, attempting to avoid all contact with anyone there, but he feels Craig's hand on his arm.

"There's Calvin."

Mark looks at the opposite side of the room and sees Calvin surrounded by a group of people.

"As he circles the room, you do the same. Stay away from him," Craig says, and then heads straight for the group Calvin is talking to.

Mark feels nervous and out of place, but he starts talking to a few people anyway. For the first half hour, he moves around the room talk-

ing about various everyday topics such as how the stock market is doing, crime rates in various cities, and other things that normal people
would talk of. He surprises himself a few times when it comes to holding a conversation about these topics, not for lack of knowledge, but
because he feels comfortable doing it. He stands near the far corner of
the room, still keeping his distance from Calvin, when a woman about
the same height as he approaches. She wears a tight black dress and
holds a half-full cocktail glass in her hand. Hanging on her arm is a
midsized leather purse. Strangely, the first thing Mark notices about her
is the diamond-encrusted choker wrapped around her neck.

"I haven't seen you at this party before." Her voice comes out
smooth.

"First time here."

She nods. "I'm Ginny." She holds out her hand.

Mark shakes her hand. "I'm . . . Damon."

"Nice to meet you, Damon."

"Not to be rude, but you don't strike me as a Ginny."

"Because I'm not . . . just like how you're not Damon."

Mark nods, but doesn't say anything.

"So what do you think of the soirée so far?"

"A little stiff."

Ginny smirks. "I agree." She looks at her watch. "But it's about to
pick up."

"I hope so."

Ginny's smirk grows to a full smile. "So what do you do?"

"I work in finance."

"Don't we all?" She stares a hole into Mark, making him feel more
uncomfortable than he already does. "I mean what do you do . . . to be
here?" She brings her cocktail to her mouth and plays with the straw
with her tongue. Her smile turns to a devilish grin.

Mark thinks for a second. *Exude confidence.* "I keep my affairs private."

"Would you turn down a willing business partner?"

"It depends. I have no idea what you do."

"There's a lot I do, but I'm one to keep my affairs private as well."

"Too bad."

"Maybe." She inches closer to Mark. "But I bet I could get you to tell me all your secrets."

"Maybe."

Mark walks away without saying another word. He continues to circle Calvin, keeping his distance and looking for Craig. Something unsettles him about this entire thing. He looks around. All the men hold their black briefcases. Mark presumes they're filled with money, but he looks at the women. Every single woman in the room carries a black bag. The bags are too small to carry large sums of money, so he doesn't know what they are for. He becomes more and more nervous thinking about everything he has experienced thus far. Ginny was clearly hitting on him, but she was waiting for a particular moment for . . . something. The nudes on the wall . . . the blocked-off area. Mark has a sickening hunch that he and Craig bit off more than they could chew.

The lights go out.

Little by little everyone's conversation dies down until it is completely silent. Then, a spotlight shines in the middle of the floor as Calvin steps into it with a microphone in hand. Mark tries to slide away toward the walls.

"Ladies . . . Gentlemen. Thank you for making our little get-together."

Making his way through the crowd, the smells of leather, mint, and expensive cologne/perfume nearly suffocate him. The smell is completely intoxicating. He sees outlines of people, as the only light available is that of the spotlight. With a quick glance toward the curtained entryway, he sees a red light shining on the floor.

"I hope you were able to get some things done this night. Before I continue, I must inform you of some recent happenings. Due to some incidents of my own making, I am forced to cancel these get-togethers for a while . . . at least until I clear the cops out of my way."

The crowd collectively groans.

"I know, I know. I apologize. This isn't a permanent change, of course. I just need a couple weeks to handle a few things. But in the meantime, we can fully enjoy ourselves this night. Ladies and gentlemen welcome . . . to Sinner's Eden."

The crowd offers up applause; not one of those claps you hear at a sporting event, but one that you would hear at some stuck-up social gathering. This leads to more confusion as the curtains are pulled back from the entryway, revealing a completely different part of the condo. It looks like a club with a dance floor, red lights above, and a bar. Twelve scantily clad women come from the room and line up, six on one side of the opening, six on the other.

"We work hard—harder than most. We deserve to play hard. With good business . . . comes good pleasure. That's the motto I live by." Calvin continues to speak. "And for our first-timers, only a few rules. Men, you do not under any circumstances approach the women first. Rule two, for everyone, especially the women," Calvin smirks. "No means no. And finally, please keep everything in the rooms that are designated for each act. Upstairs are the private rooms. On this level, the rooms where you can watch, and please, nothing more than relaxing in the hot tub. Anything nasty in there and you will immediately get thrown out."

Mark starts to go into panic mode, but calms himself down thinking about his goal. He's looking for Jade, or clues about her whereabouts. Silently, he hopes she isn't here. He doesn't want to think about what could possibly happen to her here.

Calvin leads the way into the separate part of the condo, as the music starts blaring from the large speakers. Mark slides further away from him, but someone grips his arm.

"What the hell are you doing here?"

"Get your hands off me," Mark says, ready to fight. He looks at who grabbed him and shakes his head. Without saying another word, he walks over to the far corner of the room, by the entrance just out of earshot of the crowd.

"You know I can have you arrested. How did you even get the invite?"

"You expected me to sit? While my wife is still out there . . . or here?" Mark makes sure he keeps his voice low.

"Yes, because it's *my* job to find her."

"Look, dete—"

"Don't say it. Listen, you have to leave. You don't know the kind of trouble you can get into just by being seen."

"I can't go. I'm here with someone. And I came for something."

Detective Simms paces back and forth for a few moments. He walks in close to Mark. "What goes on in there doesn't exactly make for the environment a God-fearing, church-going man can thrive in. There is no God in there. You are putting yourself at risk. You are putting the whole operation at risk. You are putting your wife's life at risk."

Mark takes a few moments to think. "Fine. But I'm not leaving without my friend."

"Where is your *friend*?"

"He's in there somewhere, I guess."

The detective sighs. "You really—"

The lights in the first half of the room cut back on, this time dimmer than earlier. Detective Simms immediately walks away and disappears into the crowd.

"I was looking for you," a woman says to him a few seconds later.

"Ginny."

"Damon." She smiles and grabs the ends of his suit coat. "Dance with me."

"I can't. Sorry."

"Still playing hard to get? I must forewarn you, I am very persistent. I always get what I want."

"I understand that but . . . ." He thinks he sees Craig on the dance floor. He smiles. "Maybe a dance or two isn't such a bad idea."

Ginny leads Mark to the dance floor. He is shocked at what he sees. In each of the open rooms that surround the dance floor, a group of people perform lewd acts upon each other. Plenty others are on the dance floor, dancing, stripping clothes off. He doesn't look too long in one direction, but as he turns to avoid seeing one thing, he ends up looking at another. In one of the rooms that are blocked off by a velvet rope, he sees a woman digging into her black purse and pulling out a set of handcuffs. He has an idea of what he was supposed to fill his briefcase with. He looks around the room, finding the scantily clad women flirting with some and dancing for others. Then he sees one woman in particular giving a lap dance . . . to detective Simms. Mark stares for a brief moment, noticing how well Simms fits into the entire mix. It makes him wonder.

"Set your case down," Ginny says, and points at a cushioned chair where she places her purse.

Mark sets the case down and starts to dance with Ginny. He looks around the dance floor but doesn't see Craig. Instead, he sees the guy he thought was Craig. The first dance was tame enough, though Mark feels sick to his stomach for what is going on around him. By the time the second song plays, the straps of Ginny's dress are falling down, and she's placing his hand all over her body. Mark does a good job of avoiding touching any major spots, but with each blocked attempt, Ginny gets more persistent, and stronger. Mark knows he has to do something because he feels he is running out of time. The music dies down a bit as the songs change, just enough for Mark to hear all the moans and groans from the surrounding rooms. For a moment, Mark wonders if this is what hell is like. The air is hot and thick, nearly choking him. The various moans and groans sound more like wails and cries to him. He hears torture instead of pleasure. Mark realizes that he blanked out, as Ginny stares at him.

"You seem pretty tense," she says. "I know this can be somewhat overwhelming for a first-timer." She grabs his hand. "Let me calm you down." She starts toward the bar.

They both sit on stools and Ginny asks the bartender for two drinks. Mark notices the awkwardness of the interaction between the bartender and Ginny. It puts him on edge. The bartender slides a shot glass in front of him.

"What's this?" Mark asks.

"It's his special blend," Ginny says. "One shot of this and everything will be right with the world."

Mark shakes his head and looks at the bartender. "Can I get a Jack and Coke instead?"

The bartender pauses and stares at Ginny. Ginny slightly nods and the bartender makes Mark a Jack and Coke. Mark takes a sip. It tastes normal enough. But he knows not to take another sip. He is still thrown off by the weirdness of the bartender.

"So who are you really?" Ginny asks.

"That's not information I hand out regularly . . . especially to people who give me fake names."

"That's a shame." She takes the shot in a gulp and sets the glass down. "Because I think you're a cop. And we have a little policy against cops . . . in general."

Mark's insides turn. "I'm not a cop."

Ginny smiles. "Never seen your face around here before."

"Like I said, this is my first time."

"And your briefcase is empty."

Mark looks around, realizing he left the briefcase on a chair near the dance floor.

"Didn't know what to bring. Again, this is my first time."

"But usually, when Calvin gives the invite to first-timers, he lets you know what to bring."

"Well, he must have slipped up."

"Let's ask him."

Mark stiffens.

"But wait . . . you've been avoiding him all night, haven't you? Circling around as he circles around."

Mark says nothing and gets up from the bar. He tries to step away, but Ginny grabs his arm.

"I would stay and sit for a little. You will find what I propose interesting."

Mark sits back at the bar.

"You see, I'm pretty smart. I have to be to survive in this world . . . in this business. You stick out like a sore thumb to me. But that's no bother. What you're here for doesn't matter to me as much as what you are going to do now. You're handsome . . . and I have a lot of tension. So, here are your choices. We could go to Calvin and see if we can jog his memory on the time he met you and gave you the invitation." Ginny smiles. "Or you can drink the damn drink the bartender gave you." She taps the bar and the bartender puts the exact same shot in front of him again. "We go upstairs and finish what we started."

Mark stares into the grizzled face of the bartender. He turns back to Ginny.

"What if I told you I'm here for some other reason than"— he motions his hand toward the dance floor and rooms—"all of this."

"I would say that's obvious."

"But what if I told you I'm not a cop, and that I'm looking for someone?"

Ginny stares at Mark and smirks. "And what if I told you I don't give a damn?"

He looks away, shaking his head. "You have no idea what you are doing."

"I do actually. I'm getting what I want."

She taps the bar again, and the bartender pulls out a gun, casually setting it on the bar.

"So now you have three choices. We can go to Calvin and he'll end your life. My friend here could end your life right now. Or . . . we could go upstairs and have some fun. Two of them end in death. The last, you may end up a bit bruised, but you get to live another day."

Mark looks around. He sees no one who could help. He looks at the shot glass and knows his darkest days are yet still ahead of him. He knows something's in the drink. He grabs it and gulps it down. The bartender puts his gun back behind the bar.

"Good boy," Ginny says. "Now upstairs we go." She gets off the stool and grabs Mark's hand.

The whole way upstairs, Mark thinks of what his goal is: to find Jade, or evidence of her whereabouts. He determines to stick with that plan, but finds it more and more difficult to do so. Reaching the top of the staircase, he finds it impossible to keep focus. Ginny leads Mark into the first private room they can get to. Once inside the glowing red room, Mark hears the click of the lock on the door. She slides her hand in his and leads him to the bed, the sole piece of furniture in the room. Mark squints, trying to keep his vision straight, but ever so often, the room twirls.

Ginny smiles, nudges him to sit on the edge of the bed, and leans over to kiss him. Mark turns away.

"Relax. It won't hurt," she says, and kisses him on the neck. "Lay back."

Mark doesn't move.

She pushes him hard into the bed. "Still resisting?" She digs into her bag and pulls out handcuffs.

Mark continues to struggle to keep his focus as his body slumps. He thinks about what Craig told him before they came to this hellhole. "Stay focused," he said. "You lose focus, you lose her." He feels he is losing her as he fades in and out of consciousness.

"I told you I get what I want. You shouldn't have come here, mystery man."

Her voice sounds like an echo from somewhere far off. He feels his arms being moved above his head and the cuffs click in tight around his wrist. He apologizes multiple times in his head to Jade, and a few more times to God. His vision blurs as he leans his head over to see what Ginny is about to do. She pulls off her dress and digs in her bag again.

Mark's vision fades to black.

CHAPTER THIRTY FOUR

MARK stirs. He slowly opens his eyes to rays of sunlight beaming on his face. He moves a bit, feeling like he has cement for blood. Every movement hurts. He rubs the back of his head. It feels like sandpaper rubbing against itself: rough and coarse, but in an instant, he pops up. He looks around and realizes he is home.

Home. In his bed.

Mark slides out of bed and stares at the closed bathroom door. He meanders to it and swings it open, hoping to see Jade; hoping that much of what he has been through the past week has been just a dream. He doesn't have to completely look into the bathroom before he knows she isn't there. He doesn't feel her presence. That notion alone brings him to a thought: Jade's essence is leaving the house. He looks at the things that belong to Jade, but for some reason, he can't connect the item to her. Yes, Jade's brush sits on her nightstand; Mark has not touched it, but to imagine Jade brushing her hair with it becomes a harder task to undertake. Little by little, he feels her slipping away.

Mark gallops downstairs and straight to the phone, where he sees there are three messages on the house voicemail. He punches in his code but stops as he sees Craig sleeping on the couch. He sets the phone down.

"Craig."

Craig doesn't budge. Mark slaps Craig's leg, calling his name again. Craig opens his eyes. They're bloodshot.

"What happened?"

Craig takes a few moments to adjust his vision.

"What happened? How did I . . . ."

"I saw you from downstairs going up with that chick. Knew it was bad news. So I followed."

"Did she?"

"I don't know what she did. When I got up there, she was gone, though."

"Gone?"

"Yeah. Gone."

Mark leans on the wall. "How long was I in there?"

"I guess from when I first saw you going up there to the time I got to the room, maybe ten minutes. Then the cops raided the place."

Mark stares at him.

"They moved quickly, taking down everyone they could. For a few minutes, we were stuck in the room."

"Because I was knocked out."

"No. Actually, you seemed somewhat alert. Well, as alert as you could have been. You kept asking about Jade and where she went, and . . . ."

"And what?"

"You kept talking about the fun time you were about to have with her."

Mark looks away, slightly embarrassed.

"So how did we get out?"

"We had some help." Craig stares at Mark. "One of the cops told me he spoke with you earlier and was hoping you would have been gone by then. He arrested us, but brought us here."

"That's it?"

"What else would there be?"

Mark starts to pace back and forth. "You knew nothing about the party. Your contact didn't tell you anything about what happens in there or anything like that?"

"He gave me what information he had."

"He held nothing back?"

"Nothing. What are you getting at?"

"Nothing." Mark shakes his head. "Nothing. What did we find out about Jade?"

"That she wasn't there."

The phone rings. Mark grabs it and picks it up, at least to stop the ringing from making his monster headache worse.

"Mark, it's Simms."

"Was she there? Any leads?"

"Are you still in your home?"

"Yeah."

"I will be over in a few. There are some things we need to discuss."

"Okay. Fine."

Mark gets off the phone and looks toward where Craig was sitting, but doesn't see Craig himself.

"Craig."

Mark walks to the front door to see Craig making his way out.

"What's going on, man?"

"I gotta get out of here. It isn't the best idea to sit in the same room with a detective . . . given the circumstances."

"Was it all for nothing?"

Craig shrugs his shoulders. "We had to know. Right?"

"But we found nothing . . . and almost got killed."

"Look, I told you from the start our chances were slim."

"I know, but . . . ." Mark begins to pace back and forth.

"We'll find her. I'm going to hit up some other people to see what they can find. But, I should really get out of here. I don't want to run into that detective again. The ride home was awkward enough."

Mark nods rapidly. "I'll let you know what happens."

Craig gives Mark an informal, relaxed salute and heads to his car.

Mark sits in the living room after having cleaned himself up, staring at a picture of him and Jade. He hears the doorbell ring and eagerly answers the door. Detective Simms looks worn, beaten almost. Mark allows him in.

"What did you find?" Mark asks.

"Wait. Hold on a second. I need to know something. How did you find yourself at that party?"

"What? That's not important right now."

"It is." Simms raises his voice. "I'm trying to find your wife and you're in my way. I don't need another missing persons case. You could have been killed in there. Don't you get it? Those people, all of them, would have shot you dead right there and not thought another thing about it."

"Well, what do you expect me to do? Sit here and wait?"

"Yes. That is what you are supposed to do. Allow the trained, experienced professionals to do what they do. It's simple. Nothing hard about it. Look, I need to know how you got into that party."

"I had an invite. It's that simple."

"And your friend?"

"Same thing."

"How did you get those invites?"

Mark looks away. "Instead of questioning me, you ought to be looking for my wife. As far as the invites go, you may as well forget about it because I'm not telling you."

"You know I can easily arrest you for this."

"Then do it. Arrest me. Better yet, put a freaking bullet in my head right now. Anything is better than this." Mark heads into the kitchen. Simms follows behind.

Mark grabs a bottle of water and downs it quickly. He grabs another and sits at the island. The whole time Simms observes him.

"We didn't find her. She wasn't there," Simms says.

"What did you find?"

"A woman in his bedroom. Strapped to the wall. Badly beaten."

"Okay."

"Her name is Karen Taylor."

"Jade's assistant when she worked for Raynard. She sold her out for Jade's position."

"She's in intensive care. We planned on questioning her when she was ready."

"You don't sound too excited."

"Well, I think were heading in the wrong direction. None of the pieces connect, and I have a feeling we are looking for the wrong things . . . for the wrong people."

"So what are you saying, Calvin is no longer a suspect?"

"I'm not saying that. I'm just saying after a few hours of questioning him at the station, I don't feel he's our guy."

"He did it. That's what *I* feel."

"Mark, we are able to dig into his life like never before, primarily because Daddy Dearest isn't bailing his behind out anymore. At least, that's what it seems."

"How do you know?"

Simms smiles. "He tried to call his lawyer. No answer. Then he called his fake daddy and they had a short five-minute conversation that left Calvin looking like he's seen a ghost. My guess is that he's been cut off. Too many incidents. Too many cover-ups. Too much money. So he's on his own. But anyway, the more information we got, the less it seemed like he was even involved."

"What about Daddy Dearest?"

"No motive."

"They are supposed to pay Jade a severance."

"That's too small-time to him. Plus he wouldn't risk the exposure. That's pretty much why he's paying the severance in the first place and why he cut Calvin off."

"I don't get it."

"Well, think about it. Why would a shady character like that want people linking any crime to his company? Why would he want anyone talking about one of his companies? In the celebrity world, that kind of exposure gets you trending, which gets you money. In this case, though, you lose money, then you lose your life."

Mark lets the thought settle in. He takes another giant gulp of water. "Anything on Alicia?"

"Nothing. She's back in Philly living with her cousin. At the time of Jade's disappearance, she was seen by many in the local market, shopping. She's stayed low since getting out. Presumably trying to get herself together. Understandable given the circumstances."

Mark winces. "So where does that leave us?"

"Well, that's what I came here to discuss with you. We need to go over our options because . . . ." Simms pauses and looks as if he is trying to find the right words.

"Just say it."

"At this point, the trail is cold. We won't be able to apply so much of our resources to finding her."

"So you're telling me you're giving up soon."

"I'm telling you we will have to assume she's dead."

Mark says nothing.

"At this point, we are sending information out to the media to see if anyone has seen her recently."

I just can't stay out of the news. "And?"

"I'll be looking around for some other leads. I'm going to dig a bit more into Alicia, but as it stands, there's nothing to find."

Mark says nothing.

"I'll send a patrol car around periodically to make sure everything is okay."

Mark nods, but he knows that the patrol isn't directly for his safety in his home, but rather to keep tabs on him.

"What about that woman . . . the one I was in the room with?"

"Carmen Tulipolo. She runs a few small-time businesses, if that's what you want to call it."

"Like what?"

"She does a little bit of everything. Drugs, prostitutes . . . murder for hire."

"Why isn't she in jail?"

"Well, she would have been if you weren't locked up in a room with her."

Mark looks down. "Look, I apologize for getting in the way. It's just . . . ."

"It's hard, I know. But I'm doing everything in my power to get your wife back. Believe me, I am."

Mark nods. "Thanks for getting me out of there. I owe you one."

Simms shakes his head. "Call it even."

"I don't see how it is."

"Don't worry about it. For now, get your rest." He heads toward the door. "We'll be in touch. I'll see myself out."

Mark waits until he hears the front door click before he calls Craig to discuss the next steps in finding Jade.

CHAPTER THIRTY FIVE

IN the corner of a dark room, she sits, curled up in a ball, praying. She hasn't seen the light of day in quite some time. How much time, she is unable to determine. All she knows is that she desperately wants to be home with her family. She screams for help, for what feels like the thousandth time, but again, her screams go unnoticed. In fact, it feels like the sounds of her voice don't go any farther than a few inches from her face, the air is so thick. She slowly shuffles her feet along the wooden floor to attempt to stand, but she finds that her screaming took a good deal of energy out of her. She doesn't remember the last time she ate. It could have been a day ago, maybe two. She remembers hearing heavy but muffled footsteps along the floor and smelling fast food. A bag was thrown in front of her, and the muffled footsteps moved away. She tore through the food in an instant.

Jade makes another attempt to stand up, using the walls in the corner for support, but slides right back down. A couple days ago, or was it a couple hours ago, she walked along the perimeter of the room. Then, she crawled along the floors at its center, getting splinters and scratches from nails that weren't driven properly into the wood. The only thing she found was a sink and toilet in the far corner of the room. Neither ran any water. Other than those two things, the room is completely empty.

She feels something crawling on her arm and shakes it off. The sudden urge to cry overtakes her as she weeps into her arms. She asks God why. She asks Him what she has done to deserve this, and then she apologizes for whatever that thing may be. She constantly thinks of Mark and the kids. She misses them dearly, and would give anything to be back with them. A feeling of dread washes over her, for she doesn't know of their condition, either. She prays for their safety.

"You pray like there's someone there to answer."

Jade snaps her head up, hearing a voice other than her own for the first time in a long time. She didn't realize there was another person in the room with her.

"And those tears . . . those tears get you nowhere. Those tears are a weakness."

That voice.

"Who are you?" Jade asks.

"No matter how much I cried, no matter how much I prayed, I still found myself in total darkness, not much unlike you right now."

Jade hears feet shuffling from the opposite direction of the voice. She slowly presses herself to her feet, using the wall for support. "Why are you doing this?"

"Do you feel it? With each passing second it squeezes, choking you. It feels like this heavy burden that no one can lighten. Yet what you feel is only a sliver of what I felt. There is no way you could fathom the pain I went through each and every day, knowing the things I held closest to my heart were ripped away from me unjustly."

Jade's blood runs cold as she realizes just who she is talking to. She hears the footsteps getting closer, accompanied by heavy breathing.

"But there is a time soon approaching, when everyone will realize what they have done, and you . . . . ."

Jade feels a grip around her arm, then a grip around her neck, choking her. She screams but a large hand covers her face, suffocating her.

"As your life flashes before your eyes . . . ."

Jade struggles mightily to breathe and begins to gag.

"As you draw your last breath, you will be left with nothing but regret."

Jade flails against the larger figure choking her.

"Let her go."

Jade's assailant releases her and she falls to the floor, gasping for air.

"See you soon, sweetheart."

Jade faintly hears the footsteps moving away from her, then the creaking of the door as she gasps for air.

Chapter Thirty Six

BERTA has remained in bed for the day. Last night she was terribly lonely, having kicked Craig out. But she knows she would rather be alone than with him and his lies. She hasn't eaten much and feels weak because of it. When she finally does decide to get out the bed, her body groans in protest. Despite the difficult time in getting up and moving around, Berta does so because she, for the first time since her tainted past was revealed, sees with a bit of clarity. There are some choices she must make and they haven't been so clear as they are now at this moment. She moves in jerking motions, like a robot, or like a person who has little energy would do, but she eventually gets into the shower and cleans up.

After the shower, she gets to the kitchen to grab a bite to eat. Part of her is tempted to turn the entire condo upside down in search of more dirt on Craig, but she figures that to be a waste of energy. Plus, what she already knows is enough . . . enough for her to make a solid decision. She goes through her rolodex of business cards and gets to Lockram-Ramses-Peterson, a law firm that supported her, Craig, and Raul throughout the years. She pauses at a thought, but quickly shakes it off. She gives them a call to get the receptionist.

"Hello. Is Mr. Ramses in today?"

"May I ask who's speaking?"

"Alberta."

Long pause. Berta hesitates because she can no longer bring herself to say her last name, married or maiden.

"I'm sorry, you said Alberta? I didn't hear your last name."

"I didn't give you one. Look, I'm not trying to be any trouble, so can you do me this favor?"

"I suppose." The receptionist sounds annoyed.

"If Mr. Ramses is in today, please just let him know Raul's daughter is on the line. He will pick it up. If not, can you let him know I called?"

"Raul's daughter, Alberta?"

"Yes."

"Please hold."

Berta waits on the line for some time and starts to fall asleep to the elevator-like music that plays over the phone. A deep and gravelly voice says hello a few times before she comes to.

"I'm sorry. Mr. Ramses?"

"Alberta! How are you? How's Craig?"

"We are fine, sir. Listen, I need to meet up with you."

"Oh, sure, how's next week?"

"No. Won't do. I need to meet up with you now."

"Is . . . everything okay?"

"Yes. No. Yes. Look, it's just very important. I need your help."

Mr. Ramses pauses. "Come now. Tell the receptionist at the front desk you have a meeting with me. She'll show you right up."

"Thank you, Mr. Ramses. I will see you soon."

Berta hangs up and starts to grab her things when that thought creeps into her mind again. For the second time, she shakes it off, fearing she's just being paranoid.

Berta gets to the large skyscraper that is in the middle of the city, not too far from where Craig works. She gets to the lobby and reads a directory that's posted on the wall. She then heads to the 49th floor where she sees the receptionist.

"Hi, I'm Alberta. I have a meeting with Mr. Ramses."

The woman wearing glasses eyeballs Berta for a few moments, then gets up from her seat. "Follow me," she says.

Berta follows her to another set of elevators that takes them a few floors up. The woman leads the way through a floor of cubicles and offices until they get to a set of double doors. She knocks and pokes her head in before letting Berta through. Berta hears mumbling, not able to hear any distinct words. The receptionist pulls her head back out and opens the door to let Berta in.

"Alberta." A heavyset man places his arms out as to give Berta a hug.

The receptionist gently closes the door behind her.

"Mr. Ramses. It has been a long time."

"It has. Too long, my sweet. Please, take a seat."

He directs Berta to a seat. His office consists of heavy woods, books, and a fireplace, making his office look more like a hotel suite than a place of work. Berta sits in a seat in front of a huge Mahogany desk. Mr. Ramses sits in a brown leather executive chair that groans under his weight.

"I know it may be an alarm for me to call and ask to meet on such short notice."

"Oh, no. It is no big deal. If anything, this is a pleasant surprise, to be visited by the most beautiful woman in the world, next to my wife, of course."

Berta smiles. "I'm flattered." Her smile turns to a frown. "But I fear what I am about to ask you isn't as flattering."

"Is everything okay?"

"It will be, Mr. Ramses." She pauses. For a third time, she thinks about what she now feels her intuition is telling her. She stares plainly at Mr. Ramses.

"Tell me something . . . ." Berta leans in. "Were you part of Daddy's network?"

"Of course. I was Raul's lawyer and friend for years."

"No. I don't think you understand what I'm asking." She shakes her head vigorously. "I'm asking if you were part of his network. The one few know about."

"I'm sorry, Alberta. I don't know what you are talking about."

Berta stares at Mr. Ramses with a cold yet intense stare. "Mr. Ramses, I know about Raul's second life."

Mr. Ramses doesn't move, but Berta can tell what she said registered.

"That's the first time I heard you call him Raul." He breaks Berta's gaze. "Look, I don't know what exactly you are looking for, but please let me advise you before we proceed any further. Nothing good can come of this, this digging up the past."

"Well, if you ask my mother, she'd say the complete opposite."

"You talked to Izabel?"

"I was talking to her for a few weeks. You see, I understand you when you say nothing good can come of digging around in the past. Nothing good came from me and mine. But nothing good can come of being completely oblivious to it, either." She taps the arm of her chair. "Look, I'm not here to get into a philosophical debate. I'm here for very specific reasons. I need your help."

Mr. Ramses sighs. "What do you need?"

"First, answer my question. Were you a part of Raul's network?"

"I was."

"So you were the legal guy that kept him covered when needed."

Mr. Ramses nods. "One of many."

"Were you the same for Courtland?"

"No. Never. I would never work with such scum."

"So you knew about his deals?"

"Some of them."

"Did you know of the one that involved me?"

"I did."

Berta nods.

"I'm assuming you know about the deal that involved you as well?" Mr. Ramses asks.

"I do."

"I'm sorry. May I ask how you found out?"

Thinking of Marcella and Jennifer, Berta says, "I can't tell you. For their sakes."

"I understand." He moves in his seat.

"Are you a part of the group that is supposed to ensure mine and Craig's safety?"

"Until the day I die."

"And you knew about Craig and the path he was headed down?"

"Yes."

"Do you know about his actions now?"

Mr. Ramses give a blank stare.

"He got in with one of his old contacts. But as far as you know, he was on the up-and-up until now."

"Yes. Is he in any trouble?"

"With me, yes. With anyone else, I don't know." Berta goes into her purse and pulls out a picture. "I believe he did it for her." She places the picture flat on his desk.

"Who is she?"

"She's the best friend I have right now. Possibly the only friend I have, and she's gone missing some odd days ago. "Her name is Jade Cooke. She's a great wife and a mother of three. I need you to find her."

"Alberta, I can't do this. I cannot get involved."

"But you can be part of a group that pulled the wool over my eyes? Made everything seem like roses when it was really garbage? You want to help me? Find her."

"That's not how this works."

"What? I need money? How much?"

"It's not about money, and I would never take your money anyway."

"Then what is it?"

"We are to ensure your safety. We are to ensure Craig's safety. We are to make sure that neither one of you steps into what Raul called a downward spiral into hell itself. That's it. I understand that you are angry, but we don't get involved in matters of that kind. It's too messy and it threatens to do more harm than good."

"So what you are telling me is that you won't help."

Mr. Ramses takes a deep breath. "No, what I am saying is that we can't help. Even if we wanted to, which I do, we can't make a move. I'm sorry."

Berta looks at Mr. Ramses, angry. "Fine. I have a request . . . and I don't want you talking me out of it."

"Okay."

"It has to do with Craig."

"I already planned on having a talk with him . . . maybe knock a little sense into him."

"No. Don't do it."

"Don't talk to him?" He gives a perplexed look.

"Don't. I . . . Just hear me out."

❦

Craig sits at his desk at work, long after Ted has gone. He scours paper after paper, throwing himself into his work to avoid the real world for a moment. His desk light is the only light in the office, only illuminating the papers on his desk and nothing more. His cell phone rings and he sees it's Mr. Ramses. He frowns but picks it up.

"Hey, Mr. Ramses. Everything . . . okay?"

"Where are you right now, Craig?" His voice comes out strained and tired.

"I'm in the office. Why?"

"I'll be there in five."

The phone clicks.

Craig twists his face in confusion and starts to straighten out the office. He cuts the lights on and starts cleaning off the couch of his clothes and a blanket.

"So, what, are you sleeping here now?"

Craig turns around to see Mr. Ramses at the door in a dark trench coat.

"You said five minutes. That was barely thirty seconds."

"It's good to see you, too, Craig. Me, I'm fine. Things are well. Janice is fine. The kids are fine."

"I'm sorry, Mr. Ramses." Craig walks over to him and shakes his hand. "How have you been?"

"Well, from the looks of it, a lot better than you have been."

"Yeah. Work is piling up. Everyone has something going on. Life happens, you know?"

"I suppose. Listen, sit down for a second." Mr. Ramses motions toward the couch that is covered with clothes. Craig sits and he brings up a chair to sit in front of him. For a few moments, he stares at him. "What's going on with you, kid?"

"What do you mean?"

"I mean I heard you've been running with some old . . . friends."

Craig makes a confused face. "Who told you that?"

"Is it true?"

Craig looks at Mr. Ramses. "Yeah."

"Who?"

"Lupo."

Mr. Ramses nods. "Why?"

"A friend has gone missing. I needed information fast. I knew he could get it."

"And there are no other motivations involved?"

"No."

"So this friend . . . they must be pretty important for you to go back to your old ways."

"She's my best friend's wife. And I didn't go back to my old ways."

"Why didn't you come to me, then?"

Craig pauses. "I don't know. Would you have helped?"

"I would have."

"Well, help me now. We can easily—"

"Craig, look at me."

Craig looks Mr. Ramses in the eyes.

"We cannot help you now. You already tipped the playing field."

"What do you mean?"

"Are you back in your old circles?"

"No." Craig stands up. "I couldn't do that to Mr. V. I couldn't do that to Berta."

"Well there's some information going around that says you are . . . and we can't have that. What we do is all about finesse. Only the bare minimum of people knows when we are involved. By contacting Lupo, you changed what people know, thereby changing how we would look in the situation. I cannot convince the others to step into this . . . mess. Why didn't you come to me first? Why go to your old righthand man? Of all people to go to, why him?"

Craig starts pacing. "My friend asked me to. Time is of the essence. Nothing more. I went to Lupo because I figured you wouldn't help. Plus, the amount of red tape you have to cut through before you get the slightest bit of info . . . it was just faster doing things myself."

Mr. Ramses watches Craig as he paces the floor. "You still have contact with him now?"

"Yeah."

"Cut all ties, immediately."

"I can't."

Mr. Ramses shakes his head. "You're forcing my hand, kid."

"I'm sorry, but I have to do this."

Mr. Ramses nods but says nothing more on the topic. "Alberta visited me today."

"Okay."

"She asked me about things in the past and more or less forced me into something."

"Forced you? Forced you to do what?"

Mr. Ramses nods. "Craig, sit down. There's something I have to tell you."

Craig walks back to the couch. "What's going on?"

"There's something you need to know. I was told not to talk to you about this and there is no real way of saying it without saying it straightforward."

Craig looks confused.

"Alberta mentioned a couple things in our conversation today."

"She's been under a lot of stress lately and—"

"She filed for divorce."

Craig stops mid-sentence, his mouth hanging open slightly.

"I'm sorry. She came in and . . . she was upset. She *is* upset; upset at Raul, me, you—"

"This is all about her past."

"And she asked for a divorce attorney."

Craig still looks stunned.

"You should be getting the papers soon."

"I . . . I don't get it. I mean, my job, my goal, my *purpose*, was to take care of her. To protect her. To love her. I made it . . . my purpose."

"I know, Craig."

"No. It's not going down like this. All because I didn't tell her a part of her past everyone would rather forget?"

"You have to be a bit more sympathetic than that. Put yourself in her shoes. We all insulated her as much as possible from her own past.

She feels betrayed by us. There were things we kept from her, and even though we had the best of intentions, we altered things for most of her adult life. And for her to find out that her husband was in on it. Her world is flipped on its head."

Craig slams the arm of the couch. "In on it? I was in on nothing. I didn't get any mandate to look after her. I looked after her because I love her."

"I understand. But sometimes our actions don't translate well to others . . . especially in light of who we were."

"Who we were? I was never really *that* person. I wasn't like you. I wasn't like Mr. V. I got into that stuff because I was still looking. I was still looking for a reason to live, a reason to get up in the morning."

"If that were the case, why did you go back?"

Craig remains silent.

After a few more moments of silence Mr. Ramses gets up to leave. Craig lets him leave without saying another word.

Eventually, Craig moves and gets up to leave the office. He grabs a duffel bag and stuffs it with his dirty clothes. He gets to his car, the only one in the garage, and throws his stuff in. When he pulls off, his tires screech and leave tire marks along the garage floor.

After an hour or so, he gets home and rushes in. He flips the switch and heads straight to the bedroom . . . then the bathroom . . . then the other bedrooms. He searches the entire home but doesn't find Berta anywhere. He wonders where she could be this late at night. The entire place looks like it has been cleaned recently. He goes back to the master suite and searches again. This time, he notices something different. It's subtle, but painfully obvious to him. He checks the other bedrooms, then goes out to the living room. He rubs his growing beard for a few moments before chuckling.

"She took down all the pictures of us."

Craig walks to the kitchen to sift through the trash. Lo and behold, broken frames and ripped pictures fill the bag. Kneeling at the bag, he pulls out a piece of the picture they took on their honeymoon. As he stares at the fragment of what seems to be his past life, keys jangle at the door. He slides the piece of the picture into his pocket and stands.

Berta opens the door and stands in the doorway, her face showing signs of shock. She shakes her head and walks in, gently shutting the front door.

"What are you doing here?" she asks.

"This is home . . . isn't it?"

"I told you to leave. I told you not to come back. I was very clear."

"Can we talk?"

"What is there to talk about? I'm done talking. It's late, and you should go."

"There's a lot we need to discuss. Mr. Ramses visited me tonight."

Berta stares at Craig for a few moments before rolling her eyes. "He told you, didn't he?"

"What were you going to do? Have someone serve me the papers and I just play right along? I feel like you're throwing me out and I have no idea why."

"You have no idea? I told you why."

"Let's just talk about this."

"I don't want to talk." Berta raises her voice. "I want you to get out. Get out now." She throws her keys onto the table and walks toward Craig.

"No. Not until we talk."

Berta goes behind Craig and pushes him toward the door. At first Craig remains calm, but on the third push, Craig flips around and grabs Berta's hands.

"Stop. Just stop for a second."

"Hit me."

"What?"

"Hit me. Isn't that what people like you do?" Berta stares at Craig with as much disdain as she can muster.

He lets go of her hands. "People like me? What do you mean people like me?"

Berta doesn't say anything and stares at Craig.

"Okay. I get it. You're mad. I understand that much. But don't let your anger get in the way of sound judgment. You know who I am. You more than anyone else know what I'm about. You know I'm not one of them. Everything we are talking about now is old. It's the past. You filed for divorce over something that happened years ago?"

Berta looks away from Craig as if she is thinking of something else. She takes a few steps back. "You know why I filed? I filed because I realized this isn't going to work. It hasn't worked and . . . and . . . I'm tired. I'm tired of trying to make something work that, in the back of my mind, I know won't. We're forcing it, but we were scared to admit it to the other." Berta smirks. "We had problems before I found out about your lies. We had numerous problems. We . . . ." She motions back and forth between her and Craig. "We simply don't fit. Yet, I was willing to force it to fit based on a silly promise I made to a man who lied to me as well. Every major male figure in my life has lied to me, in one way, shape, or form. Every one. My biological father, Raul, you. You are all the same. So please don't misinterpret what I say when I say that you are just like them. I'm not *just* saying that you are a criminal . . . a thug. I'm saying you are a liar. You are a deceiver." She sits at the dining room table. "And I want no part of it. I'm not their puppet. I'm no longer yours."

Craig stands in the middle of the floor, motionless. He feels a sinking feeling and a burning sensation in the pit of his stomach. "So that's it?"

Berta shrugs her shoulders. "I hope you find happiness in the path you choose."

Craig shakes his head and stares at Berta and her carefree demeanor. He is completely confused and wonders if she is hiding the same pain he feels at the moment. *Does she feel like she's drowning? Does she feel like she is suffocating under the weight of the world that has just dropped on her shoulders?* He shakes his head again. "Do you still love me?"

Berta winces. She considers the question, then says, "I loved the man I thought I knew. The man that stands before me is . . . different."

"That doesn't answer my question." Craig's voice becomes stern. "Do you still love me?"

Berta looks Craig in the eyes with a blank stare. "No."

For a few seconds, Craig stops breathing. He nods a few times and looks at his hands. He looks at his wedding ring and slowly pulls it off his finger. He walks over to the dining room table and slams the ring down. He goes to the back rooms and comes back out a few minutes later with suitcases. He doesn't look her way and leaves what was once their home.

CHAPTER THIRTY SEVEN

CRAIG gets his car packed up and sits inside, trying to grasp everything that just happened. He starts the car and drives to a hotel. On the way, he contends with a number of bouts of crying. When he finally makes it into the hotel room, he collapses onto the bed and stares at the ceiling. The pain he feels now is dull, but it's nagging. After a few hours of lying there, he realizes it's five in the morning, and tries to go to sleep. It takes a couple more hours for him to realize he isn't going to get any sleep any time soon, so he gets up and takes a shower. He tries to refocus. There are clear goals in front of him. First, help Mark find Jade. He grabs his phone and calls Lupo. And when Lupo picks up, it's all business.

"What did you dig up?"

Long pause.

"I've got nothing."

"What the hell do you mean you have nothing?"

"Trail's cold. Everything is silent."

"That's not acceptable. I need something in a few hours. No excuses."

"You think it's that easy? Look, I'm telling you there's nothing out there. If there was some bit of information to get to you, you know I would find it. There is nothing out there."

"For as many jobs as we have done . . . for as long as I've known you . . . how many times has the trail gone cold? How many times was there no information to pick up?"

"None."

"So you're telling me this is the first?"

"I hate to . . . but yes. People are keeping their mouths shut about this . . . or there's really nothing to say."

"Meaning?"

"The person you are looking for is gone."

"Unacceptable. Keep looking. I'm on this full-time so let me know if anything pops up."

"Will do."

Craig hangs up the phone and sits on the edge of the bed in his bath towel. He looks at his briefcase and pops it open. From one of the slots stitched to the inside, he pulls out a card with a number. He dials it. It doesn't take long for someone to answer.

"I didn't think you were going to call."

Craig rubs the back of his neck. "Yeah. Well, I could really use a friend right now. A friend who understands what I'm going through right now."

"Is everything okay?"

"Naw. Not at all."

"What's up?"

"My friend's wife . . . she's missing."

"Missing?"

"Yeah. There's a huge search going on for her, but no one has anything yet."

"I'm sorry."

"And then there's my wife . . . she wants a divorce."

"I'm sorry to hear that as well."

"And I figured, since you went through one . . . maybe you had some pointers . . . maybe you would understand how crappy this feels."

"Well, I do understand how crappy it feels, but I don't have much in the way of pointers. Remember, you were helping me."

"Yeah."

"But I can listen."

Craig sighs.

"Craig?"

"Yeah. I'm here. I just . . . I don't understand. My life was one thing one day, and just like that, everything changes."

"The more likely scenario is that things were always changing and you didn't notice it."

"I guess. I'm just under a lot of stress right now."

"Listen, why don't I come up there and we could talk in person."

"No can do. I have some other things going on up here . . . important things."

She pauses. "Hiding much?"

"Look, there's a lot you don't know about me."

"As there is a lot you don't know about me."

"Patrice."

"Okay, okay. I'm listening. Get it off your chest."

"I still love her."

"Of course you will. She is or was your wife. There obviously were some good times somewhere for that to happen."

"But how is it that she says she doesn't love me anymore?"

"She's lying."

"She looked completely sure of herself, and given the circumstances, I am leaning towards her truly feeling that."

"What happened?"

"I can't say."

"O-kay. Craig, how do you expect to me to help if I don't know what's going on?"

"I guess I really don't expect you to help."

"So why did you call?"

Craig stays silent, unable to say anything. He feels a burning in his chest, but he feels Patrice understands what he is trying to say.

"I see," she whispers. "Why don't you come down here. I'll get you a flight first thing in the morning."

"I can't. I'm . . . still married. Look, I'm sorry. I shouldn't have called. It was a jump decision . . . and . . . and . . . ."

"It's okay. Actually, it's good just to hear your voice."

"I'm sorry. I'm totally wrong here. I gotta go."

Craig hangs up. He lies back on the bed, gripping his phone with one hand, and slapping himself in the face with the other. He knows exactly what he called for, and it wasn't to discuss divorce. He again forces himself to refocus. He gets dressed and heads out the door.

CHAPTER THIRTY EIGHT

AFTER a sleepless night, Mark tries to prepare himself for another day of waiting. He tries to keep busy, but every so often, he catches himself just staring off into space, thinking about Jade. He tries to muster the fortitude to call Jade's mother to talk to the kids, but he fears he would just break down in tears, and that would do nothing but scare them. Hearing his name snaps him out of his daze. He walks to the TV and turns the volume up. He sees Jade's picture and the word "missing" under it plastered all over the early morning news. The news report talks of who she is and how long she's been missing. The reporter asks if anyone has any information on her whereabouts to contact the police. Mark turns the TV off.

Within the next ten minutes, Mark's phone starts getting calls. The house phone starts to ring off the hook. Mark ignores all the calls, every single last one of them, and continues on trying to be busy. Eventually, he sits down and starts going through the call logs on the phones. Pastor Brentwood, a bunch of church folk, and a few friends of Jade all called and left messages trying to comprehend what they just saw or heard on the news. Then, he sees on his cell phone log three missed calls from that restricted number. He doesn't recall knowing anyone with a restricted number, at least no one who wouldn't leave a message, so he starts to wonder. He always brushed it off as some slimeball bill collector, but what if that isn't the case? Mark puts his phone down, and as soon as he does, it rings again. He glances at it to see Pastor Brentwood's name again. He still doesn't pick up. Instead, he leaves the phone sitting on the coffee table and leaves the room and goes upstairs.

He goes to the bedroom and to Jade's dresser. On top of the dresser are pictures of him and her at various times in their lives. He stares at them, longing to have her back. He then pops open the top drawer and searches through it, attempting to somehow feel her through her clothes. Nothing he does works, though, and he slams the drawer shut. He makes another attempt to pray, as he has made numerous ones throughout the morning, but comes up with nothing. He finds it difficult to say anything because in part, he is mad at God. Each morning, he prays for protection. Each morning he reads in his Bible places where God takes care of, protects, and blesses those who serve Him. Mark is at a loss as to why this happened to his family. Why this happened to Jade. They serve Him in every way possible. So, why . . . .

Mark shakes his head, unable to bear the thought of God for some reason abandoning him and his family. He heads back downstairs to grab something to drink when he hears his phone ringing again. He looks to see the restricted number and immediately picks it up.

"Mark?"

"Yeah."

"I just saw on the news what's been going on. Are you alright?" A woman's voice.

"I'm . . . who is this?"

"Mark, Baby, you don't recognize my voice?"

"Baby? Look, whoever this is, stop playing games. Don't call this number again."

"Oh, I'm sure if you think hard enough you can remember who I am. And believe me, this isn't a game."

Mark listens to the woman's voice. He has an idea of who it is, but he can't believe it. He needs more confirmation.

"So what do you want?" he asks.

"I want to meet up."

"For what?" He fears the hesitancy in his voice betrays him.

She laughs. "You're still trying to figure out who this is, aren't you? That's a shame, Mark. I know it's been a while, but I would think you would always remember your first love."

"Alicia." Mark's stomach sinks.

"The one and only, Love."

"How low can you get? Jade is missing, and you call to swoop right in."

"Well, how low can *you* go, sending a single mother to jail for a made-up reason, ruining her life. And as a matter of fact, *we've* been calling you. On a number of occasions. And how dumb of you not to change your number."

"Look, I don't have time for you."

"Well, I suggest you make time. What I have to say can benefit you . . . or end you."

"Listen, I know what you are trying to do. Like I said, I don't have time for you. We didn't work out before. We will never work out. Own up to what you did, get a life, and move on."

Alicia laughs. "Mark, I don't want you."

"Then what the hell do you want?"

"I told you I want to meet up."

"No."

"Okay. So it sounds like you need a bit of motivation."

Mark hears rustling, then Alicia telling someone it's him on the line.

"Mark?" her voice comes out soft, scared almost, but he knows who it is.

"Jade. Jade, Baby, are you okay?"

"Mark, please . . . please get me." She starts to cry. "Please find me. Please."

"Jade."

Alicia takes the phone back. Then Mark hears Jade's screams. Then her screams being muffled.

"Okay, so I will text you where to go," Alicia says. "And keep this one quiet. Lord knows what I'll do to her if you don't."

Mark's breathing becomes heavy. Then, from the pit of his stomach, he releases a scream into the phone, in which afterwards, there's a long pause.

"Awww, Mark." Alicia says in a menacing tone. "I missed you, too."

The phone clicks.

A few moments later, Mark gets a text. He grabs a jacket and dashes out the house.

After a half hour of nerve-racking driving, Mark gets to the address given to him by Alicia, a small coffee shop on a street full of small shops, and parks the car. He checks the address again before getting out the car. He's never been to the area before, this small village-like town. People walk the streets carrying bags, talking, laughing, kids playing. He curiously walks to the coffee shop, dodging around people, excusing himself out of their way, and places his hand on the golden doorknob to open the door. As soon as he opens the door, the smells of fresh coffee and just-baked pastries rush his nose. His stomach growls. He visually sweeps the crowded shop, but doesn't find Alicia, so he gets in line and buys a fresh apple pastry and a cup of vanilla chai tea. He looks around again to find somewhere to sit.

"Are you Mark?" the cashier asks.

Mark hesitates, but answers still. "Yeah."

"Upstairs . . . by the window."

Mark looks around for a staircase but finds nothing. He looks at the cashier again.

"To my left. Around the other side of the counter."

Mark looks at a small doorway, presumably leading to the upper level. The cashier stares at him blankly. He moves out the way, realizing he's holding up the line. He walks to the doorway directly to a staircase and goes up the steps. Once he gets to the upper level, he sees more tables and more people, though not as many as there are downstairs. He looks straight ahead and sitting on a stool at a table by the large front window is Alicia. She stares out the window, seemingly daydreaming. Mark gets nervous, but trudges onward. He doesn't say anything, and sits on the opposite side of the small table, in front of her. She still doesn't move her gaze from window. Mark looks outside and sees his car. He realizes she saw him come in. Then Mark sees something that makes him even more nervous. The patrol car that sits outside his home on Detective Simms' orders cruises by, going slower at his car. Mark tenses, hoping Alicia doesn't pay the car any mind. He turns back to Alicia, who still stares out the window. She snaps her glance to him, but doesn't say anything.

They stare at each other, not saying a word, still taking each other in. Mark finds that she mostly looks the same, though the bags under her eyes are a bit heavier than he last remembered. Her hair is shorter, her face slimmer, but other than those things, she is the same.

"So much for that restraining order." She smirks. "Part of me wishes it was good to see you."

Mark takes a sip of his tea. "I'm not sure what you want me to say to that."

"I suppose there's nothing to say."

"Where's Jade?"

Alicia shakes her head. Mark notices she has a scar on her neck she hides well.

"I will tell you . . . when I get what I want."

"And what is that?"

"Justice."

Mark looks at her strangely. "I don't know what you mean."

"You know exactly what I mean. You know I wasn't abusing Timothy. You know I went to jail for no reason."

"I don't know that. As far I saw, it was obvious, I just didn't look at the signs because . . . ."

"Go on."

"Because I was caught up."

Alicia rolls her eyes and looks out the window again. "Jacob has good lawyers. They knew at any hint of me seeming unfit, they could get my Timothy away from me. And you . . . you testifying played right into their hands."

"I did what I thought was right."

"Or did you do whatever you could to get me away from you?"

"I told you what I did. I'm not debating the point."

"I'm not asking for a debate." She shakes her head. "Do you know what it's like in there? Especially for a person who was unjustly thrown in there to rot? Do you know what was taken from me?"

Mark says nothing.

"You will soon find out."

"What does that mean?"

"It means that you, along with others, will feel my pain."

"Is that justice?"

"Yes. For me, it is."

"So you're hurt, and you turn that to hurt others?"

"I hear a bit of judgment in your voice. What you seem to have a hard time understanding is that everything was taken from me. Everything. My house, my car, my job, my dignity, my self-worth . . . my child, all were taken from me. Everyone involved is going to feel that one way or the other, that feeling of hopelessness due to loss." She takes a breath. "Then I'm going to set things straight."

Mark takes another nervous sip of his tea. "You want me to feel pain? That's all I've felt for the past week. Pain. My family is broken . . . and for the second time, it's because of you."

"Because of me? Still to this day you can't own up to your mistakes." She chuckles. "You're in pain right now . . . and it's been only a week? Try fourteen months."

Mark becomes impatient. "What is it you want from me?"

"Right now, I want you to listen. Nothing more."

"I'm not playing your little game. I'm going to the police." Mark goes to get up.

"Then you will never see her again."

Mark stops and stares at her.

"Another point you are slow to the draw on is that you don't have a choice in this matter. You *will* do as I say, otherwise bad things will happen to her. You are in no position to make threats. You are in no position to say no. All you can do is hang on to every word I tell you as if I were Christ Himself. So do yourself and your whore wife a huge favor and sit your ass back down."

Mark looks at her. Her face is still but her eyes show intensity, none like he has seen in a person before. He slowly sits back down.

"No cops. And ease up off telling anything to your detective friend."

Mark stays silent.

"Maybe you should order another tea," she says. "We are going to be here a while."

"You wanna hear something funny? I love you, Mark. Even now, I'm thinking how mad I am at you, but if you asked me to run away with you, I would . . . in a heartbeat. And that's a problem for me . . . because there is no way that can happen . . . ever."

Mark still sits in the coffeehouse with Alicia as she talks about the trauma she has gone through over the past couple years. She doesn't speak directly, but everything sounds like it's a riddle, like there is a complete alternative to the understanding Mark has of her words. He was getting even more impatient, but feels like she just threw him a curveball.

"What do you mean, you love me? What you are doing right now isn't love. It's vindictive. It's spiteful. It's . . . evil."

Alicia looks as if she's considering what Mark said. "Like I said, it's justice. All you had to do then was say yes . . . or never lead me on the way you did. I would have left you alone. But you chose the route of ruining my life . . . to keep yours together. So if you want to talk of evil, look in the mirror." She takes a sip of her drink. "But I do love you. It pains me to see you like this . . . over her again. And we could have had such a wonderful life together . . . could have had such beautiful children."

"That's where you are wrong. I am like this, not because of her, but because of what you have done to her. And if . . . ."

Alicia snaps and reaches into her purse to pull out her cell phone (which Mark didn't hear ring).

"Hello . . . yes this is she . . . okay . . . okay . . . I will be there soon, thank you." She hangs up. "Listen, this was fun. We have to do this again sometime." She gets up from the table. "How's tonight sound?"

"What? Wait. Where's Jade?"

"Oh, I'm sorry. We'll have to save that discussion for later. I have some furniture being delivered to my home and I have to be there. You know how it is." She smiles and starts to walk off. She abruptly stops and turns around to give Mark a wink. "Be by your phone, okay, Sweetheart? And put the kiddies to sleep early. You won't want them to hear what we will discuss."

Mark hesitates just long enough for Alicia to get a sizeable head-start out of the coffeehouse. He jumps up and follows her through the upstairs level and back to the crowded downstairs, where he has a bit more difficulty keeping up with her. By the time he sees her leaving, he is still weaving his way to the front door. He finally gets outside and sees, leaning on his car, Detective Simms. Mark looks down the street both ways but doesn't see Alicia. His first thought is to find her; find her, then find Jade.

"Did you see her?" Mark asks.

"I did." Simms gives Mark a smug look.

"Which way did she go?"

"You know Mark, I am a bit perplexed. At one point, the infamous mistress was a possible suspect. Now you are meeting up with her. Even if she weren't a suspect at any point, you meeting up with her as your wife is still missing somewhere . . . ." He shakes his head. "It's not a good look for you, being this far out of town . . . with her. It's almost like you are trying to hide."

"I don't know what you are talking about."

"I think you do. What were you two doing in there?"

"Having coffee." Mark gets in his car with Simms following him. Simms knocks on the window. Mark rolls it down and starts the car.

"Mark, be straight with me. Is there anything you want to tell me?"

Mark is reminded of Alicia's threat to stay away from the detective. For the moment, he will take her seriously. "No."

"Well, a few days ago she was in Philly staying with a cousin. Now, she's here. As if answering a call." He whistles. "Let me ask again . . . just so we are clear. Is there anything you want to tell me?"

"There is nothing to tell. And I would appreciate it if you would stop stalking me and start looking for my wife." He slowly backs the car up and pulls out of the space, leaving Simms staring at him from a distance.

CHAPTER THIRTY NINE

THE rest of Craig's Saturday morning is showing itself to be largely uneventful. He went to the hotel lobby with his laptop to pretend he was doing work, but he just wanted some time to think, and he didn't necessarily want to be by himself. He waited for three hours for Lupo to call, but he never did. Growing more and more impatient, Craig gives him a quick call.

No answer.

Craig looks strangely at the phone as if something is wrong with the phone, then calls again. After many rings, Lupo picks up.

"Look, I got nothing for you."

"What do you mean? This is what you do. You find information. How is this even possible?"

Craig hears the man sigh over the phone. "Look, I've been told to back off."

"What? Who told you to back off, and why on God's green earth would you listen?"

"Ramses."

Craig is shocked at first, but quickly regains his composure. He closes his laptop and starts back to his suite. "Hold on for a second." He leaves the lobby and starts talking again when on the elevator by himself. "You sure it was him?"

"Yeah. I'm sure. He said it was for your own good."

"And you listened to him? I'm confused."

"He threatened to expose some stuff on me. I'm not even supposed to talk to you about this."

"Okay, okay, hold on. Just give me this; what exactly did he say?"

"His exact words: 'Back off or I will bury you.'"

"And his threats hold weight?"

"More than you know. A lot has changed since you left. The game isn't the same as what you last thought it was."

"So you're out?"

"I have to be. Sorry. Listen, it would be best if you never contacted me again. Get rid of this number, as it will no longer get to me."

The phone clicks.

Craig mashes the end button on his phone and grits his teeth. As he gets off the elevator, he scrolls through his contacts list to get to Mr. Ramses and gives him a call. It doesn't take long for his secretary to pick up. He skips the pleasantries and asks for Mr. Ramses right away. The secretary hesitates when she hears it is Craig, but connects him to Mr. Ramses nonetheless.

"Mr. Ramses, please tell me I'm dreaming. Please tell me you didn't contact Lupo to get him to back off."

"I did what needed to be done."

"Who do you think you are?" Craig gets to his suite and slams the door shut.

"I'm doing it for your own good."

"What about the good of my closest friend? What about the good of his wife?"

"The police should be able to handle it."

"What are you trying to keep me from?"

"I'm trying to keep you from . . . you. You're acting on impulse, and in this business you already know what happens to impulsive people. I am supposed to look out for you. I cannot let you go down that road. I'm sorry for your friend and his wife, I truly am, but this is not the way to get her back."

"But do you understand what you are doing? I have to find her. I have to be the one to find her."

"Why?"

"Because I gave up my marriage so my friend can keep his."

"So you're a martyr now?"

"No, that's not what I'm saying. But Berta sees me as someone different and a large part of that is the fact that I still had contact with those I used to run with. If I stop now, if I don't find Jade, I did it all for nothing."

"Look, Craig, I see what you are doing. It's okay to be scared of what's going on as of late, but the solution isn't to revert to a person of the past."

"I'm not scared, and I'm not reverting into anyone. I have one goal in mind and that's to find Jade."

"So you throw yourself into this cause in which you know you are over-matched. You don't have the same resources you had. Look, Alberta is reasonable. Talk to her. I believe you still have a window of opportunity here to make things right. But you can't make things right with guys like Lupo looming around."

"Things aren't going to be right. Don't you get it? We did the counseling, we talked things out, we did what we needed to make things better and they got worse. I need you to take the block off Lupo and let me operate."

"I can't. I can't do that to you. I will not do that to Raul. It's a little disconcerting that you stepped back into that world so easily, despite what Raul clearly outlined to you."

Craig's shoulders slowly slump. "I had no choice."

"There's always a choice. You always have a choice. You make the wrong ones, you pin yourself in a corner. You make the right ones and you have freedom."

"I can do without the life lesson."

"Understandable. But trust me, you are going to thank me for this one day."

"At least let me help out somehow. I can't just sit here and do nothing."

"You want to help your friend? Encourage him. Let him know everything is going to be alright."

"But how can I tell him that? I don't know that for sure."

"Look, I don't know, Craig. Raul would be better at talking to you about things like this. What would he say?"

Craig hesitates. "Thug Mr. V or Enlightened Mr. V?""

"Enlightened."

"He would tell me to have a little bit of faith."

"Well, have a little bit of faith. Go home to your wife."

"I don't have one."

Craig hangs up the phone without saying another word. He takes a few moments to regain his composure, clutching his phone, dreading the next call he must make. He starts to dial Mark, getting to the fourth number, but in anger ends up launching the phone at the wall.

☙❧

Later in the night, Mark finds himself pacing the floor, thinking of different angles to getting Jade back. After getting back from the coffeehouse, he almost broke down and called the police a number of times, but in the end realized that probably isn't the best idea. He's being forced to stay silent. He tries to watch television but the news report of Jade being missing keeps popping up, so Mark turns it off. Then, his phone rings. Restricted number again. He quickly picks it up.

"Are the kids asleep?"

"The kids aren't here."

"Oooh, even better. Come to the door," she says and hangs up.

He nervously walks to the front door and instead of opening it, he looks out through the side window. He sees Alicia carefully making her way up the driveway in high heels, wearing a short white trench coat that comes to her midthigh. It seems as if she's wearing a short skirt under because all he sees are her bare legs. He looks suspiciously at the bottle of alcohol she carries. Behind her, he sees the patrol cars that drive by his home creeping past. He knows they saw her walking toward the front door and that they likely informed Simms of her presence. He doesn't know that for sure, but it's a gut feeling. He unlocks and opens the front door and pulls her in.

"Hey, Baby," she says cheerily. "I brought a little something for our dinner tonight."

"What? What dinner? And how do you know where I live?"

Alicia looks around and for a moment stops on Mark and Jade's wedding picture. She rolls her eyes and looks at Mark. "I told you I would see you tonight, right?"

"How do you know where I live?"

"Does it matter now? Bottom line is, I'm here . . . and you're not even ready."

Mark stares at her for a second, feeling his temper rising.

"You're not going to show me around?" She sets the bottle down on an end table as she makes her way to the wedding picture she was looking at a few moments ago. Alicia lifts the picture carefully, then throws it against the wall. The frame breaks into tiny pieces.

Mark shields his face from any flying pieces of glass and looks at Alicia in disgust.

"Sorry." She smiles. "It was really bothering me. Anyway, it looks like you already ate, so let's pop the bottle."

"Where is Jade?" Mark raises his voice. "Tell me where my wife is."

"In time. But there are a few things you need to do for me first."

"What things?"

"I need two wine glasses."

Mark stares her in the eyes and Alicia stares back, unflinching. He slowly walks toward the kitchen cabinets to grab the wine glasses. Out the corner of his eye, he sees her shrugging off her trench coat, confirming to Mark that she is wearing a miniskirt. He grabs two wine glasses and hears her movement getting closer behind him. When he turns around, she is right up on him, staring at him. Slowly, she takes the glasses from him and turns around to get the bottle. She walks away as if she's hoping he's watching; as if she's trying to . . . seduce him. She pulls the cork on the bottle and starts to pour two glasses. She stares at him and smiles. Mark notices she looks genuinely happy, as if completely disconnected with what's going on around her, with what she is doing. She pours a dark liquid into the two glasses, then hands one to Mark.

"I figured we would relax a bit before getting to the business at hand."

"Business?"

"Is this pleasurable to you?"

Mark squints, then tunes his mouth up into a snarl.

"Drink, drink. Be merry. Life is good."

Mark downs the drink and slams the glass on the table. "Talk."

"I don't get it, Mark. At one point in time, you would be enjoying yourself. What happened to that Mark? I miss him."

"Enough, Alicia. Enough. I'm going to ask you but one more time. Where is my wife?"

"I'm sorry." She blinks rapidly. "But somewhere in there I think I heard a threat." She sets her glass down. "Am I correct in that assessment?"

Mark says nothing.

"Let me remind you that you have to do everything I say. Let me remind you your wife is somewhere out there and only I know where she is. I control everything in this situation. You control nothing. So if

I tell you to go kill yourself, you damn well better start figuring out a way to do so." She picks her glass back up and swishes the red substance around in her cup, seemingly in deep thought. "So we can do this the easy or hard way."

"Do what?"

She smiles. "Come on, Mark. You know what I want." She walks up to him and nuzzles her nose on his neck. She holds her glass out to the side. "You know I would give anything to feel you inside of me again."

Mark pulls away. "Stop toying with me."

"But it's so fun." She advances further, giving him a light kiss on the cheek. "You don't find me alluring? I put this on just for you."

"Alicia, stop." Mark finds it difficult to keep up with her erratic behavior.

"But you don't know what you're missing," she says in a playful voice.

Mark takes another step back.

"You might not have thought about me over the past two years, but I sure thought of you." She unbuttons the first few buttons of her blouse. "I thought of what could have been. What it would be like if we were married, if that was our picture sitting on the mantel, if it were our kids in those pictures. Mark, do me a favor. Just like how you told me when you were about to leave Jade . . . tell me you love me."

Mark's back is against the wall. He doesn't say anything but looks at Alicia in confusion.

"Tell me you love me."

Alicia presses closer to Mark, fully unbuttoning her blouse, exposing herself to him. She leans in for a kiss, and like a flash, Mark grips her neck and squeezes tightly. He pulls her in close and whispers in her ear.

"Tell me where Jade is . . . or else."

He squeezes harder as she begins to squirm, but then Mark feels a poke in his abdomen. He looks down to see Alicia pressing a gun to him. He lets go of her neck. She gasps for a few moments to catch her breath, and then she slowly backs up.

"Sit down. We have much to discuss," she says in a whisper.

Mark cautiously walks to the dining room table and sits down, with Alicia still pointing the gun at him. She moves around the table to sit in front of him, still gripping the gun tightly. She takes a few more moments to adjust.

"Would you have killed me?"

Mark looks at her strangely.

"Would you?"

"I couldn't tell you."

"Would you have killed her?"

"What?"

"If she didn't knock you out with that lamp, would you have killed her?"

"How do you know about that?"

"You would be surprised what people say when deprived of food, water . . . of light."

Mark feels his heart drop. With each passing second, he feels heavier and heavier until a tear traces down his cheek. He thinks of Jade and the torment she must be in. Silently, he wishes he had never married her, for she would have never gone through this. This, as he calls it, is his entirely fault, he believes. He looks at Alicia.

"How do I really know you have her?"

"You heard her. She needs you to *rescue* her."

"All I heard was a woman's voice that sounds like her, but I don't know for sure."

"Are you calling my bluff?"

"I'm simply saying I want to see her."

She stares him down, but he doesn't flinch.

"Fine." She pulls out her cell phone. "I figured you would need some more convincing."

She taps the screen of her phone a few times and turns the face of it toward Mark.

Mark sees a crystal-clear video of Jade. She looks worn out. A large man in a mask stands behind her.

"Plead for your life," Alicia says in the video.

"Please . . . please let me go. Just let me go."

"I can't do that. Not yet. But this is a message for your husband." She says the word "husband" with much strife. "Any words for him?"

Mark stares at the video intently. He watches Jade as she looks directly at the camera. She hangs her head. "I want him to know I love him."

The video stops.

"So what is it? What do you want me to do?" Mark asks.

"I want you to suffer. I want Jade to suffer. I want Jacob and that wench he's with to suffer. And after that, I want my son back."

Mark stays silent.

"I want you to go to where he lives, take him, and bring him to a location I tell you."

"You . . . you want me to kidnap your son." Mark shakes his head and looks in confusion. "He's with Jacob. Are you crazy?"

"Quite the opposite." Her face is stern, unflinching.

"What about Jacob?"

"What about him?" She starts buttoning her blouse. "I'll leave the finer details up to you, but I would keep it quiet for your sake."

"What are you going to do with Tim?"

"That's privileged information and you're on the outs."

"So this is it, your master plan? Cause everyone pain and get your son back. You stroll up here knowing cops are—" He thinks. "This is a show. You want them to think it was me. You want my name in the media . . . as this monster."

"Oh, Sweetheart, this is just the beginning."

"Even so, you can't get away. There's nowhere for you to go."

"You just leave that up to me to straighten out."

"I don't know if I can do it." He looks down at the floor.

"Well, you have time to think about it, I guess. I mean, the more time you take to do it, the more time Jade spends with me. And the less trusting your detective friend becomes of you. Your call, Love." She gets up from the table and packs up her things, still visibly in pain from Mark's choke. She quickly grabs her coat and puts it on. "I'll be texting you the location soon." She heads to the front door. "And get some rest, you look terrible. Maybe the sex party thing wasn't a great idea. We're not young anymore, Sweetheart."

A final jab before she leaves his home. Mark slumps in his chair, trying to find some strength. He sits for a while, considering the outlandish task Alicia asked of him. It only takes a few seconds for him to determine she somehow bugged his home, and he goes on a tear to find anything and everything planted in his home.

He ended up with a camera and two sound devices.

CHAPTER FORTY

MARK spent most of his night awake, making sure there isn't any other surveillance equipment in his home, while contemplating on how to accomplish the unthinkable. He expected a phone call from Alicia in the morning but his phone didn't make a single sound.

The doorbell rings. Mark answers the door to find Detective Simms standing at his doorway with a concerned expression.

"You have a moment to talk?"

Mark doesn't say anything but steps to the side to allow him in.

"Rough night?" He says, obviously noting the mess.

Mark simply nods.

"So there are a few things on my mind as of late and I can't seem to shake them. I'm hoping you can clarify."

"Sure. Shoot."

"At the station."

"What?"

"I'm hoping to talk to you at the station."

Mark looks at Simms, then he walks to the front door to look out the window. Two cop cars sit parked in front of the driveway.

"Why not talk to me here?"

"We need to take a couple more statements."

"So you're arresting me?"

"No. Not at all. You can refuse to go down to the station with me, though I advise against that at the moment."

Mark stares a hole into Simms. "Why do you advise against that? I've done nothing wrong."

"I'm not so sure you've done nothing wrong. But please don't fret. This isn't a back-of-the-car ride. We just need another statement or two. Just asking a couple of questions."

Mark looks out the window again to see the cops get out of their cars and make their ways up the driveway. He looks back at Simms.

"So why are they coming up the drive like they want to do something?"

Simms walks past Mark and looks out the window. He then storms outside and motions them back to their cars. He comes back in, visibly angry.

"I apologize for that. There isn't much that goes on in this town. These guys are itching for something. But anyway, are we in agreement? Down to the station, a few questions, then you're home."

Mark stares at Simms again. He knows he could easily say no, but that would only make Simms push harder. Mark determines at this moment that Simms is no longer on his side. He looks at his phone. Still no messages from Alicia. In the back of his mind, he hears Alicia telling him to avoid Simms. Jade's life depends on it. He has to make a choice, a rather easy one to make.

"If you're not arresting me, you can leave. I'm not going down to the station."

Simms stares at Mark at first unbelieving, but then nods.

"Are you sure you want to go down this road?"

"I've done nothing wrong. What road am I going down? I gave you statements already. What more do you need?"

Simms puts his hand in his pocket. "You know, Mark, I've made some mistakes in my life. Some I still regret to this day. But one thing I made sure of is that I learned from them, and I tried to find a way to avoid making the same mistake twice. Even still, there were some things I have done that I keep doing. Some things, I can't pull myself from. For example, I love my job. It takes up an astronomical amount of time. That time should rightfully have been for my son. But without ever implicitly saying it, I chose the job. It took a while to admit it. For years I'd try to be this great dad and great cop. I was failing at both. Regardless, at a point I chose the job. Now, I wish I hadn't. But that's human nature for you. We are indecisive creatures at times."

"You didn't answer my questions." Mark isn't up for any cryptic speeches.

Simms sighs. "Come on, Mark. Do you think the fact that you are hanging out with the mistress, ex mistress, whatever; is a good look for you? You think no one finds it strange that your wife is missing, and the mistress is prancing in short skirts and tight dresses to meet up with you? Twice. That's twice I've seen you with her all of a sudden. And I'm not the only one. I've received a few anonymous calls on this."

"It isn't how it looks."

"It never is."

"Look, did you find anything else that could help us? Anything else that will lead us closer to Jade?"

"I did. I sure did." Simms makes his way to the door. "Mark, you know the next time we see each other, I will be here for different reasons."

Mark says nothing.

"I'll see you in a couple days." Simms leaves.

Mark knows that means tomorrow. As he grabs his phone, he checks it again to see if Alicia has sent any messages but finds nothing. He calls Craig. At first, he doesn't pick up, so Mark calls again. Craig finally picks up, sounding groggy.

"We have to talk . . . but not over the phone. We have to meet up somewhere. Somewhere no one can hear what we are saying. Somewhere that's not here or your place. It's important."

"Wait. Slow down," Craig says. He pauses for a few moments, presumably to wake up, and comes back to the phone sounding a bit more alive. "I got a suite at the hotel down the street from my job. Is that cool? Or are you talking bomb shelter no one is going to hear?"

"That's fine. I'll be there as soon as these cops leave my house."

"What happened?"

"I'm out of time." Mark hangs up. He looks out the window, waiting for an opportunity to dodge the police that sit out in front of his home.

CʒꙨꙅ

Craig stands by the window of the suite staring down at the people in the streets, trying to collect his thoughts after Mark unloaded everything to him. Mark told him about Alicia, about her crazy plan, about Detective Simms, and the surveillance of his house.

"So officially, you're on the run?"

"It seems like it. I know I can't go back to the house."

"And no one tailed you?"

"I drove around for an hour just to make sure."

"Alright, so . . . what do you want to do?"

"I know she's alive." He pauses to think of the magnitude of that statement. It almost becomes too much for him as tears slide down his face. Craig allows him a few moments. Mark has to clear his throat a few times before continuing. "At the very least, I know she will stay that way until I give Alicia the boy."

"You plan on going through with this?"

"Well . . . what other options are there? I can't go to the police. They think I did it, so all they would do is hold me. I can't afford that to happen."

Craig brushes his hair against the grain. "So we kidnap a little boy to eventually send him back to his abusive mother." He shakes his head. "And then we get Jade back."

"We? Look, I've already asked enough of you. I gotta do this one myself."

"Naw, man. That's stupid and you know it."

"Maybe." He pauses. "But either way, we can do nothing until she gives me the information."

Craig continues to stare out the window.

"So why are you staying here?" Mark asks.

Craig looks back. "Berta and I are not on good terms right now."

"Still?"

"Yeah. It just wasn't meant to be."

"What do you mean?"

"She filed for divorce. She had enough of me, couldn't deal with my past, couldn't see that I love her . . . loved her, so she filed last week."

"Did you guys do counseling?"

Craig chuckles. "We are far from you and Jade. Counseling . . . it didn't work."

"Did you guys stick with it?"

"Nope. There was no point. It all moved too fast." He turns to face Mark. "And I doubt we could seriously go into all the details. You know, with my past."

Mark nods. "I wish there was som—"

Mark's cell phone rings. Craig watches him as he pops up and answers it. Mark grunts a few times, letting him know that it is Alicia on the phone.

"I'm in," is all Mark says before hanging up the phone. He looks at Craig. "She's sending me the addresses now."

Craig stares at Mark. He seems uncomfortable. "What else did she say?"

Mark shakes his head a few times as if he's telling himself to snap out of it. "She said if we don't have the boy to the location by sunrise, she's gonna kill Jade."

"You think she would actually do it?"

Mark looks at Craig. "Without question."

Craig nods and looks out the window again. Parts of this seems surreal to him.

"She said something else."

"What, that she's sorry and she takes it all back?" Craig tries to look far into the distance.

"I wish. But she said she will be watching."

"Watching?" Craig thinks for a moment. "So no one followed you here? And she said nothing about you being here right now?"

"I'm pretty sure no one was on me and she didn't say a word about it."

"She must have people at each location. The times you saw her, was anyone with her?"

"No. It was always just her." Mark starts pacing. "But listen to this. Simms, the detective, was there after the coffeehouse meeting. I'm not even sure how he would know to go there. And I didn't see him, but he definitely knows about Alicia coming to the house."

"You think the detective is shady?"

"I'm starting to more and more by the minute. Maybe I'm grasping at straws here, but she told me not to talk to him. I'm thinking to remove suspicion that he's involved."

"But why *would* he be involved?"

"He's one of the many people that seem to be mad at me over the incident at the school. I taught his kid, so he would have some reason to be pissed."

"But not pissed enough to help Alicia do this . . . right?"

"I guess. But that leads me to my other question. Are the cops a part of this?"

"Don't know." He shakes his head. "But that's irrelevant. The detective talk is, too. You have to avoid them at all costs either way."

"True." Mark starts walking around the room. "You've been drinking?"

Craig turns around to see him holding the wine bottle he finished by himself overnight last night. He shrugs. "It takes the edge off the pain a bit."

Mark nods as if he understands.

Before long, Mark's phone beeps again. Craig goes to his laptop to turn it on and map the addresses given to him. Mark shows him the addresses.

"This Jacob guy live in Jersey? That's like a five- or six-hour trip."

"Look at the next address."

Craig looks. "Back . . . home?"

"Philly is not my home."

"So she wants you to drive six hours to get to Parsippany in Jersey to get the little boy and drive another two to a spot in South Philly?" Craig puts the addresses on and views the online map. "A random garage."

"Let me see."

Mark stares at the screen as Craig changes the view to satellite. "Do you think she's holding Jade there?"

"I honestly don't know. But if she's been planning this for a while, which it seems like she has, my guess would be no. It wouldn't make sense, plus I'm sure she's going to want to cover her tracks. And just in case you don't follow up, she's prepared." Craig moves from the window and starts grabbing clothes. "So what's the plan?"

"It sounds like we have to get the boy. The play is at the garage. That seems to be the only opening."

"To do what?"

"Still working on it."

"And do we use force or reason to get the boy?"

"That's a good question. I don't know. Maybe prepare for both. Reason first, then force it later."

"You know the further we get into this, the harder the decisions become," Craig warned.

"I know and I'm prepared."

"We are going to have to make a few tough decisions. The more people, the tougher the decisions."

Mark nods, fully understanding what Craig is implying. "I want my wife back. And nothing or no one is going to stop me from getting her back alive."

Craig starts to get dressed. "We're going to need some tools. I'll be back."

೦೩೮೦

Mark and Craig have been on the road for a couple hours already. The setting sun shines brightly across their faces. For most of the ride, neither says anything. After Mark waited in the hotel for a few hours, Craig came back with a suitcase. When he first popped it open, his eyes glittered a bit at the sight of two handguns and enough clips for a John Woo film. Craig explained how most of his connections no longer exist, but he still had a few people he knew he could count on.

Now they drive north on I-95 to attempt what seems to be impossible. Mark shakes his head vigorously. He doesn't have time to think. The more he thinks, the more he talks himself out of what he has to do. But there's something . . . something keeps gnawing at him. He looks over to Craig, who has his focus on the road. He seems to be in deep thought as well. Maybe about their task, maybe about Berta.

"I'm not sure this is going to work," Mark says.

"It will. Just keep focused. We will be bringing Jade back home before you know it."

"But I doubt Jacob is going to give us his son."

"He won't. I don't expect him to."

"So reason was never on the table?"

"Not to me. But you can reason with him while I take the boy."

Mark gets silent.

"When I scoped the map online, I was able to get a good view of the area. Neighbors are close. No gates. Just walk up to the door and ring the bell. I'll handle the rest."

"I don't get it."

"What's not to get?"

"No. I don't get you. When did you become a kidnapping specialist?"

"Come on, this is common knowledge. I have a past."

"Yeah, but I thought what you did was mostly business and information related."

Craig pauses. "What do you think I did as soon as I got out of jail?"

"You got a job. You were working."

Craig shakes his head. "That job wasn't enough to do anything. It paid worse than minimum wage. I needed more. If I was going to make it on my own two feet I had to do more."

"So what does that mean? You sold drugs? Robbed people? What is it?"

"I did it all. I hustled. Sold drugs, stole from people, hurt people . . . ."

"Why?"

"Because that's all I could do."

"Then Mr. Valencia gave you a shot?" Mark looks confused.

"No, then I stole from Mr. V and he caught me. So I owed him."

"Why didn't you tell me this before?"

"Because I couldn't. I didn't tell anyone."

Something clicks in Mark's mind. "You couldn't tell me because you knew I would have kicked you out."

Craig nods.

"Because the same place you put your head, my daughter laid hers. We both were in danger and didn't know it." Mark turns away and looks out the window. "That's messed up."

"I know. But I never let anyone get remotely close. I would die before . . . ." Craig focuses harder on the road. "I'm sorry."

Mark doesn't say a word.

CHAPTER FORTY ONE

IT'S a cool night. The moon shines above Mark, illuminating the way to his destination. The closer he gets, the more nervous he becomes. Mark, who has been traveling by foot for the past block, walks his way to Jacob's house. The pistol he carries under his jacket feels like a two-ton boulder, yet he presses on. When he gets within visual distance of Jacob's house, he slows down. In front of the house, he sees a cop car driving by. Creeping by. He slows his pace until he's ambling along, and once the cop car is out of sight, he picks it up again, this time faster than before. It takes everything in him not to run, but he keeps a steady and even pace straight to Jacob's front door. He takes a deep breath and rings the doorbell. He checks his cell phone to see it is nine-thirty at night . . . on a Sunday night. He rings the doorbell again. Still no answer. He looks at his cell phone again to check the text from Alicia to make sure he is at the right address. He slowly opens the screen door and tries the main door to find it locked. He looks to the side window to see none of the lights are on. His phone buzzes in his pocket and he checks it.

He is in there. Keep trying the door. You're running out of time.

Mark looks around, but it's too dark to notice anything strange. He tries the doorbell again and finally, lights come on. He hears the deadbolt unlock and at the door standing in front of him in a bathrobe and slippers is Jacob. They awkwardly stare at each other for a mo-ment. It's apparent that neither man really knows what to say.

"I . . . this may seem very weird, but I need to talk to you."

Jacob looks like he is trying to find the words to say.

"It's important. Beyond important. It's life or death."

Jacob looks past Mark and out into the street. He pokes his head out the door to see if anyone is around. "You really shouldn't be here."

"Tell me about it. I just need a moment of your time."

His face twists. Eventually, he motions his head toward inside the house and allows Mark in. Mark steps in and passes his eyes over the nice-looking living room with expensive furniture.

"Who is that, Dear?" A woman asks from upstairs.

"No one, honey. I'll be back up in a few."

"I'll wait to run the bath."

"I'll just be five minutes or so." Jacob looks back at Mark. "Follow me." He turns the lights off again and looks out the window as a car drives down the street.

"Do the cops always travel your neighborhood like tonight?"

"No. But that's not the only oddity of the night."

Mark follows Jacob down a hall to a back room, presumably the family room, and Jacob cuts on a single lamp that lights the room dim-ly. He starts pacing back and forth, nervously. He stops abruptly and stares at Mark. "Did they let you know?"

"Know what? What are you talking about?"

Jacob stops and stares at Mark. "You don't know what's going on?"

"No."

"Then I don't understand, Mark, why are you here?"

"I'm here because—because I think you and your family may be in danger."

Jacob sits down, looking more overwhelmed by the moment. "I'm listening."

"Well for starters, Alicia is out of jail, and I'm sure she wants to see her son."

"She lost that privilege." He fidgets around.

"I understand, but that doesn't erase the fact that she hasn't seen her son in two years."

"I shouldn't have done it." Jacob looks down and begins shaking. "I shouldn't have done it."

"Done what? Jacob, tell me what's going on."

Jacob looks at Mark with bloodshot eyes. "I shouldn't have sent her to jail."

"What do you mean? She was treating Tim badly. She sent herself to jail."

"No. You're wrong. She never laid a hand on him . . . as far as I know. We made it all up."

Mark stands there, shocked. "How were you able to prosecute her?"

"I paid a lot of money to a lot of people to make sure she went away."

"A lot of people like who?"

"My lawyers . . . the judge . . . more lawyers to put a spin on what Tim's statements were."

"But I testified freely."

"I didn't know that, at least not until a few days ago. I always assumed you were part of the plan. My lawyers made it seem so."

Mark puts his hand up on top of his head, seemingly in his own thoughts. "She's innocent. She was telling the truth."

"Part of you had to know that."

"No. I didn't know at all. I fully believed she was abusing him."

"Maybe that's why your testimony was so convincing."

"No. No, this can't be right. Why? Why would you do this?"

"For Tim."

"But apparently he was fine."

Jacob brushes his hair with his hand. "Look, the courts always lean toward mothers . . . even if they are unfit to raise a child. I wanted my son. I knew and still know I could give a better life to Tim than she ever could."

"So you sent her to jail? Do you hear yourself?"

"I do. I hear myself clearly. I also get to hear my son tell me good morning when we sit to eat breakfast. I get to hear him tell me he loves me when I drop him off to school each day. So I went through extreme lengths to get my son. It was worth it."

Mark stands there for a second, amazed.

"You know, society always says something about the lack of real men, the lack of real fathers. What about the ones who want to be around? What about the ones who love their kids dearly but are forced away?"

"Don't give me that society crap. This wasn't totally about Tim. You wanted Alicia out of the picture and you did anything to make that happen. Now, she's back and she's taken my damn wife hostage." Mark is fuming.

"Wait. What do you mean she took your wife hostage?"

Mark hesitates and takes a few steps back. "She took my wife. I believe she has help, I just don't know who."

Jacob's face turns grave. "I'm sorry to hear that." He continues pacing back and forth. "She obviously has help. There's no way—no way she is doing all of this on her own."

"What?"

"She gave me a call recently. That's how I knew she was out of jail. She made threats. Serious threats."

"What did she say?"

"She wants me to burn. Her exact words were, 'There's a special place in hell for you. I'll make sure not to keep Satan waiting.' She somehow got her hands on some valuable information. Stuff that could expose everything. She called my lawyers and made threats. There seems to be some merit to what she is saying because now, all of a sudden, my lawyers want to wipe their hands clean."

"Did she say what she wanted in return?"

"No. I'm guessing to see me squirm."

Mark thinks back to his conversation with Alicia and how she said she was looking for justice. "Did she mention Tim?"

"No. Not at all."

Both men get silent, each in his own mind trying to cope with the destruction Alicia is causing. Mark notices Jacob's expression shift as he stares at the ground.

"So you came all this way . . . to warn me about the danger my family is in? You could have called, but I never gave you my number . . . and I never gave you my address . . . so how did you get here?"

Mark feels a bit of tension as Jacob moves to the end table with the lamp. He digs through the drawer and casually pulls out a gun.

"Now I am going to say this only once: Explain."

Mark freezes, debating if he should come out with the entire truth, or parts of it, maybe none of it. He doesn't know what to say, but he knows it must be something.

"She is trying to set things straight."

"Meaning?"

"You are not safe here. She wants everything back, I'm guessing even this house . . . including Tim. She said she was going to make everyone feel what she felt . . . then set things straight."

"We are perfectly fine here. If there is a house she's talking about, it's the one we had built."

"So this isn't the house you and Alicia lived in?"

"No. We had to move. Val didn't want to be in the place Alicia and I built together. And she was afraid of living in a place Alicia knew the exact location of."

"Val? Your wife?"

"Yep."

"You and Alicia had a house built?"

"Designed it from scratch. Bought the land. Built the house. It was ours . . . from the beginning."

"So I'm assuming when you two got a divorce, you kept the house."

"Doesn't matter." He switches the gun to his other hand. "Why are you at my house right now?"

"I . . . I was sent." Mark thinks for a moment. He thinks of the extreme lengths Jacob went through to get his son back. He finds Jacob to be not much unlike himself in the sense that Mark believes he is willing to do anything and everything to get Jade back. His soul twists and turns within him. Alicia is also willing to do anything and everything to get her son back. Three twisted and desperate people. *There has to be a better way.*

A loud thump sounds upstairs. Jacob squints and freezes altogether.

"Did you hear that?"

"I did."

"Upstairs. Now."

Mark slowly turns around and takes Jacob's directions to go upstairs, with Jacob still pointing the gun at him.

"You're not safe here."

"Shut up."

"Jacob, listen. You and your family are not safe here. Alicia knows where this is. She knows and she can end up on your doorstep any day now."

"I said shut up." He jabs the gun at Mark's spine. "Val?" He calls out.

No answer.

A fearful feeling settles in the pit of Mark's stomach as he forces bile back down his throat. It's completely quiet upstairs.

"Jacob," he whispers.

"Not another word. Keep going. Straight."

At the top of the stairs he sees a faint light coming from what Mark believes is the master bedroom. They make their way there. Mark still hears nothing.

"Val? You there?" To Mark, "Open the door slowly."

He slowly opens the door to see the room set up romantically with candles and rose petals throughout. He looks to the side of the bed to see Jacob's wife lying motionless on the floor, covered only by her bathrobe.

"What the . . . ."

Jacob moves around Mark and rushes to his wife. As he kneels down to her, Craig jumps from the closet and covers Jacob's face with his hand. After a few moments of struggling, Jacob goes limp. Craig lays Jacob's body down next to Val's.

"They're going to be out for a couple hours," Craig says. "But we have a problem. The boy isn't here."

"What did you do to them?"

"Chloroform."

"Where did you get that?"

"It was in the case. Look, we need to come up with something fast. What do you want to do?"

Mark hangs his mouth open, trying to process everything going on. "Okay. Okay. Are you sure he isn't there?"

"I'm posi—"

A loud thump sounds from above them. Mark and Craig stare at each other for a few moments, trying not to make a sound. Craig points up toward the attic and both men go on a search for the attic entrance. They get to Tim's room quickly even in the dark and turn on a small lamp near the doorway. Mark looks around to see posters of comic book characters all over the walls. He has shelves of unopened toys and decks of cards, and a keyboard on a stand in the corner. He looks at the ceiling, but doesn't find any entrance.

Craig points to the closet door that hangs open. Mark slowly moves to the closet to see the attic access point in the ceiling wide open and a chair on the floor under it. Mark motions Craig out of the room.

"I can't do this," he whispers.

"What are you talking about?"

"This isn't us, man. I mean, are we really about to kidnap this boy?"

"It's too late to start thinking of that now."

"No. This isn't right . . . this . . . all of this, just simply isn't right."

"It's also not right that Jade is being held hostage."

Mark looks away. "I have an idea. It's a little out there, but it puts us in the driver's seat. 'Cause right now, Alicia is calling the shots." He starts creeping back downstairs.

"What are you talking about?"

"Just follow me."

Craig takes a last glance at the attic access point and turns to follow Mark.

Both men silently step their way downstairs to the main level and go into the office Mark was previously in. Mark eyes the still-full glass of scotch sitting on the desk. Once in the room, Mark speaks.

"Look, this whole time, we've been playing right into her hands. We're moving in ways she would expect us to."

"There's a good reason for that, Mark." Craig looks frustrated. "She has Jade and has already proven she will cause harm to her."

"You see, that's my point. I don't doubt she will finish the job once she gets what she wants. She wants justice, she says, but this is all revenge. If I'm going to have a chance at getting Jade back, I have to find a way to take her back, because I'm almost absolutely positive she just won't give her back, even if she gets her son."

"I get you, but unless you know where she is, this whole conversation is for nothing."

"I think I may know."

"Okay, spill it, so we can go get her."

"I think she's at her and Jacob's previous home."

"Are you sure?"

Mark looks down. "I'm not. But call it a hunch."

"What's the address?"

"I don't know, but I'm hoping there is some information here that would tell us that."

"Here . . . where?"

"In this office."

"We don't have time for this."

"Dammit, then go. I'm looking for the address."

Craig, for a brief moment, is stunned by Mark's reaction. Still, he helps Mark sift through stacks of papers, even though he feels it's a dead end.

Mark opens drawers, cabinets, and boxes in search of something that would tell him the address of the home. He thinks if he found some real estate papers, maybe closing papers from when he sold it, he would be on the right track.

Both Mark and Craig search for a good fifteen minutes before Craig stops and snaps his fingers. Mark looks up and heads toward Craig.

"He sold the place for one point two million," Craig says. "Here is the address."

Mark glances over the paper before plugging the address into his phone.

A few moments later, Mark has the aerial view of the home on his phone and shows Craig. "That's a lot of land. The place is almost an hour away." He starts pacing back and forth.

"What are you thinking?"

"I'm thinking I go and check it out."

"I don't know. If you're wrong, there's no way she'll have the boy before sunrise."

"I don't think I am wrong."

"Okay so we go to this place to check it ou—."

"No. I go to this place to check it out. You go to the garage. I don't think I am wrong, but if I am, I need you to buy us time."

Craig sighs, exasperated. "What? What do you mean? You want me to go to the garage without the boy?"

"Look, I'm not playing her game anymore. And the boy, we can't do this to him. Look at what we have already done. Look at what we are turning into."

"We don't have time for morals, man. Don't you get it? Jade will die if we don't do this."

"I just can't do this. We get her back and later, there's so much to atone for. I can't have that on my conscience."

Craig stares at the carpet for a second then shakes his head. "So what do I do when I get to the garage?"

"I don't know. Buy as much time as possible."

"We traveled in the same car."

"I'll take theirs. There must be keys somewhere."

"Well . . . I guess we'd better go."

Mark and Craig tiptoe through the first floor and toward the garage. Right at the door leading to the garage, Mark sees a few sets of keys on a key hook hanging on the wall. He grabs the one with the car alarm remote.

"And if there's nothing there, I'll circle back and head to the garage."

Craig stops. "And if she is there? What if your hunch is correct? You'll be there by yourself."

Mark shakes his head. "Then I'm bringing Jade home."

Mark opens the door to the garage and looks back at Craig. He isn't able to see his face clearly in the dim lighting, but he feels the look Craig gives him. *Good luck to you, too,* Mark thinks. He presses a few buttons on the car alarm remote to make sure it's unlocked and runs to the car. Craig presses himself up against the garage wall and waits for Mark to open the main door before he sneaks out and disappears.

Mark slowly leaves the house and once clear of any cops, drives down the street and heads to Jacob and Alicia's old home.

☙❧

Craig pushes his car past a hundred miles an hour, only slowing down for tolls. He silently prays there are no cops on this particular stretch of highway, but quickly realizes what a ridiculous notion that is: praying to not get caught doing something wrong. He shakes his head. For the first half of the trip, he was angry with Mark. *Why did he have to change the plan? It was set, it was almost complete, and last minute . . . .* Then Craig realizes what he was actually getting mad at. He was mad at his friend for not wanting to take a little child from his home to give him back to his abusive mother. He goes over that notion in his head many times through. By the middle of the trip, he understands Mark's position, and feels sorry for his current state. Even with his wife in danger, he still feels the moral tug. Strangely, he feels Mark wanted to go to the home alone, as if Mark needed to get away from Craig and his amoral self. Craig then begins to feel worse because he doesn't feel that tugging at all anymore. He does some quick introspection and wonders if his faith in God was tied up into Berta and her faith. He realizes that it took too little a time for him to "revert" back to his old self, though he denied any change vehemently. He starts to think that maybe Berta was right about him. He always put up a front for her, just not the one she thought. Him loving her, that was always true.

Craig gets to the garage forty minutes earlier than the map originally said and pulls up to the side to get a good view. He looks up and down the street finding it to be, for the most part, desolate. A few beat-up cars are parked across the street. He looks at the garage and sees that it is completely dark on the inside. He gets ready to drive off when a black Escalade pulls up in front of him, then one behind him, stopping him from driving anywhere. A man in all black gets out of the Escalade behind him and strolls to his window. He taps the window with his finger and Craig lowers it a notch.

"You have the boy?" the man asks.

"Yeah," Craig says.

The man looks up at the other truck in front of him and nods. Then, a larger man steps out of the driver's side and walks to a screen door on the side of the garage.

"I want you to back up into the garage," the man next to Craig's window says.

Craig tenses as the man walks away from his window and to his truck. He knows there aren't too many good ways this could end, especially because he doesn't actually have the boy. He hears the loud screech of the large garage door opening. He takes his gun and secures it to his side, then covers it up with shirt and jacket. With luck, they won't notice he is armed. Craig takes his time to back up his car into the building that looks more like an abandoned warehouse than a garage. As he gets halfway in, the lights turn on and Craig sees a number of cars lined up with their hoods open. The large man from the truck that was in front of him motions him to keep backing up and tells him to stop when he is completely on a car lift. The smaller man shuts the garage door and walks up to Craig again. He looks through the inside of his car.

"You said you have the boy."

"I do."

"Where is he?"

"At a location of my choosing."

Craig is able to get a good look at the man. He wears dingy clothes. He has a thick beard and mustache and a bald head. *But he made sure his Escalade was nice and shiny*, Craig thinks. The man looks up at the other and smirks.

"He doesn't have the boy with him," he yells.

"So what is he here for?"

The man looks down at Craig. "Get out the car."

Craig hesitates before the bearded man takes out a gun.

"I'm only asking once."

Craig slowly opens the door and gets out the car.

"Walk to the back."

Craig looks up at the larger man at the top of a grated staircase, then back down at the bearded man.

"What did you think, you would be able to make a deal?" the bearded man asks.

"I didn't think anything. I just know what happens if I give up the boy."

The larger man makes his way to the main level and follows closely behind the bearded man and Craig. He pulls up a chair and sets it in the middle of the back room.

"Sit down. We're gonna get this sorted through." He grabs a cell phone from his pocket. He presses a few buttons and before long, he is talking to someone in hushed tones.

Craig sits and hears key words like "boy" and "crazy" while he keeps his attention on the man pointing a gun at him. The larger man walks to Craig and puts his phone on speaker.

"What are you doing, Mark? Don't you know Jade's life hangs in the balance? Do you think I won't kill her?" Alicia's voice rings throughout the back room of the garage.

Craig says nothing.

"Mark. Stop it with the games."

Still, Craig says nothing.

"He's not saying anything. What do you want me to do?"

"Keep me on the speaker."

Craig hears rustling over the phone, then footsteps. A few seconds later he hears Jade and it nearly breaks his heart. She sounds weary, drained. Then, a scream piercing the ears of everyone in the room. Craig winces at the sound of something terrible happening to Jade. The bearded man seems to flinch, but the larger remains expressionless. He then hears her weeping.

"You gonna answer me? Or do I have to do more?"

"No more. Please, no more," Craig says, strained.

There's a long pause and everyone in the room stands still.

"Say that again for me. No more, you say?"

"No more. Let her go. I'll bring the boy to you."

"And who am I speaking to right now?"

The larger man holding the phone and the bearded man with the gun exchange an awkward glance.

"This is Craig."

"Jailbird Craig?"

Craig grinds his teeth. "Yeah."

"Where is Mark?"

Craig looks down. He has to think fast. "He's dead."

His words hang in the air for a few moments as everyone tries to process what is going on. Craig thinks for a second, wondering where Mark actually is. If he had the correct address, Mark should have been there by now.

"How?" She sounds a bit choked up.

"Jacob. Jacob killed him."

"So it was you driving Jacob's car from his home?"

"Yeah. I parked far away and I couldn't just walk in the middle of the street with the boy. So I took his car and drove to my car."

"And you just ditched his? Where?"

"Where I parked my car."

"I'm asking you where. I need to confirm this."

Craig has to think fast, yet again. He thinks of a place he saw on his way to the garage. "There's a park just outside the development. It's kinda run down, but I parked the car there because there was next to no lighting. I figured it wouldn't matter by daytime because . . . because this would all be over with, one way or the other."

"I think I know that park. Grimley."

"I don't remember seeing a sign. I just know the street it is on has a lot of potholes."

"Yup, that's the one." She sighs loud enough for everyone to hear. "This doesn't involve you, Craig. You should not be here."

"I know. But I can't lose another friend. I had to do something."

"So where is my son?"

"At a location of my choosing. I just want Jade back. That's all. I'll give you your son, no questions asked."

"You know you aren't in any position to play hardball."

"I understand. But that's not the game I'm playing. I'm not playing any games at all. I just want Jade back."

Some time goes by before Alicia speaks again, so much so that the bearded man seems to be tired of pointing a gun at Craig. He rests his arm for a moment.

"I never knew what you went to jail for," Alicia says.

"Why does it matter?"

"Just—" She pauses. "Just entertain me for a moment."

He grunts. "Assault. I went for sexual assault."

"I thought you were a youth pastor or something like that."

"I was."

"Were you one of those priests? With the little boys?"

"No. Not at all." He doesn't say anything more at first, but when he realizes Alicia isn't saying anything, he explains further. "I was set up by a coworker at my night job."

"So you didn't do any of that stuff?"

"No. But I still went away for it."

"I suppose you would understand my plight then?"

"I don't get it, actually."

"Well, I never laid a hand on my son. I wasn't a neglectful mother. I treated him with love and respect. My downfall was his freaking father . . . and Mark."

"Some extreme lengths to change things, I would say."

"But that's where you lack understanding. This is what I had to do. I could never see my son again . . . ever. He was literally stolen from me. And while in jail . . . Until you know what it's like to lose a child . . . please spare me your . . . judgment."

"So I haven't lost a child. I just lost a best friend. One who through thick and thin stood by me when everyone else disappeared. I know what it's like to lose a wife because one day, she just doesn't love you anymore. I know what it's like to have time from me stolen. I know what loss is like . . . maybe even more than you . . . and some of this is because of you."

"Well, I can honestly say that I am sorry for what I have caused you. And I'm sorry for what happened between you and your wife. But there is no turning from this path now. So I present this to you now: tell me where my son is or Jade dies."

"Look, I want nothing more than to give you your son. But I can't without knowing where Jade is. It's just that simple."

"Would you be willing to lose your life for her?"

Craig's mind snaps to a time when he asked himself the very same question about Berta. "Yes."

"You are a strange man, Craig."

"Maybe. So what do we do now?"

"Well, you are in the unfortunate position of having something I want. Garrote, Chambers, I need to know where my son is. Make it happen."

The two men stare at Craig with an intensity he doesn't quite understand.

"Will do," the larger man says.

The phone clicks. And the man puts his phone back into his pocket.

"How much did she pay you?" Craig asks.

The men say nothing.

"Whatever it is, I can double it. No, triple it."

"We aren't worried about money. Your car will do just fine." He pulls out a set of brass knuckles from his pocket and slides them over his stubby fingers, and stands in a manner that dares Craig to try something. "Now you have one shot at this. Where is the boy?"

Craig looks back and forth between the two men. "The address is on my GPS. Check my recents."

The larger man nods at the bearded man and refocuses back on Craig. The bearded man walks to Craig's car. Here is where Craig sees opportunity.

"I can't find it," the bearded man yells over.

The larger man looks at Craig. "Show him."

Craig inches up from the chair and begins to make his way to the car. He tries to calm himself to stop shaking so hard, but to no avail. Craig starts walking, his footsteps echoing in his mind. He counts down from ten and steels himself. The larger man trails behind him.

Once Craig is halfway to the car, he pulls out his gun while snapping around toward the larger man. He dodges to his left while pulling the trigger three times. Craig sees two of the bullets land in the man's chest. He has no idea where he shot the other one. Craig scurries behind another car and watches as the larger man collapses, lifeless. He hears the boot steps of the bearded man, then complete silence. Craig looks around, nervously. He creeps to his left to get sight of the bearded man. He doesn't see him but he sees a wrench. Craig picks up the wrench and throws it across the garage to draw the bearded man's attention. The wrench flies in the air for a few moments and comes down with a clanging noise onto the floor. Not even a millisecond later, gunshots are fired in the direction of the wrench. Craig stealthily moves closer to the bearded man, knowing his location. Just as Craig is about to make another move, he hears a phone ringing. Craig eyes the lifeless body of the larger man and realizes his cell phone is ringing, likely Alicia trying to get an update. Craig moves down a few more cars when he sees a shadow. He looks under the car to see two boots moving toward the larger man. Craig then sneaks around and puts his gun to the back of the bearded man's head.

"Drop it."

The man startles a bit, but then flings his guns across the garage.

"Now what I want you to do is pick up the phone. Back her off. Tell her you are on the way . . . and that I have been disposed of. Understand?"

The man nods vigorously. They both walk to the body of the larger man and he kneels down to pick up the phone.

"Yeah," the bearded man says. "We're on the way to get the boy now . . . yeah . . . he got beat up but he's fine . . . on the road now, shouldn't be much longer . . . we handled him . . . the way we handled the others. Alright." He hangs up and places the phone on the ground and continues to stare at the lifeless body.

"I need you to tell me something . . . and I don't want to have to force it out of you . . . but please understand if I have to I will . . . what I need to know is where you were going to take the boy."

The bearded man says nothing, but is visibly shaken. "You killed my brother."

Craig tries to blot out the heart-wrenching sound of the man's voice.

"Answer my question."

"I don't know. He had all the information."

"Where? On his phone?"

The man nods.

"Give it to me."

With shaky hands, the man grabs the phone and raises it up to him. Craig grabs it and walks over to a table that has duct tape. He makes sure to keep his gun trained on the bearded man, who looks like he is somewhere else. Craig gets back to the man and tells him to wrap his legs with the tape and to make sure it's secure. The man does so without objection. Craig takes the tape and wraps the man's hands behind his back.

"Listen, I'm sorry," Craig says.

Craig looks around to find the chain to open the garage and pulls the door open. He moves his car out the garage and heads back in to shut the door. Once he shuts the door, he heads out the side door, giving one last glance at the bearded man staring at his fallen brother. Craig sees the sparkle of a tear dropping from his eye. Unable to bear it any more, Craig leaves the garage.

Once inside the car, Craig checks the phone of the man to see a number of text messages between the last number that called and his phone. He also sees just as many between the larger man and some other number. Craig searches vigorously for an address and comes up with one. He grabs his phone to see the address he found on the papers. The exact same address.

"So his hunch was right," Craig says in the darkness.

He sets the phone down and pulls the car over on the highway. He sits for a few moments just to concentrate on breathing. The weight of what he has done is starting to bear down on him. The look on the bearded man's face as he gazed upon his fallen brother. Seeing things like that change a man. From Craig's perspective, this isn't the first time he's seen firsthand the result of his actions. The large man isn't the first he killed. Surprisingly, this one was easier than the last, and that one easier than the one before.

He's sick of himself. It's no wonder Berta wants to have nothing to do with him. He eases back onto the highway with only a single thought.

I wish I was able to talk to Berta right now.

CHAPTER FORTY TWO

MARK drives down an unfamiliar highway, hoping and praying his hunch is correct. He consistently thinks of only one thing, and that is holding Jade in his arms again. His GPS tells him that he is arriving at his destination and Mark slows the car to a stop. He looks around, but doesn't see any houses. Rather, he sees more highway and tall standing trees on both sides. He checks his GPS again. After three more attempts, the GPS says the same thing. He is at his destination.

Mark gets out of the car and looks up and down the desolate highway. Down a ways, he sees a traffic light blinking yellow. Down the other way, more highway.

Then he sees a mailbox across the street.

Mark jogs across the highway to the mailbox and searches the area. From far away, it would look like a mailbox in the middle of the woods, but as he gets closer, he sees a faint outline of tire tracks on the dirt next to it. He jogs back to his car and turns it on, keeping the lights off, and tries to go where he thought he saw the tracks. Following along, he realizes he is driving up a hidden driveway and he takes it deep into the woods, but it eventually opens up into a park-like area. He parks the car at the end of the woods and walks a skinny muddy trail that parallels a stream.

Eventually, he comes upon a large structure lit only with landscape lights. He looks at the top to see only one room lit, as if lit by fire.

Mark takes caution when approaching the large building. The closer he gets, the more he realizes he is approaching the back of the house. In front of the house is a huge open field with various shrubbery cut to look like art.

Mark skulks to the back of the house and tries one of the doors. It's locked. He then tries another door and finds that one locked as well. Mark then looks to the side of the second door and finds a window open. He quietly presses it open and listens for any movement. After hearing none, he hops up to the window and slides in. Immediately, he realizes the window he opened and is climbing though is the one above the kitchen sink. It takes him quite a time to get in through the window and to do so without slipping or making any loud noise. Mark takes his time in stepping from the window to solid ground. Once inside, he uses his cell phone flashlight to illuminate what is in front of him. He scans the large kitchen to see a bunch of granite and stainless steel. Typical for a high-end kitchen. He moves through the kitchen to a hallway with a bunch of doors. He pauses, listening, feeling. He moves forward to the end of the hall and out to a clearing. The floors are cold and Mark aims the light to see they are marble.

He continues on his trek when he hears a woman's voice: Alicia's voice, echoing from somewhere upstairs. Mark cuts his phone light off and uses the faint light that comes through the floor-to-ceiling windows. He finds a set of stairs and takes to them as quietly as he can until he gets to the room where he thinks she is. He hears clearly now that it wasn't Alicia talking; rather, she is moaning and squealing. Mark presses his back against the wall. He looks down the hallway to a singular door at the end. He creeps his way to that door and tries it, but it doesn't open. The moans and squeals get louder and are now accompanied by a man grunting. Mark tries another door to find that one locked as well. He starts his way back downstairs when he hears a loud ringtone from the room. The moaning and grunting immediately stop and he freezes to not make a sound. Moments later, he hears Alicia talking.

"What do you mean he isn't with him?" she asks. "What? … At a location of his choosing? Put me on speaker."

He tries to make out the conversation, but knows he is at a disadvantage, so he maneuvers himself behind an accent table in the darkness, avoiding detection, to get a better listen. He slinks across the hall and tries the door to find it opens easily. He steps in to find it to be a small bathroom. He cracks the door so he can somewhat hear what she is saying, but he is still unable to really hear anything. A moment later, he sees Alicia come out of the room and go down the hall to the room that was locked. He hears the door unlock, creak open, then shut. He waits for a few moments. *Was that a scream?* Alicia comes stomping from the room.

"How?" she asks. "So it was you driving Jacob's car . . . ."

She enters the room across the hall again and shuts the door. A few quick moments later, the door opens and a large man steps out. By way of the dim light from the room, likely from a fireplace, Mark sees a man wearing a police uniform, but he is unable to make out his face. He gently shuts the door and goes downstairs without even looking in Mark's direction. The man moves in a hurry and goes downstairs. Mark takes the opportunity to step outside the bathroom to see what is in the room Alicia came from. He knows he heard a scream.

As soon as he turns, he feels a heavy force tackling him to the ground. He looks to see the large man that he thought left in a hurry. The man punches Mark a few times in the face, leaving him a bit woozy. The man gets off Mark and drags him down the long staircase and throws him to the hard marble floor. Mark immediately goes for his gun but can't find it. It is no longer on him, so before the man could do anything else, Mark gets up and charges for the man, taking him to the ground. Mark starts punching, but the man covers up well and rolls with his punches. He then lands another blow to Mark's face and that sends him reeling. Mark falls to the ground, near exhaustion, when he sees a glimmer on the floor.

His gun.

Before Mark could move to get to it, the man is on top of him again, bulldozing his face with fists that feel like bowling balls. Mark is able to cover up a bit more this time and even gets off a quick jab to the man's throat. The man starts choking and gets off Mark. Mark rushes him again and takes him down to the ground with more force. He lets his fists fly and lands a good elbow to the man's face. The man grunts and covers up and Mark takes the opportunity to get off the man and stomp him on the face. He does so twice before dashing to the gun. He grabs it and aims it at the man, but he isn't moving anymore. Mark stands there for a few moments before walking to the man and nudging him with his foot. The man doesn't move.

Mark turns away from him and stumbles back up the stairs. He feels the warm tickle of blood coming from his nose and dripping from his upper lip, but he presses forward. He gets to the top of the stairs and nearly collapses. He hangs onto the wall for support and slides his way to the last door in the hall, but before he can get there, Alicia pops out of the side room as if there isn't a care in the world. She stops when she sees Mark. Mark immediately brings his gun up to aim at her chest.

"Is she in there?" he asks.

Alicia says nothing. Mark moves his aim to the side and fires off a shot. She jumps.

"Is she in there?"

Alicia nods.

"I want you to turn around and show me. Understand? Show me my wife."

Alicia turns around and starts toward the door when Mark is tackled into the wall. He accidentally lets off another shot and Alicia jerks forward. The gun is knocked from his hand and falls to the floor as Mark is again pummeled by haymakers from the cop. Mark drives the man back away from him with his legs and pushes him into the wall on the other side of the hallway. He looks for the gun and finds it on the floor in the open bedroom. Before Mark can make a move to get to it, the cop wraps his arms around his neck, stopping all air from getting to his lungs. Mark struggles a bit and starts to flail his arms. He kicks against the wall to propel the two backward, but the man holds tight to Mark. After a few more seconds, his eyesight gets blurry and he sees random bright spots in his vision. He kicks back, putting both of his feet against the opposite wall, and sends the two of them crashing into the small bathroom Mark was hiding in earlier. The cop releases his grip just enough for Mark to twist and send a few elbows to the man's midsection. The man slumps to his side a bit and Mark punches him a few more times before leaving him there and going for the gun again; only this time, the gun isn't lying on the bedroom floor anymore. Mark limps to the bedroom and looks around but doesn't find it. Then, he hears it.

A gunshot.

Mark limps back out to the hallway and looks as the man slowly makes it up to his feet. He watches the man lean back against the wall. Then, with slow and staggered steps, the man heads for Mark. Mark heads straight for him and ducks the man's slow and weak punches. Both men tussle for a bit more, pushing each other from wall to wall, when they get to the top of the stairs. Without much regard for his own body, Mark pushes the man, sending both of them tumbling down the staircase and landing with a hard thud. Mark, lying flat on his back, looks to the side to see the man lying at an impossible angle, his eyes wide open. He immediately looks away and toward the top of the staircase.

His vision wanes as he sees a silhouette of someone coming down the stairs. Squinting, he sees Alicia, hanging one of her arms, holding a gun. Mark can't move. Alicia gets to the main level and stares at Mark. She holds the gun up to him with a shaky hand, but doesn't pull the trigger. She looks next to him at his assailant and pats him on the chest. She grabs something from his jacket and places it in Mark's hand. She stares for a few more moments before walking away from Mark and out the front door of the house. A cold wind blows through, tracing along the floor, as Alicia left the door open. Mark looks out the door to see the bright red light of brake lights, then he hears the rocks and gravel spitting from under spinning tires.

He doesn't know if it has been five seconds or five minutes, but Mark eventually starts to move. He sticks what Alicia handed him into his pocket. He summons what energy he has left to crawl up the staircase and when he does, he collapses from exhaustion and pain. Every bit of his body hurts, but he fights through the pain. He has to get to Jade.

Mark gets to his feet and staggers his way to the door to find another staircase leading up. He tries the light switch by the door but nothing comes on. He goes up anyway.

"Jade." His voice comes out hoarse. He clears his throat and calls her again. "Jade . . . I'm here, Baby."

Mark gets to the last step and pauses. He hears whimpering and heavy breathing. In the total darkness, Mark moves in the direction of the sounds. He looks behind him to see a bit of faint light from the lower level and continues forward.

"Jade. Say something, Baby. Let me know where you are."

The whimpers get louder. Mark kneels to the floor and starts crawling, placing his hand in front of him to feel around. He keeps moving in the direction of the whimpers when he finally feels something.

Her arm.

"Jade." Mark moves his face to her ear. "I'm here, Baby. I'm going to get you out of here."

Mark summons what energy he has left and picks up Jade in his arms. Slowly, he carries her from the attic and down the stairs when his legs give out on him. They fall to the floor and Mark cradles her body. Under the dim light, he sees various cuts and bruises on her face and for the first time in too long, he sees her eyes. She stares at him, un-blinking.

Tears well up in Mark's eyes as Jade lifts her hand to his face. She lets her hand fall to his collar and gently tugs on him to bring him clos-er. She kisses him softly and looks him in the eyes. Mark feels some-thing warm in his lap and lifts Jade up to see his entire leg covered in blood. He looks at her back to see her shirt soaked with blood as well.

"No." He gets to his feet again. "Hang on, Baby. Hang on."

Mark lifts her in his arms again and trudges his way down the hall-way, down the stairs, and out of the house. He sees the sun peeking out from over the horizon. Mark carries Jade to a parked truck and tries the door handle to find it open. He gently puts her in the back seat and climbs to the front, looking for keys. He finds none so he rushes back to the dead cop inside the house and searches his pockets, hoping he has a key for the truck. He finds a set of car keys and heads back to the truck. He pops one in the ignition and brings the truck to roaring life. Moments later, he speeds off, furiously tapping at his phone to find the nearest hospital. Mark finds one that is only five miles away.

After running a few red lights, Mark makes it to the hospital and pulls right up to the entrance to the emergency ward. He hops out of the truck and runs to the back door, opening it and pulling Jade out. He gets to the sliding doors.

"Help. I need help."

Everyone in the area starts rushing Mark. Doctors, nurses and the like help get Jade to a stretcher and start moving her to give her care. A few of the doctors and nurses try to take Mark back as well but he pushes them off.

"Her name is Jade Cooke. Jade Cooke," he yells as he steps back away from the hospital and heads in the direction of the truck. As he heads back, he sees red blotches leading from the truck to the hospital doors and he looks inside to see a pool of blood in the back seat. Mark grits his teeth and slams the door. He hops in the driver's seat and speeds away.

Her body was cold.

Every fiber in his body tells him he should be with his wife, but Mark continues along the highway to go to the one place he knows Alicia will be. He grabs his cell phone and calls Craig. Mark doesn't wait for a hello.

"I got her. She's at a hospital nearby. I need you to go to that hospital."

"Where is it? Where are you?"

"Put the address I gave you on a map. She's at the closest one, should be five miles down the road. Get there as soon as you can."

"Where are you headed? You alright?"

"I'm fine." Mark grits his teeth. "Just get there." He hangs up the phone and immediately dials Detective Simms.

"Simms."

"Mark, where are you?"

"Look, I'm in Jersey. I didn't run. I didn't kidnap or kill my wife. I went and got her back. I need you to listen to me carefully, and"—his phone beeps. Battery is low.— "I don't have much time before my phone cuts off. So listen."

Mark proceeds to tell Detective Simms as much as he can with the battery life left on his phone, but finds it difficult because he's being careful not to mention anything about Craig. He gets to explaining how he entered into Jacob and Alicia's old home before his phone cuts off and shuts down completely. He drops it on the passenger seat.

The sun shines brightly in his face, the sky turning from orange to blue. He is only a few minutes from where he knows she is and he slows the truck down. He gets stopped behind a school bus and waits for two little kids to find their ways into a seat. His mind switches to his own children and how much he misses them. His heart becomes heavy as he wants to break down, but he forces himself to continue.

Mark pulls up to Jacob's house and into the driveway, behind the truck Alicia hopped into at the other house. As it turns out, he was right on once again with his hunch. He just hopes Jacob took his advice and got his family out in time.

He parks the truck and cuts it off, waiting for a disturbance, a noise, something. But he hears nothing. Still sitting in the car, he looks around. Two women with reflector gear jog in the street. Another man walks his dogs, three of them. Some cars drive by, but there is nothing that would tell him something is wrong. While looking out the back window, Mark looks down at the bloodstain on the backseat of the truck. He stares at it for some time, being caught in a train of thoughts. He shakes himself from his thoughts and looks in the visor mirror. His face is marred with various cuts, bruises, and dried blood. Little by little, the events of the previous night catch up to him. He fights the waves of emotion that threaten to take over his body and labors out of the truck. He limps to the front door and tries the knob to find it locked and shuffles to the back door. He notices before he even gets there that the door is cracked open.

Mark doesn't hesitate and steps into the home again. He closes the back door behind him and slowly steps through the back hallway. He pauses to listen. Faintly, over the rushing sound of his speeding pulse, he hears talking. His head starts to feel like it's in a vice. He gets to the kitchen and everything looks undisturbed. He keeps moving through the house. Mark's mind starts racing. He expected Alicia to come here looking for Tim, yet he hoped no one was present in the home. He takes to the stairs, hobbling, but silently. He gets to the top of the stairs and looks down the hall at the wide-open door to Jacob and Val's bedroom. Now he hears talking, more like yelling. He hears Alicia and Jacob. Mark slides against the wall, making his way to the bedroom. In an instant, the yelling stops.

Mark steps in the bedroom to see Alicia and Jacob, pointing guns at each other. He puts his hands up when they both glance at him.

"Why are you here, Jacob? You should have . . . ." Mark takes another labored breath. "Alicia . . . put the gun down."

Alicia leans to the side. "Mark, you should be—"

"Dead?"

She doesn't say anything.

"So what happens now?" Jacob asks.

"Is Tim safe? Is your wife?" Mark asked Jacob.

"They're safe."

"Where, Jacob?" Alicia cuts in.

"There's no way in hell I'm telling you that."

Mark struggles to keep himself upright. "It's over, Alicia. It's over."

"No." She grits her teeth.

"Listen to the man."

Mark continues. "I got Jade to the hospital . . . Tim and Val are somewhere safe . . . ." He moves closer to her. "The cops know. They know everything." He steps in front of her, blocking her view of Jacob, but allowing her to aim her gun right at his chest. "Jacob . . . leave."

Mark hears behind him some rustling before seeing through his peripheral vision that Jacob is leaving the room. He cocks his head to the side to see Jacob motioning to Mark that he is going to call the police. Mark retrains his focus on Alicia. He looks her in her now watery eyes.

"I didn't know," he says. "It was easy to believe. Maybe I did want to believe . . . it was easier to move on that way. But I'm sorry."

Her voice comes out hoarse. "You ruined my life. He ruined my life. Why does he get to win? Why do you?"

Mark slowly and cautiously grasps Alicia's hand to move the gun away from his chest. "You know you don't need to aim that at me. I have no fight left. I can barely stand. Plus, you're not going to shoot me, anyway."

She takes a couple steps back and aims at his forehead. "What makes you so sure?"

He grabs his side, hoping to squelch the increasingly sharp pains raging through his abdomen. "I'm not. But if you were going to . . . you would have while I was sprawled out on the floor of that house."

Mark sits on the floor, his back to the end of the bed. "How did any of us win?" He leans his head back to rest.

She looks out the window, then back at Mark. She sets the gun down on the floor. "Everyone got pieces of me and I got nothing in return. Everyone got pieces of me and the *rest* of me was thrown away to rot."

"That's not what it was, Alicia. You know that."

She sits on the floor next to him. For a few moments, she stays silent.

"I truly thought I was doing the right thing . . . when it came to the case. I thought Tim was in a bad situation . . . and I cared . . . I care about him. But when it came to you . . . everything before . . . I knew I was wrong . . . I knew what we did was wrong."

"Tell me the truth," she says, "Did you love me?"

Mark lifts his head and stares out the window. He finds it difficult to breathe without searing pain, so he keeps his breaths short. "I did. I really did."

She nods. "So what did you tell her?"

"Everything I could . . . to make sure we stayed married . . . to make sure she didn't leave me."

"Because you *love* her."

Mark nods. Faintly, he hears sirens.

She gets up and goes to the window. She slightly hangs her head and begins to weep. Mark gathers some energy to make his way to her but she pulls the gun on him again.

"Stay back."

"Alicia, I kno—"

She fires a shot into the ground at his feet. She aims the gun back at his chest. Mark remains still.

"There's only one way this can end now, Mark."

"What are you saying?"

"I'm not going to run for the rest of my life. I'm not going back to jail." She paces the floor in tight, quick steps. "There are some things . . . ." She wipes her nose. "There are some things that you are going to find out. About me . . . about what I've done." She shakes the gun. "Very bad things. I just want you to know . . . they're all true . . . and I'm sorry. I am deeply sorry." She paws at her face, wiping away tears. A new batch of tears comes just as quickly.

"What did you do?"

She smirks through the streaming tears. She takes a step back, then another until her back is pressed against the window. She looks Mark in the eyes, and then turns the gun on herself, jamming it into her mouth.

"Alicia, don't do this."

She starts to sob, gun still in her mouth, and shakes her head slowly.

Alicia pulls the trigger.

CHAPTER FORTY THREE

MARK doesn't really remember much. Somehow he remembers bright lights and hands, a lot of hands reaching out to him, grabbing and pulling him down, to where, he doesn't know. He remembers seeing Craig and the nervous look on his face. He remembers seeing Berta once. Somehow, he remembers feeling the tension between the two. It takes him a good while before he realizes he's in the hospital.

Mark lies in a hospital bed with a room to himself, still trying to piece everything together. He feels like he's floating; nothing he does has that grounded feeling that tells you you're in reality. He looks around to see a whiteboard with his nurse's name and the date and time. He sees that it is Wednesday which means he has been here for two days. He lifts his arm, then lets it flop back onto the bed. He sees on the gate of the bed a few buttons for controlling the bed and one to call the nurses' station. He presses it and waits.

A few moments later, a young-looking woman walks in. She wears the normal nurse scrubs and has her brunette hair tied back into a bun. She smiles and speaks to Mark in soft tones.

"Afternoon, Mr. Cooke. How are you feeling today?"

Mark adjusts his vision to look at the whiteboard again. "I feel like trash, Mindy." His voice surprises him, coming out more like a whisper.

"Aww. What can I do to ease that for you?"

Mark tries to clear his throat, but after the third time, he feels a twinge of pain and gives up. He sticks to whispering.

"My wife. Where is she?"

Mark sees it immediately, even after the nurse tries to cover it up with a forced smile. Something isn't right. "Mrs. Cooke is in the ICU."

"Is she okay?"

"She is resting right now. Listen, why don't I get you a cup of water. Dr. Chalmers is coming this way in another half hour or so. He can explain everything then."

"That's fine, thank—"

A knock on the door. Craig peeks his head in.

The nurse looks back at Craig and smiles. She allows Craig in and steps around him, out of the room. Craig steps in and gently closes the door. He sits in the chair next to Mark's bed.

"I was in ICU with Berta. Heard the commotion at the nurses' station. Knew you woke up."

Mark notices Craig's movements. He notices the tone of his voice. Something isn't right.

"What's going on?"

Craig looks at Mark. "Well, you have two fractured ribs. A couple others were bruised."

"No, no, no. I don't need a prognosis. The doctor is going to give me that. I need to know if Jade is alright. Is she alright? Be straight up with me."

Craig winces. "You should get your rest. There's a lot ahead of you coming up. Stuff you're going to need strength for."

"What? Craig, stop playing games. The truth. Tell me the truth. Is she okay?"

Craig solemnly shakes his head. "No. She isn't."

Mark clumsily sits up and tries to get out of the hospital bed. Craig rushes over to hold him down and stop him.

"I need to see her," Mark says.

"Not yet, man. Trust me. Not yet. Get your strength back."

Mark struggles against Craig for a few more moments before giving up and lying back down. Pain covers his chest and back like a blanket. Tears stream down the side of his face. "Get out. Just leave me be."

Craig looks at Mark to see if he is serious, and when he figures he is, leaves the room. Mark notices he pauses outside the door to talk to someone, presumably Berta. After a few moments, Mark closes his eyes to rest, but as soon as he does, he sees an image he'd much rather not think about.

Alicia killing herself.

At the time, Mark wanted to look away, but part of him didn't think she was going to do it. He had hoped with every part of his being she wasn't going to do it. He opens his eyes wide. Still etched onto his eyeballs, he sees Alicia's body falling. He sees her splattering the window with her life. The way the sun shined through the reddened glass. He wishes he'd turned away.

He knows he will never be able to forget it.

Mark hears another knock on the door and looks at Doctor Chalmers walking in. The doctor is a heavyset man with a thick mustache. He wears thick glasses that seem too small for his face and walks in with a smirk on his face. The smirk doesn't strike Mark as pretentious, but rather calming. Like, whatever Doctor Chalmers has to say will make everything better. However, Mark isn't so naïve.

"Hello, Mr. Cooke."

"Doctor."

"How are you feeling today?"

"Not the best."

"Understandable." The man rolls up a stool and sits. "You have a couple fractured ribs. Two in the back, left side. Three others are bruised. So needless to say, breathing is going to be difficult for a while."

"I was out for two days? And all I have are some banged up ribs?"

"Not exactly." The doctor looks at Mark strangely. "Do you remember anything from the last couple days?"

"Not at all. The last thing I remember is . . . ."

The doctor takes out a pen and pad and starts scribbling notes. "We had to wake you every so often and we were able to do so. You're telling me you remember none of that?"

"None of it."

"I see. Mark, we believe you had a severe concussion. This matches up with the swelling we saw on the CT scan. You suffered some major head trauma. At the precise time, it is very difficult to say. We needed to keep you here for further observation."

"So I take some meds for the pain and heal up on my own, correct?"

"We need to keep a close eye on you. Is there anyone who can be with you while at home?"

"No. Yes. I don't know. What of my wife?" Mark pushes the issue. "Tell me about my wife."

Dr. Chalmers adjusts in his seat. "She sustained a lot of damage . . . and lost a lot of blood . . . much of it because of the gunshot wound. But thankfully, the bullet hit no vital organs. She was malnourished and severely dehydrated. She also suffered many lacerations on her face and a broken nose." The doctor talks in a robotic way, as if he practiced saying it many times over. "Despite the severity of her injuries, we were able to revive her."

"Wait. What do you mean, revive?"

"Sir." The doctor looks at Mark plainly. "Your wife was dead when you carried her in to us."

Mark stops breathing for a moment before realizing he was getting dizzy, and forces himself to take another labored breath. Much of what the doctor says from that point sounds jumbled to Mark. He interrupts the doctor.

"Can I see her?"

"As soon as you get your strength, we can get you down there."

"I'm good now." Mark tries to move but becomes completely paralyzed with pain.

"Please, Mr. Cooke, let your body rest for a bit more."

"I've been resting. Why can't I go see my wife?"

The doctor doesn't answer right away. "Look, give it a couple hours and—"

Another knock on the door, but no one peeks in. Dr. Chalmers stands to his feet and excuses himself. A few moments later, Detective Simms walks in. He slowly sits in the seat the doctor was in and takes in a deep breath. Mark simply stares at him, not knowing what to expect.

"How are you, Mark?"

Mark doesn't answer.

"Fair enough." Simms crosses his legs. "Well, I owe you an apology of sorts. I have to admit, I was a bit blinded by a few things. I made some incorrect assumptions."

"Like thinking I kidnapped my wife?"

"Indeed. But you should have come to me."

"It was too risky. And what were you going to do?"

"My job, Mark."

"Well, if I left you to do your job, she would be dead."

Simms stares at the green hospital wall. "A bit harsh, don't you think?"

Mark doesn't answer. Simms gets up and heads for the door. He stops and places his hand on the handle. He doesn't look back. "We had two days to look over evidence. There's a lot that comes with this case. We are going to have to review everything. Chances are we are going to need a few more statements from you."

"I understand."

"She wanted to ruin you, Mark. You're going to hear some stuff that will be tough to swallow." He opens the door. "Jacob and his family aren't pressing any charges. They feel you helped them stay alive." He waits for a response, but when he gets none, he keeps moving. "I thought you would want to know. I'll let you get your rest."

Simms leaves the room, but leaves the door open. A few seconds later, Mindy comes back in with a Styrofoam cup. Mark hears the rattle of ice chips inside the cup of water. She pulls out a straw from her pocket.

"Can I get you anything else, Mr. Cooke?"

"How did I get here?"

"Pardon?"

"In here, in this hospital. How did I get here?"

She looks around, showing her confusion as to why he's asking her. "From my understanding, you were passed out on the floor at the scene."

"Passed out?"

"Yes. I'm told from either physical trauma . . . or mental . . . possibly both. I heard it was a pretty gruesome scene."

Mark takes in what she says. He nods and says, "Thank you."

She places her hand on his arm. "Everything is going to be okay. You have to believe that. A little faith goes a far way."

"Thank you, Mindy. But I'm not quite sure what okay is."

She nods and sets the cup on the stand closest to him. Quietly, she leaves.

ÈÆÈÉ

Craig stands in the corner of Jade's room, staring at her, unbelieving of all that has befallen her. He glances at Berta, who sits in the seat next to her bed. He wants to say something, but he doesn't know what to say to her anymore. He moves to the side as nurses periodically check on Jade.

"So were we letting him know?" Berta asks.

"What are you talking about?"

"About us. About the divorce. I honestly prefer to not tell him anything. He has enough on his plate, and our issues . . . mean very little compared to this."

"I already told him."

Berta nods. "I figured I'd be too late in asking."

"But we really didn't get a chance to talk about it. Even if we did have time to go into detail, I really wouldn't know what to say."

"Meaning?"

"Meaning, this is a lot to try to explain, and I'm not quite sure I can make any sense of it."

Silence.

"What happened to us?" Craig asks.

"I don't want to talk about this right now. Not while all this is going on."

"And I have to. Otherwise I'm going to lose it. I . . . I need you. I need you to talk."

She looks down and sighs. "A lot has changed. We changed."

Craig nods. "But you know what I don't get? Why is it that we are throwing away something that was so good? Why are we throwing it away as if it doesn't even matter?"

Berta doesn't answer.

"You know what I learned? Sometimes, you have to be persistent, no matter what others say. Look at Mark. He had one goal and one goal only, and that was to get to Jade, someway, somehow. Nothing was going to stop him. Not even me, his best friend." Craig bites his bottom lip.

"So what are you saying?"

He moves closer to her. "I'm saying I want you. I want you back. Give me one night. Me and you . . . maybe over dinner . . . and we put everything out on the table. We hash out every issue, every annoyance, and find a way to move forward. We find a way we can work through this stuff, then that's what we'll do." He takes a deep breath. "'Cause I don't believe you when you say you don't love me anymore."

Berta looks down in thought. She starts to say something, but stops.

"Please, Berta. Just one night."

"You're right. I do still love you, but that doesn't mean much to me right now. Love doesn't fix this. Love doesn't fix you. Love doesn't fix . . . me."

"I know there's a lot to deal with. I understand the terribleness of what I've done, but please, give me a chance to explain . . . the right way."

"You hurt me."

"I know, and I'm sorry. Please believe me when I tell you I need you. I need you more now than ever. So much is going on . . . so much has gone on and I don't know how I can, how I can get through this stuff without you."

She looks at him, and almost makes him break down right in front of her.

"When?"

"Tomorrow night."

It takes her a few minutes, but she slowly nods. "Fine."

"Good." He takes a deep breath and exhales slowly. "Good. Did you want anything to eat? I'm headed to the cafeteria."

"No thanks."

Craig nods and quietly walks out of Jade's room. He gently shuts the door and turns around to see Detective Simms casually walking up to him.

"Do you have a second?" he asks Craig.

"I was getting something to eat."

"Sounds good. May I join?"

"I suppose." He starts walking. "What is it that you want?"

"Just to talk for a few moments. I won't take too much of your time."

"Okay, shoot."

Simms smirks. "It's funny you use that word. Anyway, I wanted to thank you for your assistance with finding Mark's wife."

"Oh . . . sure. I didn't do much. But . . . did you tell him yet?"

"About?"

"About the card in his pocket."

"Nah." Simms frowns. "Not yet. Too much on his plate now." He stares at Craig.

Both men get silent. Craig is about to walk away when Simms says, "Quick question; where were you when Mark was going to get Jade?"

He frowns. "Home."

"Do you have anyone who could confirm that?"

"What are you getting at?"

"Strange thing, I get this cell phone in a package. The phone in and of itself was wiped completely clean of all prints. Now the information on the phone was vital information. It essentially cleared Mark of all suspicion and exposed Alicia's plan in its entirety. Pieces are coming together and the info on that phone is the glue."

"Sounds like a good thing to me."

"Well, that is, but I found it strange. You see, I could account for where Mark was around the time of him getting Jade. I can't quite account for you."

"I wasn't there, so . . . ." Craig starts walking.

"Okay. I want to believe you . . . but I was thinking about when we met at that party."

"You mean that guy's perverted romper room?"

"Indeed. I asked Mark how he got his hands on not one, but two invites to this party. He glazed over much of the details and always tried to turn the tables back on me."

"Yeah? What's your point?"

"Well, I did some digging into his background. Of course, that turned out to be in error. But still, tough past, found a way to overcome, very admirable stuff . . . but then I found you."

Craig starts to slow down.

"Craig Barlow, a kid abandoned by his parents, the foster child, the demon seed. Tried to make something of his life by becoming a youth pastor. Ended up in jail for rape. Gets out of jail and somehow lands with one of the most notorious crime bosses from our area, Raul Valencia. And then, not a peep."

"Not sure what you are looking into my stuff for, nor am I sure how you got hold of any information on me, but trust me, that's not the tree you want to bark up."

"Is that a threat?"

"No. It's plainly saying there is nothing to find on me. I'm on the up-and-up. I've been on the up-and-up."

"I wish that were true. I consider myself to be a pretty good detective. Not perfect by any means, but I can put two and two together. You want to know what I surmised?"

"Not really."

"Well, I'm guessing you were at that garage. The garage that left one man dead and the other not saying a word. I'm thinking I would be able to link you to a few more 'unsolved mysteries' in the past."

"So again, what are you saying?"

"I was just giving you a chance, that's all."

"A chance at what?"

"A chance to come clean."

"I am clean."

"Maybe spiritually, and that may bode well for you in heaven, if you go, but there are still some laws you have to contend with down here. Laws that will bring you to justice, no matter how long or far you run. But I digress. I am only telling you this: once I put all the pieces together, I will come after you. But to show you some good will, I'm letting you know now, because the information on the phone was helpful."

Craig stops in front of the cafeteria.

"Aren't you going in?" Simms asks.

"No. I have to get something from my car."

He smiles. "See you soon, Craig."

"Yeah, maybe."

Craig fast-steps his way out of the hospital and to his car. He hops in, slams the door, and immediately dials Mr. Ramses. As usual, his secretary picks up and directs him to him.

"Mr. Ramses."

"Craig." He sighs, sounding aggravated. "What can I help you with?"

"I'm in trouble. Serious trouble."

"What did you get yourself into now?"

"I . . . I killed a man. And there's this detective, he's on my ass. So much so, I think he'll have a case against me in a couple days."

Another long sigh.

"Sir, please. I know . . . I know I was supposed to stay away . . . but we found her. We found her. Do you know what that means?"

"That you were in over your head. That you got too emotional and your feelings got the best of you. That instead of trying to mend things with your wife, you wanted to play hero, and you're in serious danger. Look, where are you?"

"New Jersey."

"What the hell are you there . . . Look, it doesn't matter. I want you to come straight to the office right now. Straight to the office A.S.A.P. You hear me?"

"Loud and clear." Craig starts the car. "I'll be there in a few hours."

"Before you go, were there any witnesses?"

Craig thinks for a second. "One. The man's brother."

"And do you know where he is?"

"Police custody."

Ramses sighs yet again. "You'd better hurry."

CHAPTER FORTY FOUR

MARK spent another night plastered to the hospital bed, under doctors' orders. For reasons unknown to him, they wanted to keep him another day for observation. He was okay with that because moving was still difficult, even with pain killers, but he didn't get the opportunity to see Jade. Knowing he was going to be discharged, Mark asked Craig to grab him some clean clothes, and to his delight, saw that he already had clothes waiting for him. All Craig had to do was get to the car in the parking garage to grab them. Berta stayed with Mark but hasn't said anything all morning.

"You're kinda quiet, Berta. You okay?"

Berta snaps her head toward Mark, as if she were thinking of something else. "Oh. Me? Yeah, I'm okay. How are you doing?"

"Better. Not by much, but enough. Not liking this loopy feeling, though."

"Well, you're not on just the regular Advil. They gave you some strong painkillers. Can you take deep breaths?"

"For now. We'll see how long it lasts, though."

She nods and goes quiet again.

"Look, I uhhh, Craig and I talked about . . . stuff."

"I know."

"Are you sure you want to go through with it?"

"I'd rather not talk about that right now."

"I understand, but I have to say this: Craig is a good guy. He may have made mistakes in the past, but they're in the past. Everyone has one, including you. This guy loves you, Berta. But maybe this endorsement is already too much."

Berta turns toward Mark. "It isn't. You're being a good friend. We'll find a way, Mark; we will find a way."

Craig knocks on the door and comes in with a bag. He eyes Berta before walking to Mark's bed.

"I grabbed a few pairs of everything . . . didn't know what you might want."

"Thanks, man."

Craig helps Mark to the bathroom for him to change and Berta leaves to grab a wheelchair. Mark gives her one last glance before she shuts the door behind. As Mark changes, Craig stands on the other side of the door.

"I hope you don't need help with anything else," Craig chides.

"Yeah, I'm going to need your help aiming while I pee." Mark chuckles, but not without paying for it. A sharp pain pricks at his side. At the moment, he tries to forget the rash of terrible events that has befallen him. On the inside, he feels nervous, so much so that it makes him nauseated. He steps out of the bathroom with Craig staring at him.

"Look man," Craig says. "About Jacob's house . . . ."

"Don't worry about it. It's done."

Craig nods and looks at the floor.

As soon as he signs the paperwork to officially be discharged, Mark is wheeled to the ICU. Craig doesn't say anything while wheeling Mark to Jade's room, and Mark appreciates that. Mark feels more and more uncomfortable by the moment, and when Craig stops him in front of Jade's room, he almost panics. Mark feels Craig's hand on his shoulder.

"It's going to be all right."

Mark nods and struggles to get out of the wheelchair. Once on his two feet, he places his hand on the door handle and takes as deep a breath as he can without forcing on the stabbing pain. Mark waits at the door. He turns slightly to his left to see Craig standing there, looking at him. Craig's face is tight, as if he's trying to hold back tears. Mark then switches to his right to see a number of nurses and doctors at a nurse's station simply staring at him. At the end of the hall, he sees Berta walking briskly toward him, seemingly with something on her mind, but stops when she sees him at Jade's door. It's an awkward moment for Mark, to have everyone that can see him staring at him, Craig holding back tears, Jade on the other side of the door in the ICU of a hospital. It's all surreal to him.

Mark takes another semi-deep breath and turns the handle. Everything moves slowly and he can hear almost everything, including the clicks of the handle as he turns it. He takes one glance back, then opens the door. The first thing he notices is the beeping—a lot of beeping of various machines. The lighting is low, as most of the bright lights are outside the room, shining in. He sees a curtain blocking Jade from his view. Mark takes another step. In the far corner, he sees Jade's mother, and goes to say something. Without looking his way, she gets up and storms right by him, leaving the room. Mark looks confused at first, then hurt, but he refocuses on Jade. He tries to control his breathing, to lessen the amount of short, rapid breaths he's taking, but without being able to take a deep breath, he fails. He raises his hand to the curtain and slowly pulls it back to see Jade lying in the bed.

She's Jade, but she isn't.

A number of tubes link from her body to different machines, leaving Mark unable to comprehend what is going on. He stands there, frozen. He can't remove the look of shock from his face. After a few moments of taking it all in, he takes another step forward. He places a shaky hand on hers.

"We got authorization from her mother."

Mark turns around to see Dr. Chalmers.

"We revived her, but she wasn't able to sustain a heartbeat for long."

"How long does she have to be on this?"

"For as long as it takes her body to heal and do things for itself. If it does things for itself."

"What are her chances . . . of coming out of this?"

"It's hard to say. There are so many—"

"Make an educated guess. I want to know her chances."

Dr. Chalmers clears his throat. "Slim. She just . . . lost too much blood. Her body had to work too hard to compensate and she didn't have much energy to begin with. That's the negative, I suppose. A bright note is that she *is* still alive. In her condition, that's a miracle."

"So what now? What am I supposed to do now?"

"I . . . I can't answer that for you. I can give you your options, but it's a good idea to discuss with family and friends what course of action to take. I'm sorry."

Mark hears the doctor's footsteps as he leaves the room. He stares at Jade.

"Jade, Baby, I need you to wake up. We need to get out of here." He holds his tears in even though it hurts because he knows the contractions of crying would hurt even more.

"Jade, Sweetheart, please move. Give me something. I know it's hard, but give me something. Please."

Mark moves his hand from hers. In an instant he realizes he is face-to-face with what he feared most.

His personal failures leading to the downfall of whom he loved most.

He tries to feel for her, not on a physical level, but an emotional one, a spiritual one, but he feels nothing. It reminds him of the morning after the crazed and twisted party. He felt for her presence. But even right in front of her, he can't feel *her*. He bites his bottom lip and turns away. He takes a quick glance at Berta, who stands at the doorway, and then at Craig, who stands behind the wheelchair, and hobbles over to sit. Craig holds the chair as Mark labors into the seat. He still tries to hold in tears, but now some come out, lining the sides of his face. His nose gets stuffy as he hears his heartbeat in his ears. Through somewhat blurred vision, he sees Jade's mother, sitting in a chair in the hall, dabbing her eyes with a napkin. Craig wheels him to her, and Mark places his hand on her lap. She doesn't look him in the eyes, still, and abruptly gets up. She walks back to Jade's room and shuts the door, leaving Mark in the hall holding his hand out. Mark swallows down the pain and places his hand on his lap. He looks around to see yet again, nurses and doctors staring at him, some of them turned red from crying.

"Let's get you home," Craig whispers.

Mark lets Craig wheel him out the hospital and whispers, "There isn't a home without her."

Chapter Forty Five

MARK looks out the window for most of the trip, still trying to get a grip on the recent events of his life. He notices Craig glances over at him every couple miles or so. Mark wants to close his eyes to sleep, but each time Craig drives over a bump in the road, a searing shot of pain reverberates up and down his body.

Craig's cell phone interrupts his thoughts. Craig snatches it up, but only says yes or no. After a quick few seconds, he throws the phone on the dash.

"Listen, man, we have to talk," he says. "I gotta dip off for a while. Things are heating up for me and . . . ."

Mark looks at Craig. He visibly is shaken by something.

"I have to get out of town."

"What are you talking about?"

"I can't go back home, at least not until some things get cleared up."

"What happened?"

"Look, I talked to that detective guy. Simms, right?"

"Yeah." Mark looks awkwardly.

"I came upon some information while at that garage in Philly. I handed it over to him, but there's no way he could have known it was me. It was a phone and I wiped it clean of prints. Somehow, he knows I was there at the garage. That puts me at a crime scene I really shouldn't be in. But even beyond that, he's been digging into my past, the shady parts . . . the parts that could send me back to jail. Apparently, he gets a hard-on for taking down the business types."

Mark immediately thinks of Calvin and how obsessed Simms seemed to take him down.

"I called a few people who have been backing me and practically begged them to clean it up."

"And?"

"They agreed, but I can't be anywhere near him. I gotta go some-where far for a bit while they back him off."

"How long?"

"Don't know."

"Where will you go?"

"Don't know."

"And that leaves you where with Berta?"

"I don't know. We were supposed to meet up tonight to work on things. I . . . don't know what to do."

"Call her."

Craig reaches for his phone and dials Berta. Mark hears the ring-ing, but no answer.

"Nothing."

Mark stares out the window, wincing in pain. "I don't know what to say."

"I don't, either. I don't want to leave. And now is the worst possi-ble time to do so. I just . . . I don't want to go back to jail. I can't do it. And if I go back, I know it would be for life."

Mark doesn't say anything as Craig lets his words hang in the air a bit more.

"But I will be back. Trust me. I'll be back to see you and Jade and the kids and . . . ."

Mark looks at Craig to see a tear drop from his eye.

"You have to do what you have to do . . . right?"

Craig nods. He clears his throat. "But if you need me, just call. It doesn't matter when. Just call."

"I appreciate it." Mark says, but he knows Craig's words ring hollow. "When do you have to leave?"

"Tonight."

Mark nods. "Listen, I'm sorry for dragging you into this. I didn't . . . I mean . . . it wasn't supposed to be like this. Life wasn't supposed to be like this."

"It's not your fault."

Mark looks out the window as they drive through his neighborhood. Somehow, he feels completely disconnected from his home, and it looks like a strange place as Craig pulls the car up into the driveway.

"Most of this *is* my fault."

Craig puts the car in park and helps Mark get his things inside. Mark doesn't move much once he steps foot inside his home. He looks around to find everything exactly as he left it.

"You going to be alright?" Craig asks.

"I'll be fine. Don't worry."

Craig looks at his watch. "Listen, the doctors . . . they suggested you shouldn't be here by yourself. I was supposed to stay with you . . . ."

"I'll be fine. I know you have to go. Just make sure you take care of yourself out there."

"I will. Keep me updated on Jade's condition. Even if I don't pick up, please leave me a message."

Mark nods and puts out his hand. Craig looks down for a second, and then shakes Mark's hand. Visibly struggling, he then leaves Mark, with phone in hand, attempting again to call Berta.

Mark stands in his empty and too-silent home for so long he loses track of time. For that stretch of time, he doesn't move, but tries to mentally fill the house with sounds; sounds of the kids running around, sounds of Jade in the kitchen or on the phone talking to someone from the church. He actually hears none of that. The air is filled with a silence so painful he feels it in his head, in his body. He eventually sits down in his comfortable chair and decides to listen to the messages on the answering machine. The voicemail box is full and he plays through each and every message, one by one. He listens to the well wishes from church folk, a few messages from Pastor Brentwood, other messages from bill collectors, and finally a single message from the community college. The college decided to withdraw its job offer. Mark listens to every message with a straight face. By the time he gets to the final message, it's nighttime and he sits in total darkness. He struggles to get out the chair and walks to the kitchen. He opens the refrigerator, grabs a bottle of water, and guzzles half of it before popping a few of his pain meds. He shuts the door, cutting off the only light in the house. Suddenly, swiftly, he feels a chill go up and down his spine. He tries to move, but is paralyzed in pain. Then, he hears it again. The muffled gunshot. He is yet again reminded of Alicia. But this time . . . .

"Why did you let me go, Mark?"

Mark tries to control his rapid breaths.

"You remember when you said it was me and you forever? You remember when you told me you loved me? Why, Mark? Why let me go?"

"You are not real. You're dead." He gets to his feet.

"I am real. I'm the most real person you know. I'm the most real you will ever know."

"I saw you kill . . . you killed yourself."

"No. You killed me, Mark. You killed me."

Mark limps to the kitchen light and flips the switch. When light fills the room, he looks around frantically, but finds no one. He turns on every light in the house and checks everywhere—bedrooms, bathrooms, closets. He finds no one. Beads of sweat form on his forehead and pool with other beads to trace down his face. He still hears Alicia's voice, but faintly.

"And now, I'm with you forever."

03☙

Craig's mind is on a million things at once. He reluctantly backs out of Mark's driveway and heads straight for the office. By the time he gets there, Ted is already making his way out. Craig runs into him in the lobby.

"Sir. How are your friends?"

"They're okay, I guess."

"I'm sorry to hear everything that has happened to them."

"As am I. Listen, we need to talk, and I know you've been trying to meet with me for some time."

"Yes, ummm." He digs into his messenger bag. "Here." He hands Craig a folded sheet of paper.

Craig opens the paper and reads. "You're resigning?"

"Yes, sir. I got a job offer . . . in New York."

"Wall street?"

"Not quite. But close enough. I . . . it's the best opportunity for me to—"

"No need to explain. This is what hard work gets you. This is what the studying and getting the licenses was for."

Ted smiles. "I thought you would be upset."

"I'm happy for you. You will do well there."

"That . . . that is a big weight off my shoulders. I—"

Craig notices that Ted looks behind him, so he turns around. A short man in plain clothes approaches Craig.

"Craig Barlow?"

Craig doesn't say anything but observes the man. He sees an envelope in his hand and immediately knows what this is about. He sighs.

"Yeah, that's me."

"You have been served."

Craig takes the envelope and the man walks away briskly. Ted looks at Craig in confusion.

"Listen, Ted. There are some things I need to deal with. I'm going to be gone for a while and unfortunately, I won't be able to see you on your last day. Why don't you take your last two weeks off to get things set up and all."

"Sir?"

"Trust me. You don't want to know what is going on. Just take the two weeks off, and I'll catch up to you somehow. Okay?"

Ted nods slowly. He puts his hand out and Craig shakes it.

"I really appreciate it, sir. I pray God has something for you . . . for what you have done to help me."

Craig gives Ted a nod.

"I'll give you a call sometime. Maybe we can do lunch in New York?"

"Sounds good. Take care of yourself, Ted."

Craig waits until Ted is completely out of the building before heading to the elevators and to his office. He gets to Ted's desk . . . Berta's desk, and stares at it for a moment. He looks around for a second before carefully opening the envelope. He sees in big bold letters the heading.

Petition of Dissolution of Marriage

He slides the papers back into the envelope and closes it again. He stands there a few moments, tapping the envelope on his chin. He snaps back out of his thoughts and moves with haste into his office and grabs his laptop and a few other documents. He's sure the detective is going to check the area, so Craig makes sure there's nothing to find.

He fills a duffel bag with folders of papers and his work laptop and makes his way out of the office. He tries to call Berta again.

Still no answer.

⋯

Berta lies curled up in the bed weeping. Since coming from the hospital, that's all she's been able to do. She cries for her friends. She cries for her broken marriage. She cries for her broken life. She hears her cell phone go off again, but she doesn't move to look at it. She knows it's Craig again. In the background, she plays the CD Marcella and Jennifer sent her, and she plays it on repeat. All she could think of is what Raul and the monster said of Craig.

"I've been in contact with your protégé . . ."
"He's not like us."
"I get the impression that he is. I've seen his work . . . Does he know I'm Alberta's father?"
"He does. And he knows why she's with me."

She hears the doorbell ring and fixes herself up before answering. As soon as she slightly opens the door, Craig barges in, pulls her close and kisses her. She resists at first, but eventually finds the kiss to be familiar territory, and that's comforting to her. She just starts to go in for more when he pulls away.

"We have to talk," he says.

"I know. Isn't that why you are here?"

"No. Yes." He looks distraught. "We have to postpone that talk."

"What are you saying?"

He paces back and forth, incessantly looking at his watch. "I have to disappear . . . for a while."

Berta feels like she's been punched in the gut. "What do you mean disappear for a while?"

"I mean exactly that." He stops pacing. "I got into some trouble . . . ."

She already knows where this is going. "Stop." She pauses to think. "This is not what I signed up for. This is not the marriage I—"

"Is that Mr. V?"

Berta looks around for a picture, forgetting she had the CD still playing the phone messages. She pauses. "Yes."

"How on Earth . . . ?"

"Look," she rushes over to the computer to stop the playback. "I didn't sign up for this. Wait, what is that face for?"

Craig sighs. "You're acting like this is how I wanted things to be."

Berta tightens up. "You chose to do this, Craig. This *is* how you wanted things to be. Otherwise, they wouldn't be like this. And now, before having the most important discussion of your marriage, you tell your wife you can't make that dinner. You can't have that conversation, because *you* have to disappear. So, let me cut to the chase, since it seems there's somewhere you have to be that's more important: Once you walk out that door, don't bother coming back. And I mean it. Don't show up. Don't call."

"But you don't understand. Even if I stay, chances are, I will never be able to come back. If I leave now while things get better—"

"What did you do?"

He freezes.

"What did you do that's so bad you have to disappear?"

He looks down. "I can't tell you."

"Craig . . . ."

"I killed a man, okay?" He raises his tone, but is careful not to yell. "It was me or him."

Another blow to the gut. "What do you mean? Like, you actually took someone's life?"

Craig nods solemnly.

Berta stares at Craig, trying to understand him. For a long and awkward silence, Berta tries to process this situation. "You're . . . ." She finally says, "You're a murderer?"

"No." He winces and takes a step toward her. She quickly steps back. "Please, Berta. I can make things right. I can . . ." He looks exasperated.

"Have you done this before?"

"Berta, please."

"Have you done this before?"

Craig nods. Berta finds it difficult to breathe. "Even back when you called yourself a rapist? You were really a murderer?"

Craig remains still.

"Please leave." She softens her tone. "Please leave and never come back."

"But—" He takes another step closer.

"Don't come closer. Please leave, Craig."

Craig looks stunned. She knows he's hurting, and part of her wants to console him, but a bigger part is scared of him. She watches him as he saunters to the front door, and just before he leaves he whispers, "I'm sorry."

⋘⋙

Craig gets to the parking lot of Lockram-Ramses-Peterson, and pulls up next to a black limousine. He grabs his bag from the passenger seat and gets out. Without hesitation, he gets into the back seat of the limousine. Mr. Ramses is seated next to him.

"What's in the bag?" Ramses asks.

"Work stuff. Paperwork."

"Computer? Phone?"

"Yeah."

"Leave that with me."

Craig looks at Ramses to see if he is serious.

"We can't have them trace anything to your location." He hands Craig a briefcase. "A new cell phone, credit card, and laptop. I advise against contacting anyone you know. And as far as work goes, you took a two-week vacation. Any communication will run through us. If it's work-related after the two weeks, we will relay, if it is other, we will run interference."

Craig nods.

"You know they will go to her, too."

"I know. But you already have that handled. Right?"

"We do." For the first time since Craig entered the limousine, Ramses shows some emotion. "For what it's worth, I'm sorry . . . you know. For you and Alberta."

"I'm sorry, too. But sorrow doesn't change things. Action does, and I took the wrong ones." He swallows hard. "You know I went to see her before I came here."

Ramses looks over. "And?"

He shakes his head before leaning back on the headrest. "She was listening to this recording, a conversation. I believe it was Mr. V's voice. I have an idea of whom he was talking to."

Ramses looks perplexed. "Courtland?"

Craig slowly nods.

"How would she get ahold of that?"

"No idea. But I figured you'd want to know. Anyway, where am I going?"

"My ranch out in Texas."

"Great. Texas."

"What's wrong with Texas?"

Craig looks at Ramses. "It's not home." He looks out the window. "When do you think I will be able to come back?"

"That's hard to tell. It depends on how determined this detective is. Could be a week. Could be two months. Could be longer. One thing on our side is that the most recent activity occurred in a different state . . . out of his jurisdiction. That won't stop him, but it will surely slow him down."

"And the divorce? I obviously won't be able to show up in court if this doesn't blow over soon enough."

Ramses sighs. "The courts will proceed with her request. The judge will easily sign off on it."

"Can you buy me time . . . if I'm not back?"

"That would be tough. You not showing up is synonymous with saying you are not contesting the divorce. And all the lawyers have to say is, 'Mrs. Alberta Barlow and her husband no longer share the same moral and ethical values, so it is not possible to live in harmony and trust,' or something along those lines, whatever is in the petition." Ramses looks at Craig. "Did you get it yet?"

"Yeah. It's in my bag."

Ramses nods. "We'll work on getting this cleared up for you quickly."

"Thank you."

"No thanks needed." Ramses looks outside. "Listen, we are pulling up to the jet now." He puts his hand out in front of Craig. "You take care of yourself, you hear me? Clear your mind."

"Yes, sir." Craig shakes his hand.

"See you soon."

Craig steps out of the limousine with a briefcase and a duffel bag, both of which an attendant of the jet takes onto the plane. He stands at the steps leading into the plane and looks up at the sky. A gust of wind sends chills up and down his spine. Each step he takes toward the opening of the plane makes him feel more and more disconnected from the world. He feels completely and utterly alone.

Cؒؒ

She feels like she's floating, unable to find anywhere solid to stand. She feels her eyes are open, but she sees nothing but darkness; black, suffocating, and oppressive darkness.

"Hello?"

It doesn't sound like her voice travels very far, so she screams. She screams for everyone she knows hoping someone would answer.

No one does.

Jade remembers being held against her will. She remembers spending a large amount of time in a dusty and dark room. She knows she isn't back in that room because things are . . . different. She feels around on her body. No clothes. She kneels down and sits, wrapping her arms around her legs, pulling her knees close to her chest. She remembers talking with Alicia. She remembers . . . she remembers being shot. She feels around her body again, but finds no wounds. In fact, she doesn't feel any pain. She returns back to her curled-up position. *Someone took me from the room. No, Mark took me from the room . . . Mark rescued me. Mark rescued . . . me.* She screams again for Mark but is greeted with more silence. Now, more than ever, does she feel vulnerable. She thinks back to the last time she saw him, under the dim lights of that place. He looked so worn. But there was a glint in his eye. Nothing was going to stop him from getting to her. She's his wife. That thought makes her smile. She closes her eyes and lets thoughts of him warm her. Memories flood her mind and fill her area with heat. She opens her eyes to see different images, floating through the air. All the images are of Mark. Slowly, the images get closer and cover her like a blanket. *So warm.*

But then, seemingly far off, a dot appears. It's a bright dot, like that of a distant star. She reaches her hand toward it. As she motions toward it, her hand is engulfed by total darkness. She snatches her hand back and brings it to the warmth of her new blanket. Something in her is urging her toward the bright dot. She yearns to be in the same area as that dot, that star, but she would have to leave the images behind. She's not quite ready to do that.

And the darkness is so very cold.

⊰⊱

Mark is awakened by the sound of the doorbell ringing. It takes him a few moments to realize he fell asleep in his comfortable chair. He moves slowly as his joints crack and pop in every movement. He waits a moment before attempting to stand to his feet. As he holds the arm of the chair for support, he places his feet on the floor and reels himself up. He shuffles to the front door hunched over, as he finds it nearly impossible to stand upright. He cracks the door open to see Pastor Brentwood. Mark tries his best to straighten up, but finds it to be too difficult.

"I hope I'm not intruding."

"No, sir, you aren't. I got your messages. I just . . . ."

"No need to explain. May I come in?"

Mark opens the door more to allow him in. "Would you like anything to drink?"

"No. Thanks. Please, I know it's a struggle to stand. Can we sit and talk for a few?"

Mark nods and shuffles over to the living room.

Once seated, Pastor Brentwood stares at Mark, as Mark does everything he can to avoid looking him in the eyes.

"How are you holding up?"

"As well as I can."

"Any more news on Jade's condition?"

"Nope. Still critical. Still . . . not awake."

"And the kids?"

"I haven't talked to them in some time. They're with Jade's mother." He looks up and notices Pastor Brentwood isn't looking at him but at the end table where Mark's pain meds are. "I have some banged up ribs."

Pastor nods. "Is anyone here with you, helping you . . . or even checking up on you, maybe?"

"He has me."

Mark shivers. He feels a hand on his shoulder and looks to see a woman's hand. He looks back toward Pastor Brentwood to see the old man look at him strangely.

"Mark?"

Mark looks to his side again to see Alicia coming into view. She stares at Pastor defiantly.

"Get out of our house," she says.

"No, sir. I don't have anyone helping out. But I should be good."

"You sure? Why don't you see if you could stay with Jade's parents as well? At least then you would be able to be with your kids."

"I can't face them. Not yet. And I believe Jade's mother is angry with me. I'm not sure why as of yet, but when I'm able to grapple with all of this, I will find out."

Pastor grunts. "I'll stop by every now and again to check up on you, if that's okay. For now, I want to pray with you."

Mark closes his eyes and starts to bow his head when he feels a tap on his chin. He looks up to see Alicia standing directly in front of him, in between him and Pastor, her face not even an inch away from his.

"I am all you need. When will you realize that?"

Mark slowly shakes his head.

"Give me a kiss, Mark."

Mark doesn't move.

"KISS ME."

On the verge of tears, Mark closes his eyes and bows his head. "Sir, I feel like there's darkness all around me . . . everywhere I go." He hears footsteps headed upstairs. "I don't know what to do . . . or what I did to warrant this. What did we do?"

"You must look toward His everlasting light. God will make a way for you . . . for your family."

"But what if it's too dark to see the light?"

"Then you have faith, Son. Faith allows you to see in the darkness. Come now. Let us pray."

Thank You for Reading
this J. Evan Johnson Book

Sign up for his FREE newsletter and be first to get updates on
new releases, sneak peeks of future stories,
completely free books and short stories, bonus content,
AND MORE!

Visit him online to sign up at
www.thejejstory.com